Erebus

Jo could see a dark figure standing near to one of the fridges at the far end of the room. It was Mark Bates. She watched in silence as he opened the fridge door and took out a large piece of raw steak, the blood dripping from it as he removed it from the metal tray. He lifted the steak in one, hairy-palmed hand, looked at it for a moment, then tore off a chunk with his teeth. He chewed with difficulty, blood dripping from his chin. Bates grunted in satisfaction as he indulged his gluttony. Dark, rusty stains smeared his cheeks and some of the red liquid dripped from his long nails. When he opened his mouth, a gobbet fell to the floor and, quick as a flash, he scooped it up and rammed it back into his mouth.

Jo turned away, revolted, and fled from the kitchen.

Downstairs, Bates stuffed the last of the steak into his mouth then he fastidiously licked every last drop of blood from his fingers . . .

Also by Shaun Hutson

Slugs
Spawn

Erebus

Shaun Hutson

A STAR BOOK

Published by

the Paperback Division of

W.H. ALLEN & Co. PLC.

A Star Book
Published in 1984
by the Paperback Division of
W. H. Allen & Co. PLC
44 Hill Street, London W1X 8LB

First published in Great Britain by
W. H. Allen & Co. PLC, 1984

Phototypeset by Input Typesetting Ltd, London
Printed and bound in Great Britain by
Anchor Brendon Ltd, Tiptree, Essex

ISBN 0 352 31498 2

To Peter Williams
Make mine de-caffeinated with honey

Acknowledgements

To everyone who helped with this book, thank you. On the research side, I would like to thank Mr Peter Milton. Regarding the actual writing, many thanks to Niki, who helped me even more than usual. Thanks also to Bob Tanner who, at the beginning, gave me the kick up the backside I so richly deserved. And I am grateful to everyone at W. H. Allen concerned with the production and distribution of this book.

Shaun Hutson

Erebus (er-u-bus): 1. A region beyond Hades; the abode of the Dead.

2. The Greek God of darkness, born of chaos.

PART ONE

'The motions of his spirit are dull as night,
And his affections dark as Erebus . . .'
   – *The Merchant of Venice*; Act V; scene 1

'Shame on the night.
For places I've been
And what I've seen . . .'
   – Ronnie James Dio

One

The gravel of the driveway crunched loudly beneath the wheels of the Rolls Royce as Terence Bristow brought the vehicle to a halt.

He switched off the engine and glanced across to the passenger seat where his wife, Laura, sat. They exchanged smiles and clambered out of the car. The drive from their home some eight miles from Wakely, to the stables, had taken less than fifteen minutes and they had passed just two vehicles on the way.

It was still early and Laura pulled her white mink jacket tighter around her in an effort to ward off the slight chill in the air. Fingers of mist drew patterns across the grass which surrounded the complex of white-washed buildings. She wasn't normally up so early in the morning, and, glancing down, she saw that the hands of her solid gold Cartier watch had barely reached 7.06 a.m.

Bristow rubbed his hands together, smiling as he saw the senior stud-groom approaching from one of the stables. They exchanged pleasantries and proceeded up a narrow path towards another building.

'How are things today?' asked Bristow.

'Fine, Mr Bristow,' said John Peters, scratching at his left ear. 'We had the foal out in the paddock yesterday. He's feeding well and he looks strong.'

Bristow nodded approvingly. The foal had been late, born just two days ago. A May foal. Something of a rarity in the world of racing but, Bristow reasoned, the animal would be worth millions. Sired, as it had been, by Regal Gent, winner of both the English and Irish Derbies the previous year. After the second win, Bristow had decided to put the animal out to stud. Now, as he leant on the gate of the box and looked in, he smiled contentedly.

The smell of fresh straw was strong in his nostrils and, inside the box, one young studman was busily turning the yellow strands over with a small pitchfork. Another lad, a rotund, red-faced youth in his teens, was brushing the tail of the mare which stood quietly before him. Bristow's eyes strayed to the foal and he was suitably satisfied by the sleek sheen of both animals' coats. The mare was a bay, a large animal perhaps eighteen or nineteen hands and she seemed to dwarf the foal which nuzzled her flanks.

'A winner if ever I saw one,' said Bristow reaching across to grip his wife's hand.

Laura was looking at the mare which had begun to move its head back and forth somewhat agitatedly.

'She's lathering up a little, isn't she?' Laura said, noticing some flecks of sweat around the animal's neck.

The studman brushing the mare's tail merely continued with his task. He stepped back, accidentally treading in some droppings. His companion held back a chuckle and continued turning the straw. But, as he looked up, he too saw that the bay was beginning to sweat. She continued to swing her head back and forth for a moment longer then she suddenly froze. But her ears were pricked, her nostrils flared wide and, as he watched, her eyes seemed to roll in the sockets. She snorted loudly.

With lightning speed, the mare lashed out with her offside hind leg, driving her hoof back savagely, catching the younger studman in the solar plexus. There was a sickening thud, accompanied by the strident

4

cracking of bone as several ribs splintered under the impact and he was propelled backward by the blow, crashing into the far wall of the box. In the twelve foot square area all hell suddenly seemed to break loose.

'What's wrong with her?' Bristow shouted at Peters who was already slipping the catch on the door in an effort to get inside the enclosure but, as he saw the mare rear up, he slowed his pace.

The first studman dropped his fork and pressed himself against the wall, heart hammering against his ribs. He glanced at the mare and then at his companion who was slumped against the rear wall, blood dribbling over his lips. He had no means of restraining the mare for she wore no harness of any kind. The foal took a couple of nervous steps back, whinneying softly.

'For God's sake do something,' Bristow demanded as he watched the mare turn its attention to the foal.

The larger animal struck swiftly, its head snaking forward cobra-like to strike at the bewildered foal. Powerful teeth were clamped together like a vice and the mare bit hard, twisting its head for a second, tearing a large lump of flesh and muscle free. The bite was a lethal one for it severed one of the foal's carotid arteries. Blood exploded from the savage wound with the force of a high pressure hose, spraying the horrified onlookers.

Laura Bristow screamed as the crimson fluid splattered across her face and body, turning her white mink the colour of poppies. Bristow himself could only watch mesmerised as the mare reared high in the air before bringing both front hooves crashing down onto the smaller animal's back, smashing its spine. The foal crumpled beneath the onslaught, its legs collapsing under it. The little animal raised its head as if soliciting help but a piledriver blow from the mare caught it above the right eye. The sharp edge of the hoof shaved away a portion of the skull and tore the glistening orb from the socket. Still attached by the optic nerve, it dangled like some bloodied table tennis ball from the gaping hole in its head.

The first studman took his chance and ran for the unlatched door. The mare struck at him but missed and the youth vaulted the partition, rolling over in the gravel on the other side.

'Get some help! Hurry!' shouted Peters and the lad scrambled to his feet.

Laura had fainted but Bristow himself could only stand and stare, as if entranced by the horrendous tableau before him. He failed to notice that Peters had turned away and was shouting to several other men nearby, motioning for them to join him.

The foal was already dead and the mare stood over the body, her mad eyes fixing Bristow in a challenging stare. The air was thick with the stench of blood and excrement, the only sounds now the low snorting of the horse and the moans of pain from the injured studman.

Bristow heard voices drawing closer. He felt his stomach begin to churn and then, as he took one last look at the foal, he bent double and retched until there was nothing left in his stomach.

Two

The mist hung thickly around the hills and hollows which surrounded the town of Wakely. But, as a watery sun began to haul itself across the sky, those shreds of condensation began to disperse, as if a veil were being drawn back to reveal the small town.

It stood amidst a patchwork of woods and fields, some of the many farms which dotted its outskirts clung to the sides of the low hills. Others, like the town itself, seemed to be hiding away in shallow valleys.

The closest town to it, about twenty minutes drive along the main road which bisected the countryside, was Arkham. The two places could not have been more different. The latter being a thriving, bustling centre of industry and commerce whilst Wakely depended largely on its livestock and arable farming. The economy of the whole place seemed to revolve around the dozen or so farms nearby. The land rewarded the efforts of those who toiled on it. The soil was rich in minerals and, other than a disastrous failed harvest back in 1964, no one in Wakely could remember when nature had denied them full bounty.

The town itself was a curious amalgam of ancient and modern. In the high street, one or two half-timbered houses sat almost reluctantly alongside red brick shops and small offices. The town was regarded affectionately by its older inhabitants, sometimes reviled by the younger members of the community due to its lack of leisure amenities. But for a bingo hall and a twice weekly disco (held in the small youth club) Wakely offered little in the way of entertainment. Days were spent at work, nights in front of the television or at one of the six pubs. Once more the clash of chronology showed itself in the architecture of the pubs themselves. There were those which still burned real fires in their grates in winter and refused the intrusion of a juke-box, whilst others sported pool tables and drinking was done to the accompaniment of pop music and the electronic bleeping of Space Invaders.

The town seemed to represent a polarisation of styles

and opinions but its inhabitants were united by one thing. Their reliance on the land.

Butchers bought local livestock at the weekly market. The numerous grocers purchased their goods from those farmers who maintained arable lands. Even bakeries made their own flour from wheat and corn supplied locally. Outsiders came to buy, naturally, but the town seemed to guard its yields jealously and buyers from anywhere other than Wakely itself usually went home with little or nothing.

But, if the produce of the surrounding countryside was something to be horded, friendship was not. Isolated it might have been but Wakely's inhabitants were not imbued with the coldness which sometimes afflicts residents of isolated communities. Nonetheless, it remained a town in hiding. Nestled within its cocoon of hills, trees and fields Wakely and its residents survived admirably without the help or hindrance of outsiders.

In the stillness of the morning, sounds of men at work were already beginning to fill the air. Those who worked on the farms had been on the go since before the break of dawn and now, as the sun burned away the last wraith-like vestiges of mist, Wakely began to come to life.

Three

Ken Hargreaves put down his slice of cake and grunted irritably.

'Do you have to do that at the bloody table?' he

rasped, looking across at his companion who was busily inspecting the contents of one nostril on the end of his finger.

Nick Daley apologised and returned to his cup of tea instead. At just twenty-nine he was almost twenty years younger than his thick-set colleague opposite. Ken Hargreaves took one more fleeting look at the younger man then stuffed what was left of the cake into his mouth, his attention shifting to the newspaper spread out before him. All around other men chatted, smoked, drank tea or coffee and ate. Some with hearty appetites, others more perfunctorily. Hargreaves saw this same ritual every day and had done for the past thirty-two years.

In the canteen of Wakely abattoir men discovered whether they really *were* hungry or not. Of the younger men, Daley amongst them, few ate with such gusto as Hargreaves and his older workmates. He, himself, had just demolished three rashers of bacon and two eggs before his cake. Daley had prodded at a piece of apple pie, more interested in gazing round about him than eating. Or, Hargreaves reasoned, somewhat reluctant to fill his stomach, imagining the sight he would shortly be witnessing.

The only thing which Hargreaves had not been able to get used to in all his years at the place was the smell. He expected it to smell like a charnel house downstairs because that was what it was. The stench of blood and excrement was almost palpable, such was its intensity. But, even now, in the light, air-conditioned canteen, that smell still followed him – the smell of death which clung to him after work like a second skin, resistant to even the strongest soaps, unremovable by countless showers and baths. His clothes were washed every night yet still that pungent odour seemed to permeate the very fibres as an ever-present reminder of the job he did.

9

Wakely abattoir employed just over fifty men engaged in tasks ranging from the unloading of live-stock, the inspecting of those animals for disease, preparation of the carcasses and, naturally, killing. That was the job which Hargreaves performed. As many as 500 animals a day passed through the slaughterhouse, arriving in twos and threes, brought by individual farmers. Some arrived in the huge two-tier trucks which could hold as many as eighty pigs.

Hargreaves had been given the task of showing young Daley the ropes and, as he glanced up periodically from his paper, he could see that the younger man was nervous. He had only worked at the slaughter-house for two days and it was to be his first time in the killing room, nicknamed 'the carcass cave' by the men who worked in it. In five minutes' time, when the hands on the wall clock crawled round to 10.15 a.m., he would follow Hargreaves down to the pens where the various livestock were waiting to be despatched. Already he looked pale and the older man smiled to himself, wondering if Daley would be like the last youngster they'd assigned to him. The youth had watched fascin-ated as Hargreaves had loaded the humane killer then, as it was pressed to the cow's head he had keeled over, falling face down in the sea of crimson which swam ankle deep on the floor of the killing room. No one had seen him since.

'If you think you're going to throw up, go outside and do it,' said Hargreaves, glancing up at Daley.

The younger man swallowed hard.

'What?'

'If you want to puke,' Hargreaves expanded. 'Don't do it in the meat room.'

Daley nodded, a thin film of perspiration sheathing his forehead as he saw Hargreaves down the last of his tea and get to his feet. He motioned for his younger companion to follow.

They left the canteen and headed down a flight of stairs which brought them into a long corridor, sealed at the far end by a heavy steel door. Hargreaves opened it and ushered Daley through. They emerged onto a high walkway which ran around the cavernous interior of the meat room. The slatted metal cat-walk had a handrail and Daley leant against this in order to look down into the pens below. Tethered there were up to two dozen bullocks, some standing still, others pawing the blood-soaked floor in bewilderment. The stench was unbelievable. Despite six powerful extractor fans which hummed loudly inside the large room, the smell still drifted up in invisible tendrils, causing Daley to recoil slightly. A large set of double doors to his right were open and he could see two men pulling away the carcass of a dead bullock, a large hook driven through its nose. He swallowed hard as he saw that the body was still twitching. The lowing of the cattle seemed to bounce off the walls, rolling around inside Daley's head like slowly breaking waves.

'Put these on,' said Hargreaves, handing the younger man a pair of what looked like waders. They fastened by a strap at his thigh and he saw that the older man also wore a pair. When both were suitably attired, Hargreaves led the way down another flight of steps to the floor of the room. Daley saw the blood lap around his ankles and he gritted his teeth as a portion of bone floated past on the sea of gore, bound for one of the many drains which dotted the concrete floor. One or two had already become clogged with pieces of animal debris and excrement and Hargreaves decided that the place would have to be hosed down before he started on the next group of animals. However, he intended to dispose of the bullocks first.

Near to the animal pens was a wide, stainless steel-topped bench. On top of it lay an assortment of tools. Daley noticed a small sledgehammer, a couple of saws and what looked like a large air pistol. It was that particular device which Hargreaves picked up. It had a vicious looking metal bolt extending from it, protruding about an inch from the end of the barrel.

'The humane killer,' Hargreaves announced, holding up the weapon. He then crossed to the nearest of the pens and approached a bullock which was licking the metal struts of the enclosure, apparently unconcerned by the presence of the two men. Hargreaves leant forward, pressed the bolt to the animal's forehead and pulled the trigger.

There was a loud thud. The implement bucked in the older man's hand as the bolt slammed into the bullocks's skull then quickly retracted, bringing with it a sizeable lump of bone. The animal let out a low grunt then dropped as if pole-axed. Streams of blood erupted from the hole in its forehead. The sphincter muscle gave out and, as the bullock underwent its death-throes, Daley heard the rapid splattering of excrement in the sea of red fluid beneath. He blenched, gripped the pen with both hands and coughed.

Hargreaves watched him for a second, noticing that his skin had taken on a pale, yellowish tinge.

A blast of coppery-smelling fumes swept over them both and, almost immediately, the two men from the double doors to the right emerged and headed for the dead bullock. They nodded a greeting to Hargreaves who exchanged brief words with one of them. Both men were sweating profusely.

'There's eighty pigs coming in at eleven, Ken,' said the first man. 'If you can shift this lot,' he made a sweeping gesture towards the penned bullocks, 'I'd be grateful.'

Hargreaves nodded.

Daley was still gazing down at the body of the dead animal.

'First time in here, is it?' asked the man with the meat hook.

The youngster could only nod.

Hargreaves suppressed a grin as he saw the first man squat down beside the dead bullock. He pulled back the animal's lips and bared its teeth, turning the head in Daley's direction.

'Say cheese,' said the first man, grinning.

Hargreaves and the other two cracked out laughing but Daley didn't see the joke. He merely watched in silence as the carcass was dragged away.

'You all right?' Hargreaves asked him.

The younger man nodded although the gesture was a mechanical one. He could feel his stomach somersaulting.

They moved to the next pen.

The animal inside it was still but it watched the slaughterer with rheumy eyes that seemed to hide a glint of fear. Fear? Anger? Realization? He had often wondered, during his years in the abattoir, whether the animals actually knew what was going to happen to them. Did this particular bullock somehow understand what was about to take place?

He steadied the humane killer in his hand and took a step closer.

Suddenly the animal lunged forward, slamming itself into the metal pen. The impact shook the small enclosure, causing the two bullocks next to it to spring into action as well. There wasn't much room inside the pen for it to gather momentum but, nonetheless, the bullock still managed to attain sufficient impetus to bend the top two struts of the enclosure.

'Jesus,' muttered Hargreaves, stepping back for a second.

The steer let out a low rumbling bellow and launched itself at the frame once more.

Daley saw the gate buckling.

The other two bullocks by now were also slamming repeatedly against their pens and Hargreaves realized that he must act quickly. He stepped forward and lowered the bolt. However, the animal brought its head up sharply and knocked the device from the slaughterer's hand. It flew into the air, disappearing beneath the tide of crimson.

'Christ,' he growled. Then turning to Daley.

'Get the other one – it's on the workbench.'

Daley was frozen for long seconds but the sight of the pen gate bending spurred him on. He waded through the blood, nearly slipping once, and snatched up the second of the bolt-loaded killers.

'Hurry,' shouted Hargreaves.

The first bullock let out a booming roar and drove its way through the battered metal of the pen.

Rivets, screws and pieces of aluminium exploded into the air, showering the two men who raised their hands to shield their faces. The large animal skidded on the slippery floor but then regained its footing and turned on its would-be executioners. Hargreaves managed to leap aside, blood spraying up in a crimson wave as he went sprawling in the mess, but Daley was too slow.

The bullock hit him in the stomach with its left horn, driving him up against the metal work-bench, the lethal stubby protuberance gouging his skin. He screamed in agony as he felt his stomach wall give way beneath the unbearable pressure. The stench of the bullock mingled with the powerful odour of his own viscera as the crushing impact first mangled the lower part of his ribcage to a pulp, rupturing both lungs, then tore open his belly, releasing a tangle of intestines.

'Oh my God,' gasped Hargreaves, rolling over. He was lying less than two feet from the maddened bullock and its victim, his hand still firmly clamped around the humane killer. Daley's screams filled his ears like the cries of the damned, echoing off the walls.

The slaughterer dragged himself to his feet and pressed the bolt to the bullock's side.

With a roar of rage and pain it backed off, the hole in its left shoulder gradually growing bigger as the flesh seemed to rip like tearing material. A mess of entrails began to bulge from the riven hide. The beast snorted, blood spilling from its nostrils. It tried to turn but staggered and fell as its bolt-blasted shoulder gave out. Hargreaves leapt back, hearing the sound of tearing metal from behind him.

The other two bullocks had broken free.

The meat room had become a madhouse, a deafening cacophony of bellows, roars and screams, both human and animal. Hargreaves found his breath coming in gasps and he looked around desperately for a means of escape. There was an alarm bell on the far wall. Whether he could reach it or not was another matter.

The second bullock spun round and headed towards him, stumbling momentarily, giving him precious seconds. But, the waders slowed Hargreaves down. In his mind's eye he could see the bullock. Head lowered, charging towards him, ready to grind him into the ground beneath its crushing weight.

The alarm looked a hundred miles away.

'What the fuck is happening?'

He heard the shout of surprise and horror as the first of the men with meat hooks appeared and looked in upon the scene of carnage. He barely had time to shout a warning to them and they slammed the metal doors, dropping the locking bar in place as the third bullock smashed into it. Then they stood helpless, listening to the unholy commotion from inside the meat room itself.

Hargreaves reached the alarm and smashed the glass with one bloodied fist, the strident shriek of the siren immediately joining the fierce bellowing of the maddened cattle. There was no more sound from Daley.

Hargreaves turned.

The bullock slammed into him, shattering his pelvis, destroying kidneys and liver in the fearful impact. He felt as if his internal organs were being forced upwards first into his chest and then into his throat. What was, in fact, filling his throat was a mixture of blood and bile which, seconds later, gushed from his mouth like water from a broken dam. As the animal backed off, the slaughterer slumped to his knees and found himself gazing into the burning eyes. The beast fixed him in an insane stare, eyeballs bulging madly in red rimmed sockets, thick streamers of saliva hanging from its mouth.

The bullock drew back a foot or so then butted him again, pushing him down into the ocean of blood, pressing hard on his chest until the sternum collapsed and his body seemed to fold in upon itself.

A moment before he lost consciousness he heard footsteps above him on the metal cat-walk, the metallic rattle as a shotgun cartridge was chambered and, a second later, the deafening blast as the weapon was fired. The bullock was hit just behind the left eye, most of its head exploding, showering Hargreaves with a confetti of bone, blood and brain. The creature lowed and its legs buckled as a second discharge tore a hole in its side the size of a football.

The body collapsed beside the fallen man.

Hargreaves could only lie motionless as footsteps drew nearer. He heard shouts then another thunderous gunshot this time close to him.

Then he heard nothing at all.

Four

The light breeze set the curtains billowing, fluttering like the membranous wings of giant moths. The cool air was welcome because the room was stifling.

Vic Tyler lay on his back watching as the curtains danced softly at the bidding of the wind. A single bead of perspiration trickled from his forehead and he wiped it away with the back of his hand. Beneath him the sheets felt damp, a legacy of the warm night, and he shifted uncomfortably, finally swinging himself upright. Perched on the edge of the bed he sat motionless, head lowered, inhaling deeply in an effort to draw some sweet fresh air from the atmosphere of musty stale sweat and freshly laundered linen.

Outside the window birds sang in the clutch of willows which bent and sagged in the bright sunlight. Despite the fact that it was still relatively early, the burning orb in the cloudless sky blazed with savage intensity. Tyler glanced at the clock on the dressing table and saw that it was 10.30 a.m.

He muttered something to himself and ran a hand through his short brown hair. He'd overslept, or rather he'd been allowed to oversleep. If his father had still been alive . . .

The thought trailed off and Tyler swallowed hard, getting to his feet. He padded out of the bedroom across the landing to the bathroom where he switched on the shower, testing the water. He studied his reflection in the mirror, satisfied with what he saw. Tyler stood about six foot two, his body thick with muscle. At thirty-two he was in reasonably good shape for a man who had spent the last six years of his life working behind a desk. The transformation had not been easy for him. Born and brought up on a farm in Wakely, the farm to which he had now been forced to return, Tyler had always known and loved the freedom of the country-side. The city made him feel like a prisoner, an outsider. He had felt like a child, thrust into a strange environment.

At his father's suggestion he had left the farm just after his eighteenth birthday to attend agricultural college. Jack Tyler had seen the wisdom of allowing his son to learn that there was more to farming than driving a tractor and shovelling manure. Tyler himself had left with mixed feelings. Nevertheless, he settled to his new task. However, when his mother died three years later, he had been devastated.

He had returned to Wakely for the funeral and considered whether or not he should even contemplate making the trip back to college but his father persuaded him. He returned and completed the course, but the death of his mother was something which obsessed him. Guilt began to loom large in his mind. Would it have been any different if *he'd* been there? The spectre of that guilt still plagued him. From college he had moved on to work for the Ministry of Agriculture itself. He was good at his job, he earned an excellent salary and he had his own flat in Bayswater. He had friends too. Tyler was a likeable man, always quick to smile, ever ready with a warm handshake and a pleasant word. There had been a succession of girls, mostly one night stands but that was sufficient for him. It was how he wanted it. Yet still he felt a curious ambivalence towards the city. He welcomed what it gave him but he hated it for what it was. And he missed the country.

On hearing of his father's death his actions had been instantaneous. He had handed in his notice, packed his belongings into every available suitcase and carrier he could find and headed back to Wakely, leaving London and his memories behind him.

Now he stood beneath the shower, eyes closed, his mind full of thoughts and ideas yet somehow able to appraise the situation clearly and rationally. He was back where he belonged. Back in Wakely on the farm which had been his home for so many years and which, he promised himself, would remain so until his own death. There was a savage irony to the entire scenario which Tyler was not slow to consider. His father had originally sent him off to college and now, with Jack's death, he was home once more.

The last of the Tylers, he mused to himself. He smiled thinly but the gesture faded rapidly, as if washed from his face by the swiftly flowing water. He was back where he belonged but God alone knew that he would have given anything for it to be under different circumstances.

He turned off the shower and stood for long moments, watching the last of the water swirl away down the plughole. Then, he stepped out, wrapped a towel around himself and began drying his hair.

From the bathroom window he could see the red bulk of the Massey-Ferguson moving slowly across one of the fields to the North of the farm. It was driven by Russell Jenkins, one of two farmhands who Jack had employed. The other, Jim Harrison, was feeding the livestock elsewhere. Both men were in their forties and had worked for the family for as long as Tyler could remember.

Both had been present at yesterday's funeral.

Indeed, Tyler had been surprised at the number of people who had turned up. It had seemed as if the whole of Wakely had come to stand at his father's graveside. Each one of them carrying their individual memories of the man. Tyler had been both grateful and moved by their gesture. The townspeople had welcomed him back amongst them as if he had never been away. The place seemed to radiate cordiality, the homecoming only soured by the circumstances which necessitated it.

Tyler dried himself thoroughly then wandered back into the bedroom where he pulled on a pair of jeans and some old wellingtons. There was a crack in one of the toes and Tyler muttered irritably. There had been several violent thunderstorms recently and the earth of the farm was caught in a curious kind of limbo. Some parts were cracked and parched, others were like a quagmire. From the humidity in the air, Tyler had every reason to believe that they were in for another storm that night.

He went downstairs and, unable to face anything cooked, devoured six rounds of toast which he washed down with several large mugs of tea. Formica cupboards and stainless steel glinted in the rays of the sun which streamed through the open windows. The farm might be old and traditional on the outside but its amenities were strictly modern. The only concession to a bygone, less hectic and mechanised age were a couple of antiques housed in the sitting room: a full size man-trap which hung over the fire place and the rusted blade of a horse-drawn plough. Both had been put there by his father.

His father.

He exhaled deeply then got to his feet, wandering out of the house into the yard itself.

He winced momentarily, shielding his eyes from the glare, but then he relaxed, drawing in a deep breath which smelt of wet grass, hay and manure. The smell had a welcome familiarity about it and Tyler smiled as he headed towards the pig-sty which stood near to the farm's main gate. There was a barn close by which housed the sows and boars but the sty was used for weaners and it was obviously well populated judging by the noise which was coming from inside.

Tyler saw Jim Harrison standing amongst the hungry piglets, his gloved hand dispensing meal to them.

'Morning, Jim,' said Tyler, approaching the sty.

The farmhand looked up, the sun glinting on his bald head.

He nodded at Tyler, momentarily stopping his task.

'Me and Russ thought it best to let you sleep in, Mr Tyler,' said the bald man. 'With all what's happened, like.' He swallowed hard, as if embarrassed.

Tyler nodded.

'I appreciate it but I've got to get used to being up at dawn again now I'm here to stay.'

'Well, the work's underway anyhow, Mr Tyler.'

'Thanks. And you can drop the *Mr* Tyler bit too, Jim. Call me Vic.'

Harrison smiled, mischievously.

'OK,' he paused. 'Vic.'

Tyler peered into the sty and ran an appraising eye over the pigs inside.

'I thought we just used this sty for weaners,' he said, puzzled, looking at the size of the pigs rummaging around for the food which Harrison dropped.

'We do.'

'*These* are weaners?' asked Tyler, almost incredulously. 'But the bloody things are twice the size they should be. You're trying to tell me that these pigs are only ten weeks old?'

'We found it hard to believe at first,' Harrison told him. 'But it's the same with all the animals fed on that new meal.'

Tyler frowned, looking first at Harrison and then at the pigs again. One of them raised its head, nostrils flared, small eyes fixing him in a glassy stare.

'Your father,' Harrison said, dropping his gaze as he spoke, 'he bought some new multi-purpose feed a few weeks back. The fellow who sold it to him said it would increase growth in livestock.'

Tyler nodded approvingly.

'What about the milk yield from the cows, has it affected that?' he wanted to know.

The farm hand shook his head.

'Where did my father get this feed?' asked Tyler.

'There's a new company just outside town,' Harrison said, struggling to remember the name. 'But I'm buggered if I can remember what they're called.' Harrison shrugged. 'Anyway, they make and sell the stuff.'

Tyler nodded.

'Well, it obviously works. We should get a better price for the stock at market.'

'Most of the farms around here are using it,' Harrison added. He tossed what was left of the meal into a small trough then unlatched the sty and eased himself out. He lingered for a moment then wiped his head, leaving a dark smear on his bald dome.

'If it's all right with you, Mr Ty . . . sorry, Vic, I'll get on with my other jobs.'

'Right, I'll be along to help in a minute,' Tyler said, listening as Harrison picked his way across the muddy yard, his boots squelching in the thick ooze.

The younger man leant on the wall of the sty and gazed in at the weaners gathered around the trough. As he had first noticed, for their age, most of the animals inside the enclosure were twice their normal size. It looked as though he was going to make a sizeable profit at the market in two days' time.

Tyler stroked his chin thoughtfully.

He wondered how big the weaners would be when they had finished growing.

22

Five

The first low rumblings of thunder rolled across the bruised sky, banks of blue-black cloud giving it a mottled appearance. The first silent forks of lightning pushed their way tentatively across the darkened heavens.

The lights in the laboratory flickered once then regained their initial brilliance. The banks of fluorescents in the ceiling reflected off the work tops in the large room. The animals in the rows of cages scurried back and forth nervously as the storm drew nearer.

Geoffrey Anderson crossed to the lab door and peered through the meshed glass panel near the top then, still not fully satisfied that he was alone, he pushed the door open a fraction and peered out. The corridor on either side of him was deserted, the floor sparkling as if someone had been over it with a gigantic buffing machine. The white walls reflected the glow from the strip lights overhead making it seem brighter in the corridor and Anderson felt suddenly conspicuous. But he was satisfied that he was alone.

The clock behind him ticked noisily in the silence, the hands having crawled around to 10.15 p.m. Apart from the rhythmic sound of the timepiece the only disturbance in the solitude was the distant thunder and the agitated squeaking of the animals.

Anderson locked the door behind him, flicked off the lights and stood silently for long seconds. There was a film of perspiration clinging to his face which he hurriedly wiped off with the sleeve of his white overall. As he looked down, the red and silver V C, the logo worn by all Vanderburg employees, seemed to wink at him. He swallowed hard then moved across to the wall phone, looking over his shoulder once more towards the meshed window.

His hand was shaking slightly as he began to dial.

The staccato clatter of typewriter keys sounded like machine-gun fire in the confines of the small office and Jo Ward sighed as she read and re-read the piece she had just finished. There was something not quite right about it but she couldn't put her finger on what it was. To hell with it, she thought, at least she'd make the deadline with time to spare. The stories didn't have to go to press until eleven in order for them to reach the morning edition of the *Arkham Comet*. Elsewhere in the office things were at various stages of organized pandemonium as other reporters rushed to complete their assignments, some hampered by the fact that their typewriting dexterity had not yet extended to more than one finger.

The phone on Jo's desk rang and she picked it up.

'*Arkham Comet*,' she said, her American accent sounding as strong now as it had been when she had first come to work for the paper six months ago.

'I want to speak to Joanna Ward,' the voice at the other end said, breathlessly. It sounded as if the man had been running.

'Speaking. Who is this?' she wanted to know.

'There isn't much time. My name is Anderson. Geoffrey Anderson, I've spoken to you before.'

Jo ran a hand through her chestnut hair, brushing two or three long strands from her forehead.

'Oh, the guy who works at Vanderburg Chemicals,' she said, finally recognizing his voice. She had, indeed, spoken to him before but his voice sounded different this time. There was a strong note of urgency in it, fear even.

'I have to meet you,' he said. 'Tonight.'

Jo reached for a pencil and began drawing irregular shapes on the pad before her. She glanced briefly at her watch.

'It's getting late, Mr Anderson, surely we could discuss it tomorrow or . . .'

He cut her short.

'No.' He almost shouted the word at her. 'It must be tonight.' She could hear him breathing hard.

'Whereabouts?' she wanted to know. 'A pub maybe, there's . . .'

Again he interrupted.

'No. Nowhere where there are people. What I have to say . . .'

The sentence trailed off and, for long seconds, Jo thought that the phone had gone dead. Outside there was a loud growl of thunder.

'Mr Anderson,' she said.

Silence then a burst of static.

'Mr Anderson, are you still there?'

'Yes.' His voice was lower but still strained. 'There's a lay-by on the main road between Wakely and Arkham, it's near an old roadside café. The place is deserted now. Meet me there at eleven-thirty.'

She scribbled something on her pad.

'Hello,' he babbled. 'Did you hear me?'

'Yeah, I got it. Eleven-thirty. I'll see you then.'

'Don't tell anyone,' he gasped. 'I . . .'

The line went dead.

Jo flicked the cradle but there was just the steady hum of static. Finally she put down the receiver, replacing it slowly as if she expected it to burst into life once more. Whatever it was that Anderson wanted he was certainly in a hurry to tell her. She chewed the end of her pencil thoughtfully then glanced down at the location she had scribbled on the pad. A lay-by in the middle of nowhere – what the hell would he want to meet her there for? She wondered if the guy was some kind of creep, maybe he was going to try and jump her the minute he got her alone. She shook her head. He didn't sound like that sort of person. He *did* sound frightened however.

She got to her feet, slipped the notepad into her handbag and headed for the door.

Outside, the storm was drawing closer.

Geoffrey Anderson drew in a deep breath, held it a second then opened the door of the darkened lab. The corridor outside was still empty, all the doors leading down to the lifts tightly locked. He had removed his white coat and stood now in his two-piece suit, his tie undone. He felt as if it were strangling him and, when he swallowed, the muscles of his throat seemed to be swollen. He wiped a hand across his face, salty drops of perspiration stinging his eyes. Overhead, the strip lights buzzed like indolent bluebottles and Anderson paused momentarily as he heard the distant thunder growl menacingly.

He locked the lab door and began walking along the corridor, his shoes beating out an urgent tattoo in the preternatural silence of the deserted building.

Anderson turned a corner and found himself at the lifts. He jabbed the button which would take him to the ground floor, shuffling impatiently as the car rose. His eyes were fixed on the glowing white numbers which lit up as it passed each floor.

It stopped at 3 and his heart missed a beat, the breath frozen in his lungs, but when the lift finally arrived it was empty. He stepped in and rode down to the ground floor.

The reception area of Vanderburg Chemicals was vast, large enough to hold a football pitch. Doors and corridors led off from this carpeted central chamber like the tunnels in a termite nest. At the far end were six sets of reinforced glass double doors. Rain was already coursing down them as the deluge outside began and now bright forks of lightning tore through the blanket of clouds. There were just three lights burning in the reception area, the shadows in the corners seeming thicker, conspiratorial. As if they were hiding something.

Anderson walked quickly towards the exit, his feet now cushioned by the carpet. In the dull light its normal orange colour reminded him of congealed blood.

He reached the doors and paused for a second. His car, a blue Ford Granada, was parked on the other side of the car park. There were other vehicles out there and he counted six large Scania lorries, each one with a tanker attached. The black tankers bore the familiar red and silver logo of Vanderburg Chemicals, the two letters joined together at the curve of the C.

Rain was beating heavily against the glass doors of the main building and, every so often, Anderson would shield his eyes as the sky exploded into a patchwork of searing lightning which left an afterburn on his retina.

There were one or two lights still glowing in windows on the East side of the building and Anderson wondered who could still be working at 10.45. He just hoped they hadn't seen him.

The large sheds to his right were silent, huge black leering shapes, they seemed to grow from the night itself. These were the warehouses and manufacturing buildings where hundreds of tons of the new Vanderburg multi-purpose feed were stored and created using a formula which Anderson himself had worked on. Beyond them stood the well-lit living quarters used by all but a handful of Vanderburg's employees.

There was movement behind him.

He spun round, the breath catching in his throat. In the abyss of the large reception area he could see nothing. The shadows seemed to grow darker, the lightning momentarily abating as if even the elements were combining to conceal the source of the sound from him.

It came again.

A soft, swishing sound, close to him.

A particularly vehement crack of lightning suddenly

lit the entire area, bathing it for precious seconds in cold blue light and, in that light, Anderson saw what was making the noise.

Someone had forgotten to close a window and the broad leaves of a rubber plant were swatting the glass nearby. He smiled thinly, a whisper of relief escaping him.

He almost laughed aloud at his own foolishness. He was, he told himself, becoming paranoid. Nevertheless, his heart would not stop pounding.

There was a loud ring as the lift purred into action.

Someone was descending.

Anderson moved quickly, pushing open the exit doors, ignoring the rain which drenched him. He ran across the tarmac to his car, fumbling in his jacket pocket for his keys as the heavens exploded in a deafening symphony of power above him. He jammed the key in the lock and slid, gratefully, behind the wheel. For long moments he sat there, his breath coming in gasps, head bowed. Then, he pulled the handkerchief from his pocket and mopped his face as best he could. His breathing began to slow down somewhat. Anderson inserted the key in the ignition and gripped the wheel, glancing down at the clock on the dashboard as he did so.

It was almost 10.59.

He prepared to start the engine.

The dark shape rose from the back of the Granada as if it had materialized from the blackness itself. Something cold and thin was looped around Anderson's neck and it was a second or two before he realized what was going on. He was slammed back in his seat as the wire was pulled tight.

He tried to grip the lethal strand, to ease the mounting pressure on his oesophagus, but the more he struggled, the tighter it was pulled. A second tug nearly hauled him over the back of the seat and now the

28

cheese wire began to cut through his flesh, through his windpipe. Jets of blood sprayed the windscreen as veins and arteries were cut. Anderson's eyes bulged in their sockets and his attempt at a scream came out as a liquid gurgle. Blood poured down the front of his shirt as his body began to go into an uncontrollable spasm.

The dark shape in the back seat made no sound but merely pulled harder on the wire, wrenching Anderson several inches up from his seat.

His bladder gave out and a dark stain spread rapidly across his crotch, mingling with the blood which was puddling on the mock leather beneath him. His eyes rolled upwards in their sockets, bulging like swollen boiled eggs, as he felt the tide of unconciousness roll over him. There was a sound in his ears like that of the sea. A great pounding, churning noise which blotted out everything else.

The sound of fluid excretion signalled his death but Anderson's executioner pulled the wire tight against the dead man's spinal cord. Only the bone prevented Anderson from being decapitated.

The car smelt like a slaughterhouse.

The dark shape in the back sat perfectly still for long seconds just gazing at the body of Anderson.

Outside the rain lashed the car unmercifully. Inside, blood trickled down the windscreen like crimson tears.

Six

Jo Ward wiped the condensation from her windscreen and peered through the lashing rain which slammed against the glass. The wiper blades seemed unable to clear the torrents and she wondered if she was going to have to stop.

The road between Wakely and Arkham was badly lit, framed as it was on both sides by trees. They bent and bowed beneath the driving rain, spidery branches reaching down towards the slowly moving Chevette. The headlamps cut a swathe through the blackness but still Jo found visibility was down to about fifty feet. The dull orange glare of the sodium lamps were like pools across the road, islands of light in a sea of darkness.

Why the hell did Anderson have to pick a place like this to meet her? she thought.

She caught sight of the disused transport cafe from her side window. Just beyond it, shrouded by trees, was the lay-by which Anderson had spoken of.

Jo eased the Chevette along the last few tortuous yards of slick tarmac then drew to a halt, the car facing Wakely. She wondered whether or not to switch off her headlamps. Surely he would find her anyway? She decided to leave just the side lights burning. A rolling crack of thunder seemed to shake the car and Jo shuddered involuntarily. She reached for her handbag and pulled out a pack of cigarettes, easing the window down slightly to let the smoke out but rain poured in too freely and she hastily wound it up again. The car began to fill with a blue haze.

Jo smiled thinly to herself. It was like breathing New York air. The smile faded rapidly. Even the thought of that dirty city sent a shudder through her. She'd been born and brought up on Manhattan's East Side, over-looking the slimy brown tongue which was the East

30

river. Some days, she and her friends would stand on the Queensboro bridge and look down at the small boats and tugs which moved along that aquatic thoroughfare. Jo often wondered where the boats were heading, her curiosity more usually extending to the men who worked on them as well. Were they going home to loving wives? To endless rows? Had some of them even got homes to go to? All through her early years Jo's interest in other people had been something which amused and surprised those who knew her. Not least her parents. Her father worked for a cab company while her mother cleaned rooms at the Hotel Roosevelt, less than three blocks from where they lived.

Jo began her own working life at the hotel, earning enough money to support herself while she pursued a faltering career as a freelance journalist. Her interest in people and her curiosity seemed to find a pefect outlet in the articles she wrote. Forever probing and searching for something, she would work an eight hour day at the Roosevelt then begin anew when she got back to her home at night. But journalism was her real love and, as the years passed and her payment cheques totalled just 1,500 dollars, she began to despair of ever making a real breakthrough into the profession she craved so much to be a part of.

Then she met Tony.

Tony Hagen was a guest at the Roosevelt when he first met Jo. Immediately impressed by his appearance and looks she was at first taken aback by his advances. She was a very attractive girl and she was aware of that fact but they came from such vastly different ends of the social spectrum that contact seemed impossible. However, as she got to know him better she found that the fancy suits and expensive jewellery came from an unexpected source. Hagen worked for Alberto Scalise, great grandson of one of Al Capone's top trigger men and then head of the largest of New York's five families.

31

The temptation was too great for her. She slept with Hagen, she used him, remembering each little piece of information he let slip until she had enough material for an article which she managed to sell to *The New York Times*. They wanted more and they were willing to pay a high price. The opportunity was irresistible.

After the third article appeared she was offered a job on the paper which she took immediately. However, Hagen became more evasive, frightened even. He warned her off, telling her not to write anything else about Scalise but Jo had always been stubborn.

She continued seeing Hagen who, she realized, had fallen in love with her despite the dangers to himself. But she could prise no more information out of him. Or so it seemed.

When he asked her to marry him she agreed and Hagen once more allowed his tongue to flap.

The next story she wrote made the front page.

Within two days it was all over.

They had been sitting in a bar on Lexington Avenue when two men walked in who Hagen instantly recognized.

Now, as Jo sat in the Chevette sucking hard on her cigarette she could still see the scene, printed indelibly on her mind. The first of the men had been carrying a coat over his right arm, the second merely stood in the doorway. Hagen had turned to face them, the beer glass still mid-way between his mouth and the bar top. The first man had let the coat slide away to reveal what he held beneath. Jo had recognized it as a .45 automatic. The man had fired three times.

The first shot caught Hagen in the face, shattering the beer glass before ploughing into his chin, blasting away most of his bottom jaw. The second shot hit him in the chest and lifted him off his feet. The third blew a fist-sized hole through his left shoulder, the impact spinning him round. He dropped to his knees, the screams of the customers ringing loud in his ears.

Jo had thrown herself over the bar, pulling her legs up and shielding her head as more slugs ploughed into the thick wood, blasting long shards away. She heard the hammer slam down on an empty chamber and she took her chance. Leaping to her feet she pushed past the terrified barman and scrambled for the rear exit.

Neither of the men followed her.

Naturally, the incident itself made front page news but Jo had been shaken nonetheless, and then when someone blew the windscreen of her Lincoln away with a shotgun as she was driving home one evening, it was the last straw.

She left America and came to London where she found freelance work relatively easily, but London seemed too central. Too exposed. She moved to Arkham and had worked on the *Arkham Comet* for six months.

She ground out the cigarette in the ashtray and lit up another, glancing at her watch as she did so.

11.48 p.m.

Where in the hell was Anderson?

No other vehicles had passed by, coming from or going to Wakely. She drummed on the wheel irritably and peered out into the storm blasted night.

Away to her left stood the old transport café, now a hollow shell. The only thing moving was a rusty old sign which swayed and rocked precariously as it was buffeted by the wind. The large windows which had once formed the front of the dining area had been smashed and scores of stones lay in the forecourt. There was even the wreck of a Volkswagen rusting in what used to be the car park. The entire, decaying complex was cloaked in blackness, illuminated only occasionally by the bursts of lightning which ripped across the rain-sodden sky.

Jo ran both hands through her hair and glanced at herself in the rear-view mirror. Considering some of the things she had been through in her life she looked remarkably fresh for her twenty-eight years. There wasn't a worry line to be seen and the almost perfect curve of her skin was broken only by a small scar near her right eye – the legacy of that night in the bar on Lexington Avenue. She wore little or no make-up, except for some eye-liner. Even in the darkness of the car, those twin green orbs seemed to glow like jade beacons. She wore a pair of jeans, cut off at the bottom, the material slightly frayed, and a dark blue sweatshirt accentuated her breasts.

She was in the process of lighting another cigarette when she heard the loud drone of a car engine.

Seconds later, powerful headlights cut through the night, shining brightly in her face for fleeting moments as the car drove past.

'Goddamit,' she muttered as the vehicle disappeared in the direction of Arkham.

Jo looked at her watch again. It was almost 12.15. After another five minutes she intended leaving. She'd stop at the first phone she came across and ring Anderson's home. Maybe the stupid son of a bitch had forgotten. Jo quickly dismissed the thought. He had sounded too anxious on the phone, too distraught. He needed to see her and she believed him. Perhaps his car had broken down. She quickly ran through a list of reasons why he hadn't turned up then looked at her watch once again. Three more minutes and she was going.

She snapped her fingers. She'd noticed a phone box on the forecourt of the deserted transport cafe. If it was still working she could ring from there. She had his number at Vanderburg too in case something had prevented him leaving. Jo decided to ring there first.

She twisted the key in the ignition and started the

engine, swinging the Chevette around, heading back towards the night shrouded derelict cafe. She pulled into the kerb and pushed open her door. Leaving the engine idling she sprinted the twenty yards to the phone box.

In the Stygian gloom of the rain-soaked woods something moved.

Something large.

Across the other side of the road, hidden by the impenetrable blackness and the stifling confines of the trees, a portion of the night seemed to detach itself and find animation. The shape moved slowly through the trees, watching as Jo first stopped her car and then clambered out to scuttle to the phone box. She could be seen quite clearly because the lightning now lashed the sky with increasing rapidity, casting a cold bluish glow over the landscape.

The shape watched intently as Jo lifted the receiver, then, like a shadow, it seemed to spread as it approached the roadside.

There was a particularly vehement explosion across the heavens and the shape paused, ducking down behind some bushes.

Jo's car was just ten yards away.

The box smelt fusty and Jo wiped the dirty receiver on her jeans when she lifted it, relieved to hear the steady purring which signalled that it was still in working order. She fumbled in the pocket of her jeans for some change and pulled out a handful of ten pence pieces which she laid on the metal shelf beside her. She dialled Vanderburg Chemicals.

Behind her, the wind whistled mournfully through the smashed windows of the deserted café. A sign proclaiming

HOT MEALS SERVED HERE

hung crookedly, one end of it having come loose. It slapped against the wall of the main building beating out an intermittent rhythm.

The ringing tone sounded and Jo prepared to push one of the coins into the slot.

It continued to ring.

No one answered.

She let it ring fifteen times then put the receiver back down and pulled a piece of paper from her coat pocket which had Anderson's home number on it. She dialled once more. This time it rang just three times before it was picked up. Hearing the rapid pips, Jo pushed her money in.

'Mr Anderson?' she said.

Silence.

'Mr Anderson. Hello.'

Just a low hiss of static. Nothing more.

'Do I have the right number?' she asked.

There was a thunderous explosion of lightning which caused the receiver to crackle alarmingly. It was so loud that Jo held it away from her ear for a second. When she listened again, the line was dead. She put the receiver down angrily.

'Shit,' she muttered, scooping up what was left of the change and shoving it back into her pocket. She paused in the phone box for a moment, preparing herself for the dash through the rain to the car. Then she pushed open the door and scurried across to the waiting Chevette. Was Anderson playing some kind of game with her? she wondered. If so, why? She exhaled deeply and reached into her purse, pulling out her diary. Jo reached back to flick on the car light, puzzled to find that it didn't come on when she touched the switch. She sat in darkness for a second before turning slightly in her chair to see why it hadn't come on.

The bulb was missing.

Not just blown, the entire bracket which held the light, including screws, was gone.

She frowned. It had been fine before she got out of the car . . .

It had been removed. Torn out.

But by whom she wondered? her heart unaccountably beating that little bit quicker. She put the Chevette in gear and stepped on the accelerator, anxious to get away from this place, to get home. However, her curiosity was aroused and she was already determined to visit Anderson the following day.

The light and bracket from inside the Chevette lay on the roadside until a foot came down slowly and deliberately on them, grinding them into splinters. The dark shape watched as the tail lights of Jo's car disappeared around a bend then, as stealthily as it had come, the shape dissolved back into the trees and became as one with the night once more.

Seven

Ronald Faber barely heard the alarm. As he woke he reached out instinctively to switch it off but the clock had already run down. Instead he lay beneath the sheets his eyes crusted shut as if someone had sealed the lids during the night. He raised both hands to his face and murmured something to himself. The sheets beneath him were sodden with perspiration and, as he swung himself upright, he swept some matted strands from his forehead. His breathing was shallow, asthmatic almost, and when his body was suddenly racked by a powerful spasm of coughing he gripped his chest in alarm. It certainly wasn't smoker's cough. He hadn't touched the damned weed in any form in all of his forty-two years.

The spasm passed and he got slowly to his feet, a strange gnawing pain in the pit of his stomach. He rubbed his mountainous belly gently as he crossed to the window and looked out.

Sunlight blazed brightly through the chink in the curtains and Faber closed his eyes tight once again, recoiling from the blistering heat and brightness. Below him, the main street of Wakely was starting to come to life as early morning shoppers moved about and some of the other businesses opened their doors for the beginning of another trading day.

Faber knew that he too must have his shop open at nine o'clock, just as he had done every day for the last twenty years. As sole owner and proprietor of Faber Menswear he prided himself on not having missed a single day through illness or anything else. But, today, he would have given anything not to have to go down into the shop and work.

He was a big man, perhaps twenty stone, and the dressing gown which he pulled on barely met around his ample stomach. His black hair was plastered to his head by perspiration and, when he tried to swallow, it seemed as if his throat had seized up. His mouth was dry, his tongue felt as if it had been turned to chalk.

He passed slowly into the bathroom and gazed at himself in the mirror, a little disturbed at what he saw.

His skin was milk white, not just on his face but all over his body. And it had a uniformity to it, there didn't seem to be one part of him that had any colour. Even the dark mole which stood out so prominently on his chin appeared to have been drained. He raised one hand to his cheek and rubbed gently at the skin, his eyes narrowing as some pieces of flesh came away. He looked as though he'd been exposed to the sun for a great length of time but for the deathly pallor of his skin. The flesh around his nails was cracked and split, the nails themselves broken. His lips were swollen, puffy and thick and when he opened his mouth, a strangled cry escaped him.

As he pulled his dressing gown open he saw that the skin on his chest was coming away in great coils. Like some kind of obscene sloughing he looked like a man in transition, shedding one skin for another. And, everywhere was the bloodless colour of his flesh.

He splashed his face with water, quivering slightly when he stepped back and saw that there were fragments of skin floating on the surface of the water.

'Oh God,' he muttered, his words strained.

He turned to the toilet and began urinating.

As the first spurts of blood jetted from his penis and spattered the white porcelain of the lavatory bowl, Ronald Faber fought back a scream.

The water began to turn a dark red colour as the thick fluid continued gushing forth. It was as if his bladder were filled with red ink. His eyes bulged in horror as the bowl seemed to fill with the crimson liquid then the coppery odour reached his nostrils and he realized that his urine wasn't merely the *colour* of blood.

It was blood.

At that point he did scream.

Eight

From its exterior it could well have been a concentration camp. All it lacked were the machine-gun nests.

The complex of buildings which made up Vanderburg Chemicals stood in the middle of thirty acres of country-side about a mile or so off the main Wakely-Arkham road. The entire collection of monolithic structures was enclosed by a wire fence fully twelve feet high. A daunting enough prospect as it was, topped by several lengths of barbed wire, the fence also bore a sign. Stencilled in large red letters, it proclaimed:

DANGER ELECTRIFIED FENCE

Beneath that, as if any would-be interloper should be foolish enough to ignore the warning, another, smaller, sign read:

THESE PREMISES ARE PATROLLED
BY GUARD DOGS

Jo Ward pushed her sunglasses back onto her nose and ran an appraising eye over the array of fortifications before her. She was driving parallel to the high fence, looking alternately through her windscreen and open side window. A cool breeze wafted into the car and for that she was thankful. High above her the sun had already risen in the cloudless sky, its powerful rays bathing the countryside beneath. Jo drove slowly, the Chevette bumping over the uneven road.

So, she thought, this is where Geoffrey Anderson works. She turned the name over in her mind, wondering just what the hell he'd been playing at the previous night. Two or three things still puzzled her about the events surrounding the mystery. She had recognized the click on the other end of the phone as she'd reached Anderson's house. It had been an answering machine switching itself on. But, she reasoned, why no message? What good was a goddam answering phone without a tape in it? Secondly, the light bracket which had been taken. She glanced up at the place where it had been. Taken. That was something of an understatement. It had been ripped out, by hand too from the look of it. Jo pressed her foot down on the accelerator a little harder. The sooner she saw Anderson the better. Besides, she was anxious to find out what he had to tell her.

After another minute's drive she found herself approaching a set of gates. They were topped with barbed wire like the fence but both stood open and only a narrow yellow barrier separated her from the long driveway which led up to the Vanderburg complex. Jo took off her sunglasses, ran a hand through her hair and pulled up at the barrier. She banged her hooter twice, trying to illicit some response from the blue uniformed men seated in a yellow Porta-cabin to the left of the barrier. They were drinking tea and chatting but one finally sauntered out, brushing the sleeve of his uniform as he approached. Jo caught sight of the red and silver VC on his breast pocket as he drew closer.

'Good morning,' said Jo.

'Morning, Miss,' said the guard, eyeing first the car and then Jo, his attention drawn momentarily to the valley between her breasts, visible in the vee of her white blouse.

'I have an appointment with a Mr Anderson,' Jo told him.

'Who are you?' the guard wanted to know.

She told him her name.

'What do you want to see him for?' the man asked, his eyes now turned on Jo's face.

The lie was ready on her tongue.

'I represent a company which is interested in amalgamating with Vanderburg. Mr Anderson told me he could introduce me to the right people.'

The guard licked his lips, gazing once more at Jo's breasts. His brow furrowed. She hoped he wouldn't notice how tightly she was gripping the steering wheel. The plastic felt clammy beneath her sweaty palms.

She played her trump card.

'Call him – you must have a phone in there,' she motioned towards the yellow cabin.

The guard took a step back.

Jo felt her heart beating faster. He had called her bluff; now she had to hope it worked.

'What was the name of your company?' he asked.

'That's really between Mr Anderson and myself,' she told him. She pushed open her door and stepped out. 'Look, let me call him.'

The guard appreciated the chance to see her standing upright and he nodded approvingly as she walked towards him. He held up a hand to halt her.

'OK, we'll let you through,' he said.

Jo slid back behind the wheel, her whole body shaking in a mixture of anxiety and triumph. The barrier was raised and she drove through, smiling at the guard as she passed. She watched him in the rear-view mirror for a moment, relieved when he didn't go back into the cabin. He might just decide to alert the main building while she was on her way up the drive. The macadamized surface was wide enough to accommodate four or more cars driving abreast of each other and, a moment later, Jo saw why.

A huge Scania rolled towards her from the opposite direction, the sun glinting off its metal tanker. The juggernaut sped past and she felt the Chevette tugged momentarily into the larger vehicle's slip-stream. The large lorry rumbled away towards the main gate.

She finally reached the maze of buildings and pulled up before the main block. There were numerous other cars parked outside. She spotted a Jensen, even a Porsche, amongst the lesser vehicles. Her own car she left right outside the six sets of double doors which led into the main reception area.

It was cool inside the cavernous arena, a welcome change from the heat outside and Jo felt the perspiration chill on her skin. Two large fans, set near the doors, rotated full circle, ensuring that the whole reception was kept at a comfortable temperature. Her high heels sank into the thick carpet as she approached a desk behind which sat a girl of about her own age. She was dressed in a dark blue skirt and jacket which reminded Jo of an Air Hostess. The only difference was the familiar VC on the breast pocket. The girl wore a name tag on her lapel which identified her as Julie.

She gave her perfect practised smile as Jo approached the desk.

'Good morning,' said Jo. 'I'd like to see Geoffrey Anderson please.'

'Do you have an appointment?' asked Julie, the smile apparently bolted to her face for it didn't fade even when she spoke.

'He's expecting me.'

'Who shall I say is here?'

'My name's Joanna Ward.'

Julie flicked a switch on the console before her, reaching for a small set of earphones as she did so. There was a loud bleeping, rather like an overloud pager.

'There's a Miss Joanna Ward in reception,' said Julie, into a mouthpiece, the smile still not slipping. 'She says she wants to see Mr Anderson.'

There was a moment's silence, mutterings at the other end of the line and Julie listened. Jo took the opportunity to glance around. There were a number of people moving about in and around the reception area, coming and going through the corridors which led off, spoke-like from the central chamber. Some were in pairs, others alone. All wore the dark blue uniform of Vanderburg or white coats, some even had overalls on. Two young men, both in their early twenties, passed by and cast approving looks at Jo. Even their overalls bore the red and silver VC. The reception smelt of carpet cleaner and polish. The drone of muzak added a background to the chatter of typewriters and the almost constant purring of lift doors as people came and went.

'Someone will be down in a moment,' said Julie, flicking the switch on her console to 'Off'. 'Would you like a cup of coffee?'

Jo availed herself of the offer then went to sit down in one of the soft leather chairs near the lifts. She had hardly seated herself when a tall, white-haired man in a three piece suit emerged from the lift nearest to her. His shoes, she noticed, were in need of cleaning. He headed straight towards her, as if he'd known her for years but, she reasoned, considering she was the only person in sight not sporting a Vanderburg logo, it was safe for him to assume she was a visitor.

She got to her feet as he drew closer.

'Miss Ward,' he said, smiling. He extended a hand which was dotted with liver spots but there was a warmth in his handshake. Jo looked at him carefully. He was in his fifties, perhaps older but his blue eyes twinkled with a radiance which belied his years. His skin was wrinkled, a double chin wobbling fluidly as he shook her hand.

'What can I do for you?' he asked.

'You're not the guy I spoke to last night,' she said. He smiled.

'No. My name is Glendenning. Martin Glendenning.'

'I wanted to see Geoffrey Anderson.'

'So I understand.' He motioned her towards a door on the left and she began walking towards it. When he opened it, she found herself in an office. It was a small

44

room, the desk and filing cabinets making it seem over-crowded. He invited her to sit down, taking up position himself on the other side of the desk. The room was obviously sound proof because Jo could no longer hear the muzak from the reception area once Glendenning closed the door.

'As I was saying,' he began. 'I realize that it was Mr Anderson you wanted to see. Might I ask in what connection?'

'I'm a journalist,' she told him. 'He rang me last night and said he wanted to speak to me.'

'Really,' said Glendenning, his smile fading slightly. 'How did you manage to get past the security men at the gate? They have instructions not to let members of the press in.'

'Something to hide?' said Jo, grinning.

Glendenning chuckled.

'I wish it were that exciting here, Miss Ward,' he said. 'No, it's nothing like that but we're a new company and our backers are somewhat shy of publicity.'

'Who are your backers?' she asked.

He smiled.

'Do journalists always leave the office in the morning with the intention of finding a story?'

'We do our best.'

Glendenning nodded. He rested his elbows on the desk and propped his chin on his hands.

'Well, Miss Ward, I'm afraid there seems to have been some kind of misunderstanding. Mr Anderson doesn't work here any more. In fact he moved on some time ago.'

'He spoke to me from here last night,' Jo protested.

'That's impossible. Besides there is no record of a call, all phone messages are monitored you see.'

'You mean the phones are bugged?' said Jo, flatly.

'Not in the sense you mean,' Glendenning told her. 'It's just part of security procedure.'

45

Jo exhaled in exasperation.

'He called me about eleven last night, maybe a little earlier.'

Glendenning shook his head.

'Most of our employees leave the main building at seven,' he said. 'It's extremely unlikely that anyone would be working at such a late hour in any case. Besides, as I said, Mr Anderson has not worked at Vanderburg for some time.'

'What do you call some time?' Jo demanded.

The older man shrugged.

'Weeks.'

The American shook her head.

'If you'll excuse the expression, Mr Glendenning, someone's been shafted and I get the impression it's me. Some guy calls me last night, says his name's Anderson. I know the man's voice for God's sake. He says he has to meet me. Now you tell me he's been gone for weeks.'

'I'm sorry I can't be more helpful, Miss Ward,' Glendenning said, getting to his feet. He walked to the door and opened it, a gesture which was unmistakable. Jo rose and walked past him into the reception area.

'You never did tell me how you got past the Security men,' the older man asked her, smiling.

'I lied to them,' said Jo. 'All part of the job.'

He chuckled and they exchanged pleasant farewells. Glendenning closed the door behind her and, only then, did his smile dissolve into a frown.

'Left weeks ago, my ass,' Jo rasped, fumbling for the pack of Marlboro. She lit one and sucked hard on it. On the seat beside her was a piece of paper.

It bore the address of Geoffrey Anderson.

One way or another she was going to find out where he was.

Nine

The cow tried to rise but then dropped forward onto its
spindly front legs. It raised its head and snorted in pain,
its body lathered in thick white sweat. A Friesian, it
was virtually all white due to the creamy coating of
fluid it exuded. The barn smelt of damp straw, mingling
with the fusty odour of cattle and the more pungent
stench of excrement. The cow twitched its tail frenziedly
as if trying to brush away some non-existent flies and,
as he watched, Tyler saw blood trickling from both its
anus and also from the gaping opening to its womb.

'Did you call the vet?' he asked, agitatedly, looking
round at Russell Jenkins who was carrying a bucket of
hot water and some cloths.

'He said he should be here in ten minutes,' Jenkins
replied setting the bucket down.

Tyler looked back to the cow.

'I hope to God she lasts that long,' he murmured.

The animal had managed to lift itself up onto its
forelegs once again and stood swaying uncertainly, its
eyes bulging in pain. Its stomach and much of its hind
quarters appeared grossly swollen and, as he watched,
Tyler could see rapid undulations beneath the skin. The
calf was a large one and it was due to be dropped very
soon. Tyler crossed to the cow and laid his hand on its
muzzle, disturbed to see that there was blood coming
from its nostrils too. The animal was bleeding
internally.

'Come on, Hawley, for Christ sake,' he rasped under
his breath.

'Is there anything more we can do?' asked Russell
Jenkins, watching as the cow's hind legs buckled as
if unable to bear the immense weight they were supporting. Tyler coaxed the animal into lying down
but it seemed unable to do so adequately. The huge

protuberances in its hindquarters making this almost impossible. It was as if someone had inflated the creature with a high pressure pump. The undulations became more rapid, more violent and the cow tossed its head about spraying Tyler with the foam like perspiration.

From outside the barn, both men heard a car pull up. A door slammed and Jenkins ran across to see who it was.

Dan Hawley walked in carrying a large black bag which he swiftly opened, pulling out a stethoscope.

'Get her up if you can,' he said, tugging off his tie, hurriedly unfastening his shirt. He crossed to the stricken cow and pressed the stethoscope to its ribs. The heart beat was faint. He moved down and tried to locate the calf's upper-body. There was no sound but the animal was obviously still alive because Hawley could see the frantic movements inside the cow itself. He pulled off his shirt, quickly washed his hands in the bucket of hot water then approached the rear end of the cow which was now on its feet, partially supported by Tyler and Jenkins.

'What the hell is wrong with her?' asked Tyler, perspiration coursing down his face.

'The calf's stuck lengthways by the looks of it,' Hawley told him. 'I'll have to right it.' He steadied himself. 'Hold her tight,' he said. Ignoring the vile odour which was coming from the groaning beast, Hawley slid first one then two dripping hands into the bleeding orifice before him, feeling for the calf's head. He found the feet, the fore-legs he guessed.

'Give me some rope, quick,' he snapped, withdrawing his hands, both of which were dripping crimson.

Tyler scuttled across to the other side of the barn and snatched up a piece of stout hemp, almost knocking a pitchfork over in the process. He cursed and threw the rope to Hawley.

'Why didn't you call me earlier, Vic?' asked the vet.

'Because things didn't start to get bad until about twenty minutes ago,' Tyler told him.

'Here,' said Hawley. 'You'll have to help me, we're going to have to pull the calf free.' He plunged his hands back inside the cow's riven uterine passage and tried to loop the rope around the forelegs of the calf. He cursed as he attempted to complete the difficult task, sweat running off him in salty rivulets. He was a thick set man, powerfully built but he showed remarkable dexterity when dealing with animals, and now Tyler saw a slight grin spread across his face as he succeeded in fastening the rope around the calf's legs. He gripped it hard and Tyler did likewise.

'Hold her head,' the vet told Jenkins.

The cow let out a bellow of pain which sent shivers through all three men – a low rumbling ululation the like of which Tyler had never heard before. Jenkins stepped back in surprise.

'Hold her, dammit,' snarled Hawley but, a second later, he too stepped back as he saw blood begin to pour even more rapidly from her gaping median vagina.

'Oh Christ, the Müllerian duct has ruptured,' the vet rasped. 'The bloody thing could bleed to death.'

'Is there anything you can do?' Tyler demanded.

'We can at least save the calf,' Hawley told him.

The cow bellowed once more, even more loudly this time. The sound seemed to thunder from the very walls themselves then, as that roaring sound of agony subsided, another very different noise took its place.

There was a sound like tearing fabric and the cow's side began to split open. Blood burst from the gash and, a second later, what looked like a hoof tore through the rent.

Tyler stepped back in horror and, even Hawley could only stand transfixed as part of the cow's rump seemed first to be sucked in and then to rapidly bulge, the

49

flesh straining to the point where it became shiny, as if pushed from the inside by some impossible force.

There was a rasping sound and the skin broke. Blood and excrement sprayed upwards in an obscene fountain and, from the ruins of the cow's hindquarters, a head appeared. It rose on a long, snake-like neck. It was the head of the calf, but no calf any of them had ever seen before, and it gazed defiantly at them for long seconds. Then the rear end of the cow literally exploded as the calf tore itself free.

Tyler and Hawley recoiled, splattered with blood, watching as the calf, which they could now see was huge, struggled to free itself from the torn body of its mother. Pieces of cow and calf became momentarily as one and it was as if the men were witnessing some monstrous kind of binary fission as one animal became two. Like the nuclei of two cells, the animals separated, the cow going into spasm as the calf continued to tear itself free. It burst from the torn remnants of its mother, lumps of the allanta chorium hanging from it, the membranous sack sticking to it like grotesque streamers of translucent flesh.

'What the fuck is it?' gasped Jenkins, looking at the calf which now stood upright.

The creature was at least four feet high at the shoulder. A living nightmare. A patchwork of life. Bumps and growths seemed to cover it, leaving not one square of skin unaffected. Its head was heavy, weighed down by what appeared to be a large tumescent protuberance on one side. Tyler noticed with horror that this additional growth had an eye and for fleeting seconds he thought the monstrosity had two heads. It stood perfectly still, watching them, blood and pieces of internal tissue dripping from its gore soaked hide. Then it moved towards Jenkins.

The calf opened its mouth to reveal a set of powerful

50

teeth and Jenkins pressed himself back against the wall of the barn.

Tyler leapt to one side, grabbing the pitchfork, lowering the two prongs at the deformed calf.

'Don't touch it,' screamed Hawley, as the abomination spun round to face him, lips drawn back in a grimace of rage. It uttered a low sound in its throat, a noise which gradually grew in volume, impossibly loud for a creature of its size.

Tyler gritted his teeth and thrust the pitchfork forward, driving it into the chest of the calf, ignoring the fresh gouts of blood which sprayed him. He wrenched the weapon free and struck again, this time piercing the calf's side, pushing deeper until he caused it to topple over. He leant on the fork with all his strength, holding the creature down as it bucked and twisted frantically, trying to escape the twin prongs which pinned it to the floor like a butterfly to a board. The calf raised its head and tried to bite him but Tyler merely stepped back a foot or two, tore the fork free then rammed it through the dying monstrosity's head. One of the prongs punctured an eye on the way and, amidst the cracking of bone, the thing writhed one last time then was still.

Panting, Tyler staggered away, looking down with digust at the calf and what was left of the cow. Blood had sprayed everywhere and the barn reeked of the coppery smelling substance.

'What is it?' Jenkins asked once more, looking down at the body.

Hawley knelt beside the dead calf.

'It's a mutation of some kind,' he said. The vet turned to look at Tyler. 'I'll have to do an autopsy.'

Tyler nodded, wiping some blood from his face.

'What the fuck would make it grow like that?' he said, his voice a hoarse whisper.

'I won't know that until I've done the autopsy,' Hawley told him.

'Call me as soon as you've got any information,' said the farmer.

'I'll need something to put it in,' the vet told him.

'Russell,' Tyler hooked a thumb towards the other barn and Jenkins scuttled out to fetch something in which to wrap the monster.

'I've never seen anything like this in my life,' Hawley confessed, prodding the calf with his index finger. 'Mutations yes, but never as advanced as this.'

'Could the growths be tumours?' said Tyler.

'I doubt it, not as large as this, especially the one on the head.' The vet looked at the bulge with its extra eye. 'What about the bull that serviced this cow. Is *it* all right?'

'I told you, Dan, there was nothing out of the ordinary until about thirty minutes ago when the cow started bleeding. I thought it was an ovarian rupture like you did but . . . not this.'

'I'll need to examine the cow as well, chances are there was some kind of genetic fault with either the bull or the cow – some kind of change in the DNA, perhaps a translocation of chromosomes.' He exhaled deeply. 'I won't be able to say until I've given them both a thorough going over.'

The two men stood in silence for long seconds, their gaze fixed on the mutation at their feet.

'Have you had any other breeding problems?' Hawley asked.

Tyler caught the note of concern in his voice.

'No, why do you ask?'

'Just curious,' said the vet.

'I *have* got weaners and lambs that are twice the size they should be for their age,' Tyler said.

'You're not the only one, Vic,' said Hawley, flatly.

52

'You know Stuart Nichols over in Western Orchard farm and old Ben Thurston? So have they.'

Tyler looked puzzled.

'But no mutations?' he said.

Hawley shook his head.

Both of them returned their gaze to the deformed calf, its third eye fixing them in a glassy stare.

Tyler exhaled deeply, the blood starting to congeal on his hands.

'What the hell is going on?'

Ten

The multi-coloured awnings which adorned the stalls of Wakely market flapped in the wind. The central square of the town was awash with colour. It resembled the palette of a mad artist, greens, blues, reds and all manner of stripes alongside each other in bright rows.

Jo drove slowly past, glancing over at the market. The clock on the council building across the square struck eleven, trading was in full swing. Why then, Jo wondered, were there so few people around? She had been in Wakely on market day before and had always found it practically impossible to walk around the central square let alone drive. But today was different. People moved about quietly and few voices were raised for there was no need to shout. Everything had a calmness about it and a serenity which was almost unnerving.

Anxious for some fresh air, Jo stopped the car and

53

got out. She had parked next to a large fruit van and two men were unloading it, one of them struggling across to a nearby stall with crates of oranges. The man seemed to be managing without too much trouble but, half-way to the stall, he sagged and dropped the crate which promptly burst open. Jaffas went rolling in all directions like huge orange marbles.

'Oh sod it,' grunted the man and began picking them up.

His companion chuckled, jumped down from the van and they set about gathering the dropped fruit.

Jo ran an appraising eye over them. Both men were in their early twenties, stripped to the waist, one of them with dark hair that reached his shoulders. Yet what struck her as most odd was the colour of their skin. Considering it had been so hot during the past few weeks and these men were obviously from one of the farms around Wakely, both were milk white. There wasn't the slightest trace of sun tan on either of them which was something Jo found surprising. She walked past, aware that the one with the long hair was gazing at her legs.

'Morning,' he said, cheerfully, looking up at her.

Jo smiled, even more aware of her own smoothly tanned skin as she looked into the pale face of the farm hand. His eyes were narrowed against the sun as he looked at her, his glance shifting furtively from her face to her breasts.

'I thought you were supposed to sell your goods,' she said, motioning towards the oranges. 'Not throw them around.'

The two men finished gathering up the fruit and succeeded in placing it amongst the other produce. The stall seemed unusually well stocked.

'Business not too good?' Jo asked.

'There aren't that many people around today,' said the one with the long hair.

Jo scanned the first aisle, flanked on both sides by stalls selling everything from wet fish to brass antiques. It stretched for at least a hundred yards ahead of her yet there were barely two dozen people in it. They seemed, some of them, to be moving in slow motion, as if every step were an effort.

'I thought it was usually busy in town on market days,' she said.

'It is,' the first man said, touching his cheek. Jo frowned, noticing how sunken his features were, the dark rings beneath both eyes which looked as though someone had smudged soot there. She put it down to a rough night.

'Can we interest you in anything, love?' said the second man brandishing a cucumber before him. Both he and his companion laughed.

Jo grinned.

'Maybe some other time,' she said and wandered off.

The town square of Wakely was cobbled and she found that she had to walk slowly for fear of overbalancing in her high heels. As she passed up the aisle, glancing at each stall, she noticed again just how quiet it was, even in the centre of the market. A few people chatted animatedly and every so often a peal of laughter would ring out but, in the main, the shoppers and traders were subdued.

Jo paused at a stall which sold miniature glass animals. All of them, she guessed, made by the proprietor. He was sitting at the rear of the stall reading a tatty paperback, his face hidden from view. The journalist looked at him, studying his hands which were large, comfortably enclosing the book. She frowned slightly.

The fingernails of his left hand were long and pointed, the skin of the cuticles cracked and raw. The nails of the other hand were the same, the index finger particularly long to the point where it had begun to curve over.

Jo picked up one of the glass animals, an elephant sitting up balancing a ball on its trunk, and inspected it.

'Need any help, lady?' said the man, his voice low.

The American looked up and, once again, found herself looking into a face the colour of sour cream. Only this time the man's lips were cracked too, as if he'd been exposed to the sun for a long time. Yet he had no colour. His cheek bones were high, the skin looking as if it had been stretched over them. She saw that it was peeling in places, just small fragments which flaked off as he rubbed his chin.

'These models are very nice,' she said, replacing the elephant.

'All my own work,' said the man, proudly.

'I was saying to some guys back there, it's not very busy for market day,' said Jo.

The man shook his head.

'It might buck up a bit later on,' he explained. 'The livestock market is held this afternoon.'

Jo nodded.

'Nice talking to you. I like your models very much,' she told him as she walked away.

The man returned to his paperback.

It must have taken Jo thirty minutes to walk up and down all six aisles of Wakely market and she found that she managed it without the customary barging and bumping which usually occurred on this, the town's busiest day of the week. She headed back to her car, passing the fruit stall where the man with the long hair winked at her and smiled. She returned the gesture, noticing that he too had long, hooked fingernails on at least four of the spindly digits. Her initial surprise and curiosity had diminished somewhat and, by the time she slid back behind the wheel of the Chevette, her mind had returned to more important things.

She glanced down at the piece of paper beside her which bore Geoffrey Anderson's address.

Jo started the engine and drove off. She wriggled uncomfortably in her seat at first. The sun, pouring through the windows, had turned the plastic seats of the car into a hot plate which seared her legs and even burned her backside through the thin material of her skirt. As she drove, she rolled her head back and forth in an effort to release some of the tension which was gnawing at her shoulders.

Anderson's house stood amidst a large expanse of garden, separated from his neighbours on both sides by a high wooden fence. The grass, Jo noticed as she got out of the car, looked short, freshly mown even. The man she sought might indeed have left Vanderburg Chemicals but he certainly hadn't left Wakely. The garden looked immaculate. She approached the front gate, inhaling a heady mixture of blossom from the trees and the numerous fragrances of flowers growing in abundance in all the gardens before her.

There was a sign on the gate which read: 'Avalon'.

She double checked her piece of paper, although it was a formality. This was definitely Anderson's house. Jo walked briskly up the path, noticing as she did so that the curtains at the front of the house were drawn – doubtless to keep out the scorching sun. She knocked on the door and waited.

There was no answer. No sounds of movement from inside.

She tried again.

Still nothing.

She pushed open the letter box and tried to peer into the gloom inside the hall. It was like looking into a pit. She could see nothing. Jo followed the path around to the back of the house where she banged on the rear door. Once again she noticed that the curtains, both upstairs and down, were drawn. The American tapped on the kitchen window with her car keys and still she received no answer. She wandered down the garden to a large shed, surprised to find it unlocked. It smelt fusty inside, an odour of damp wood and earth. The windows were dirty, the tools inside caked with dried mud.

Jo walked back to the house, around to the front and along to the house next door.

The curtains there were drawn too.

She banged the front door twice, stepping back to look up at the red brick dwelling.

She waited for five minutes but there was no answer.

She was becoming increasingly irritable by now and walked back the way she had come, to the house which stood on the other side of Anderson's.

She almost breathed a sigh of relief when she saw a woman, a little older than herself, emerge from the front door, a plastic bucket in one hand, a wash leather in the other.

'Excuse me,' Jo called.

The woman looked up as the journalist walked up the path towards her.

'Sorry to intrude,' said the American. 'I won't keep you a minute.'

'If you're a Jehovah's Witness I'm afraid I'm busy,' said the woman, taking a step back.

Jo smiled.

She held out her hands.

'No Bible, see.'

The woman smiled, running a hand through her tousled blonde hair. She was a trifle on the plump side, the jeans she wore just that little bit too tight around the thighs. Her face was aglow, her ruddy complexion making it look as though someone had scrubbed her cheeks with a wire brush.

Jo could hear the sound of a record player from inside the house.

58

'I'm sorry to stop you working,' said Jo. 'I won't take up a minute of your time.'

'Who are you?' the woman wanted to know.

'I'm a journalist, my name's Joanna Ward. I work for the *Arkham Comet*.'

The woman nodded.

'I'm looking for the guy who lives next door, Geoffrey Anderson. I wondered if you'd seen him.'

'You're American, aren't you?' the woman said, smiling as if she'd just made some earth-shattering discovery.

Jo nodded.

'About Mr Anderson,' she persisted, 'I wondered if you'd be able to tell me anything about him.'

'Is he in trouble?' asked the woman almost excitedly.

'No, it's nothing like that. *Have* you seen him lately?'

'Not since Sunday, he was out there cutting his grass,' the woman told her. 'A nice man. He kept himself to himself but there's nothing wrong with that is there?'

Sunday, Jo thought. 'He was here two days ago?'

'Yes.'

'But you haven't seen him since?'

'No. You could probably contact him at work. I think he's got something to do with that new chemical place.'

Jo fumbled in her pocket and produced a card.

'Look, if you see him, could you call me on that number, please.'

'I can't really tell you much about him,' said the woman, apologetically. She ran her eyes over the card which Jo had given her.

'Do you know if he finished working for Vanderburg Chemicals recently?' Jo enquired.

'He's worked for them since they started.'

'So he hasn't left or been fired in the last three or four days?'

'Not as far as I know.'

Jo nodded.

'Thanks very much, you've been a great help.' She turned and headed back to her car.

The woman looked at the card once more then pushed it into her back pocket. By the time she had done that, Jo had driven off.

Eleven

'I reckon you must be using the wrong soap, Jack. You've frightened all the bloody customers away.'

A chorus of laughter and cheers greeted Stuart Nichols' remark. He downed what was left in his cider glass and ordered another round, pushing the other empty glasses towards the barman. Nichols was a big man, a year or two older than Tyler. He ran a farm to the west of Wakely, a large holding on which he kept a herd of more than two hundred cattle. He and his wife, Bet, had lived there for the past twelve years.

'It's not me,' Jack Vernon told him. 'It's you lot, come trooping in here with your sodding great boots covered in cow shit.'

The group of men gathered around the bar of 'The Black Swan' laughed.

'That's a fine way to talk to your best customers,' said Tyler, taking a hefty swig from the fresh pint which Vernon handed to him.

'It is quiet in here though,' said Reg Gentry, looking around the bar. He chewed thoughtfully on the stem of his pipe and scratched his face, careful to avoid the nasty scar on his left cheek. He'd been kicked in the face by a pony when he was eleven. It had broken his jaw in four places and cost him five teeth as well as leaving him with the scar.

As he sat on the bar stool he glanced up at the light above him and winced slightly.

'I bet you don't know where you are, now you're back doing some real work again, Vic,' said Nichols, taking a hefty swallow from his pint pot.

'Well, it beats sitting on your arse behind a desk I'll say that,' Tyler told him.

'How are you settling in?' asked Ben Thurston.

'Fine thanks, Ben,' said the younger man warmly. 'It's great to be able to breathe clean air again.' He chuckled.

Tyler had always reserved a certain affection for Thurston. The man was in his early sixties, the oldest of the landowners around Wakely. He and his three sons ran a fifty acre farm to the North. Thurston had intended to retire when he reached his sixtieth birthday but, with the passing on of his wife, that had not transpired. He reminded Tyler of his own father in many ways; his dogged determination, sharp business mind and other, less noticeable features further endeared him to the younger man.

Nichols took another swig of his pint, wiping his mouth with the back of his hand.

'One of my sows gave birth to a litter,' he said. 'About two days ago and every one of the little buggers was dead. All seven of them. I can't understand it.'

'Dan Hawley told me you'd been having trouble with your weaners,' said Tyler, wondering whether or not to mention the incident with the calf.

'When did you see Dan?' asked Nichols.

'This morning, about three hours ago,' Tyler told him. He decided *not* to mention the deformed animal. 'I said to him that my weaners were twice the size they should

61

be and he mentioned that you and Ben too were getting the same results.'

'I'm not complaining,' said Thurston. 'With the stock as big as it is we should all get better prices.'

'Bloody right,' echoed Nichols. 'I'll be asking more than usual I'll tell you that.'

'Bred a super-pig have you, Stuart?' asked Jack Vernon, grinning.

'You could say that,' Nichols told him, smugly, then he laughed.

'It's been the same with my lambs,' Thurston added. 'Only three weeks old but some of them are as big as collies.'

'What do you think's causing it?' said Reg Gentry.

'I couldn't give a sod what's causing it,' Stuart Nichols told him. 'All I know is my profits are going to rise.'

Tyler was the first to notice Jo when she walked into the bar. She strode past the farmers, smiled softly at them and ordered herself a drink.

'If there's any more like that come in today, profits won't be the only thing rising,' Nichols said, lecherously. He watched as Jo seated herself on a stool at the far end of the bar, hitching her skirt up until it was well above her knee, revealing her slim tanned thigh. She took a notepad from her handbag and began scribbling something down.

'I've not seen her around before,' Gentry said.

Tyler didn't speak. He had his eyes fixed firmly but discreetly on Jo, watching her over the rim of his glass.

'I believe we were talking about livestock,' said Ben Thurston, smiling.

The other men seemed to come out of their trance, their eyes turning away from Jo who could see them out of her eye corner. She smiled to herself and continued writing.

'What about you, Vic?' said Nichols. 'You're the one

with the brains, you went to college. What do you think's causing the accelerated growth?'

Tyler shrugged.

'It's difficult to say. My farmhands were telling me about some new multi-purpose feed they'd been using.'

Nichols nodded.

'That stuff from Vanderburg or whatever the hell it's called?' he asked.

'I don't know the name of it,' Tyler said.

'It's from Vanderburg Chemicals,' the other farmer continued. 'The bloke who sold it to me said it would increase growth.'

Jo sat up at the mention of the word Vanderburg. She swung round on her stool and faced the men.

'Pardon me,' she said. 'Don't think I'm eavesdropping but I did hear one of you mention Vanderburg Chemicals, didn't I?'

The men were a little taken aback by her accent but Tyler broke the sudden silence, hesitantly at first perhaps but thankful for the opportunity to converse with such an attractive young woman.

'Yes you did,' he said. 'Do you know something about them?'

'Not as much as I'd like too,' said Jo. She picked up her drink and walked over to the group of men. Thurston offered her his stool.

'You're a Yank, aren't you?' said Nichols.

'I'm an *American*, yes.'

'What are you doing here?' asked Gentry.

'I work for the *Arkham Comet*. I'm just covering a local story,' she said.

'Anything interesting?' asked Nichols.

Jo shook her head.

'Not really.' She sipped at her drink. 'Are you all in town for the cattle market?'

Tyler nodded.

'Was that an educated guess?' he asked, smiling at her.

'I've been to it before,' she told him.

Jo looked deep into his blue eyes and could almost feel the warmth there. She afforded herself a quick inspection of this tall, hard-faced man dressed in jeans, boots and a check shirt. His face was pleasantly tanned, the material of his shirt unable to conceal the powerful body beneath.

'To be accurate,' said Thurston, 'it's a livestock market.'

Jo shrugged.

'Whatever it is I was surprised there weren't more people around.'

'So were we,' Nichols told her. He eyed the newcomer up and down, noticing that her full breasts were unfettered by a bra, the twin peaks of her nipples dark beneath the fabric. 'What's a Yank doing working for the *Arkham Comet*?'

'It's a living,' she told him.

Gentry looked at his watch. The hands were approaching 1.00 p.m. He downed what was left in his glass and got to his feet.

'If we don't get a move on we'll miss the bloody market,' he said and the other men also finished their drinks. Tyler hesitated.

'Want to come along?' he asked her. 'You can see how we yokels spend the day.'

He smiled at her and Jo responded. Tyler found himself drawn to those twinkling green eyes of hers, hypnotized by them.

'I have to make a phone call first,' she told him.

He nodded.

'Jack, the lady would like to borrow your phone,' he said.

The barman smiled and ushered Jo towards the end of the bar where, from beneath the counter, he produced a

64

phone and set it down before her. Tyler watched her as she jabbed at the numbers, drumming agitatedly on the bar top as she waited for the receiver to be lifted at the other end. When it finally was, she recognized the voice.

'It's Jo Ward,' she babbled. 'Put me through to Doug Clark, please.'

Another moment's silence at the other end then she heard the familiar voice of the editor.

He wanted to know where she was.

'I'm in Wakely,' Jo said and then, before he could ask why, 'Listen, Doug, this could be important.' She told him about the phone call of the previous night, about her visit to Vanderburg Chemicals, of Glendenning's lie about Anderson and of that particular man's disappearance. 'I think Anderson is still in Wakely. I have to find him.'

He asked how long it would take her.

'That's impossible to say but, whatever it was he wanted to talk about must have been pretty goddam important. I have to stay here until I find him.'

Clark suggested that her imagination might be getting the better of her.

'For Christ's sake,' she blurted, 'you know me better than that. Besides, when I asked Glendenning who Vanderburg's backers were he changed the subject. I'm sure Anderson knows something worth knowing and I want to hear it.'

She hung up and rejoined Tyler.

'Do you want to follow my truck in your car?' he asked her.

'What's wrong with me riding in the cab with you?' she wanted to know.

Tyler smiled.

'Fair enough, if you don't mind the twelve cattle and sixteen pigs in the back. It doesn't exactly smell like a rose garden in there.'

He led her out to the waiting truck, a large van that looked like a container lorry, its sides painted white. He opened the passenger side door and helped her up onto the running platform. From there she scrambled into the cab.

'You weren't joking, were you?' she said, wrinkling her nose.

Tyler chuckled and scuttled around to the driver's side where he hauled himself up and started the engine, the smell of diesel mingling with the odour of livestock.

'I did warn you,' he said and, this time, they both laughed.

Twelve

The livestock market was held in a maze of yards and sheds on the main road leading out of Wakely. It always attracted a sizeable gathering of people: buyers, livestock breeders and interested onlookers. It was, like the other market in the town square, something of an event for Wakely's inhabitants and also those who made the trip from outside the town be it for business purposes or just plain curiosity.

The trucks and vans which carried the animals were parked in a large tarmac area to the rear of two corrugated iron sheds. From there, the animals were herded through a series of pens and enclosures, separating them into varying sizes, breeds and species.

Some of the farmers were under contract to the various butchers, restaurants or hotels in and around the town so business was done briskly. It was just a matter of deciding on a price. The livestock would then be herded back into their respective transporters and driven straight to the abattoir for slaughtering. The whole process took less than a day from arrival at the market to delivery of the prepared carcasses to the appointed destination.

Those animals belonging to farmers not under contract were open for auction to anyone who cared to pay the right price for them. Tyler's stock came into this latter category but he felt confident about making a healthy price on all his stock. Some of the animals were occasionally bought by other farmers. Particularly dairy cattle and pigs. One or two of the small-holders specialized in one type of livestock, so bidding for what was termed 'independent stock' was also their privilege.

Jo lit up a cigarette and offered the pack to Tyler.

He declined.

'I don't smoke.'

Jo lit one and blew out a funnel of the bluish haze.

'Does this place always smell as bad as this?' she asked, waving a hand in front of her as if to drive away the odour of animal excretion and damp straw.

Tyler grinned.

'Country air is good for you. You've lived in towns too long.'

'I intend staying in towns if the country smells as bad as this.'

They were standing beside a small enclosure which housed a sow and six piglets. Tyler ran an interested eye over the smaller creatures, at once impressed and puzzled by their exaggerated size. The largest was at least twelve inches high at the shoulder. Nevertheless they had, as he'd expected, brought him an excellent price and he'd already negotiated a deal for the litter with a buyer from a restaurant in Arkham. He watched as the animals moved agitatedly around the sow, one

67

or two trying to reach her swollen teats in order to feed. The sow herself grunted and moved around the pen as if attempting to keep away from her hungry offspring.

'Look, mum.'

The shout startled Tyler and he turned to see a small boy, about twelve, clambering onto the metal struts of the enclosure, leaning over to get a better look at the animals inside. His mother, who had two other younger children with her, trudged wearily over to her son and joined him at Tyler's side.

The farmer looked at the little group and then at Jo who smiled, as the boy began to make grunting noises like the pig.

The sow had finally stopped her agitated pacings and remained still long enough for one or two of the piglets to begin feeding. They were swiftly joined by the others, all jostling one another in an effort to reach the milk secreting glands.

'They're sucking her tits,' said the boy loudly, laughing raucously.

'*Teats*,' said his mother, slapping him on the back of the head, looking around to see if anyone else had heard. She looked at Tyler and coloured slightly. He smiled.

The piglets were becoming more excited and Tyler could hear a series of low grunts coming from the sow. A grunt that suddenly turned into a bellow of pain.

One of the litter had gripped a teat in its mouth and, with a powerful twist of its neck, wrung the swollen appendage off.

Blood jetted from the gash, splattering the other animals.

It was like a signal for them.

Almost as one, they began gnawing and tearing at the teats, ripping them free, swallowing them, the mixture of milk and blood cascading from their jaws. Then, as the sow toppled over they moved in frenziedly upon her, almost burrowing into the soft flesh of her underbelly, seeking out the vital organs inside.

Tyler began to clamber over the rail as he saw two of them use their trotters to gouge a cleft in the bloodied flesh. A foul-smelling flux of viscera erupted from the wound and the piglets squealed excitedly, devouring the bulging intestines which presented themselves, bursting forth from the sow's mutilated stomach. She tried to rise, to shake off the cannabalistic horde but it was no good.

The boy on the fence had turned the colour of rancid butter, his sisters screaming hysterically, his mother trying to drag all three of the children away.

Tyler grabbed one of the piglets and pulled it off. He hurled the animal to one side, horrified when it rolled over and then came at him, trying to bite his leg. He kicked it hard in the face, the blow momentarily felling it.

Jo saw two men nearby, dressed in dark green overalls, one of them carrying a small sledgehammer. She called to them, one eye still fixed on Tyler who was trying to save the dying sow.

The men in the overalls were stockmen, employees of the livestock market and both came running when they heard the commotion. The one carrying the hammer vaulted the rail, heading for the nearest piglet.

'Kill them,' shouted Tyler, driving his foot into the side of another of the litter.

The stockman needed no second bidding. He brought the hammer down on the head of the nearest piglet and killed it with that one crushing blow.

The sow was trying to crawl away, her intestines dragging in the straw like bulging bloodied party streamers. Jo gripped the rail tight, the cigarette stuck to her bottom lip. She watched as the squealing piglets were despatched, each one killed by a blow of the sledgehammer. Except for the last which Tyler himself finished off. Sliding his sheath knife across its throat he dropped the writhing body to the ground and watched as it quivered violently. Blood jetted from the slashed throat.

'What happened?' asked the stockman with the hammer.

Tyler told him.

'I've heard of sows eating piglets before,' said the man. 'But not the other way around. What the hell caused it?'

'How should I know?' snapped Tyler, irritably. He looked down at the sow. The animal was dead, sprawled amongst her dead litter. One of the stockman hurried off to get something in which to conceal the carcasses.

Jo merely stood gazing at the scene of carnage. She looked at Tyler who was shaking his head slowly, trying to wipe some blood from his hands.

The stockman returned with a number of sacks, one of which Tyler took from him. He bent and lifted the nearest dead piglet by the ears, tossing it into the hessian bag then he clambered back over the fence, clutching his grisly acquisition in one gore-soaked hand.

'Come on,' he said to Jo, walking briskly towards the car park and his waiting truck.

'Where are we going?' she asked, hurrying to keep up with him.

'To see about this,' he told her, holding up the sack.

They were back in town in less than ten minutes.

Thirteen

Dan Hawley's veterinary surgery stood in a quiet, residential area of Wakely about two minutes' drive from the centre of the town. A large, detached house with white-washed walls and a spacious garden, it looked more like a rest home than a place of work. Hawley worked alone, helped out during the day by his receptionist, Mandy Potter, a lively girl in her early thirties who, because of the enormous glasses she wore, reminded Tyler of a barn owl.

The house had a sign outside with Hawley's name and credentials engraved on it and, on either side of the front door, two large stone dogs stood sentinel. It was a garish touch which never failed to amuse Tyler but, as he pulled the truck into Hawley's driveway, the last thing he felt like doing was laughing.

Jo followed him as he got down from the cab, clutching the sack and its bloodied load. He had hardly spoken during the drive from the livestock market and his face was set in tense lines as he approached the front door of the surgery. He walked into the reception and found that there were perhaps half a dozen other people waiting inside.

Dogs began to howl and bark at him. An elderly man who was balancing a parrot in a cage on his knee coughed as the bird began squawking, sending feathers and sand in all directions.

The smell from the sack which Tyler held began to fill the waiting room.

'Hello, Mr Tyler,' said Mandy, eyeing the sack curiously.

'Is Dan in there?' Tyler asked, motioning towards a green door to his right which led into the surgery proper.

'Yes, he is but . . .'

The farmer spun round and headed for the green door, Jo right behind him.

Mandy got to her feet, pushing her glasses back on her nose.

'You can't go in there yet,' she protested, but already Tyler was pushing his way in, leaving Mandy to cope with the complaints of the other visitors.

'Knock before you come in for Christ's sake,' said Hawley, without looking up. He was hunched over his desk writing something in a large red book. The vet turned when he heard the door slam.

'Vic, what the hell do you want?' he asked, his gaze quickly shifting to Jo.

Hawley got to his feet, watching as Tyler upended the sack and dumped the dead piglet on the stainless steel work top nearest to him.

'First calves, now weaners,' said Tyler angrily. 'Six of the fucking things, from the same litter, have just torn one of my sows to shreds.'

Hawley frowned and moved over to look at the still body of the piglet.

'It was like they were crazy, rabid or something,' said Jo.

The vet momentarily transferred his gaze from the dead pig to Jo. Tyler made hurried introductions then all three of them returned their attention to the carcass before them.

'What exactly happened?' asked Hawley, pulling on a pair of rubber gloves and reaching for a probe.

Tyler told him.

The vet nodded almost imperceptibly, using the probe to open the jaws of the piglet. A thick slush of blood and bile oozed from the open mouth and puddled beneath the piglet's head.

'What about that calf?' asked Tyler. 'Have you had the chance to examine it yet?'

Hawley shook his head.

'As soon as I find anything I'll let you know. No doubt you're expecting there to be some kind of link between the calf and this weaner?'

'Yes,' said Tyler. 'Perhaps some kind of genetic defect that's peculiar to both of them.'

'It's unlikely, Vic.'

'Then what's your bloody answer, Dan?'

'I haven't get one yet. I wish to Christ I had. Deformed calves, still-born litters, weaners that tear their own mother to pieces, baby animals that are growing at four times the rate they should be. I can't come up with answers to problems like those in a couple of hours.'

'How long has this been going on?' Jo asked.

Hawley shrugged.

'Well, for one thing, we don't even know if any of the incidents are related.'

'Don't tell me that these things are coincidence,' Tyler snapped.

'I didn't say they were,' Hawley muttered. 'But you can't put your finger on a calendar and say "it started then".'

'But when *would* you say the incidents began?' Jo asked again.

'Four, five weeks ago,' Hawley told her.

Jo nodded, her eyes flicking around the large surgery as the vet returned to the animal before him. The room was large, with a table and what looked like two operating tables inside. Powerful arc lamps on adjustable arms were arranged over each one. Rows of filing cabinets filled one wall and above those hung Hawley's certificates of practice. The other three walls were covered with shelves. Medicines, tonics and pills of all descriptions were contained there and, as Jo looked more carefully she saw that there was a larger jar containing some amber coloured fluid.

Floating in it was a small dog, which, on closer

73

inspection, she noticed had just three legs and no eyes. The journalist shuddered involuntarily.

'Like I said, Vic, I can't tell you anything until I've done autopsies on the animals. You'll just have to wait for my call.' Hawley pulled off his rubber gloves, muttering to himself as some skin flaked off in the process. He rubbed the back of his hand gently, more flesh peeling away to reveal a raw area beneath.

Jo looked at the hand and then at the vet's face which was pale, dark rings beneath his eyes. He turned off the light over the table, massaging his temple as he did so.

'I *will* get back to you,' he said again.

They all exchanged brief farewells and Hawley showed them to the door. As he walked back inside the surgery he took a last look at the dead piglet and pulled a sheet over it.

'What do *you* think is going on?' said Jo, studying Tyler's profile.

'I wish I knew,' he said.

Tyler drove slowly through the narrow streets of Wakely, heading back towards the pub where Jo had parked her car.

'For a quiet town this place sure has its share of mysteries,' she said, smiling.

Tyler nodded.

'It seems like we both have problems,' she said. 'You need answers, so do I, I have to find Geoffrey Anderson.'

'What's so special about this bloke anyway?' asked Tyler.

'Well, between you and me, I think he knows something that someone doesn't want him to talk about.'

'Like what?'

'If I knew that I wouldn't have a problem would I?'

'Ask a silly question . . .' Tyler let the sentence trail off.

'Look, you've lived in this place for most of your life. You know the people, you know the places.'

'You're asking me to help you find Geoffrey Anderson?'

'Right.'

Tyler brought the truck to a halt alongside Jo's Chevette. He switched off his engine and looked across at her.

'Look, Jo, I don't know anything about Anderson. I don't even know much about you.'

'We can soon put that right,' she said. 'How about dinner tonight?'

Tyler grinned, finally chuckling aloud.

'What's so funny?' Jo wanted to know.

'It's the first time any woman has asked me to dinner.'

'So, is it a date?'

'How could I refuse? What time?'

She checked her watch and saw that it was almost 3.45 p.m.

'I've got to go back to Arkham and pick up some stuff, then I'll check into a hotel here. I need to be in town. If Anderson's in Wakely and I'm damn sure he is, I mean to find him.'

'And dinner?'

'How about eight-thirty?'

He nodded, watching her as she jumped down from the cab.

'Eight-thirty in the hotel, I'll meet you in the bar,' she nodded in the direction of 'The King George', one of two hotels which overlooked the main square of the town.

Tyler nodded.

He watched her as she crossed to her car, started the engine and drove off. Then he himself turned the key

75

in his ignition and the big truck roared into life. He swung it around, squinting up at the burnished sun as he did so.

By 4.00 he was back at the farm.

Fourteen

The late afternoon sunlight crept like an intruder through the chinks in the venetian blinds. Vera Duggan stood at the sink peering at the partially hidden glowing orb which still burned brightly in the cloudless sky. As she watched it she felt her skin begin to tingle and her eyes begin to water. Vera looked away, moving across to one of the yellow painted cupboards on the wall by the fridge. She moved slowly. Arthritis had eaten deep into her joints and now, at sixty-eight, there were times when she could hardly move her hands. Ordinarily the sun eased the tightness in her joints but, for the past two or three weeks, it had been having the opposite effect. She felt stiff all over and she had been forced to retrieve the thick walking stick which she had discarded ten years before.

It had belonged to her husband, now dead for more than fifteen years. But his slippers were still in the same place in the hall, his photo still on the wall. He had looked so handsome in his uniform. Arthur Duggan of the King's Own Yorkshire Rifles. He had been wounded at Amiens in 1917. Gassed at Passchendaele. It had been that which had brought on his bronchitis. The same complaint which had taken him from her those fifteen years ago. Since then she had lived alone but for her succession of cats. Her sons rarely visited her but she didn't really miss them. One was an engineer, the other a plasterer. They took turns to look after her at Christmas but, other than that, she hardly saw them from one year to the next.

She hobbled to the pantry and retrieved a tin opener, working it with difficulty around the lip of the tin until she finally managed to open it. She scooped out the contents with a fork, pushing them into a bowl which bore the name 'Beth'. The cat finished preening itself and looked up, smelling its food.

'Come on,' said Vera, holding the bowl before her.

The cat, impatient for its food, leapt up onto the table and pawed at her hand.

'Get off,' Vera told it.

The cat continued trying to reach the food.

'Get down, now,' she snarled.

The cat hissed and tried once again to reach the dish of food, only this time it scratched Vera's hand. The claws cut easily through her thin flesh and she yelped, dropping the bowl, looking down at the four gashes on the back of her hand. The cat remained standing on the table, looking at her as if it realized that it had done wrong. It meowed and jumped down off the table, eagerly devouring the spilt food.

Vera muttered something under her breath and raised the walking stick above her head, steadying herself against the table.

With a grunt she brought it crashing down again.

There was a strength and ferocity to the blow which belied her years and condition for, so powerful was the impact, she heard the crack of bone as the walking stick connected with the cat's head. It screeched and tried to run but the blow had stunned it and, as Vera struck again, blood burst from its skull. The animal fell forward and Vera drove the end of the stout stick into its side, pressing down until she heard the breaking of ribs. The cat rasped, blood spilling from its mouth. The sight of the blood seemed to inflame Vera even more for she brought the walking stick down once more on the creature's head. This time the force was enough to rend bone and a gobbet of grey and red brain matter welled up through the smashed skull.

Still Vera continued beating at it until the kitchen floor was spattered with blood. Only when the cat was completely motionless did she sink to her knees, hands in the mess of grey and crimson. She was panting from the effort but there was a crooked smile on her face and, as she gazed at the dead animal, she began to salivate madly until streamers of sputum hung from her false teeth.

She shielded her eyes from the sun and began to laugh.

Fifteen

Despite the approach of evening, the sun still remained dominant in the sky. Now bleeding some of its colour into the heavens it retained its heat and Jo wiped a bead of perspiration from her forehead as she parked the Chevette in the car park beside 'The King George'. It had taken her just over an hour to drive back to her home in Arkham and pick up a few clothes.

Now she checked that the vehicle was securely locked up and walked around to the main entrance of the hotel.

Ivy grew thickly all over the old stonework, so thick in places it seemed that if it were cut down the entire building would collapse. The dining room was as yet in darkness, the only lights burning were those in the reception.

It was cool inside the hotel and Jo welcomed the respite for the cloying humidity in the air was making her feel uncomfortable. She smiled to herself, realizing that she must already have been away from New York too long. Out there residents learned to cope with eighty per cent humidity during the summer. But, the heat had unpleasant side-effects. Jo knew that the murder rate rose by almost double during those dog-days.

Now she carried her suitcase up to the reception desk and scanned the place for a member of staff. The hotel smelt of polish and new wood and, from somewhere nearby, there was a tempting aroma of food. Jo rubbed her stomach as she heard it rumble. There were two old pikes crossed on the wall over the open fire place behind her and on either side were metal pots which looked like witches' cauldrons. The entire place was panelled in dark oak, the beams, from the look of the tiny holes in them, being genuine.

Jo spotted a bell and shook it.

She looked around to see if anyone was going to respond. There didn't seem to be any guests or staff about.

The man rose from behind the desk, a tall fellow who towered over Jo.

'Can I help you?'

She spun round, shocked at the sudden sound.

'Damn,' she gasped, her hand going to her throat. 'Where did you come from?'

'Sorry if I startled you, Miss,' the man said, apologetically. 'I was down behind the desk, I didn't hear you come in.'

Jo nodded, regaining her breath.

'I'd like a room please. For a week.' She gave him her name and address. When she filled in the confirmation form she charged it to the *Arkham Comet*.

He turned and selected a key.

'Number 24,' he told her. 'On the second floor.' When he spoke, his voice was low and rasping, his teeth reducing the sounds he made to harsh whispers. His teeth looked huge, to the point where he had difficulty closing his mouth.

Jo nodded, looking more closely at the man. The badge on his lapel read 'Mark Bates'. He was in his late thirties, although it was virtually impossible to guess his age accurately. His skin was pale, shrivelled around the eyes and lip corners, sunken around the cheeks. It was peeling in places, particularly on the backs of his hands which, she noticed, bore the long, hooked nails she had seen earlier in the day on other Wakely residents. But his most striking features were his eyes. The irises glowed with an unnatural brilliance, quite in contrast to the yellowish, vein-infested whites.

Jo picked up her case.

'There aren't any porters,' said Bates. 'But I can help you with that.' He nodded towards the case.

'No that's fine. Thanks anyway,' Jo said.

She'd got as far as the lifts when he called her back.

'You forgot your key,' he informed her, walking out from behind the desk.

Jo smiled.

'One of these days I'll forget my name,' she said, reaching out to take it from him.

For a second she almost gasped aloud but she clenched her teeth together, the breath caught in her throat.

She could see it. There before her. The key was in his hand but she hesitated.

She looked at Bates and then down again.

There was hair growing on the palm of his hand.

Sixteen

'There's no one else for me to see is there, Mandy?' Dan Hawley asked, peering out from inside the surgery.

The receptionist was sitting at her desk glancing at *Cosmopolitan*. She put the magazine down and ran a finger through the list of names in the appointment book.

'No, Mr Hawley,' she said. 'But Stuart Nichols rang about half an hour ago and asked if you could go out to his farm tomorrow.'

'Did he say what was wrong?'

'Something about his lambs losing wool.'

Hawley nodded. He pulled off his rubber gloves and balled them up, pushing them into a pocket in his apron.

'You can drop the formalities now, Mandy,' he said.

She smiled and got to her feet.

The vet pulled her close, their mouths meeting, tongues probing urgently. She snaked her arms up around his neck, eager to prolong the sensation. When, finally, they did separate Mandy found that her glasses were misted over. She removed them, laying them on the desk behind her. Hawley brushed a speck of dust from her long lashes then kissed her softly on the end of the nose.

'If you're going to call me Mr Hawley during working hours,' he said. 'Perhaps I ought to call you Miss Potter.'

She chuckled.

'I don't know why we bother keeping up the pretence, Dan, everyone in Wakely knows what's going on between us.'

'You make it sound like something from a Barbara Cartland novel,' Hawley said, brushing a strand of hair from her forehead.

'You know what I mean.'

'People in Wakely are what you might call traditional-ists. They have their standards and they expect everyone to conform to them. But they turn a blind eye when what they see starts to offend their moral sensibilities.'

'Very philosophical,' she said.

'And very true,' he added, kissing her again.

They had lived together for nearly a year in the vet's house. Prior to that, Mandy had been married to a plumber named Andy. There had been two children from the marriage, both boys. With Andy, she had endured a secure and steady way of life. He was a dependable, even predictable man. But that had not been enough for Mandy. She deplored his lack of ambi-tion, his willingness to settle for what life gave him rather than taking it with both hands. And, over the years, she had seen her children being moulded into the same shape as their father. Neither of the boys had any desire to leave Wakely or the surroundings they had grown up in. At thirteen and eleven, she could see them as mirrors of their father and she began to resent them for it.

Hawley had been everything she had always hoped to find in a man.

She'd met him quite by chance. One day, taking the family dog along for its distemper shot, she had encoun-tered the thick set, dark-haired man who was to become her lover.

Hawley had been in partnership with an older man for some time and, eager to have his own practice, he had often thought of leaving Wakely and setting up somewhere else. The problem had been solved for him when his partner had been killed in a car crash some eighteen months earlier. The practice had automatically come to him and since taking over he had expanded it until he alone now served Wakely and all areas for thirty miles round about.

She had found him so easy going on that first meeting. Mandy relaxed in his company until it felt as if she had known him all her life and, before she left the surgery, he asked her to have dinner with him one night.

She had agreed, thinking for days beforehand of an excuse which would not arouse her husband's insane jealousy and suspicion. She had gone to Hawley's house where he had cooked them a lavish meal and, afterwards, as if it were the most natural thing in the world, they had gone to bed together. Through him she had found her true self, discovering passions which she had thought dormant, finding others she never knew she possessed. He helped her shed her inhibitions until *she* became the teacher. Revelling in her newly awakened sexuality, overcome by Hawley's own expertise, she became insatiable. They were fused together by a ferocity of feeling which surprised them both.

She had found it easy to leave Andy and the two boys. At least, she had in the emotional sense. When he found out where she had gone he turned up at the house carrying a crow bar and he broke every window he could until, that night, Hawley had emerged to face him. The two men had exchanged blows, the vet sustaining a hairline fracture of the left tibia from a blow with the metal bar but he had left Andy with a broken nose and two fewer teeth.

It had been Hawley's suggestion that Mandy become his receptionist. At first she had been reluctant, realizing how quickly word of what had happened would spread around Wakely. However, she agreed eventually and, after the first few weeks of knowing looks and sly remarks, she had come to accept and enjoy her new way of life.

She didn't intend to contest the divorce case. She

didn't want anything from Andy and she certainly didn't wish for custody of the children. She had all she wanted with Hawley.

The cuckoo clock on the wall above the desk signalled its presence by screeching six times.

Mandy touched Hawley's cheek, tutting when some skin came off. Small flakes of it stuck under her nails.

'You look pale, Dan, are you feeling OK?' she asked, noticing also that his lips were swollen and cracked.

'I'm a bit tired, nothing more,' he told her.

'Then don't you think it's time you packed up?' She began undoing her white overall. 'I'll go and get dinner ready.' He ran an appreciative eye over the figure previously concealed by the overall. She was blessed with large but firm breasts, her figure narrowing slightly at the waist before filling out again into a well rounded bottom. Her stomach was flat, her legs long and slender.

'Are you going to eat some proper food tonight?' Hawley asked her, smiling.

Mandy feigned irritation.

'And what's that supposed to mean?'

'It means, when are you coming off that bloody stupid diet?'

'A fish and fruit diet is good for you. I've already lost three pounds in the last two weeks.'

He slapped her backside.

'From where?' he japed.

Mandy stuck her tongue out at him.

'I won't be long,' Hawley said. 'I've got something to do first.'

She hesitated.

'I promise,' he said and headed back into the surgery. Mandy disappeared into what were the living quarters of the house.

Hawley crossed to the work top nearest him and slipped on a fresh pair of rubber gloves. Then, slowly, he pulled back the sheet which covered the remains of the piglet brought in by Tyler that afternoon. The vet pulled one of the arc lamps over and flicked it on, wincing at the powerful light. He closed his eyes for a moment, a sharp pain jabbing at his temples, and when he finally opened his eyes it was as narrow slits. The light felt hot on his skin.

He reached for a scalpel and steadied his hand then, with consummate skill, be began to cut a hole in the pig's skull.

Jesus, the light was bright. His eyes were almost watering now, making it difficult to concentrate. He put down the scalpel and blinked hard. His eyes felt gritty, as if he'd gone for too long without sleep.

The lamp felt even hotter on his skin.

He took a small saw and set about opening the cranium of the piglet, finally exposing the brain. This done, he cut two thin sections, small enough to fit on a microscope slide. He carried them across to the magnifying instrument and slid one beneath the powerful lens.

'Now,' he murmured to himself, relieved to be out of the rays of the arc light. 'Let's see what we've got.'

Seventeen

The bar of 'The King George' was empty but for Tyler, the barman and a couple of other people. The barman, dressed in white shirt and jacket and a pair of black trousers which had gone shiny around the backside, was busy cleaning glasses. Hardly for the rush of business, Tyler mused.

He pulled self-conciously at the top button of his shirt, anxious to loosen his tie a little. He had got out of the habit of wearing one and it was beginning to feel a little uncomfortable. Nevertheless, he had made a special effort for this night. As soon as he'd returned to the farm he'd taken his blue suit from the wardrobe where it had hung since his father's funeral and pressed it over, careful not to burn it. Then he'd showered, shaved and dressed, discovering that he'd been too early, so he drove into Wakely anyway and had a pint or two at 'The Black Knight' enduring the warmly sarcastic comments of his friends who had only once seen him in a suit.

Now he sat glancing alternately at the clock in the corner and his own watch.

It was 8.30 p.m.

With the timing of an actress who has just received her cue, Jo emerged from one of the lifts to the right. Tyler smiled at her across the darkened bar, immediately impressed by her appearance.

Her thick hair had been recently washed and allowed to dry naturally, making it look shaggy. She wore little make-up, the near perfect bone structure of her face making her features glow in the dull light. She wore a black dress, slashed across one shoulder and also up as far as the thigh. The curve of her tanned legs was accentuated by the silver high heels which she wore.

'Hi,' she beamed, seating herself beside him.

'Hello,' he said, smiling at her. 'What will you have to drink?'

She asked for a vodka and lime and, when the barman had poured it, heaping the glass with ice first, she sipped slowly at it, regarding Tyler over the rim.

'So, you hung up your wellington boots for the night, huh?'

86

'Yes, ma'am,' he said, saluting. He raised his glass. 'Cheers.'

'Here's to secrets,' she said and smiled that radiant smile once more.

Tyler nodded.

'Secrets,' he muttered. 'I still don't know what it is you're looking for, apart from this bloke called Anderson.'

Jo sighed.

'Maybe I don't either. Doug said it was just my suspicious mind.'

'Who's Doug?'

'Doug Clark. My editor and . . . friend.'

'What's that supposed to mean?'

'We had a thing going for a time. Notice I use the past tense.'

'Serious?'

'It would have been if I'd let it go that far. He wanted it to. I didn't.'

'So you split up.'

She ran the tip of her index finger around the rim of her glass.

'There was never too much there to begin with,' she told him. 'It wasn't long after I came to Arkham. I was lonely I guess. If it hadn't been Doug it would've been someone else.'

'And now you're not lonely anymore is that it?' he asked.

'Hey, you ask a lot of questions. I think you're in the wrong job. You should be a private detective.'

'Just curious.'

'What about you? Any sordid truths to tell?'

'I should be so lucky.'

They both laughed.

At nine they got up and walked through into the dining room. But for one man alone in a corner the place was devoid of people. They ordered, the menu brought to them by a thin waitress whose face looked like a skull in the dim light. Jo frowned.

'I'll tell you one thing I've noticed,' she said. 'There seem to be a hell of a lot of people in this town who need some sun. Did you see that waitress? She looked anaemic.'

Tyler scratched his chin thoughtfully.

'Now you come to mention it I *have* noticed. Perhaps it's a virus of some kind.'

The first course arrived and they began eating. Both had prawn cocktail.

'So, how did you come to be a farmer?' Jo asked him.

'My father died, not long ago, left me to look after the place.'

'I'm sorry.'

'That's OK.' He smiled at her, mesmerized once more by her raw beauty, her mixture of sensuality and pure animal magnetism. She reminded Tyler of a caged beast, forever on the move, her questions probing, her manner relaxed and yet possessing a certain urgency. 'I'd been brought up on the land, it's what I know best.'

'I didn't even see anything green until I was seven and that was Central Park.' She laughed, sardonically. 'Muggers parade. Do you know that one in three families in New York have had someone amongst them mugged? That's a lot of people.'

'It's a lot of muggers.'

'They tell us to feel sorry for minority groups. You know, Negroes, Chicanos, Puerto Ricans. The underprivileged.' She shook her head. 'The underprivileged are beating our goddam brains out.'

'It's the same in some parts of Britain. I used to live in London. That's going the same way, you can't walk the streets in some areas without getting attacked. It's the political situation as much as anything, if people can't get money by working, then they'll nick it. No jobs, no money, no future.' He stuffed a spoonful of prawns into his mouth.

'Some of the city cynicism rubbed off on you,' she said.

'Perhaps. Why did you leave America?'

She told him about Tony, about the stories in the papers, about the murder, about the attempt on her own life.

'Christ,' he muttered when she'd finished. 'It must be quite boring living in Arkham after what you've seen.'

'I'd rather be bored and *alive*,' she told him and they both laughed. 'Anyhow, it's fine here for me. There's no pressure on me now like there used to be.'

The waitress returned and took away the empty dishes.

'You said your father was dead,' Jo said, softly. 'You haven't told me about your mother.'

Tyler lowered his gaze momentarily, staring into the bottom of his glass as if seeking an explanation of some kind.

'She died when I was twenty-one. A heart attack.'

Jo sensed she'd struck a wrong chord in his emotions.

'I still blame myself for her death in a way,' Tyler continued. 'She never wanted me to go away to college. It was all my father's idea. I knew that whatever I did I'd end up hurting one of them. It turned out to be my mother. She never did forgive me for going.'

'You shouldn't feel guilty about her death,' said Jo.

'I've come to terms with it now but it was difficult in the beginning.'

The main course arrived. Tyler had fish. Jo had chicken.

'Why not steak?' she asked, smiling, grateful for the opportunity to change the subject.

'I work with meat, so I don't feel like eating it too,'

he explained. 'I haven't touched meat or poultry for years.'

He re-filled Jo's wine glass. Then, he watched, amused, as she cut up her food, switched hands and began picking up the pieces, holding her fork in her right hand.

'Have you heard anything about this Anderson bloke?' he asked.

Jo sighed.

'No, but I know he had something important to tell me. I know he sounded frightened when I spoke to him on the phone.' She paused to swallow. 'And, what's more, I also know that the people he worked for lied to me about him. I'm sure he's around here somewhere, it's just a matter of finding him.'

'He could have left the country.'

'He had no reason to, besides, one of his neighbours saw him two days ago.'

'There's probably a perfectly simple explanation for it.'

'Terrific. If there is then I'm happy but I'd like to know one way or the other, you know what I mean?'

'And how do you intend doing that?'

'By breaking into his house.'

Tyler looked at her carefully across the table.

'What the hell will that solve?' he asked. 'You're a reporter not a bloody copper, you can't just go around breaking into people's houses.'

'Got any better suggestions?'

'And you want me to help you?'

She nodded.

'When do we do it?' His tone had lost some of its surprise.

'Tonight.'

'Fair enough.' He couldn't resist a smile. 'I reckon the Mafia should have tried to recruit you, not kill you.'

They both laughed.

90

Jo found herself gazing deep into the blue pools that were Tyler's eyes. Like twin circlets of June sky they seemed to glow with a radiance which she found both sensitive and arousing. As she ate she looked closely at him, the chiselled features, the broad shoulders, and she felt a stirring within her. She was drawn not just to his physical appearance but also by his easy manner. Christ, she was hot for him. It was as simple as that.

Tyler himself found his gaze drawn to her. She looked like something from an erotic dream, sitting opposite him with one tanned shoulder bare, the hair cascading over it. The tips of her nipples nudging the material of the dress. When she moved her foot he felt one of her legs brush against his and a feeling much akin to an electric shock ran up his spine. He watched her eating, fascinated and attracted by the way she licked her pouting lips after each mouthful. He saw the pink tip of her tongue flick forward, snake-like before disappearing back inside that moist orifice.

'You said you had some problems of your own,' said Jo over coffee.

The farmer nodded, as if reluctant to talk about them.

'It's the animals,' he said, finally. 'Well, you saw what happened at the market today with the weaners.'

The American shuddered at the recollection.

'It's not just that, it's other things and not only on *my* farm either. Those fellows you saw me with this afternoon in the pub, each one of them has been having problems with his stock.'

Jo rubbed her stomach and pulled a face, remembering the chicken she'd eaten.

'Thank God it seems confined to the bigger animals. Cattle, sheep and pigs and it's mainly affecting the young.'

'You say "it", what do you think it is?'

He shrugged.

91

'I don't know, I'm just hoping that Dan Hawley can come up with some answers.'

Jo sipped at her coffee and considered the farmer's troubled expression. He had his hands clasped on the table before him.

Putting her cup down, she reached forward and gently squeezed Tyler's arm.

He looked up, a little surprised then responded by pressing her slim hand between his. Their eyes locked.

'A town full of secrets,' he whispered.

She nodded almost imperceptibly, enjoying the contact with him. The strength in those hands.

'Maybe we won't like the answers we find,' she murmured.

They regarded each other a moment longer, as if disturbed by her words. Tyler finally managed to look away from those hypnotic green orbs of hers, the pupils now dilated.

He paid the bill and they left.

A cool breeze had sprung up and Jo shivered as they walked to her car. Above them, dark clouds conspired to blot out the watery moon. She shuddered as she slid behind the wheel, taking a glance at Tyler as she started the engine.

She guided the Chevette out into the road. The drive to Geoffrey Anderson's house should take about ten minutes.

It was almost 10.48 p.m.

Eighteen

The ticking of the wall clock sounded deafening in the silence of the kitchen. There was no other sound and the dull green luminosity of the clock hands was the only thing which was able to infiltrate the totality of the darkness. The room, in fact the entire house, was swamped in a gloom as impenetrable as pitch. All curtains were drawn, as they had been for the last two days. Not even the sodium glare of the street lamps outside was able to penetrate the abyss.

But, inside the home of Geoffrey Anderson, there was movement.

The darkness may have been almost palpable but there was a part of it which seemed to move independently of the rest. It was no shadow for there was no light to cast one. As if a piece of the gloom had gained form, the shape moved effortlessly through the black house. It walked slowly, noiselessly, completely at one with the cloying funereal surroundings.

It moved through the kitchen, opening the fridge door. There was a pool of water near the door, a spillage from the melted ice inside. The shape pulled out drawers and rummaged through them but all with an economy of movement which caused little sound.

It passed through into the sitting room, discovering a bureau. This it inspected more thoroughly, pulling open the cupboards and drawers but discovering nothing. Still it made no sound and even its breathing was muted and low, scarcely audible.

The shape froze in mid-stride as it heard a car drive past. It stood for long seconds then, satisfied that it would not be disturbed, it headed for the door which led to the hall.

The stairs creaked slightly as it ascended. Four closed

doors confronted it as it reached the landing and it moved towards the closest one.

It was open and the shape entered quickly.

Outside a car pulled up, the powerful headlamps cutting through the blackness.

The shape moved cautiously to the window and pulled the curtain back slightly, gazing out. It looked down upon the two people who had clambered out of the car and who, it now saw, were coming towards the house.

It watched as they approached then it let the curtain go and retreated back into the gloom.

There were sounds of movement from outside the house but, hidden within, surrounded by the cocoon of blackness, the shape waited.

Tyler closed the car door behind him and ran an appraising eye up and down the street. But for the odd light burning in sitting rooms or bedrooms, the tree-lined thoroughfare was in darkness broken only by the dull glow of the street lamps. A moth fluttered lazily around one of them, its wings skittering against the housing.

Jo pulled a torch from her coat pocket and flicked it on. Satisfied that it worked she headed towards the house which bore the sign 'Avalon'.

'It looks quiet enough,' said Tyler as he opened the gate.

'That's how it looked earlier,' Jo told him.

She moved impatiently forward but the farmer blocked her way. He shook his head.

'Let me go first,' he said, softly.

She agreed, allowing him to lead the way, furtively, up the garden path. They decided to break in via the back way in order to make themselves less conspicuous. Jo looked to her left, watching for any lights in the house of the woman she'd spoken to that morning. There were no lights to be seen anywhere.

94

The moon had been well and truly smothered by dark cloud so they hadn't even the advantage of natural light.

As they reached the back door Jo flicked on the torch.

'Shine it on the lock,' whispered Tyler, fumbling in his pocket. 'Shit,' he grunted. Then, turning to Jo, he asked, 'Have you got a hair clip or something like that?'

She hadn't.

Tyler pulled off his jacket, wrapped the garment around his elbow and, looking around one last time, drove it into the glass panelled door.

The pane spider-webbed but didn't break.

He hit it again, wincing as some glass smashed loudly on the kitchen floor inside. Then the farmer hurriedly slipped his hand through and unlocked the door. They both scuttled inside.

'Burglar I'm not,' he muttered, pulling his jacket back on. 'Now tell me what the hell we're looking for?'

Jo shone the torch around the kitchen, playing the beam over the beige walls. She picked out a calendar, a rack of knives, a couple of shelves and cupboards.

'I'm not even sure myself,' she told him, walking cautiously towards the door which led into the sitting room. Her high heels clicked loudly on the lino.

Tyler followed, noticing that one of the knives was missing from the rack. It was nothing extraordinary in itself but, with the rest of the room being so well ordered, this particular abberrance seemed all the more prominent.

The shape moved quietly from one bedroom to the next, listening to the muffled sounds of movement below. Finally it emerged on the landing and peered over the banister into the seething pit of Stygian blackness beneath.

The long-bladed kitchen knife, held in one black hand, seemed almost to be floating on air.

'Does this place look lived in to you?' said Jo, shining the torch around the sitting room.

'Well, someone's been here recently,' Tyler proclaimed, motioning towards an open drawer in the bureau. He hunted through it but found nothing. Jo moved to join him, picking up some pieces of paper which she discovered elsewhere on the cabinet.

'There might be notes of some kind,' she said.

'About what?' he enquired.

'I don't know. Anything, just to tell us where the hell Anderson is.'

Tyler moved into the hallway where he discovered the phone and the answering machine.

'Jo,' he called.

She joined him, shining the torch over the machine.

The cassette had been removed, the tape torn out. It hung like long streamers from the shattered cassette case. Even the plug on the machine itself had been removed.

'I told you there was something going on,' she said almost triumphantly.

'Let's not jump the gun,' said Tyler. 'There could be a logical explanation for this.'

'Like hell,' she rasped.

The American shone the torch around, bringing the beam to bear on the doormat.

There were two letters lying there, both addressed to Anderson and both bearing postmarks two days old. She looked at Tyler and an unspoken acknowledgement passed between them.

'Let's check upstairs,' said the farmer, taking the torch from her and mounting the first step.

The dark shape heard the sound of footfalls on the steps and it melted back into the darkness. It stepped into the bath and drew the shower curtain slowly around to

96

conceal itself still further. It gripped the knife tightly and listened intently as the stairs creaked.

'We can get it done quicker if we check the rooms separately,' said Jo. 'If you find anything, shout.'

He nodded and pushed open the door of the nearest room. She, for her own part, took the one to the left.

Tyler found himself in what appeared to be a spare bedroom. A single bed was made up neatly and the room smelt of fresh linen. There was a wardrobe too and he tried the key, wincing at the squeak as he turned it. The door came open and Tyler shone the torch inside.

Apart from a set of blankets, it was empty. No clothes, no shoes. Even the coat hangers were gone.

He pushed the door to and crossed to a bedside cabinet, sliding open a top drawer.

It too was empty.

Tyler frowned, repeating the procedure with the solid oak dressing table which stood beneath the window. The entire thing had been cleared, all the drawers were empty.

He exhaled deeply.

Jo, meanwhile, found herself in what looked like an office of some kind. There was a desk, a couple of filing cabinets and piles of paper and envelopes of varying sizes. The desk itself had just two pencils and a small writing pad on it. She checked the drawers which, to her surprise, were empty. Puzzled, she ran a hand through her hair and decided to flip through the pad. Several pages had been torn out, the tops of the perforated paper still in place.

She crossed to the filing cabinets and pulled the top one open. There were about three dozen manila files inside. All unmarked. All empty.

'Christ,' muttered Jo, her voice a mixture of anger and frustration. She pushed the cabinet shut a little too hard, the sound of metal on metal ringing around the silent house.

Tyler heard it and called to her.

She answered that she was OK.

The farmer moved into a second, larger bedroom.

Once more he was confronted with a wardrobe, a bigger one, and this one was locked. He tugged at the recalcitrant fastening. Finally putting down the torch and using both hands. It wouldn't budge. He looked around for something with which to break the handle and retrieved a brass paper weight from a nearby sideboard. He struck the handle twice and, on the second impact, it dropped away.

Jo heard the clatter but paid it no heed as she moved into the bathroom. She blinked hard, her eyes having become accustomed to the gloom, but in this particular room it seemed darker still. It was small, with just a toilet, a wash basin and a bath. The shower curtain, she noticed, was drawn.

Her heels sounded loud in the stillness as she crossed to the nylon curtain and prepared to pull it back.

Behind it, the shape raised the knife.

Jo took a firm hold on the curtain.

'Come here.'

The shout startled her. She spun round, letting go of the curtain, and headed in the direction of Tyler's voice.

She found him in the larger bedroom, two suitcases lying on the floor before him. They were both open. Both filled with clothes.

'If he'd gone away,' said the farmer. 'I think he might have taken his things with him.'

Jo nodded, looking down at the cases. Someone had gone through the wardrobe, removed every item of clothing and meticulously packed them into the tan suitcases.

'The wardrobe in the other room is empty too,' Tyler told her.

'I told you there was something wrong here,' she said.

'That still doesn't explain where Anderson is.'

'No,' murmured the American.

'I think we should call the police but not from here. This is out of our hands now. We'll report him as a missing person, tell them what's happened.'

'When?'

He looked at his watch beneath the torch light.

It was approaching 11.42.

'If he's already been missing for two days another few hours won't hurt. We'll wait until morning.'

Jo agreed.

They left everything as it was and made their way back down the stairs then outside once more. Tyler flicked off the torch as they reached the back door and they scuttled across the front lawn back to the waiting Chevette.

From the window of the larger bedroom the shape watched the car pull away, the kitchen knife still cradled in its hand.

Nineteen

As the sound of the Chevette's engine receded into the night, the curtain was slowly pushed back into position and the inside of Geoffrey Anderson's house once more became as black as pitch. Nevertheless, the lone intruder moved, as he always did at night, with an assurance few others possessed. His footsteps were as noiseless as before and he crossed to the larger bedroom, retracing his own steps and also those of Tyler and Jo.

He stood, a dark shape amongst so much gloom, gazing down at the open suitcases, the long bladed kitchen knife still gripped firmly in his hand. He hefted the lethal blade before him a second then dropped it onto the bed. His breathing was shallow but more guttural now and he suppressed a cough as he reached into his jacket pocket for a pack of Rothmans. There was one in the box, crumpled. What the hell, he'd make do. He'd started smoking when he was five and now, at fifty-three, he was on over eighty a day. His fingers, long and slender, were stained almost black with nicotine. He lit the cigarette and sucked hard on it. A spasm of coughing racked his body and he banged his chest angrily.

Carlo Fanducci was dying.

He knew it, he didn't need any doctor to tell him. He was fucking dying. The mornings when he coughed until he spat blood, the pains in his chest, the bouts of wheezing. They had told him that, he didn't need any goddam medical genius to confirm it. But what the hell, everybody had to die sometime. Fanducci smiled thinly, running a hand through his lank grey hair. Despite the fact that his hairline was receding, the lustrous grey strands still grew in abundance over his ears and the back of his head. Deep creases scarred almost every inch of his face, particularly his forehead which looked as though someone had pulled a fork across it. Someone had once told him he had a face like an unkept grave and he smiled once more at the recollection.

He sat down on the edge of the bed to finish his cigarette, the glowing tip the only light in the room.

Fanducci inhaled painfully.

He'd thought he was going to have to kill the man

and the girl when they'd entered the house. He didn't recognise the man but he'd seen the girl before. He'd listened in on the phone tap the night Anderson had called her then he'd watched her from the trees as she'd used the call box. He'd ripped the car light from inside the Chevette with his bare hands. He smiled and flexed his fingers. There was enormous strength in those hands. He might be dying but he sure as hell didn't intend going down weak and enfeebled.

The vision of the girl floated into his mind once more. He thought he'd seen her before that night in the lay-by. She was American, like himself. He had detected her accent – East Side, New York. Different from his own which was a curious amalgam of Italian and Lower Manhattan. He'd been born in Mott Street, at the very centre of 'Little Italy'. His father had been a bartender, running one of the joints owned by the Molinaro family, one of New York's largest and most powerful families. Fanducci himself had graduated, over the years, from collector to soldier and, finally, to trigger man.

Cosa Nostra. He almost said the words aloud. *Our thing. Our* fucking *thing.* Only he was no longer a part of it. Don Vito Molinaro had seen to that. The old bastard had given him a job to do. There had been a Union boss called Bishop. He wouldn't toe the line, wouldn't pay his dues to the collectors. Had even pulled a .45 on them, told them to fuck off and stop bothering him. Fanducci had been told to warn the Union leader off, frighten him a bit. So he had paid a visit to the man's factory, spoken to him. Ended up sticking the barrel of his .357 between the motherfucker's legs.

It hadn't been warning enough.

Old man Molinaro had finally given Fanducci the go ahead to push the button on Bishop. The Union Leader had to go and Fanducci was only too happy to do the job. He'd trailed the man home one night, then sat in his car until late finally emerging around midnight.

He'd cut through one of the windows with a glass cutter and entered the building.

Bishop had woken up as the Italian had entered the room and Fanducci could still remember the look of horrified realization on the Union leader's face as he saw the .357 being drawn. The big gun had not had the benefit of a silencer and the bang when it came had been thunderous. The hollow-tipped bullet had caught Bishop in the chest, exploding as it shattered bone, ripping an exit hole the size of a fist as it punched its way out of his back spraying Mrs Bishop with gobbets of lung and smashed scapula.

She'd started screaming when Fanducci had fired the second bullet into the nape of her husband's neck.

In the darkness her screams had seemed to be coming from some disembodied ghost but, in the pale light from outside, he could see her, drenched in her husband's blood. She continued to shriek. Then the two kids appeared from another room and *they* were screaming.

All of them were fucking screaming.

The only way to shut them up was by blowing their heads off and that was precisely what he'd done.

It had been plastered all over the papers the next day. Fanducci had been summoned before the Don and told that he was outcast. The family didn't want him any longer. Fuck them, he thought, and he went.

There was no shortage of buyers for his services. During his years as a family member he had met many top industrialists. These powerful men always needed bodyguards and Fanducci had found himself another employer with ease. He'd enjoyed that way of life. There had been more women in those years than he'd ever had before. One of them had become his wife.

By that time in his fiftieth year, Fanducci had married a girl half his age. She had the face and body of a movie star and a mind like a child. However, in bed she was something else. And, she was too much for him to handle. She had, he'd later discovered, a string of lovers but it wasn't until he walked in one night and found her being well and truly shafted by some goddam nigger that he'd found out. He'd beaten them both with a chair leg. Then he'd broken the nigger's fingers for good measure and thrown the girl out. Little bitch.

At roughly the same time, he'd been approached by John Stark. A mysterious man about six years younger than Fanducci himself. He'd asked the Italian what he was earning, then offered to double it. The condition was, he would have to up roots and move to England. Stark was opening a chemical research plant of some kind and he needed someone like Fanducci working for him. The Italian had agreed and, for the past three years he'd lived in England, working for what was to become Vanderburg Chemicals. He saw little of Stark, taking most of his orders from a guy called Thorndike, an Englishman who he could not learn to trust but then, Fanducci reasoned, trust was a hard thing to come by.

It had been Thorndike who had told him to kill Anderson. He hadn't reckoned on any interference though. Now, as he sat on the edge of the bed he tried to remember where he'd seen that dark-haired girl who'd not long ago left the house. Quite a looker, not the sort you'd easily forget – nice tits. No. The memory eluded him. He took one last suck on the cigarette, nipped it out and dropped the butt into his jacket pocket.

Then he set about his task.

Twenty

It was just after midnight as Jo and Tyler stood facing each other in the car park of 'The King George'. She had locked her own vehicle and now they stood beside the farmer's landrover.

'I'll meet you in the morning,' he said. 'We'll go to the police, tell them everything. They'll find Anderson.'

Jo nodded.

'Thanks for your help,' she said. 'I appreciate it.'

He leant forward and kissed her softly on the lips, feeling that familiar tingle run the length of his spine as he did so.

Jo felt the same sensation and she pulled Tyler closer, her lips parting, brushing the hard edges of his teeth before probing deeper into his mouth. He responded fiercely and they remained locked together for long moments, each enjoying the touch of the other. He felt her soft hair brush against his hand and he shuddered. As she slipped one hand inside his jacket it was all he could do to contain the erection he felt beginning. They finally broke apart, gazing into each other's eyes.

'I'd better go,' he said, opening the door of the landrover.

She watched as he climbed in and started the engine. He smiled at her, then spun the wheel and drove off. Jo stood in the car park for a moment longer, then she headed for the side entrance to the hotel.

There wasn't a soul in the reception as she entered. The American wandered into the darkened bar and found that too was deserted. She felt a sudden pang of hunger and knew she would have to eat something before she turned in for the night. Just a sandwich would do. Jo crossed to the reception and rang the bell.

No one appeared.

There were some papers on the desk top and a half

finished glass of beer but there didn't appear to be anyone around to claim them.

'Hello,' she called, her voice sounding strangely muffled in the silent confines of the reception.

The night porter or some member of staff had to be around she reasoned. Maybe they'd gone for a leak. She waited a moment longer, walking across to the open fire place, looking up at the two large pikes crossed above it. The weapons had been polished recently and glinted in the half light. Jo wandered back to the desk and rang the bell once more.

When the second attempt failed to secure any response, Jo lifted the flap which led behind the counter and walked through. There were two doors before her, both closed, both marked 'Private'. She knocked on the first one, peering inside when she got no answer. It was a small room, one wall being lined with leather chairs. There were a couple of coffee tables in there too, some magazines lying around. Jo guessed that it must be the staff room, a suspicion confirmed when she saw a rota pinned to a notice board on her right. There was another door before her which led through into the kitchen. This door was slightly ajar and she could see light spilling through the crack. There were vague sounds of movement from inside so she headed towards the door.

Of four banks of fluorescent lights set into the ceiling of the kitchen, only one was lit and, from where she stood, Jo could see a dark figure standing near to one of the fridges at the far end of the room.

As he turned, she saw that it was Mark Bates. She watched in silence as he opened the fridge door and took out a large piece of raw steak, the blood dripping from it as he removed it from the metal tray.

Jo was hidden from him by the darkness and by a rack of cooking utensils which hung before her. She watched, mesmerized, as he lifted the steak in one

105

hairy-palmed hand, looked at it for a moment, then tore off a chunk with his teeth. He chewed with difficulty, blood from the meat dripping from his chin. Bates grunted in satisfaction as he indulged his gluttony. Dark, rusty stains smeared his cheeks and some of the red liquid dripped from his long nails. When he opened his mouth, a gobbet fell to the floor and, quick as a flash, he scooped it up and rammed it back into his mouth.

Jo turned away, revolted, and fled from the kitchen. She felt sick and, when she finally reached her room, she drank several glasses of water before she felt the nausea pass off.

Downstairs, Bates stuffed the last of the steak into his mouth, then he fastidiously licked every last drop of blood from his fingers.

Twenty-one

The following morning, Jo ate a light breakfast of toast and jam washed down with a cup of coffee. She couldn't face the bacon and eggs which she saw one of the other guests tucking into, not after what she'd seen the previous night. She hadn't slept too well and there were dark rings beneath her eyes. Dressed in a pair of jeans and a red T-shirt she was already beginning to feel warm as, outside, the sun rose in a cloudless sky and began its merciless grilling of the land beneath.

She had looked for Bates but not seen him. There were just two waitresses and a porter, all three of whom looked lethargic and pale. Perhaps Tyler had been right? There might be a virus going around. She sipped at her coffee. A virus which caused hair to grow on the palm of a man's hand and made him eat raw meat? Jo almost chuckled aloud.

Her thoughts turned to other things. The incident at Anderson's house last night had unsettled her. Although at least now she felt secure in the knowledge that her hunch had been correct. There *was* something going on which he had known about and which someone at Vanderburg didn't want him to talk about. At least it looked that way. Obviously they wouldn't know for sure until they found him. She paused. *If* they found him. Jo hastily dismissed the idea. After all, this was England, not New York. Things like that didn't happen here. She finished her coffee, seeds of doubt already sown and growing in her mind. The American lit up a cigarette, took a few drags on it and left the dining room.

Tyler was waiting for her in reception.

'I wondered if you'd be up yet,' he said, smiling.

'With the lark,' she told him as they headed out to his waiting landrover.

As they drove to the police station she told him about Bates and the raw meat.

'Christ, what would make him do that?' Tyler wondered aloud.

She mentioned what he himself had said about a virus.

'It's possible I suppose but if it is a virus which is affecting so many people how the hell is it transmitted?'

'I'm a journalist not a doctor, Vic,' she said.

'Curiously enough, neither of my farm hands have turned up this morning but no one's rung in to say if they're sick or not. One of Stuart Nichols' blokes is taking care of things for me.'

They drove slowly through the quiet streets, noticing

just how few people there were about. Granted it was only ten o'clock but Wakely town centre was usually bustling by now. Those few people who were on the streets seemed to be moving in slow motion, heads bowed as if searching for something on the ground beneath them.

Tyler turned a corner, braking hard as a man stepped out in front of him.

'You silly sod,' Tyler shouted angrily. 'I could have killed you.'

The man merely looked round and both Jo and Tyler saw how bloodless his features were, the cheeks sunken, the eyes dark rimmed and yellowed. The man narrowed them against the glare of the sun. He gazed at the occupants of the landrover in bewilderment and, as he did so, Jo noticed that the flesh was flaking from his hands and curling back in almost transparent wisps. His nails were hooked, those that weren't broken. He stood motionless for a moment, then walked on as if nothing had happened.

Tyler looked anxiously at Jo and started the engine again.

'Maybe we should stop off at the doctor's surgery,' Jo said. 'See if he's had many cases like we've been seeing.'

'First things first, eh?' said the farmer. 'Let's find out where Geoffrey Anderson is. Besides, we don't know there *is* anything wrong with the people in Wakely yet.'

Jo opened her mouth to speak but Tyler cut her short.

'And even if there is, I don't see that there's much we can do about it.'

'But if it's affecting so many of them it must be communicable. What the hell is to stop us catching it?'

The farmer seemed not to have considered that possibility. As if troubled by the realization, he drove the rest of the way in silence.

There were two Panda cars parked outside Wakely police station, both with their windows wound down in an effort to let some air into the stifling confines of the vehicles. The police station itself was a large, white-washed building; just one storey, it was about the size of a supermarket and quite disproportionately large for the number of men on the force. Tyler knew four of them well, the other three just well enough to nod to.

He swung the landrover around and parked in front of the main doors, then he and Jo climbed out and strode down the six wide stone steps which led to the forecourt.

Inside the building it was cool, two powerful fans droning in opposite corners of the entry-way giving some respite from the blistering heat outside. Tyler crossed to a meshed glass partition and rapped sharply on it.

There were sounds of movement from behind, of a bolt being slipped and then the partition opened to reveal a red-faced man with a thick growth of beard. He had his white shirt rolled up to the elbows but there was still perspiration glistening on the thick hairs of his forearms. Rotund and quick to smile, he reminded Jo of a dark-haired, sweaty Santa Claus.

'Hello, Vic,' said Sergeant Don Mason. 'How are you?'

'Not so bad,' said Tyler, then he introduced Jo.

Mason smiled even more broadly and shook hands with the American who did her best to retain her smile as she felt her hand engulfed by the sticky puffiness of Mason's appendage.

'What's wrong? One of your pigs got lost has it?' Mason said, chuckling.

'I want to file a missing persons report,' the farmer told him.

Mason raised his eyebrows quizzically. He reached for the appropriate form and stood there, pen poised.

'What's the name?' he asked.

'Geoffrey Anderson,' Jo told him. 'He's been missing since Sunday.'

'Three days,' said Mason to himself, scribbling on the form. 'Description?'

There was an awkward silence.

Mason looked up.

Tyler exhaled deeply.

'We don't know what he looks like. Neither of us have ever seen him.'

'So how do you know he's missing?' Mason wanted to know.

'We broke into his house last night,' Jo said. 'All his clothes were packed as if he was going away but there was no sign of him. I think someone had been through the house.'

The policeman tapped on the desk top with the end of his pen.

'*You* broke into someone's house?' he said.

They both nodded.

'Perhaps I should be filling out a bloody charge sheet, not a missing persons form. What the hell were you doing breaking into somebody's house?'

'Don, for Heaven's sake listen to me,' said Tyler. 'I'm telling you, Anderson has disappeared.'

Mason wiped a bead of perspiration from his forehead.

'We'll soon sort this out,' he muttered. 'Peck.'

A constable appeared from one of the back rooms. He was tall, perhaps six five and he moved slowly as if each step were an effort. Both Jo and Tyler noticed the pallor of his skin, the way his teeth protruded from his swollen lips.

'Peck, drive out to this address,' said Mason handing the P.C. a page from his notebook. 'See what you can find.'

Peck nodded, blinked hard and rubbed his eyes.

'Come on, move yourself, lad, we haven't got all day. Radio in as soon as you've found out what's happening there.'

The constable nodded and made his way slowly out to one of the Pandas. They heard the engine being revved up, then the car pulled away.

'He needs a bloody bomb behind him that lad,' said Mason. 'He's been moping around looking like a wet weekend for the last week or so.'

'He looks ill,' said Jo.

'Well, if he is, he's not the only one on the force who is. Two of my constables called in sick five days ago and I haven't heard anything from them since and the others here, apart from myself and P.C. Dagless, look like death warmed up.'

'So do most of the people we've seen,' said Jo.

'I reckon there must be a virus or something going round,' Tyler added.

'Probably bloody flu,' Mason said, scornfully. He considered the missing persons report again. 'What makes this Anderson so important anyway?'

'He works for Vanderburg Chemicals,' Jo said. She paused. 'Or *worked*. He was a research scientist. He wanted to speak to me about something but he never got the chance.'

'So you two thought you'd break into his house and see if you could find him?' Mason said, sarcastically.

'Goddamit, we had no choice,' Jo snapped.

'Perhaps he's gone on holiday,' Mason insisted.

Tyler shook his head.

'No,' he said, emphatically.

The sergeant offered them some tea and they sat in the entry-way and drank it, waiting for Peck to radio in.

'When he gets inside he'll find the suitcases,' Jo said to Tyler. 'They'll know we're telling the truth then.'

There was a hiss of static from the microphone on

111

the desk close to Mason. He picked it up and flicked the transmitter switch. Tyler and Jo got up and crossed to the partition in an effort to hear the conversation.

'Tango One come in,' said Mason.

More static.

'Peck, for Christ's sake come in you idiot.'

'Sorry, sarge, I was having trouble with the handset.' The constable's voice sounded tinny.

'Have you checked the house out?' Mason asked.

'I didn't have to.'

'Why not?'

'Anderson's here.'

'What?' snapped Tyler.

Mason waved a hand for him to be quiet.

'You're sure it's him. Geoffrey Anderson. You have got the right address haven't you?'

'Sarge, it's him, I'm telling you. He said he was leaving for a few weeks' holiday. I saw his cases in the hall.'

Mason exhaled through clenched teeth, his eyes fixed on Jo and Tyler.

'OK, Peck, come back to the station. Over and out.' He flicked off the set.

Mason held up the missing persons report and very carefully tore it up.

'Next time, Vic, get your facts right before you come bothering me. Now clear out before I charge you both with breaking and entering.'

The two men glared at each other for long moments, then Tyler spun round and, followed by Jo, left.

As they clambered into the landrover Tyler banged the steering wheel angrily.

'What the bloody hell is going on?' he snarled.

'Vic, it couldn't have been Anderson,' Jo insisted.

'Well, as far as the police are concerned, it *was* and the case is closed.' He started the engine and turned the vehicle around, heading in the direction of his farm.

112

'I'm not letting it drop, Vic.'

'We were taken for mugs,' he snapped. 'Someone fooled both of us.'

They drove the rest of the way in silence.

Carlo Fanducci stood in the doorway and watched the Panda pull away. He couldn't resist a smile. Jesus, what a dumb bastard that cop had been. He hadn't even asked him for any I.D. A real lame fuck. Fanducci had said he was Geoffrey Anderson and the cop had believed him, even fallen for the line he'd shot him about going away for a few weeks. Dumb motherfucker. The ex-Mafia man chuckled to himself and closed the door.

He wondered if he'd get any more trouble from the two bastards he'd seen in the house last night.

If they wanted trouble, fine.

As he moved, the .357 Magnum felt heavy in its shoulder holster.

Twenty-two

The cow walked by slowly, followed by its calf. The larger of the two animals paused momentarily and looked at the two onlookers, then it found some grass and began eating. All over the field animals were doing likewise. In some places, the young were almost as big as the parents. It was difficult to distinguish them.

'See what I mean,' said Tyler, indicating one of the over-developed calves. 'Twice as big as they should be for their age.'

Jo nodded.

'But you said it wasn't just the cows.'

'It isn't,' said Tyler, heading back across the yard towards a barn. Jo followed him, trying to avoid the mud patches, muttering to herself when her heels sank into the sticky ooze. Tyler looked down at her feet and grinned.

'Not the most practical footwear for a farm,' he japed.

The American was about to say something when her left shoe was actually pulled off by the clinging mud. She hopped about on one leg, hurriedly tugged the shoe free and slipped it back on.

The farmer led her into a barn which contained a number of pigs. In small pens were about two dozen sows, most with litters. The noise in the building was almost deafening. Jo looked into the first pen and saw three large weaners feeding from their mother's teats. She shuddered involuntarily, remembering what had happened at the livestock market. In the next pen were more piglets, only here some of them were normal size. One lay motionless in the straw whilst another, larger one, sniffed at it.

'Some are affected, some are normal,' said Tyler, wearily.

'I don't know what to make of it.'

He turned and headed for the exit but Jo lingered for a moment, her attention caught by the small pig before her. It was still lying in the straw but whether or not it was dead she didn't know. Its larger companion continued to nuzzle against it until finally it gripped one of the creatures floppy ears in its mouth and tore it away.

Jo winced.

'Oh God,' she murmured, then she found the breath to call Tyler. He scuttled back to the pen and glanced in at the tableau before him. The larger piglet had taken another chunk out of the dead one and was chewing hungrily. The smell of blood had created squeals of excitement amongst the remainder of the litter and, in seconds, they were crowding around the body of the dead weaner. Tyler reached for a nearby broom and, stepping over the rail, drove the litter away. He picked up the dead pig by one of its hind legs and lifted it out of the pen. The others returned to the sow as if nothing had happened.

Jo had turned pale and she headed for the door ahead of Tyler who carried the torn carcass of the dead weaner with him. He tossed it onto the ground outside and sighed.

'Are you OK?' he asked the journalist.

She nodded.

'When is this going to stop?' she wanted to know.

'I wish I knew.'

There was a large compost heap nearby, the stench even more unbearable due to the fact that the sun had been baking it for the past few weeks. Tyler tossed the weaner onto it and pitched a few forkfuls of the muck over the carcass. Beside the heap Jo noticed some large bags, like the bags supermarkets sold potatoes in. They were of a strong plastic, silver in colour and she could also see some red letters on them. The American squatted down and pulled one of the bags free.

'What was in here, Vic?' she asked.

'A new multi-purpose feed,' he told her.

They looked at one another as Jo uncovered the label: VANDERBURG CHEMICALS.

The same thought struck them simultaneously.

'Then it is something to do with the feed,' she said. 'I mean, what's been happening to the animals? The accelerated growth, them turning crazy?'

Tyler nodded.

'I'm pretty sure none of this started happening until the Vanderburg feed was introduced to the stock. Hawley said that other farmers around here have been having the same sort of problems as I have.' He scratched his chin thoughtfully.

'Christ,' he muttered. 'Stuart Nichols was using it, so was old Ben Thurston. They *did* both mention peculiarities in their stock.'

'Increased growth,' Jo added. 'I heard one of them say that when I was in the bar before the livestock market.'

'Still-born litters and Ben said his lambs were as big as dogs. It has to be the feed.'

'Maybe Anderson ties in to this somehow,' she said. Tyler frowned.

'Come on, Jo, you're obsessed with this bloody bloke. How could he have anything to do with what's been happening at the farms in Wakely?'

'Look, Anderson worked for Vanderburg Chemicals. These sacks belong to Vanderburg Chemicals. The feed they produce has caused abnormalities in livestock. There . . .'

He cut her short.

'We won't know that for *sure*, not until Dan Hawley completes the autopsies.'

'Goddamit, Vic, there has to be a link,' she shouted at him. She threw the bag down angrily.

'You want there to be a link,' he countered. 'Anderson probably doesn't even know anything about this multi-purpose feed, let alone its effects.'

'He was a research scientist for Christ's sake, he was one of the guys working on the project.'

'Where's your proof?'

She was silent for a moment. Her breath was coming in short gasps, her eyes aglow with anger.

'Let's see what Hawley says first,' Tyler said. 'But I think you're wrong about the link between Anderson and what's going on here.'

'Maybe you're right,' she conceded. 'Maybe I am

116

paranoid about Anderson but it's one hell of a coincidence.'

Tyler nodded. They stood for a moment longer, then he walked back to the house with her. He asked if she wanted a coffee. She said yes.

'I'll make you a cup when I've tried to reach my two farmhands.' He crossed to the phone.

'I can do it. Just tell me where everything is,' said Jo.

'In the kitchen, you can't miss it, it's still out from breakfast time.'

She wandered through into the kitchen. Tyler picked up the phone and dialled Harrison's number.

No answer.

He let it ring half a dozen times.

Still there was nothing.

Tyler put the phone down. If Harrison was that ill, then surely his wife would have called in for him. Unless she too was sick. But too sick to reach the telephone? He tried Jenkins's number. The result was the same. No answer.

He replaced the receiver and wandered into the kitchen where he found Jo standing over two steaming mugs of coffee. She handed one to him.

'No luck?' she asked.

He shook his head.

'Maybe they've got that virus,' she offered.

Tyler smiled thinly.

'Now you *are* clutching at straws. You'll be telling me next that Anderson's mixed up with that as well.'

Jo smiled wryly.

'I don't discount the possibility.'

'Don't journalists ever stop speculating?'

'No.'

They carried their coffee into the sitting room and Tyler seated himself on the sofa. Jo sat next to him, lighting up a cigarette. She looked around the room, taking in every detail.

'It's a nice house,' she said. 'Not what you'd expect a farmhouse to look like.'

'You mean where are the horse brasses and carved wood furniture?'

She chuckled.

'A bit of a cliché that,' he said, smiling. 'Farmers are businessmen these days. We're more concerned with stock figures and V.A.T. than we are with weaving our own sweaters and making oak tables.'

'I *never* had you figured as a cliché, Vic,' she told him. She noticed two photos on the mantelpiece over the fire.

'Your parents?' she asked, motioning towards them.

'Yes.'

Jo got to her feet and crossed to the fireplace, looking at the photograph of the man and then at Tyler.

'There's a resemblance.'

'Same face, same temperament my mother used to say.'

'Don't you ever get lonely out here by yourself?' she asked, returning to the seat beside him.

'No. I could ask you the same question, you're thousands of miles away from home. Don't you ever miss it?'

'I don't miss New York. Though maybe one day I'll go back, just to see if things have changed.'

She looked down into her coffee as if trying to discover her next few words there.

'Who am I kidding?' she confessed. 'I wouldn't dare go back.'

'You mean because of the Mafia?'

She nodded.

'They're like the goddam Mounties, they always get their man.'

Vic squeezed her hand and she turned to look at him. As on the previous night, Tyler sensed that curious duality within her. The raw, smouldering sexuality

118

mingling with the softness. It was a combination which aroused him deeply and he found himself gazing deep into those jade eyes. He leant forward and kissed her softly on the lips. Jo touched his stubbled cheek with one long nail, listening to it rasp across the bristles. Then she pulled him closer, her mouth eager to find his, her tongue probing deeply.

Tyler slid his right hand up her back until he felt her soft lustrous hair. Without breaking the kiss, Jo moved closer to him, her hands sliding inside his shirt to explore his muscular chest. He felt her long nails rake his flesh and the sensation sent waves of pleasure through him.

He slipped his free hand up her T-shirt, his eager fingers brushing her left nipple. It stiffened to a hard bud and he transferred his attention to the other one. Jo let out a low gasp of pleasure and lay back, allowing the farmer to reach her more easily. She pulled the T-shirt over her head and dropped it behind her, treating Tyler to the sight of her firm breasts. He bent forward and kissed each nipple in turn, drawing it between his teeth, leaving a trail of saliva as he licked his way down to her navel.

She loosened the button of her jeans, closing her eyes as he eased her zip down. She lifted her bottom so he could pull the denim free. He removed her jeans and panties in one movement. He nuzzled the area between her legs, his hands parting her thighs a little more. He kissed her mound, allowing his tongue to snake lower until he was flicking her clitoris.

Jo arched her back, pushing her pelvis hard against his questing, darting tongue, wanting him to push it into that most sensitive area. Her entire body felt as if it was on fire and, as he probed her moist cleft, she jerked spasmodically beneath the attentions of his tongue.

She opened her eyes and looked at him as he knelt

before her, freeing his own bulging erection. Jo reached for it eagerly, moving her hand gently up and down the shaft until Tyler himself began to shudder.

He entered her with ease, both of them gasping at the sensation and he began to move rhythmically inside her. Jo raised her hips to meet each of his thrusts, her hands resting on his buttocks as she drew him in deeper.

Tyler bent his head and lapped at her swollen nipples and he felt her body begin to tense.

She murmured something in his ear, her hair brushing against his shoulder as she leant forward. She licked some perspiration from his face, gritting her teeth as she felt the first sensations of impending orgasm. Tyler quickened his pace and, seconds later, Jo was moaning loudly, raking his back with her nails as the fury of her climax racked her body. Tyler tensed and, a moment later, he too joined her in ecstasy and she writhed with renewed pleasure as she felt his hot seed spurting into her.

For long moments they lay breathless, Jo running her fingers through his hair. Her body seemed to be glowing and both of them were covered by a thin film of perspiration. He withdrew gently from her, allowing his eyes to trace a pattern once more over her shapely body. Jo lay back, naked, on the sofa, her eyes closed.

Tyler ran his hand up her leg, pausing just short of her slippery cleft.

'It's more comfortable upstairs,' he said.

They both laughed.

Twenty-three

Wakely's only General Practitioner's surgery was crowded as usual. The waiting-room, which seated twenty people, was full and there were even patients standing in the corridors waiting their turn. A chorus of coughs and mutterings drifted from the room, mingling with the strident ringing of the phones on the front desk. One harrassed receptionist tried to deal with patients wanting appointments and manage those who already had them.

In a room to the right sat half-a-dozen more people, some clutching green cards, others pink ones. The pink cards signified blood tests and nurse Jan Williams peered through her appointment book to see how many more she had to do before she finished at one o'clock. She had a splitting headache, not helped by the glaring fluorescent lights above. As she swabbed the arm of a patient and steadied the syringe over the bulging vein, she blinked hard. The needle seemed to swim into separate images for a second before clarifying.

She'd had the headache for the past two days but the tablets which usually relieved it had not worked this time. She'd thought about phoning in to say she was going to have a day off but had decided against it. Besides, if she was at home she would only sit around feeling sorry for herself and the kids would drive her potty. They always did during the school holidays. They got so bored and ended up fighting. Jan had two children, both boys, both ten years old, identical twins in fact. They were the image of their father. Joe Williams had been made redundant two months ago from his job in Arkham and now spent his days sitting around the house worrying where the rent was going to come from. Jan didn't fancy a day at home in *that* atmosphere.

The patient got up and left and Jan transferred the

blood to a phial, placing it alongside the other eight which she had already collected that morning. As she gazed at the crimson liquid she felt her stomach churning and, for a moment, she thought she was going to be sick. She bowed her head and massaged her temples, a little disturbed to find flakes of skin coming away beneath her finger tips. Her hands and arms looked milk white and, when she caught sight of her face in an upturned kidney bowl, she thought she was looking at a skull. The distorted vision leered back at her, eyes sunken, the orbs bulging from the sockets. The blood vessels seemed swollen in places as if threatening to burst but the whites were sepia coloured.

Jan Williams closed her eyes, hoping that the pain in her head would go, but it showed no signs of abating.

She called her next patient.

A urine test this time. She gave the man a small bottle and directed him towards the lavatory, reminding him that the sample must be 'mid-stream'. He looked vague and she started to explain but then he smiled as if something had clicked and he marched off to the toilet.

Jan consulted her book once more, readying a fresh syringe as she saw that she had yet another blood test to do. She ushered the woman behind the curtain and sat her down, fastening the velcro pad around her bicep. Jan blinked hard under the light and stuck the needle in.

It missed the vein and the woman yelped in pain and surprise.

The nurse apologized and tried again. This time the needle punctured the pulsing vein. She let the tourniquet go and drew the required amount of blood. As before, she deposited it in a tube and reached for the seal but, as she held the bottle in her hand, she began to salivate wildly until streamers of sputum dribbled from her mouth. The pain in her head seemed to grow in intensity until it felt as if her eyes were going to burst from her skull.

The woman who had just had her blood taken sat mesmerized, watching the nurse who had clamped her hand around the bottle and was squeezing. With her free hand she reached for two more of the phials, crushing the glass inside her fist.

There was a loud crack as it broke.

Blood cascaded from her hands, pieces of glass falling also, other shards slicing open Jan's palms. She opened her hands to see that the glass had lacerated her hands badly. Broken pieces of crystal protruded from the torn flesh as thick crimson liquid pumped out.

Jan raised both hands to her mouth and lapped at the swiftly flowing blood.

The woman in the chair fainted.

The man returned from the lavatory, apologising for only having half filled the bottle but, when he saw what the nurse was doing, his bladder seemed to find hidden reserves and a dark stain appeared at the front of his trousers.

Jan Williams sank to her knees amidst the blood and glass, both hands held up, the crimson liquid running down her arms to stain her white overall. Ignoring the pieces of glass which cut her tongue, she sucked and licked frenziedly at the life fluid.

When a doctor tore back the curtain and looked down at her she merely turned and smiled, her teeth and lips dripping red, her hands in bloody tatters.

Her wild laughter began to fill the room.

Twenty-four

Dan Hawley wiped some perspiration from his forehead with the back of his hand and steadied the scalpel above the calf. The animal was lying spread-eagled on one of the dissection tables, the vet's trolley full of implements beside it. He cut carefully into it, just above the anus and opened the alimentary canal. A vile-smelling dark fluid spilled from the rent and, even though he was wearing a mask, Hawley winced slightly. He cut a piece of the slippery internal tube and placed it carefully on a microscope slide, then he turned his attention to the calf's stomach.

The accumulation of gas had caused it to swell up so that when the vet cut into it, it deflated rapidly. Bile spurted onto his gloved hand. He sliced off a section of the stomach wall and placed that on a slide too.

He coughed and supported himself against the work bench for a moment, wincing beneath the powerful overhead lights which blazed like minute suns. Then he pressed his eye to the microscope, slid the specimen beneath the powerful lens and peered at it. He adjusted the focus until things swam into crystal clarity, carefully scrutinizing what he saw before him.

Hawley exhaled deeply and reached for the second slide.

What he saw was the same.

Ordinarily, bacteria will survive in a dead body for anything up to three days before dying. The microscopic organisms which he saw before him had come from an animal that had been dead for two days and yet they were still moving amongst the other debris. But what surprised Hawley was the fact that they were multiplying.

Instead of dying, the bacteria were increasing.

He stepped back from the microscope and crossed to

a small incubator nearby. From it he took a third slide, one which held a section of the piglet's brain which Tyler had brought in the day before.

Hawley looked once more at the third slide.

The bacteria had begun to form spores.

He swallowed hard, his mouth feeling as if it were full of chalk. His tongue seemed swollen, his lips dry. He crossed to the sink and filled a plastic cup with water but, instead of slaking his thirst, it made him feel sick. The vet held his stomach for a moment, then returned to the spread-eagled calf. He took a saw from his trolley and set to work opening the skull. The tumescent growth on the side of the head had begun to shrivel like an old grape but, Hawley noticed, the eye which was attached to it still gazed glassily at him.

He prized away the portion of skull he'd cut, exposing the brain, then he retrieved his scalpel and carefully cut a sliver of the grey-red matter, dropping it onto a slide as he had done the other specimens.

There were spores in there too.

Whatever kind of bacteria it was, Hawley had never seen its like before. It was multiplying at a greatly accelerated speed, forming spores in order to hibernate. But why? He coughed again and pulled off his rubber gloves, then he walked across to a small bookshelf on the far wall. From it he took down a heavy tome and flicked agitatedly through it. There were diagrams of every known bacteria but nothing remotely like what he'd seen on his slides. He slammed the book shut and stood there for what seemed like an eternity then, pulling the gloves back on, he returned to the calf.

He'd already examined the cow which had given birth to it and found traces of exactly the same bacteria in both her bloodstream and placenta. It had also been present in the remains of the stomach.

The cow, the calf and the weaner. All three had

become breeding grounds for the new strain of bacteria, their carcasses infested with the microscopic life form.

Hawley took one last look at the writhing shapes on the slide, then he hurried to the phone and dialled Tyler's number.

Mandy Potter opened the door when Tyler and Jo arrived. She ushered them through into the surgery, then disappeared.

The hands of the wall clock had just crawled past noon.

As the farmer and the journalist entered the surgery they were immediately struck by the foul smell. The body of the calf had been covered by a rubber sheet but, nevertheless, the strong odour hung heavily in the air making Jo cough.

Hawley was sitting on a stool beside the microscope. The room was stuffy, the blinds down, the overhead lights having been turned off.

The vet looked up wearily as his two visitors entered.

'What have you found, Dan?' asked Tyler.

Hawley exhaled deeply.

'I wish I could tell you,' said the vet, enigmatically. He motioned for the farmer to look into the microscope which he did, squinting down the eye piece. He saw the bacteria moving rapidly amongst the tissue, then he stepped back to let Jo have a look.

'It's bacteria,' said Hawley, answering an unasked question. 'There are four separate specimens taken from the weaner, the calf's brain and stomach and from the cow. They're all identical.'

'What does that mean?' asked Jo.

'A virus?' asked Tyler.

'I don't think so,' the vet told him. 'The bacteria which cause viral infections in livestock aren't as. . . .' He struggled to find the word. 'They're not as powerful.

126

This bacteria is not only multiplying, it's creating spores.'

'Meaning what?' said Tyler.

'Meaning that it intends or intended to go into a period of dormancy, of hibernation. Now, very few bacteria are able to do that and those that do are normally confined to plants. This is a completely new strain. Not different. New. *I've* never seen anything like it before.'

'How does that explain what's been happening to the animals lately?' the farmer enquired. 'The cannibalism, the still-born litters, the increased growth?'

Hawley exhaled deeply.

'As I said, I took samples from the stomachs of all three animals. There was a greater abundance of the bacteria in the stomach of the cow. She ate something which induced the growth of this bacteria. It was passed on through her bloodstream to the calf. That was what happened with the sow and her piglets. That's what's been happening with *all* the livestock around here. The parent animal has been passing on the bacteria through the bloodstream to the unborn young which have been developing more rapidly. The bacteria have, somehow, caused a change in the DNA of the young animals.'

'What could they have eaten that would do this?' asked Jo.

'It's a toxic agent of some kind. It's impossible to say without a sample of it,' Hawley told her. 'All I do know is, whatever it is, it's inorganic.'

'You mean it's man-made?' said Tyler.

Hawley nodded.

'The feed,' said the farmer, wearily. 'The Vanderburg feed. It's the only inorganic compound that any of my animals have had lately.'

'What about the other farmers?' asked Jo.

'We'll have to find out.'

'I need to run some tests on this feed,' said Hawley. 'Break it down, find out what exactly it's comprised of.'

Tyler nodded.

'And then what?' Jo asked.

'I'm going to see how long the bacteria survive for,' Hawley told her. 'I need to know as much as possible about it if I'm going to help. Get me a sample of it.'

Tyler turned and headed for the door. Jo followed.

'I'll be in touch, Dan,' he said.

'Where are we going now?' she asked.

'Visiting,' Tyler said, enigmatically.

They sprinted across to the waiting landrover and climbed in and, in seconds, were heading out towards Stuart Nichols's farm.

Hawley stood before the bathroom mirror, reluctant to turn on the light above it. As if the sight of his own face were too abhorrent to him. But finally he did so, wincing painfully as the fluorescent sputtered into life. The vet inspected his skin, both surprised and anxious by its pale, dry appearance. He put a tentative finger to his cheek and rubbed, watching as a thin coil of skin came away. It left a red patch beneath and Hawley swallowed hard.

Perhaps Tyler was right. Perhaps there *was* some kind of virus going around.

The vet moaned and pressed both hands to his temples. The light seemed to sear his eyeballs until he could stand it no longer. He shot out a hand and switched if off.

In the silence of the bathroom he listened to his own low, guttural breathing. His body felt tight, his skin itched. With clumsy fingers he began unfastening his shirt finally pulling it free to expose the wasted flesh beneath.

Skin was coming off in great long tendrils, hanging from him like leprous rolls.

128

Hawley sucked in a frightened breath. He pulled at one of the coils and it came free, much like sunburnt flesh, but it felt moist. He dropped it into the sink and tried to wash it away. His throat was dry and sore and he scooped a handful of water from the swiftly flowing tap. It made him feel sick and he steadied himself against the basin, gazing through bloodshot eyes at his own ghastly visage.

He pulled another of the flesh coils from his chest, held it in his hand for a second, then pushed it into his mouth and chewed hungrily.

Twenty-five

The windows of the landrover were open but the slight breeze which they allowed in offered no respite from the scorching heat. Tyler wiped a hand across his forehead and brushed away the film of perspiration. Above them, the sun blazed with unrelenting fury.

Jo tossed the butt of her cigarette out of the window and gazed at the surrounding countryside. The road which led out of Wakely towards Stuart Nichols's farm was flanked on both sides by thick forest and gently sloping hills but, as they left the town further behind, the land flattened into rolling fields.

Ahead of them on the right, Jo spotted something.

'What's that?' she asked, pointing.

Tyler smiled and slowed down as they reached it.

'It's Wakely football club,' he told her.

'It used to be one of the best equipped non-League

clubs in the country. The old chairman was a builder. Now he's dead the whole place has gone to ruin.'

The ground was compact, surrounded on all sides by a high wooden fence which was now broken in many places. The six floodlight staunchions still rose into the air although somewhat less majestically than in the past. The steel girders were rusted, weeds and overgrown grass lapping at their bases like some kind of floral sea. The smaller stands were roofed with corrugated iron looking more like enlarged sheds and they too carried a patina of rust, so bad in some places that there were holes in them. The pitch was like a jungle, infested with weeds. Grass grew wildly in places but, in others, it had been trampled flat. The kids from the town cycled out to the old stadium in the summer and played in the disused goals but there were none to be seen on this particular day. Wakely Town F.C. had gone broke in the end after many years of struggling with low attendances – the same fate which was befalling many other league and non-league clubs. However, Tyler could still remember the days when people had come from all around to watch, filling the ground to capacity.

'I used to go there with my father when I was a kid,' said the farmer as they left the place behind. Soon, it was nothing more than a vague outline in the rear view mirror.

'How far to the farm?' asked Jo.

'It's just up ahead,' Tyler told her, pointing through some trees.

He swung the landrover off the main road onto a sun-baked track. The vehicle bounced over the hardened ruts and Jo gripped the door handle to prevent herself being shaken too badly. There was a clatter in the back as the farmer's shotgun fell from its hooks and skittered across the rear of the landrover. Tyler stuck it into a low gear and slowed down, lessening the effect of the bumps. As he drove, he scanned the fields around them. His forehead puckered into a frown.

Jo glanced to one side and caught his worried expression.

'Something wrong?' she asked.

'I don't know yet,' he murmured.

The gate which led into the farm yard itself was open. Tyler swung the landrover around and brought it to a halt beside a large shed which he knew Nichols used for milking. They both got out.

Immediately, the silence seemed to wrap itself around them like a glove.

Tyler looked around and exhaled deeply.

'Where the hell are all the animals?' he mused.

There was a sty to the left but it was empty, the gate open. Even in the fields there was nothing to be seen and yet Nichols owned a herd of over 200 cattle. Tyler wandered into the milking shed, alert for any sign or sound of movement. Jo followed him, wrinkling her nose at the cloying stench inside the shed. It seemed even hotter inside the metal construction, like walking into an oven.

Tyler was the first one to spot the dead cow.

It was lying near the far exit of the shed and he walked cautiously across to it. The buzzing of flies could clearly be heard and there were dozens of the things crawling on the carcass. Tyler got as close as he needed to and peered at the cow. Its eyes were open, its tongue lolling from one side of its open mouth. Flies crawled eagerly over the glassy orbs. There were no external signs of damage to the animal. No wounds. No blood. He and Jo stood there for long moments, gazing down at the body, then they turned and headed outside once more.

The yard was rectangular, sheds and barns forming the enclosure which led up to the farm house itself.

Lying in the open doorway of another barn were two dead pigs – big boars, saddlebacks by the look of them.

Tyler held up a hand for Jo to stay back, then he crossed to the door of the barn and looked in, careful to avoid the carcasses. The stench from them was appalling, exposed, as they were, to the sun. And, this time, as well as flies, the carcasses had drawn the attention of some ants. The insects crawled frenziedly over the bodies, some of the flies feasting on a gaping sore near one boar's ear.

Inside the barn were a number of pens, designed to hold pigs, very similar to the ones Tyler had on his own farm.

The gates to every single one were open, the animals gone.

'What is it?' asked Jo, appearing at his shoulder.

'See for yourself,' he said.

She peered into the barn, then stepped outside again, almost tripping over one of the dead boars. She looked down and noted with disgust that a large blow-fly was just disappearing into the animal's nostril.

'What could have killed them, Vic?' she asked.

'There's no sign of injury on any of them,' said the farmer. He shrugged helplessly.

'A disease?' she said, cryptically.

'Could be. But where the bloody hell are the rest of the stock?'

He turned and headed towards the farm house itself. It was a two-storey, pebble-dashed building with a grey slate roof and a genuine nineteenth-century chimney stack. In fact, the whole building looked somewhat anachronistic amongst the modern machinery which lay around in the yard.

As they approached the house, Jo noticed that the curtains, both upstairs and down, were drawn.

Tyler reached the front door and knocked hard.

It swung open.

'Stuart. Bet,' he called. 'It's Vic Tyler.'

Silence.

'We'd better take a look inside,' said Jo.

They walked into the hall, squinting in the gloom.

'Stuart,' Tyler shouted once more, passing into the sitting room. He bumped his leg on a table and cursed. It was so dark in the room. The place smelt fusty, the humidity wrapping itself around them like a sweaty glove. Jo felt her T-shirt sticking to her back and she ran both hands through her thick hair.

Tyler pushed open the door to the kitchen.

There was some food on the table. A piece of cheese and a couple of slices of bread, the edges curled up. The silence in the room was broken, yet again, by the loud buzzing of flies.

'Let's try upstairs,' said Tyler, leading the way.

As he opened the door from the hallway to the staircase he had to stop for a moment. The steps were immersed in a blackness so total it was virtually impossible to see a hand in front of him. He moved cautiously, slipping on a step half way up.

'Shit,' he grunted and continued his ascent, finally reaching the landing. There, he was grateful to find that the powerful rays of the sun had managed to find a chink in the curtains and a single powerful ray of light lit up the area. Jo joined him and they approached the first of three doors which confronted them. Tyler knocked loudly on the closest before turning the handle.

'Stuart,' he shouted.

They walked into the room.

It was empty. The bed was unmade, the sheets rumpled, one pillow lying on the floor close by. The room smelt of copper, a strange metallic smell which reminded the farmer of rotting meat.

'Let's try the next one,' he said.

133

He repeated the same procedure, banging loudly on the door, calling Nichols' name and then entering.

It seemed darker in the second room, a blanket having been pinned across the window as well as the drawn curtains.

Lying prone on the bed, arms by his sides, was Stuart Nichols.

Tyler and Jo moved quietly into the room, the only sound being the low, guttural breathing of the other man. His chest rose and fell almost imperceptibly, his mouth open to reveal protruding teeth. Even in the gloom, Tyler could see how pale Nichols's skin was. His hands, palms turned upward, bore the long hooked nails which both Jo and Tyler had come to recognise by now.

Tyler took a step closer, recoiling slightly from the stench which seemed to be emanating from Nichols's body. A combination of rancid sweat and an overpoweringly fetid odour which made the farmer cough.

'Stuart,' he said, reaching out a hand but not touching the motionless form of his friend.

Nichols didn't stir.

The pillow beneath his head was dirty and, as Tyler looked more closely, he saw that there were several sizeable growths of hair lying there. Not mere strands of it but thick hanks. Nichols's scalp was bared in places where the hair had come out, raw and angry as if it had been torn away.

'He looks as if he's in a coma,' said Jo. 'Maybe we ought to ring a doctor.'

There was a low rasping sound from nearby and both of them spun round, their eyes searching the gloom.

It came from behind them, from the other bed in the room.

So mesmerized had they been by the sight of Nichols, neither had noticed the hunched form of his wife lying on the other bed.

Bet Nichols was, Tyler remembered, a large woman but now, she looked as though she was suffering from anorexia. Her body, covered only by a thin nightdress, was emaciated, as if she hadn't eaten for days. For weeks. The pallor of her skin was even more alarming than that of her husband and her hair, usually done up in a bun, was hanging loose.

Tyler reached forward and shook Nichols, trying to rouse him from his deathly slumber.

'There's a phone downstairs,' said Jo, 'maybe we ought to ring a doctor.'

Tyler didn't speak, he was still gazing down at his friend. He touched Nichols's cheek, withdrawing his hand quickly as he felt how clammy the skin was but, after a moment's hesitation, he cautiously opened the other man's crusted eyelids. His eyes were dark ringed, the whites flecked with yellow, the normally steely eyes now dull and lifeless. Tyler shuddered. It was like looking at a corpse.

'Stuart,' Tyler called, shaking Nichols hard until he saw his eyelids flicker open.

He turned his head to look at Tyler, his cracked lips sliding back in a bestial sneer.

Tyler took a step backwards.

'What do you want?' Nichols croaked, trying to swing himself upright. He finally managed it and sat on the edge of the bed, head bowed.

'How long have you been like this?' Tyler asked him.

'I don't remember,' said the other farmer, sounding as if he had gravel in his throat. He put both hands to his temples and winced. Tyler crossed to the window and pulled down the blanket, then he dragged the curtains open, flooding the room with sunlight.

Nichols let out a howl. A deafening shriek torn raw from his throat, from the depths of his soul. A sound which was a mixture of rage and pain. He staggered to his feet, shielding his face from the powerful rays of

135

the sun and Tyler looked on in horror as the flesh on his friend's arms rose swiftly into half a dozen reddening welts. The flesh was actually blistering as surely as if a red hot iron had been pressed to it.

'Shut them,' screamed Nichols.

He crashed into the bed and overbalanced, trying to slide down beside it to hide from the sunlight. He had one hand across his face, the other outstretched before him. Jo, too, saw the skin rise into a series of liquescent blisters which, all at once, burst. They left dark crimson gouges in the flesh and Nichols's fingers curled round, his nails tearing the palm of his hand.

'Shut the fucking curtains, for God's sake shut the fucking curtains,' he roared, dragging himself to his feet.

Tyler was in the process of doing what Nichols wanted when he heard the click of a shotgun hammer. The other farmer, his face now a malevolent mask of pain and anger, had snatched a twelve bore from beneath his bed and was aiming the barrels at Tyler.

'Shut them,' he bellowed once again.

Tyler complied hurriedly.

'Now get out of here,' snarled Nichols. 'Leave us.' One side of his face looked as if someone had thrust a blow torch at it. Huge suppurating sores dribbled their sticky contents down his torn cheek, one of them having formed over his left eye, nearly closing it.

Bet Nichols writhed silently on her own bed, her flesh similarly scorched. But Nichols had taken the full brunt of the intruding sunlight and he swayed uncertainly, the shotgun levelled at Tyler's stomach. He edged cautiously towards the door, ushering Jo before him.

'Get out now,' rasped Nichols, licking his swollen lips. He raised the shotgun and, for one interminable second, Tyler thought he was going to fire but, as the farmer and the American stepped out of the room, he lowered it once again.

Tyler closed the door behind him.

There were sounds of movement from inside and, a second later, Nichols burst out of the room, staggering drunkenly.

'Don't come back here,' he said. 'If you do I'll kill you.'

'Stuart, you need help,' Tyler said, his eyes never leaving the gaping mouths of the twin barrels.

'I told you, just get away from me,' Nichols growled and he stood sentinel at the top of the darkened stairs as Jo and Tyler retreated. 'And don't try sending anyone else or I'll kill them too.'

Jo was the first to reach the hallway and she pulled open the door, hurrying out into the blazing sunlight. Tyler followed a second later.

'My God,' muttered Jo. 'What the hell happened to him?'

Tyler could only shake his head vacantly.

'It must be a disease of some sort,' he said, almost incredulously.

'Rabies?'

'No. He isn't exhibiting the symptoms.'

'Hawley said that the bacteria was a new strain. Maybe he's got a new kind of rabies.'

Tyler was unconvinced.

'Did you see what the sunlight did to his skin?' said Jo. 'I mean, it burned him for Christ's sake.' There was a note of desperation in her voice. 'Vic, what are we going to do?'

'Calling the police won't help, especially after that fiasco about Anderson. They'll probably lock us both up.'

'We should get a doctor out here,' she insisted.

'You heard what he said and I believed him. If anyone sticks their head around that door he'll kill them.' They stood facing one another for a moment, then Tyler turned and headed back towards the landrover. 'Come on,' he said.

Jo hesitated, her eye caught by something close by, something which she hadn't noticed when they'd first approached the house.

To the right of the building was a small wooden shed, its door open. The sunlight was glinting on something silvery.

'Vic, come here,' she called and the farmer spun round.

Jo was standing in the doorway of the shed.

'Look at that,' she said.

Inside the shed, piled three or four high in places, were sacks of the Vanderburg multi-purpose feed.

Without a moment's hesitation, Tyler lifted one of the heavy sacks onto his shoulder and, together, they headed back to the landrover. He opened the rear door and threw the sack in alongside his own shotgun then he clambered into the driver's seat, waited until Jo was settled beside him, then turned on the engine. Tyler swung the vehicle around and floored the accelerator. The quicker they left this place the happier he'd be.

They were back in Wakely in less then ten minutes and only when they were safely back in the confines of the town did Tyler ease the pressure on his accelerator. The needle on the speedometer bounced from sixty to thirty and hovered there.

He drove slowly through the tree-lined streets, both he and Jo noticing how quiet things were. There weren't above six people moving about in the blossom-shrouded streets. Garden tools and toys lay discarded in some places, most houses had their curtains drawn and the few people who *were* moving around looked pale and lethargic.

And there was something else, something which

Tyler found even more disturbing than the absence of people, because it was even more inexplicable.

There were no dogs or cats to be seen.

Wakely was becoming a ghost town.

Carlo Fanducci lit up another cigarette, coughing as the acrid fumes burnt his chest, searing his lungs. He spat out of his open window, noticing that the sputum was flecked with blood. What the hell? It was nothing new.

Parked across the road from Dan Hawley's surgery, he had a clear view when Tyler pulled up.

The Italian watched as first the farmer then Jo clambered out, Tyler retrieving the sack of Vanderburg feed from the rear of the vehicle.

Fanducci ran an appreciative eye over Jo and sucked hard on his cigarette. The red T-shirt clung tightly to her body, highlighting the smooth swell of her breasts. Great tits, thought the Italian. He wondered what she was like in bed. A regular little ball-breaker no doubt about it.

And, he was sure now, he'd seen her somewhere before.

He watched as she followed Tyler up the path to Hawley's front door, then he lit up another cigarette, using the butt of the other one to do it. This time he didn't cough.

Fanducci loosened his tie slightly and relaxed back in his seat.

In time it would come to him. Eventually he would remember exactly who that girl was. His memory was one of the things he prided himself on. Names, places, dates. All filed away, waiting to be recalled.

A thin smile spread across his face.

The reporter from the *New York Times*. He'd seen her with that scum-bag Tony Hagen a couple of times. She'd blown the whistle on old man Scalise's rackets and he'd put out a contract on her.

Well, well. What a small world it was turning out to be. Fanducci chuckled to himself and eased the .357 from its holster. He released the cylinder, spun it once, then snapped it back into position. The Italian patted the butt gently.

Twenty-six

Helen Piper sat back on her haunches, laying the trowel before her. She was perspiring despite the fact that she only wore a bikini top and a pair of cut-off denim shorts. The sun had moved full circle in the sky and now, with the advent of afternoon, its rays weren't so powerful. Helen ran a hand through her long black hair and got stiffly to her feet. She'd been out in the garden for most of the day, digging, weeding, planting. Now she decided that it was time to go inside, she was parched. Besides, she'd have to start getting something to eat for herself and the children.

Phil wouldn't be home for another few hours. He'd gone to London on business and she didn't expect him until after seven. He'd been putting in extra hours for the last six months but still Helen was not satisfied. As she passed the pram which stood beneath the porch the sight of their five-month-old daughter, Lorraine, seemed to remind Helen just how badly they needed the money now. Of course everyone had been delighted when she'd announced that she was going to have another child, but she and Phil had already been saddled with a mortgage which they could just about pay and now, with the arrival of the baby, it looked as though they were going to struggle again.

He told her not to worry but she took no notice. It was in her nature. She worried about the bills, she worried about the children. She worried about World War Three. Helen looked in at Lorraine as she passed and smiled down at the sleeping baby. Then she padded inside and put the kettle on.

The house was unusually quiet considering her five-year-old son, Kevin, was upstairs. He'd been up there for hours and she'd not heard a peep out of him. There must be a reason why. Helen decided to find out what he was up to.

As she passed the mirror in the hall she patted her stomach approvingly. She'd worked hard to regain her figure after Lorraine's birth and now, at thirty, she was in as good shape as she'd ever been. Helen moved quietly up the stairs, hoping to surprise her son in the act if he was doing anything he shouldn't be. She tip-toed across the landing and opened the door with the 'Star Wars' poster on it.

The room was in semi-darkness, the curtains drawn.

'Kevin,' she called, unable to see him at first, angry that he'd shut out the light. Then, in the gloom, she saw him crouched by the bed. There were toy soldiers spread across the carpet, the boxes emptied wantonly.

'What are you doing up here?' she asked him, crossing to the window and pulling open the curtains. 'You've been stuck in your room all day. Go out and get some fresh air while I get your tea ready.'

'Oh Mum,' he muttered, his brown hair plastered to his forehead by perspiration. 'I'd rather play in here.'

'Outside, Kevin, please,' she insisted.

'No,' he snapped.

'I told you to go outside, it's not good for you being cooped up in here and with your curtains drawn too.'

'I don't want to go outside. Leave me alone.'

Helen slapped him across the backside.

'Don't talk to me like that, Kevin,' she said. 'Now go on.'

She ushered him out, watching as he shuffled irritably down the stairs. Helen walked into her own bedroom and peered out of the window in time to see the boy emerge in the garden below. He kicked at a stone and, hands dug in the pockets of his jeans, began wandering up and down. She pulled the window closed, leaving just enough room to let some of the late afternoon breeze in.

In the garden, Kevin Piper shielded his eyes from the glare of the sun, glancing alternately up at the window where his mother had been and then at the pram where his baby sister lay. He had a headache and his stomach felt as though he'd eaten too much but he knew that wasn't true. He hadn't been able to eat all day. He hadn't felt like it. His head hurt. He didn't like the sun. Kevin kicked a stone and it banged against the side of the pram. He looked up at the window. No sign of his mother. He picked up a stone and threw it at the pram. The impact rocked it and, from inside, Lorraine began to whimper. He smiled and picked up another stone. A larger one.

This one he hurled with all his strength.

It struck the pram near the hood and Lorraine began to cry.

The shrill sound made his head hurt more.

He threw another stone, this time lobbing it into the pram.

Lorraine screamed and began sobbing loudly.

'Shut up,' grunted Kevin. 'Shut up.'

The crying went on. Louder.

'Shut up,' he shouted, advancing towards the pram.

The window above him opened and Helen looked out. She could hear Lorraine crying, but the porch obscured her view of the pram and also of Kevin.

He gripped the pram by the handle and began to pull on it, using all his weight.

Lorraine was screaming now, her sobs punctuated with racking gasps.

'Lorraine,' Helen called. 'Kevin, what are you doing?' She left the window open and hurried out of the room.

With one final surge of strength, Kevin managed to tip the pram up. It tottered on its back wheels for a second, then pitched forward, catapulting Lorraine out onto the grass. The baby continued screaming, lying helpless on her back before Kevin who was glaring down at her.

He reached for the trowel.

Helen ran down the stairs, tripping at the bottom, nearly losing her footing. She scrambled on, tugging open doors in her haste to reach the garden.

Kevin lifted the trowel in both hands and raised it above the screaming baby.

Helen burst from the back door in time to see him bury the pointed blade in the baby's stomach.

Now it was her turn to scream.

She tried to move towards him but her legs buckled and she could only crawl. Helen saw him bring the weapon down again, this time piercing the little girl's throat. A fountain of blood erupted from the wound, most of it splattering Kevin who bent his head to the jetting flow of crimson, allowing it to flood into his mouth, swallowing hungrily.

Helen Piper passed out.

Twenty-seven

'The one on the right is the broken-down Vanderburg feed, the one on the left is from the bloodstream of the calf.'

Hawley stepped back from the twin microscopes and invited Tyler to look. The farmer pressed his eye to the first of the magnifying instruments and peered at the rapidly moving organisms on the slide beneath. Then he passed to the next one. He looked at Hawley but said nothing. Jo was the next to inspect the findings. It was she who broke the brooding silence.

'They're identical,' she said.

Hawley nodded.

'The same strain of bacteria is present in both the calf's blood and the Vanderburg feed.'

'So the inorganic compound which caused the trouble with the animals *is* the one in the feed? said Tyler.

Hawley nodded.

'But what it is I don't know. It's bacteria, that's true, but what I'm getting at is the fact that the compound itself is made up of proteins. From a breakdown of the Vanderburg feed the other constituents are what you'd expect to find in any animal feed. Maize, barley, wheat, that kind of thing. It's just this protein that shouldn't be there.'

Tyler exhaled deeply.

'What do you mean, it shouldn't be there?' He looked agitated.

'It's been specially introduced into the feed. Manufactured and then added. But it's a synthetic protein. It has no peptide links.'

Tyler held up a hand.

'Look, Dan, can you keep it in a language we can all understand?' he asked.

Hawley apologized, then continued.

'A protein molecule is made up of hundreds of thousands of amino-acid molecules. They're joined together by peptide links. By combining with oxygen, the amino-acid forms bonds which help keep the protein molecule together. The proteins in the Vanderburg feed have not been synthesized from amino-acid. They've been created artificially. That's another reason why the bacteria are still flourishing when they should have been dead ages ago, the proteins have been created from some kind of autotrophic organism. From something inorganic.'

'Man-made, like you said before,' Jo added.

Hawley nodded.

'That's right. This bacteria is virtually indestructible.'

A heavy silence fell over the trio in the room. The vet looked at his two companions, wondering if what he had said had made any sense to them. From the worried looks on their faces he assumed that it had. Tyler peered into the microscopes once more.

'Who could create protein like this?' he asked.

'Someone with very specialized knowledge in this particular field.'

'Like a research scientist?' said Tyler, looking at Jo.

'Anderson,' she said, quietly.

The farmer nodded.

'But why should the protein be consumed by bacteria?' asked Tyler.

'Because with normal protein molecules if you immerse them in water or salt solutions they form colloids. It's like a protective mechanism. These proteins are artificial, they have no protection so, after a while, they simply become engulfed by bacteria which feed off them.'

Tyler wiped a thumb across his eyebrow and swallowed hard.

'There's something else,' said Hawley, crossing to one of the dissection tables where the body of the weaner lay covered by a sheet. He pulled it back, pointing to a small patch of grey coloured skin on the animal's side. 'Spores,' he said. 'The same ones that have been showing up in the bloodstreams and stomachs of the other animals.'

'Have they moved to the outer skin?' asked Tyler.

Hawley nodded.

'On a living animal they'd be invisible.'

'My God,' said Jo. 'What does it mean?'

The vet swallowed hard.

'It means that the idea about a virus spreading through Wakely, amongst its *human* population, is more than likely right,' he announced, wearily.

'But how?' Jo wanted to know. 'You said you didn't know how it was communicated.'

'I didn't before today,' the vet told her.

'So,' demanded Tyler. 'What's the answer?'

'All animals fed on the Vanderburg multi-purpose feed are likely to be carrying this bacteria in them, some more advanced than others. The bacteria, once it has formed spores, then transfers itself to the skin of the animal, sometimes on the hide itself, sometimes in the first layer of muscle.' He paused. 'Anyone who's eaten meat is liable to be infected.'

'Oh God,' muttered Tyler.

'Beef, pork, lamb, mutton, sausages, pies. *Anything* that contains meat is more than certainly contaminated and anyone consuming that meat will be infected.'

'What about poultry and fish?' asked Tyler.

'It hasn't affected them. The feed, as far as I can gather was only designed for use on larger stock.'

'That's something at least,' said Jo.

'At Stuart Nichols's farm we found some dead animals,' Tyler told the vet. 'Could the bacteria have killed them?'

'Some bacteria, once they've finished with the host animal or plant, form spores in order to disperse. To move around. Most are air carried, others water carried.'

'What are you getting at?' asked the farmer.

'We don't know what form the dispersal of these spores takes,' Hawley said. 'The spores from the dead animals you found may already be in the air.'

'Then other people could be infected with this virus?' said Jo. 'People outside Wakely?'

Hawley was silent for long moments.

'Look, at the moment, the only thing I know for sure is that it's confined to animals fed on the Vanderburg compound. They're the ones carrying and transmitting the virus.'

There was another troubled silence.

'Anyone eating meat is at risk,' Hawley reiterated.

Tyler sucked in a weary breath.

'Have you any idea what this disease or virus might be, Dan?' he wanted to know.

'None at all,' the vet said. 'I'm not a doctor.'

The farmer looked at Hawley, noticing the paleness of his skin, the deep black rings around his eyes, the yellowed whites so heavily veined.

Hawley looked at him, aware that he was being stared at. He squinted as the bright lights overhead seemed to sear his eyes.

'Are you feeling all right?' Tyler asked.

'Yes,' he said, defensively. 'Shouldn't I be?'

'Just wondered.'

Hawley tried to swallow but his mouth tasted dry. He said nothing.

'I need to use your phone,' said Tyler.

Hawley motioned him through into reception, keeping his head bowed.

The farmer passed through into the other room and picked up the receiver. He thought for a moment, then dialled. At the other end the phone began to ring.

He let it ring a dozen times, then tried again.

There was still no answer from Wakely's doctor's surgery.

Tyler pressed the cradle down, listening to the persistent buzz for long seconds. There was no point in driving over to the surgery. He felt instinctively that it would prove fruitless. There was obviously no one there.

He dialled Ben Thurston's number.

Nothing.

He tried Reg Gentry's farm.

It was the same story.

Tyler hesitated for a moment, then dialled Thurston's farm once more. God, he hoped nothing had happened to the old boy. As he stood listening to the ringing at the other end, Tyler frowned, thoughts of his own father suddenly coming, unbidden, into his mind. Perhaps, he reasoned, it was because he identified old Ben so closely with his own late father. It would be like losing a parent all over again if Ben was dead.

The phone was still ringing.

'Come on, come on,' muttered Tyler, gripping the receiver more tightly.

He actually had it poised over the cradle when he heard the click which signalled that it had been picked up. He lifted it swiftly to his ear.

'Hello,' he said. 'Ben?'

Tyler heard low, guttural breathing.

'Ben. Is that you?'

A cough.

'It's Vic Tyler.'

'What do you want?'

He recognized the voice. It belonged to Frank Thurston, the eldest of Ben's boys. But the voice had a harsher, deeper quality to it which it didn't usually possess.

'Are you all right?' asked Tyler.

'I'm all right.' The voice was becoming weaker.

148

There was a long silence.

'Frank, let me talk to Ben will you?'

Another long silence.

'Frank, are you still there?'

'Still here.'

'I want to talk to Ben, is he there?'

There was a bang and Tyler heard footsteps shuffling away from the phone.

'Frank,' he called.

Jo, meantime, had appeared at his elbow.

'Did you reach anyone?' she asked.

Tyler held up a hand for her to be quiet.

More silence. A hiss of static.

'Hello, Vic, what can I do for you?'

Tyler smiled as he recognized Thurston's voice, as bright and cheery as usual.

'Ben, are you feeling OK?' asked Tyler.

'*I* am, but I can't say the same for my boys,' Thurston told him. 'They both look like death warmed up, they've been like it for a few days now. I've tried getting the doctor but there's no bloody answer from the surgery.'

Tyler exhaled deeply.

'What's on your mind, Vic?' Thurston asked.

Tyler looked at Jo. Should he tell Thurston about the virus?

'Nothing Ben, I called Reg Gentry's place but I couldn't reach him. I thought I'd try you. There's nothing wrong.'

'Well then, if you'll excuse me I'll get back outside, I'm doing everything here at the moment.' He chuckled.

Tyler nodded.

Thurston hung up.

'So,' Jo said. 'Not everyone's infected.'

'Not everyone.'

She reached for the phone.

'What are you doing?' he asked.

'Calling my paper, someone's got to know what's happening here,' she announced.

'Don't mention the virus,' Tyler said.

'Why, Vic? The people in Wakely need help.'

'Well, they're not going to get it by having reporters swarming all over them.'

She stepped back and looked deeply at him.

'What's that supposed to mean?' she demanded.

'If you tell your paper what's going on, word will spread. There'll be newsmen from all over the country converging on Wakely.'

'The public have a right to know what's happening. Especially if Vanderburg Chemicals are in back of all this. People's lives might be at risk, we don't know if this virus or disease or whatever it is càn kill.'

'Exactly. That's why we don't want more people in the bloody town. They might pick it up, carry it to other places.'

'Goddamit, Vic, this is one hell of a story. Don't try to get in my way. The rest of the country has a right to know.'

'All right,' he said, softly, his voice muted but full of anger. 'Ring your office.' He lifted the receiver and pushed it towards her. 'Do it.'

She took it from him and dialled.

He saw her forehead wrinkle into a frown.

'What's wrong?' he asked.

She flicked the cradle.

'The line's dead.'

She tried again but still there was nothing.

She dialled her own home number.

No sound. Not even a hiss of static.

'The internal lines were all right,' he said.

Jo looked at the receiver for a moment then replaced it.

'Wait,' said Tyler, taking it from her. He dialled 100

150

and waited for the operator to answer. 'What's your home number?' he asked Jo.

She told him.

Tyler asked the operator to connect him with the number.

There was a moment's silence then a metallic voice told him: 'I'm afraid the number you have requested is no longer in use.'

Jo snatched the receiver from him.

'I want Arkham 62671,' she said.

'The number you have requested is no longer in use.'

Tyler left her with the recalcitrant phone and scuttled back into the surgery. He found Mandy Potter standing beside Hawley. She smiled at the farmer.

Jo re-entered the room a moment later, a worried expression on her face.

'They won't connect me with anywhere outside Wakely,' she said.

Mandy looked surprised.

Tyler glanced down at his watch and saw that it was nearly 7.00 p.m.

'There might be something on the local news,' he said, hopefully.

Mandy led them into the sitting room and turned on the television.

A blue screen greeted them, words spelt out in red letters gleaming like fresh blood against the glowing background:

THERE HAS BEEN A TRANSMITTER FAILURE
NORMAL SERVICE WILL CONTINUE SHORTLY.

Mandy tried the other channels but it was the same on each one. She excused herself and hurried upstairs to try the portable.

'Where's the nearest transmitter?' asked Jo.

'It's in Ducton, about thirty miles from here,' Tyler told her.

Mandy returned a few moments later.

'It's the same message,' she announced.

Tyler switched off the set, gazing at the blank screen for a second.

Through the open door into the surgery he could see Hawley slumped forward across one of the work-tops.

'Is he all right?' the farmer asked.

'He's been a bit under the weather lately,' Mandy explained. 'But he won't go to the doctor.' She shrugged.

'We'd better go,' said Tyler. Both he and Jo left via the surgery. 'Dan,' he called and Hawley turned. 'If you find anything else, anything at all, call me.'

Hawley nodded.

Tyler closed the door behind them as they left. They hurried from the surgery to the waiting landrover and climbed in.

The sky was stained darkly with the colour of the dying sun. Dusk settled over the countryside, the evening clouds gathering in the distance to form a purple shroud which would soon blacken to form the cloak of night.

Twenty-eight

The cassette whirred to a stop and ejected with a loud click.

'Oh sod it,' grunted Gordon Thompson.

Beneath him, her blonde hair plastered across her face, Tina Phillips moaned softly. As he went to pull away she held him close, the touch of their naked bodies causing sensations in her which she did not want to curtail.

'Leave it,' she whispered, running her fingers through his long brown hair.

She leant forward and kissed him, their tongues probing urgently against one another. Tina drew Thompson's bottom lip between her teeth and sucked gently, chuckling as she did. They broke and he rolled to one side, allowing her searching hand to find his erection. She began to move it rhythmically up and down the shaft, bringing her right leg over so that the sensitive area between her legs was rubbing against Thompson's thigh. He felt her wetness on his skin, mingling with the perspiration which was already there.

They had been living together for three months and, to Gordon Thompson, it seemed as if they'd spent all their time in bed. Not that he was complaining. Tina, twenty years old and a year younger than himself, was always eager. Her sexuality knew no bounds. They had never had much time together before, their love-making confined to hurried lunch hours at her home or snatched evenings at friends' dwellings. But now, in the security of their own place, they were taking full advantage.

She leant forward and kissed him again before sliding down and nibbling the flesh of his shoulder, drawing it between her white teeth, nipping him. He groaned, the pain of the small pinch tempered by the building pleasure he was feeling from her hand.

Still stroking his erection, she raised herself onto her knees and turned slightly. Thompson slipped a hand between her legs, his fingers tracing a pattern inside her thigh, probing at her liquescent cleft. He felt her stiffen as he gently stroked the hard bud of her clitoris.

Tina sucked at his chest, leaving a red mark, then

she lapped her way down to his stomach, repeating the procedure.

This time she bit a little too hard and Thompson let out a small yelp of pain but he said nothing, tensing as he felt her hand speeding up on his penis. Allowing him to move his eager fingers inside her, she sat back and looked into his face and, in the darkness of the room, he noticed how her eyes seemed to be ablaze. He had known her passion was intense but he'd never seen her quite so restless as tonight. She kissed him again, fiercely. This time she took his lip between her teeth and sucked harder.

'Jesus,' he gasped, pulling his head away and raising a hand to his mouth.

She had drawn blood.

'Be careful, love,' he said, dabbing a tentative finger at the small gash in his bottom lip.

She didn't speak but merely bent forward again and, this time, Thompson felt her warm breath on his swollen penis head. She manoeuvred herself above him, lowering her slippery sex towards his mouth. His tongue darted forward and he himself felt waves of pleasure run through him as she began to nibble at his stiff organ, finally slipping it into her mouth.

Tina's saliva mingled with the clear liquid which was seeping from the head of his shaft. He thrust forward into her hot mouth.

He felt her stiffen as, for his own part, he lapped at her vagina. She rubbed herself harder against him as she felt her orgasm approaching. Her eyes glowed and Thompson felt her chin nuzzling his pubic hairs as she continued to suck at him, her teeth raking his erection.

For fleeting seconds he realized what was happening.

She bit his penis in half, severing muscle and veins as she clamped her teeth together.

He let out a shriek of agony but it was muffled as she thrust herself at him. Thompson blacked out at once.

Tina sucked hard at the torn root of his manhood, eagerly swallowing the blood which pumped from it, staining the sheets beneath and gushing over his thighs. Her sharp nails tore his scrotum to bloody streamers, shredding the tender flesh.

She lay on top of him, her lips and chin dark with his life fluid.

Finally satiated, she rolled onto her back, ignoring the stench which emanated from Thompson's body.

The breeze which wafted in from the window stirred the strands of her hair. Those that weren't matted with blood.

She closed her eyes, a thin smile on her crimson lips.

PART TWO

'Turn up the lights, I don't want
to go home in the dark . . .'
  – O. Henry

'And the day burns through their blood,
like a white candle through a shuttered
hand . . .'
  – Roy Campbell

Twenty-nine

The meshed glass partition swung open as Tyler banged on it. The sound of squealing hinges was deafening in the unearthly silence of the police station. Even the two big fans which normally stood over the entry way were silent, the blades immobile.

'There's got to be someone here,' said the farmer, glancing out of the window to where the two Panda cars were parked.

During the short drive to the station that morning, they had seen perhaps two dozen people on the streets. No more.

Tyler reached round and slipped the bolt on the half-door. Jo followed him through. They stood behind the desk, the ticking of the clock above them the only noise in the stillness. The radio stood nearby and Tyler flicked at the 'On' switch. There was a loud crackle and a scream of feedback. He adjusted the volume.

'Ever used one of those things before?' Jo asked him.

Tyler shook his head, fiddling with the frequency regulator in an attempt to pick up a signal of some kind. All he got was a fluctuating buzz and occasional bouts of silence.

'Shit,' he muttered, glaring angrily at the radio. 'We'd better have a look around, the place can't be deserted.'

Jo moved towards a closed door on the left but Tyler stepped in front of her, his hand closing on the knob.

They found themselves in what he took to be the rest

159

room. There was a large notice board with rotas pinned to it and a couple of photos of cars. On the far wall was a dart board, the arrows jammed into the bull's-eye. The blinds were drawn in the room, plunging it into deep gloom but, in the corner, Tyler saw someone sitting down.

'Who's there?' a voice asked and Tyler recognized it as belonging to Don Mason.

He moved towards the sergeant who tried to rise from his seat. It seemed an effort and he gave up finally, sinking back into the plastic covered chair.

'Don, are you all right?' asked Tyler, drawing closer to the policeman. As he did, he saw that the sergeant's normally lustrous beard was greying, patches of raw skin showing through in places where the bristles had come out in thick hunks. As he raised his hands to his temples, Jo noticed how long his nails had become, the cuticles cracked and riven.

'I feel so bloody tired,' croaked Mason, accepting the hand which Tyler offered.

The farmer shuddered involuntarily as he felt the cold clamminess of the policeman's flesh against his own.

Mason swayed drunkenly for a second, then seemed to regain his footing.

'Where are the other men?' asked Tyler.

'Not here,' Mason told him, heading towards the door. He recoiled slightly as he reached the light and stood in the frame, momentarily frozen. He narrowed his eyes and groaned, one hand pressed to his temple, the other supporting him.

'I don't know what the hell is wrong with me,' he said.

'How long have you felt like this?' Jo asked him.

He shrugged.

'Started to feel bad yesterday afternoon. The wife, she's . . .' he hesitated, as if he'd forgotten what he was going to say next.

160

Jo and Tyler helped him into the other room where he groaned aloud at the lights and the sun pouring through the unshaded window.

'Is your wife ill too?' Jo wanted to know.

'I couldn't wake her up this morning. So tired.'

Tyler and Jo exchanged anxious glances.

'Look, Don, we've got to contact someone outside Wakely,' explained the farmer.

'Phone them.'

Jo picked up the nearby phone but the line was, as she'd expected, dead. She shook her head and replaced the receiver.

'The lines are down. You'll have to use the radio,' Tyler insisted. 'Get in touch with the Arkham police.'

'Why?'

'Because people here in Wakely could be in danger. We need help.'

'A virus of some kind,' Jo added.

'What the hell are you going on about?' rasped Mason.

'Call the Arkham police,' Tyler said, firmly.

'No good. We're out of range. Arkham's too far from here, besides, they use a different frequency.'

'So find the frequency,' the farmer demanded.

Mason rounded on him.

'They're out of range,' he growled, his yellowed eyes glowing, the veins in them bulging.

'Try,' roared Tyler.

The two men faced each other for a moment, then Mason nodded painfully and reached for the modulator. He turned the dial, the high pitched screams of interference making him wince. Voices drifted, phantom-like, over the air-waves until, finally, Mason grunted and raised the microphone to his mouth.

'This is Wakely Police Station,' he croaked. 'Sergeant Don Mason speaking. Come in Arkham. Over.'

161

The hum of static was punctuated by sharp crackles, then a distant voice answered:

'This is Arkham. Go ahead. Over.'

Tyler took the microphone from Mason who offered no resistance.

'Arkham Police Station?' said the farmer.

'Affirmative. Please identify yourself.'

'Vic Tyler, I live in Wakely. Listen, send some men over here now I . . .'

'Are you a policeman?'

'No, I told you, I live in Wakely. Will you – '

Again he was cut short.

'You have no right to be using police property, it's an offence.'

'There's no one else here you silly bastard,' snarled the farmer. 'The people in Wakely are in danger, send some men. It's urgent.'

'We've received no reports from Wakely to that effect.'

'That's because the policemen here are gone. For God's sake listen to me . . .'

A hiss of static.

'Did you hear what I said?' Tyler rasped.

'We have received no reports concerning Wakely.'

'Well I'm giving you a fucking report now,' the farmer shouted. 'People are dying. We need help.'

'There have been no formal reports made.'

Tyler gripped the microphone until it threatened to break.

'Let me speak to someone in charge,' he demanded.

'We have received no formal reports. Over and out.'

There was a loud click and then silence.

Tyler hurled the microphone to one side in a paroxysm of rage.

'Bastards,' he fumed. 'Stupid bloody bastards.' He looked down at Mason who was shielding his face from the encroaching sunlight. He pushed past them, heading back into the darkened rest room.

Tyler exhaled deeply.

'There's nothing we can do here,' he said. 'Let's go.'

Tyler was surprised to see one or two members of staff present in 'The King George' hotel. The bar was open and there was even a man sitting on one of the stools sipping at a pint of beer. A rotund chambermaid was hoovering the carpet in reception. She looked up briefly as Jo and the farmer entered.

The American crossed to the desk and rang the bell, wondering if Mark Bates was going to appear. She thought back to the incident the other night when she'd discovered him devouring the raw meat. Was he going to emerge from the staff room with blood dripping from his hands? She hurriedly dismissed the thought.

'I'll have to get your key, miss,' said the chambermaid, appearing beside her. 'There's only a few of us here today.'

'Why is that?' asked the journalist.

'Some of the staff are off sick,' the maid explained. 'My husband, he's not been too good lately.'

'What's wrong with him?' asked Tyler.

'He looks so pale, sir, and during the day all he wants to do is sleep. He's not so bad at night though.' She shrugged.

'But *you* feel OK?' said Jo.

'I'm fine thank you.' The maid looked puzzled and she coloured slightly beneath the combined gaze of Jo and Tyler.

'Is there something wrong?' she asked, handing Jo her key.

The American smiled.

'No.'

The maid crossed to her hoover.

'It seems pointless doing this,' she mused.

'Why,' Tyler wanted to know.

She looked up.

'Well, what with there being hardly any guests here. And I can't see us getting many more in the near future the way things are.' She leant on the cleaner like a navvy on a shovel. 'I'll tell you something else, a lot of people have left the town. Don't ask me why but only two days ago the family who live next door to us moved out. And I've noticed how many people seem to be feeling off colour. You know, ill. I can't understand it.' She paused, shaking her head. 'It's a good job Mr Bates isn't here.'

'Who *is* Bates?' asked Jo.

'The Manager,' explained the maid. 'Why?'

Jo shook her head.

'I was just curious.'

The three of them stood in silence for another moment, then the maid started up her cleaner.

'I suppose I'd better get this done all the same,' she said and bustled off across reception.

Jo and Tyler headed for the lifts, both of which stood empty before them. For some unaccountable reason, the sight of people in the reception and lounge made them feel easier but, as the lift bumped to a halt and the doors slid back, the corridor which stretched away ahead of them seemed curiously forbidding.

They reached Jo's room and went inside.

It was large, containing a double bed, a sideboard and even a desk. The wardrobe had mirrors on its doors and through a white door was the bathroom. A latticed window looked out onto the car park at the back of the building. There were tea-making facilities so Jo filled the kettle from the tap in the bathroom and plugged it into the socket nearby.

Tyler sat down on the edge of the bed.

'If there are people leaving the town, like the maid

said, then that would be one explanation why there aren't so many about.'

'And the ones who haven't left?' said Jo, cryptically.

'We've got to assume they're infected with this virus, whatever it is.'

'You know I've noticed with a lot of them, sunlight or artificial light frightens them. It hurts them. Like that guy Nichols.' She sucked in an anxious breath. 'What kind of virus makes people afraid of the light?'

There was a long silence broken finally by Jo.

'I was thinking about what Hawley said. About the synthetic, man-made proteins in the Vanderburg feed. Geoffrey Anderson *would* have known about it. He would have known the effects it was going to have too. Tests must have been done.'

'What are you getting at, Jo?'

'That night he tried to talk to me, maybe that was what it was about. Anderson must have known what was in the feed. Someone didn't want him shooting his mouth off.'

'He may have known the effect it would have on animals but how could he have known what it would do to human beings?'

'I think he was told to keep quiet. When he wouldn't someone shut him up. Killed him.'

'Come on, Jo, this isn't New York,' said the farmer, wearily.

'Then where is he?' she barked. 'He was scared that night he rang me. He knew someone was on to him.'

'Like who?'

'That's what we've got to find out.'

Tyler exhaled deeply.

'We don't know he's dead. We don't know anything.'

'We know that this town is infected with some kind of virus. We know it's spread by eating contaminated meat. And we know that the victims can't come out in sunlight.'

'That adds up to nothing,' said Tyler. 'Why hasn't everyone in Wakely got this virus? Why haven't you and I caught it?'

'You don't eat meat. I haven't touched any since I arrived in Wakely.'

Tyler stroked his chin thoughtfully.

'If Vanderburg Chemicals are responsible for the virus,' he said, slowly. 'They wouldn't want any publicity. No outside interference.'

'You think they're behind the phone and TV blackouts?' Jo said, incredulously.

'It's a thought, although I doubt if they'd be able to do anything on that scale without help.'

'Help from whom?'

'That's what we've got to find out. We've got to get inside Vanderburg Chemicals.'

Jo looked at him, dumbstruck.

'Are you kidding? That place is like Fort Knox.'

'There has to be a way. We've got no choice.'

'When do we do it?'

'Tonight,' he announced, flatly.

'And in the meantime?'

'I think it would be best if I moved in here with you. I'm not leaving you alone. Not now.'

She kissed him softly on the cheek and he brushed a strand of hair from her forehead.

'What about your farm?' she asked.

'What farm?' he said, sardonically. 'Diseased animals are no good to a farmer. They'll have to be destroyed.' He got to his feet. 'I'll be back in an hour or two,' he said. Then he was gone.

The kettle had begun to boil but Jo didn't notice it. She was gazing out of the window, watching the scudding clouds.

It was just after 1.00 p.m.

166

Thirty

The oak table sparkled like ice beneath the fluorescent lights. The room smelt of polish and nicotine, the air filled with a bluish haze. It was a large room, twenty feet wide and thirty long, the table being its centre point. The white painted walls bore framed pictures, including an original Turner over the fire place. The painting looked somewhat anachronistic set over an electric fire. Indeed, the entire room seemed to be caught in a kind of chronological limbo. A clash of cultures and times mirrored in what it contained. Antique furniture sat side by side with such modern encumbrances as a computer terminal which, at present, showed a blank screen. The windows, large and airy, were double-glazed, offering added sound proofing.

Five men sat around the table, each with a note pad and pencil before him.

The wall clock ticked noisily in the stillness, the hands having crawled round to 3.00 p.m.

Sir Oliver Thorndike looked at his own watch and coughed exaggeratedly as if to still a babble of conversation, but all eyes were on him anyway.

Thorndike was fifty-three, a tall but heavy set man with thick white hair and sad eyes. He had been knighted in 1978 for his work in the field of genetics. He had worked for Vanderburg Chemicals since 1980. He coughed once more, brushing an imaginary speck of dust from the sleeve of his navy blue suit.

'Gentlemen,' he said. 'If we could begin.'

There were nods of approval.

Thorndike looked at the man closest to him on the right. Charles Muir finished lighting his pipe and sucked contentedly on it.

'The new synthetic compound is almost completed,'

said the older man, his voice a harsh Scots drawl. 'It should be ready for introduction within a week.'

'It will be treated with ultra-violet rays this time,' added Richard Neville.

At forty-five, Neville was the youngest man at the table. He pushed his glasses back on his nose and shuffled in his seat.

'It should have been treated before,' said Muir.

'We had no way of knowing what the effects of the synthetic protein would be,' Neville protested.

'You're a bacteriologist,' the Scot said, challengingly. 'You should have had some idea.'

Thorndike raised a hand.

'Gentlemen, please,' he said. 'We all appreciate that the first batch of the additive was, how shall we say, unproven. The results were merely unfortunate.'

'Why was it not thoroughly checked?' Muir persisted.

'For God's sake,' snapped Martin Glendenning. 'The damage is done now. We made a mistake. That mistake can be rectified this time.'

'Whatever we do now can't be of any help to the people of Wakely,' Muir said, chewing on the stem of his pipe.

'We all knew we were taking a chance,' said Thorndike, sweeping back his white hair. 'We were unfortunate.'

'A masterful understatement,' Muir chided.

'Do we know exactly how the viral infection is affecting the residents of Wakely?' asked Neville, toying with his wedding ring as he spoke.

Thorndike picked up a manilla file and flipped it open.

'First reports indicate that it's manifesting itself as something like pernicious anaemia. We haven't been able to discover the exact effects yet.'

'Does it really matter?' said Glendenning.

'Well, it only matters in as far as knowing its communicability,' Thorndike said. 'It seems confined to the town at the moment so it's reasonably safe to assume that the virus is passed on through ingestion of the affected meat.'

'Is there any possibility of outside interference?' asked Glendenning, plucking at the back of his hand.

'In what form?' Thorndike wanted to know.

'Police. Other authorities.'

Thorndike shook his head.

'If the need arises, we can seal Wakely off,' he said. 'From what I can gather, many of the residents have already left.'

'Infected or virus free?' Muir wanted to know.

Thorndike held up his hands.

'Charles, there's no possible way we could know who was or wasn't infected. Wakely has a population of just under 4,000. From that amount of people it would be impossible to guess how many had the virus.'

'*Try* guessing,' the Scot insisted.

Thorndike looked at the fifth man seated at the table, who was yet to speak, and then at Neville.

'From a population of 4,000,' the younger man began. 'One could expect perhaps a quarter of that number to have contracted the virus in some form.'

'What about those who aren't infected?' asked Glendenning.

'What about them?' Thorndike said.

'What's the likelihood of them contracting the virus?'

'Unless they eat the contaminated meat, they should be safe from the primary infection,' Thorndike told him.

'What about secondary infection?' asked Muir.

Thorndike exhaled deeply.

'As I said before, we have no way of knowing how or even if the virus is communicable except by ingestion.'

'There is the problem of cure,' said Neville. 'Can we find one?'

'It's not our business to find one,' snapped

Glendenning. 'This project is designed to maximize the growth of livestock by the infusion of synthetic proteins. Any adverse effects caused by that work are regrettable but, nonetheless, not our concern.'

'Not our concern,' said Muir, angrily, the pipe bouncing about in his mouth. 'We virtually wipe out an entire town and you say it's not our concern.' He paused. 'I say we should call off the project for the time being.'

A chorus of mutterings greeted his remark.

Thorndike stilled the babble and looked at the Scot.

'That is impractical and unnecessary, Charles, and you know it,' he said.

'Geoffrey Anderson agreed with me,' Muir said.

'To hell with Geoffrey Anderson.'

The voice came from the fifth man who got to his feet and walked to one of the windows which looked out into the grounds of Vanderburg Chemicals. He was tall, nearly six five and his black hair glinted beneath the lights. When he spoke it was with a strong American accent, Mid-West. He was wearing an expensive suit and, when he smiled, which was something of a rarity, a single gold tooth sparkled amidst the expanse of white enamel.

He reached into his pocket and pulled out an engraved silver hip-flask. Unscrewing the cap he took a hefty swig, then turned back to face the men around the table.

'Anderson was a pain in the ass,' said the dark haired man, vehemently. 'This project demands top secrecy at all times, that's why we're working with the co-operation of your Government.' His voice took on a hint of sarcasm. 'To further Anglo-American relations. Now if anybody else wants out that's fine with me but hear this, if one of you bastards breathes a word of what's been said in this room, you'll be wearing your asses for hats.'

170

John Stark took another swig from his flask, then returned to his seat. As chief financial backer to Vanderburg Chemicals he relished his own importance and was never slow to remind those around him of it too. He had founded the company three years earlier, shortly after the death of his wife, using her maiden name for the concern. She had been killed in a traffic accident, the brakes on her Trans-Am failing as she pulled in front of a Mack truck carrying a tank load of amyl nitrate. There hadn't been much left to bury.

'I don't think any of us want to leave, Mr Stark,' said Thorndike.

'Then what the hell is he bitching about?' snapped the American, pointing at Muir.

'Look, I'll work for you,' said the Scot. 'But that doesn't mean I have to stop caring about the people my work affects. Especially when it's something on this scale.'

'You win some, you lose some,' snapped Stark.

'And in this case we lost an entire town,' said Muir.

'You were the goddam scientists, you should have got it right first time. If anyone's to blame it's you.'

'Well,' said Thorndike, 'I'm sure matters have been put to rights this time.' He smiled at Stark but the gesture was not returned.

'Yeah, well there's something else.'

The men looked, vaguely, at the American.

'I'm talking about that girl and the guy in town, whoever the hell he is. They're too goddam curious.' A rare smile crept across Stark's face. 'Still, curiosity can kill more than cats.' He chuckled.

'What do you propose to do?' asked Glendenning.

'*You* spoke to the girl didn't you?' said Stark.

The older man nodded.

'She did seem rather . . . inquisitive. Especially about Anderson,' the scientist said.

'Too inquisitive.' He turned to Thorndike. 'I want

Wakely sealed off. Cops, telephones, TV, I know that's already been taken care of but, from now on, I don't want anyone leaving. I want this town sewn up tighter than a fish's ass and I mean water-tight. Make that phone call.'

Thorndike reached unhesitatingly for the phone close to him and dialled a London number. It rang for a moment, then the others sat watching as he spoke.

'I'd like to speak to the Minister,' said Thorndike.

The secretary asked for his name, then what he wanted.

'Tell him it's Erebus.'

There was a moment's silence at the other end of the line. A confusion of clicks and crackles as Thorndike was re-connected on another line.

Muir chewed on his pipe.

Stark took another swig from his hip-flask.

The other two men watched Thorndike as he moved the receiver agitatedly from one hand to the other.

Glendenning plucked at the flesh on the back of his hand.

Neville continued twisting his ring.

Thorndike suddenly became animated as he heard a voice at the other end of the phone.

'Yes, sir,' he said. 'This is Erebus.'

He swallowed hard.

'There have been difficulties. We need the town sealed off. No passage for residents or visitors.'

The voice asked what kind of difficulties.

'Project Erebus has precipitated some unforeseen confusion here. We need time to rectify the situation.'

How long, the voice wanted to know.

'Until further notice,' said Thorndike looking across at Stark.

The American nodded.

Thorndike listened for a moment.

'Yes, sir, I understand. No, there is no danger to the project itself.'

There were more hasty enquiries, then Thorndike spoke again.

'Yes, sir. Everything will be taken care of.'

He put the phone down and turned to the waiting American.

'It's done.'

'What, may I ask has been done?' Muir enquired.

'Within forty-eight hours,' Thorndike told him. 'Wakely will be completely sealed off from all outside contact.'

'How?' the Scot wanted to know.

'That's not your worry,' Stark told him.

'What's your solution, *Mr* Stark?' Muir began. 'Complete the annihilation of Wakely that was begun by Project Erebus?'

The American rounded on him.

'Listen to me,' he growled. 'This project is worth millions and we're not the only ones who are going to benefit. Why the hell do you think your Government is behind me too?' There was a long silence. 'Now, there's nothing else to be said. I don't think I have to keep you *gentlemen* from your work any longer.'

The assembled scientists rose and filed from the room. Stark took a swig from his hip-flask, then crossed to a desk in the far corner of the room. He flicked a switch on the console before him and muttered something into the intercom. A moment or two later there was a knock on the door.

'Come in,' he called.

Carlo Fanducci walked in, a cigarette hanging from his mouth. He closed the door behind him.

'The guy and the girl who've been doing the digging in town, who are they?' asked Stark.

Fanducci coughed, fighting to keep down the bitter phlegm.

'The girl's a reporter. She's from the East Side,' he said, his voice raw and gravelly. 'I knew I'd seen her someplace before. She was the one who fingered old man Scalise back in New York. She's been fucking around with this guy, Tyler, for a few days now.'

'Do you know where they are?' Stark asked.

'Tyler runs a farm about a mile outside town. The broad's staying at a hotel in Wakely. But, from what I've seen, he spends most of his time there.'

'What do they know?'

Fanducci shrugged.

'Waste them,' said Stark, flatly. 'And anyone who's with them.'

'When do you want it done?' asked Fanducci.

Stark took another swig from his flask.

'As soon as you can.'

The Italian nodded.

Thirty-one

The attic smelt fusty, the dust of neglect having settled thickly on everything. Particles of it swirled in the beam of Tyler's torch as he clambered up onto the thick rafters. It was a part of the farm house which he used to visit regularly as a youngster, sitting for hours with his father, listening as the older man spoke. Young Tyler would sit cross-legged before the man he held in awe, watching him clean his beloved guns. He had learnt all he knew about guns from his father and now, as he shone the torch around the attic, those memories came flooding back. The beam glinted on some of the trophies which hung on the walls of this most hallowed retreat. Plaques, statuettes, certificates. Everything covered by a film of dust. On the far wall, however, was a canvas sheet. Pinned at either side, it protected the valuable collection beneath.

Tyler reached forward slowly and pulled it down.

There were four shotguns on the rack. Two nickel plated Purdeys, a Franchi automatic and a single barrelled Baikal. Beneath them, in a large cupboard, were countless boxes of ammunition. Tyler still held his own Purdey by his side. It had been given to him on his sixteenth birthday by his father, the stock still bore his faded initials. They had been carved by his father.

Tyler's mother had never been keen on guns, her own brother having been wounded in a hunting accident, but Jack Tyler had taught his son how to use them carefully and skilfully. Many hours of practice and aching shoulders had turned Tyler into a proficient marksman and, at seventeen, he had won the county championships for clay pigeon shooting. Still the youngest person ever to do so.

Now he looked at his own gun and at those of his father.

Already he could feel the tears welling up inside him, not so much for the fact that the memories of his father were so strong but for the purpose to which he intended to put these beloved weapons.

He took down the top gun from the duo of Purdeys and hefted it before him. Then he selected the Franchi. That done, he unlocked the ammunition cupboard and took out as many shells as he could stuff into the pockets of his jacket. He could, he reasoned, come back for more if he needed them. Then, carrying all three weapons, he made his way back down the rickety step ladder which led up to the attic. He paused at the

175

bottom and loaded his own gun and the other two, thumbing five cartridges into the automatic.

When he emerged into the late afternoon sunlight, Tyler felt sick and he had to steady himself against a fence for a moment.

He sucked in huge lungfuls of air, realizing what he had to do but feeling something akin to disgust with himself.

Many of the animals were already gone. Pens and fields were empty. Elsewhere, animals lay dead, some partially decomposed in the heat. But there were still three or four dozen in and around the farm.

Tyler knew they were diseased. He knew they must be destroyed but it made his task no easier. He looked up at the attic window as if expecting to see his father standing there watching him, shaking his head reproachfully as he saw what use his guns were being put to.

Tyler picked up the Franchi and worked the pump action, chambering a round. He crossed to the pig sty and looked in at the oversized weaners, raising the weapon to his shoulder.

He aimed and fired in one movement.

The first animal dropped into the mud as the roar of the shotgun was joined by another. And another. The weaners made no attempt to move as the shot tore into them and, finally, when the hammer slammed down on an empty chamber, the sty was full of carcasses. A bluish haze of smoke wafted gently into the air and the stink of cordite was strong in Tyler's nostrils.

He re-loaded and walked purposefully across to the nearest shed which housed half a dozen cows due for milking.

Tyler gritted his teeth and opened fire, tears now flowing swiftly from his stinging eyes as his ears were filled with the deafening retort of the gun and the loud bellowings of the cattle. And there was another sound.

His own moans of distress.

The smoke cleared slowly and, before it had dispersed, he was firing again. Choking back sobs, trying to keep his aim straight. His shoulder ached from the constant thudding against it of the stock as each fresh impact slammed against him.

He was muttering soundlessly to himself as he fired, passing from one shed to the other. From cattle to pigs, to sheep. The Franchi began to glow red in his hands so he dropped it and, with bloodstained hands, broke the nickel-plated Purdey and checked that it was loaded.

It was.

He gave both barrels to a large bull, watching as the animal went down as if pole-axed.

He felt hot salty tears running freely down his cheeks now because he realized that, in the thundering discharge of those shotgun blasts he was destroying not just diseased animals. He was destroying everything his father had built up. He was slaughtering his own memories. The Purdey roared in his hand.

Each blazing explosion was like an accusatory shout.

Tyler shouted aloud at each discharge, his sorrow gradually giving way to anger as he continued with his grisly task.

The ground was littered with empty shell cases, but there were always plenty more at hand.

'Vanderburg,' he muttered, his jaw set firm.

The rage seemed to grow.

'Bastards,' he growled. He would find out why this had happened. Someone would pay. Tyler was determined that somebody would suffer for what had been done.

The slaughter continued.

It took Tyler over an hour to despatch what livestock he could find on the farm. By the time he'd finished, his arms felt like lead weights. His eyes stung and his nostrils were full of the stench of gun oil and cordite. He dropped to his knees and gulped down the air, trying to ignore the pungent odour of blood which was so strong.

Finally, he got up and trudged wearily back to the house. He collected as much ammunition as he could carry and put it into the landrover with the three shotguns, then he climbed into the vehicle and sat behind the wheel for what seemed like an eternity.

'I'm sorry,' he whispered, wondering whether the words were spoken to the memory of his parents or to appease his own tortured conscience.

He started the engine and swung the vehicle out of the yard. He didn't once look back.

Jo sat on the edge of the bed listening. But for the odd sound of movement from downstairs, the hotel was in silence. The American got to her feet and crossed to her door. She paused for a moment, then opened it, peering to her right and left.

The corridor was empty, the doors to the other rooms were closed.

Jo dropped her own key into the back pocket of her jeans and quietly closed her door behind her. She moved noiselessly towards the first and nearest door and turned the knob. It wouldn't budge. She dropped to one knee and squinted through the keyhole.

The room was well lit inside, the curtains drawn back.

Jo got to her feet and moved down the corridor. It turned at right angles as it approached the lifts, both of which were stationary. The American moved to another door, glancing behind her at the lifts, as if expecting someone to emerge at any second.

She wondered how many of the guests were infected with the mysterious virus, if any. Some of the staff of the hotel certainly were – she knew that only too well after the incident with Bates – and of the other guests she knew nothing.

The second door she tried was also locked.

Jo was about to move away from it when she heard a noise from inside.

She pressed her ear to the white wood and listened.

It came again. A low, guttural rasping. Like asthmatic breathing.

She knelt once more to try and look through the key hole, but all that greeted her prying eye was darkness.

The breathing seemed to grow louder for a moment, then ceased.

The American knocked gently.

The breathing began once more, slow and strained.

Jo paused a moment longer, then moved along to a door which, she noticed, was ajar.

It was dark inside the room and she opened the door inch by inch, allowing the light to dispel the gloom.

It was as quiet as a grave in that room and Jo shuddered involuntarily as she passed across the portal and into the blackness.

The room was like her own except for the fact that it showed no signs of being inhabited. The bed was made, the smell of carpet cleaner strong in the air.

She moved towards the bathroom and pushed open the door, slapping on the light as she did so.

There was hair in the sink. Thick dark hunks of it. Not strands but tufts which had clogged the plug hole. Jo prodded at it with her key, noticing something else too. A thin, almost transparent substance which reminded her of mucous. She turned away, stifling a scream as she looked into the bath.

The white enamel was splashed with blood.

Jo swallowed hard and leant over the bath, dipping one finger tentatively into the crimson liquid.

It was fresh.

She got up and hastily left the room, intent on

179

returning to her own. **The corridor turned at right** angles again and Jo realized that she had come almost full circle in her search. Out of curiosity, she tried each door as she went. Finding every one locked.

However, the room next to hers was not locked.

The handle turned smoothly in her grip, the door opening a fraction.

The American hesitated. This was no bedroom. From the smell of freshly laundered sheets she realized that it was the linen cupboard. She wondered whether or not it was worth looking into, then something caught her eye. Something crumpled lying on the floor about two feet inside the room.

She stepped inside.

Had Jo been in the corridor, she may well have seen the lights on the lift flash brightly but, hidden inside the laundry room, she was oblivious to what was going on.

One of the lifts was rising.

Jo took a closer look at the crumpled mass on the floor, prodding it with her key.

It looked like the transparent stuff she'd seen in the sink of the other room. But what the hell was it? She looked around and found a pile of towels nearby. She pulled the top one down and wrapped it around her hand.

The lift bumped to a halt and the doors slid quietly open.

Jo picked up the sticky substance, noticing how tendrils of it hung like rotting streamers. It had a revolting familiarity about it. As she held it before her, it seemed to take on a shape.

Unfolding, the slimy mass fell away like unravelling paper.

Jo saw hair attached to it and she finally realized what she was holding.

It was a large coil of human skin, shed as a snake would shed its old hide.

She dropped it in disgust and got to her feet, backing out of the room, eyes fixed on the lump of skin as if it were a living thing.

The hand closed on her shoulder.

Jo screamed and spun round.

'Sorry,' said Tyler, apologetically.

She could only stand and stare at him, her heart hammering madly against her ribs.

'Didn't you hear the lift coming up?' he asked.

Jo shook her head.

'What's wrong?' Tyler wanted to know.

'Well,' she panted. 'Aside from the fact that I nearly had a goddam heart attack, I've found a couple of things.'

'Like what?'

'Like that.' She pointed to the sloughed skin.

Tyler knelt and glanced at it.

'Skin?' he asked.

She nodded.

'That's not all.'

Jo showed him the blood and hair in the other room, then led him to the locked bedroom where she had heard the breathing.

'There's someone asleep in there,' he said.

'It's four thirty in the afternoon,' she snapped. 'Who sleeps at this time of the day?'

'And what do you propose we do? Kick the door down?' he said. 'There's probably a perfectly logical explanation for . . .'

She cut him short.

'Don't give me that crap,' she rasped.

The door was suddenly pulled open.

Both of them stepped back, surprised to see Mark Bates standing there.

'What are you doing here?' he rasped.

'I heard you breathing,' said Jo. 'I thought maybe you were sick.'

Bates regarded them warily and, in the light, they both saw how the skin had peeled from his face and neck, leaving red and angry patches beneath. He shielded his face from the light, the thick growths of hair on the palms of his hands clearly visible.

'What do you want?' he demanded.

'Nothing,' said Tyler, pulling Jo aside. 'Sorry if we disturbed you.'

Bates glared at them, then slammed the door once more and locked it.

Jo and Tyler were left in the corridor, gazing at the closed door. It was the farmer who made the first movement, urging Jo to join him as he walked back to their own room. Once inside he locked the door behind them.

'Do you think it's safe here?' the American asked him.

Tyler nodded. He crossed to the window and looked out. Jo studied his broad outline as he stood there, unusually silent.

'Vic.' She spoke his name softly. 'What's on your mind?'

He told her what had happened at the farm prior to his return.

'My father built that place up from nothing,' he said. 'Every time I pulled that trigger it was as if I was destroying a piece of his dream.'

Jo crossed to the window and slid her arm around his waist. He pulled her closer.

'You had no choice,' she said.

The words brought him little comfort, but the sadness which had lain so heavy inside him had now turned into a knotted ball of fury. He wanted revenge.

The sun vanished momentarily behind a bank of dark cloud and, in the distance, they could both see the shadow which it cast over the land. Jo shuddered and Tyler held her tighter.

'It'll be dark in a few hours,' he said.

At 7.30 p.m. they returned to the room where they'd found Bates and, surprisingly enough, found the door open.

Tyler checked out the entire room.

Bates was gone.

Thirty-two

Night lay heavy over Wakely. An impenetrable blanket of darkness denied even the welcoming glow of the moon. A few stars glinted against the velvet back-drop but even they were mostly obscured by banks of thick cloud which spread across the gloomy heavens like ink stains on a blotter. There was a storm in the air. The heat of the day had become a cloying humidity and, even as Jo and Tyler sat in the dining room of 'The King George' prodding at the remnants of their dinners, the first low rumblings of thunder could be heard away to the north.

'The fences around Vanderburg Chemicals are electrified,' Jo began. 'If we get past those there's Security guards and patrol dogs. Vic, I'm telling you, it'd take a team of Green Berets to break in there.'

'We'll see,' said Tyler, defiantly.

'So, once we're in, assuming we can *get* in, we're not even sure what we're looking for.'

'Somebody's been doing everything they can to stop us finding out the facts about what's going on in Wakely. The only people who would need to do that are the people at Vanderburg Chemicals.' He paused. 'No phones, no television, not even any police or newsmen. The whole set up is too . . . organized to be a coincidence.'

'You said you thought that Vanderburg couldn't do anything like that without help,' she said.

'I don't. I think someone else is involved. Don't ask me who.'

'Who's powerful enough to seal off an entire town?' Jo said, the question hanging lazily in the air.

Tyler had no answer for her.

A troubled silence descended over them.

Carlo Fanducci brought the car to a halt across the street from the hotel. He lit up another cigarette and inhaled the smoke, gritting his teeth as he felt the pain begin to gnaw at his chest and throat. He coughed, wincing at the effort. Son of a bitch, he thought. It was getting worse. Fucking cancer must have eaten away most of his lung by now. What the hell, there was no good crying about it. He hawked and spat onto the pavement, the bloodied sputum looking black beneath the dull glow of the street lamp.

The lights on the front of the hotel glowed with a rare brilliance and Fanducci noticed how none of the people on the streets went near to the building.

He could see them in the gloom, moving furtively. Like tangible shadows they scuttled about in side streets and doorways, always careful to keep clear of the puddles of yellow light given off by the sodium lamps. Fanducci himself felt at home in the darkness and, as he drew the .357 from its shoulder holster, he did not need to see the heavy cylinder. He knew, from the sound it made as he spun it that every chamber was full. Each one carrying a lethal hollow tipped bullet.

Satisfied, he slid the revolver back into position and reached onto the back seat where he found the Ingram. The machine gun, no bigger than a shoe box, was also loaded, the thirty-two round magazine rammed tight into it. Fanducci pulled back the bolt, priming it.

His little baby. It fired over 1,500 rounds a minute and, from close range, would cut a man in half. He wrapped the leather carrying strap around his wrist and hefted the weapon before him. When he got out of the car, the Ingram dangled at his side.

Fanducci stood for long moments watching the front of the building. Nothing stirred, only the long strands of ivy which clawed at the stone work moved in the shallow breeze.

There was a back entrance which he'd found the other day. Shit, he'd go in that way. Give them a little surprise.

The Italian smiled to himself and set off towards the hotel.

Overhead, the first soundless flash of lightning tore its way across the heavens.

Jo and Tyler walked through the darkened reception towards the lifts and the American jabbed a button. The lights on either side glowed brilliantly for a second, then dimmed. There was a loud rumble of thunder. The lights blazed with their usual power once more.

'Bloody storm,' muttered Tyler.

They were now the only ones in the reception. Off to the left the door to the staff room stood closed. To the right, the bar was empty as well.

The lift purred to a halt and the doors slid open. Outside there was a whiplash crack of lightning followed by a growl of thunder which seemed to shake the building to its foundations. They both stepped into the lift and Jo pressed the button marked 'l'. The car began to rise.

Even inside the lift, insulated to a certain degree against the noise from outside, the storm raged with nerve-shredding fury, the celestial explosions continuing at an ever increasing rate as the storm reached its full magnitude.

The lights went out.

The lift was plunged into a blackness so total that Tyler could not see his companion even though she stood just two feet from him. At the same instant, the lift stopped dead.

'Oh Christ,' murmured the farmer.

They stood for interminable seconds, waiting for power to be restored but nothing happened.

'Perhaps the storm's brought down a power line,' said Jo.

'We must be between floors,' Tyler said. 'Perhaps I can get these doors open, then we can see.' He fumbled his way across the small compartment to the sliding doors and worked his fingers into the tiny gap between them, then, with a grunt, he began to pull in both directions. His muscles bulged as he fought to open the doors, the veins throbbing at his temples.

They began to open a fraction.

Jo held up her lighter, the meagre light which it gave off being sufficient to show them that they were, indeed, between floors. But the top of the car showed about two feet above the floor of what would be the first storey.

Tyler suddenly let the doors go as the pressure became too much to bear.

Jo flicked off her lighter and the two of them stood in the gloom. Disembodied voices floated on a sea of darkness.

'Can we climb up through the gap?' asked Jo.

'*You* can,' Tyler said. 'I'll hold the doors open as far as I can, you'll have to try and squeeze through.'

'What about you?'

'There should be an emergency exit in the top of the lift. A maintenance opening or something. If I can get through that, perhaps I can make it to the second floor.'

'No, it's too dangerous. Maybe we should wait until the power comes back on.'

'And if it doesn't?'

The question hung ominously in the air.

'I'll try the doors again,' said Tyler, bracing himself. Jo slipped her shoes off, realizing that she was going to have to clamber over the farmer to reach the small gap. The floor of the compartment felt cold beneath her bare feet and a chill ran through her though she was convinced that not all of it was induced by the cold. She shuddered involuntarily.

Tyler, by now, had managed to force the doors open far enough for her to attempt to slip through. Jo was grateful that she was slim, a few more pounds around the backside and she'd be stuck.

'Ready?' grunted Tyler.

'Ready,' she assured him.

The entire lift was rocked by a powerful impact from above.

Tyler fell back, the doors sliding swiftly shut, nearly trapping his hands.

The car was shaking slightly and they could both hear loud scratching sounds coming from above.

'What the hell is that?' Tyler said, looking up.

Jo was silent, straining her eyes to see.

There was someone on the top of the lift.

The shaking continued for a moment, only to be replaced by what sounded like heavy footsteps.

'How could they have got up there?' asked Jo, a note of fear in her voice.

'From the second floor,' Tyler offered. 'They must have climbed down the cable.'

There was a loud scraping sound filling the lift now and, as Jo flicked on her lighter, they both saw that the maintenance hatch was being opened.

Whoever was up there would be through in a minute or two.

The lighter grew hot in Jo's hand and she dropped it, plunging them back into darkness once more. She dropped to her knees, fumbling to find it. Groping like a blind person, her ears ever alert for the sounds from above as the hatch was pulled away.

Tyler felt helpless. Unable to see a hand in front of him, he could only stand there impotently and wait for the intruder to drop from above.

The lights suddenly came back on, the lift simultaneously bucking into action. It rose the required few feet and bumped to a halt on the first floor.

'Get out, quick,' Tyler shouted, pushing her through the half-open doors.

Jo stumbled and fell into the corridor, looking behind her to see Tyler following.

The maintenance hatch was torn free.

Tyler backed off slightly, looking around for something to defend himself with. There was a small fire extinguisher nearby and he snatched it up, hefting it before him like a club. But no one came from the lift and, as the doors slid quietly shut, the farmer lowered his make-shift weapon.

Jo had struggled to her feet and was standing behind him.

'Who was it?' she said, breathlessly.

Tyler merely shook his head.

'You go back to the room, lock yourself in,' he told her. 'Don't open the door for any reason.'

'Where are *you* going?' she demanded.

He dropped the fire extinguisher and headed for the stairs.

'To get us some protection.'

Jo stood for long seconds, listening to his footsteps receding, then she turned and headed up the corridor towards their room, fumbling in her pocket for the key.

She glanced anxiously to her left and right as she walked, watching for the slightest signs of movement from any of the other rooms.

She was in the process of inserting the key in the lock when the lights went out again.

Jo suppressed a scream, relaxing as, a moment later, the power came back on. The thunder rolled ominously around the building and, through the window at the far end of the corridor, she glimpsed jagged barbs of lightning ripping through the thick clouds.

She stepped inside the room and hurriedly locked it.

Across the corridor, the door directly opposite hers opened a fraction.

Carlo Fanducci gripped the Ingram sub-machine gun firmly by its butt and leant against the door. It opened effortlessly and the ex-Mafia man moved silently through the kitchen of the hotel. He strode through the darkness with assurance, his own black shape causing him to melt into it, only his low breathing signalled his presence at all.

He stopped as he heard footsteps in the reception beyond but then he scuttled to the door in time to see Tyler disappear out of the front entrance.

Fanducci smiled. The girl was obviously upstairs alone. Both together or one at a time – it didn't bother him how he had to take them out. He pushed against the door and found himself in reception, behind the desk. The Italian cursed as the light above it flickered again but he flipped open the registration book and ran one nicotine-stained finger down the list of names.

He found Jo's name and checked it against the number of her room.

Behind him, the door to the staff room opened slightly.

Fanducci released the safety catch on the Ingram and steadied the weapon in his hand, eyes fixed on the front entrance. On the glass doors which he knew Tyler must use to re-enter the building.

Away to his left, just out of his field of vision, there was movement. Two shadowy figures, hidden by the gloom, moved closer.

Fanducci ducked down behind the desk, just enough to keep himself hidden but to provide a good view of the main doors. Finger resting on the trigger, he waited.

Tyler unlocked the rear door of the landrover and pulled out the nickel plated Purdey. He broke it and thumbed two cartridges into the hungry chambers. As he looked up the sky seemed to grow darker, clouds gathering like predatory birds above him as the thunder and lightning continued their deafening symphony. The farmer stuffed a box of shells into his jacket pocket then, taking care to lock the vehicle once more, he turned and headed back to the hotel. The rain would not hold off for much longer, Tyler reasoned, although a possible downpour was the last thing on his mind as he trekked back towards the hotel. His mind was in a turmoil.

What *had* happened while they were in the lift? Tyler tried to think of a logical explanation but, lately, things in Wakely had begun to defy rationality.

As he approached the front of the hotel, the farmer glanced behind him.

Across the street, hidden by the deep shadows in a shop doorway, he could see two people. Further down the pavement there were others. Even though he couldn't see their faces he knew they were watching him. Tyler paused for a moment, trying to count the dark shapes, but it was useless. They seemed to move and writhe as one, a large undulating mass which defied close scrutiny.

He walked into the hotel, slowing his pace as he entered the darkened reception. For some reason, it seemed even more forbidding than the storm-blasted street.

Tyler saw the staff room door open and he took a step back.

Fanducci, who was already straightening up, saw the farmer move and thought he'd been spotted. The Italian rose from behind the desk like a malevolent Jack-in-the-box, the Ingram pointed towards Tyler. The farmer barely had time to hurl himself behind one of the oak beams near the door when Fanducci opened up. The hit-man squeezed the trigger and the reception was filled with the staccato rattle of automatic fire. Bullets, sprayed in a wide arc, ploughed through wood, plastic and ricocheted off metal. The sound of breaking glass added to the racket as the shells shattered the doors. Shards of crystal sprayed in all directions and Fanducci kept his finger on the trigger until the hammer struck an empty chamber. He swiftly pulled a fresh magazine from his belt and rammed it in, opening up immediately. Spent cartridge cases rained down like brass confetti as he raked the area where Tyler had been standing.

Tyler hugged the beam, the Purdey gripped in one hand, wondering what was happening. The room smelt of gun oil and cordite and a thick haze of smoke was drifting in the air.

The firing suddenly ceased and Tyler took his chance. He leapt out from behind the beam, throwing the shotgun before him, rolling over until he was sheltered behind a couple of chairs. From his vantage point he could see Fanducci reloading.

He could also see two figures who had emerged from the blackness and were almost upon the Italian.

Despite himself, Tyler shouted a warning.

Fanducci spun round and, for a second, he froze.

Both the figures facing him were dressed in the uniform of the hotel. One of them a maid, the other a chef. The latter of the two carried a kitchen knife.

He struck with lightning speed, slicing open Fanducci's left arm from shoulder to elbow. Blood spurted from the rent and the ex-Mafia man yelped in rage and pain, his finger tightening on the trigger of the Ingram. It spat out its stream of hot lead, the impact blasting both figures against the wall. Bullet holes the size of fists gaped in their chests and stomachs and the wall behind them was splattered crimson.

Immediately, Fanducci turned his attention back to Tyler, the machine gun stuttering loudly.

The farmer ducked low but it was useless.

One of the high powered slugs caught him in the shoulder. It slammed him backward, erupting from his back just above the right scapula. He rolled over, trying to fire the Purdey, pressing the butt to his injured shoulder. He screamed in agony as he fired, the stock slamming into the wound as the recoil shook him. The twin barrels erupted, the discharge missing Fanducci. The power of the explosion blew a hole in the reception desk itself and Tyler fumbled in his pocket for fresh cartridges. He could see his assailant emerging from behind the desk, drawing a revolver.

The first of another two figures in the bar reached up and tore the long pike from the wall, levelling it at Fanducci.

The Italian heard the noise and turned, not sure, for the first time in his life, what to do. He knew Tyler was re-loading but he now found he had two more enemies to deal with.

Tyler saw the figures, a man dressed in a dark suit

192

who held the pike and a girl in her late thirties, her hair hanging loosely to her shoulders. Patches of her scalp were exposed, raw and angry. Both of them were as white as milk. The man's face was dotted with streaming blisters, his cracked lips drawn back to reveal long teeth now brown in colour.

Fanducci heard the loud metallic snap as Tyler successfully closed the Purdey.

Pike or shotgun?

It all seemed to happen at once.

The diseased man thrust forward with the pike, the vicious point burying itself in Fanducci's side just below the armpit, knocking him over. He went down in a bleeding heap, one hand clapped to the gaping wound which the girl leapt for with a speed that amazed Tyler. She was upon the Italian in seconds, her mouth hungrily seeking the bloody gash. He writhed in agony as she tried to tear his shirt free in an attempt to reach the wound now spilling crimson fluid so freely.

Tyler, his shoulder burning with pain, pulled both triggers, watching as the concentrated shot struck the woman in the back. It lifted her off Fanducci, tearing open her back, snapping her spine as it ripped through her torso to burst forth from her chest, destroying one breast and spattering the pike-carrying man with gobbets of viscera.

The man seemed intent on reaching Fanducci however and he drove the pike forward again, putting all his weight behind it. The wicked point punctured the dying man's stomach, pinning him to the floor like a butterfly to a board. He let out a keening wail of agony which was smothered as blood bubbled up his windpipe and filled his mouth.

Tyler managed to get to his feet, holding the shotgun in one hand, the pain in his shoulder gnawing away at him. He ran for the stairs, by-passing the scene of slaughter before him and ignoring the man who had his face buried in the torn hollow of Fanducci's stomach. The farmer could hear liquid slurping from behind him as the man feasted on the Italian's blood.

He stumbled half way up the stairs, the shotgun falling from his grasp. Tyler turned to retrieve it and saw that the man was now following him. And he was moving with surprising speed.

Tyler snatched up the shotgun and stumbled on, not daring to look round.

As he reached the landing he saw Jo standing in the corridor. She'd heard the noise from downstairs and come to investigate.

'Get back,' screamed Tyler.

The diseased man caught up with him as he stopped to load the shotgun.

Tyler's attacker launched himself at the farmer, crashing into him with the force of a steam train. Both of them slammed into the nearby wall, Tyler already weakened from loss of blood. He rolled onto his back, trying to keep the man's hands away from his throat. He felt long nails gouging his flesh as his attacker fastened both hands around his windpipe in a vice-like grip. Tyler could smell the fetid stench from his opponent, he could feel the strength in those hands, see the fire in the eyes.

The farmer struck out with his good hand, driving two fingers into the man's left eye.

He shrieked but merely tightened his grip.

Jo stood mesmerized for a second, then snatched up the shotgun.

'Do it,' croaked Tyler, his face turning the colour of dark grapes.

The American levelled the shotgun until it was pointing at the man's head. He was straddling Tyler now, using all his power to throttle his victim, but he turned his head and opened his mouth in a defiant roar.

Jo saw blood and pieces of intestine sticking to his

long teeth, more of the red fluid and ragged pieces of flesh hanging from the gaping maw which was his mouth.

'Kill him,' Tyler urged, now a second away from unconsciousness.

Jo gritted her teeth and pulled the trigger.

The roar was deafening, the barrels flaming white for devastating seconds.

From such close range the effect of the blast was incredible. The man's head was literally torn from his shoulders. A sticky mess of crimson and grey porridge was splattered against the far wall and the body, the arteries still jetting blood, remained upright for a second before toppling over.

Tyler was on the point of blacking out. He managed to roll away, gazing up through pain-blurred eyes as Jo dropped the gun and fought to keep down the hot vomit which was clawing its way up her throat.

Further up the corridor, unseen by either of them, Mark Bates moved silently from the room opposite Jo's. He paused, then slipped inside her room, closing the door behind him.

He waited.

Tyler propped himself up on one elbow, his free hand reaching for the handkerchief in his trouser pocket. He pressed it to the wound in his shoulder, alarmed at how quickly the linen was soaked with blood. He coughed, finding it difficult to swallow. There were several deep indentations in the flesh of his neck from his attacker's powerful hands and the farmer spat as, once again, he felt his throat stinging from the pressure which had been put upon it.

Jo stood against the other wall, trying to look away from the headless remains of Tyler's assailant. The Purdey lay at her feet, the open chambers smoking.

'Jo,' Tyler rasped.

She was milk white, her breath coming in short gasps.

'Jo.' He said it more forcefully and she seemed to regain her senses somewhat. She looked at him, her green eyes a little glazed.

'Help me,' he said, trying to get up.

She finally tore her gaze from the dead man and aided Tyler as he struggled upright. He took his hand from the wounded shoulder and slipped one arm around Jo for support. His right arm and hand felt numb and he kept flexing his fingers to ensure that he still had control over the appendage. He wondered, for one terrifying moment, whether the bullet had severed some vital nerve, but as he continued flexing his fingers he realized that it hadn't.

Outside, the storm continued to rage across the sky and, as the two of them moved slowly towards their room, the lights in the corridor flickered once more.

'What happened?' Jo asked, finally. Her voice low. 'I heard shooting.'

He nodded.

'There was someone down there with a machine gun,' Tyler said.

'One of the townspeople?'

'No.'

'Is he still down there?'

'He's dead. Two of them killed him.' He paused. 'Tore him apart.'

'Oh God,' she murmured. 'That man who attacked you . . .' The sentence trailed off.

'Diseased. And there was a woman with him. I shot her.'

They reached the door of the room and Jo pushed it open. She frowned, flicking at the light switch.

'Dammit, I thought I left this on,' she said. She tried the switch again but there was still no light.

'The power's on,' said Tyler. 'The corridor lights are working.'

'The bulb must have blown,' she surmised.

Tyler walked across to the bed and sat down, pulling off his jacket carefully, wincing as he did so. The blood had congealed thickly in and around the wound, the material of his shirt and jacket stiff with the red substance.

'You'd better come into the bathroom,' said Jo. 'I'll clean that up for you.' She indicated the wound.

Tyler got up again and crossed to the door, grimacing as he turned the handle.

'Let me,' said Jo.

She twisted the knob.

From inside the bathroom, a clawed hand snaked out and gripped her by the wrist.

She screamed uncontrollably as she felt the hairy palm pressing against her flesh, the long nails tearing into her skin. The door was opening, the attacker emerging.

They both saw that it was Mark Bates.

Jo tried to pull away from him but the strength of his grip was too great. Eyes bulging madly, saliva dripping in reeking ribbons from his swollen lips he advanced from the darkness of the bathroom, pulling Jo towards him.

Her screams drummed in Tyler's ears and he looked around for some way to fight this new horror.

Forgetting the pain in his shoulder, he leapt at Bates and all three of them went down in a heap, Bates releasing his grip on Jo. He seemed more interested in the blood which was now flowing once again from Tyler's bullet-torn shoulder. The farmer may have been injured but he fought with a new-found strength born of desperation. He grabbed Bates by the hair, stepping back in horror as a huge tuft of it came away in his hand to reveal bloodied scalp beneath. But his reactions

197

were fast and he drove his knee up hard into Bates' face. The impact sent the man reeling. He crashed against the open bathroom door, slipping on the floor inside. Tyler was upon him in an instant, driving kicks into his torso, almost shouting in triumph as he heard ribs cracking.

Tyler dragged Bates to his feet and forced him over the bath, bending his back at an impossible angle.

Despite his wound, the farmer was still too heavy for Bates who clawed impotently at his opponent.

Tyler, his face a mask of rage and fear, brought one forearm crashing down on Bates' throat.

There was a sound like splintering wood and the man's spine broke.

Tyler remained lying across the body, pressing down ever harder as if he feared Bates would get up if he released his hold but, finally, he slid off. The corpse dropped to the floor with a forlorn thump.

Jo stood frozen in the doorway, unable to speak.

The farmer hauled himself upright, looking down at the body of his attacker. Bates' eyes were open and staring, the pupils now dilated and glazed. His face, like that of the man further down the corridor, was covered in numerous large blisters, some of which had burst and were weeping watery pus. Others, just forming, appeared like bulges beneath the pale skin.

'Let's get out of here,' said Tyler.

'But where are we going to go?' Jo asked, exasperatedly. 'There could be more of them outside. We can't leave the hotel.' There were tears in her eyes and the farmer could see that she was having trouble holding them back. He pulled her close to him, the burning pain in his shoulder having lessened somewhat.

'Vic, what are we going to do?' she whimpered.

'It's OK,' he said. 'We'll be OK.'

He wasn't sure if he was reassuring Jo or himself.

She looked up at him, wiping the tears away angrily. 'I'm sorry,' she said, 'coming apart on you, like this.'

He said nothing.

Jo laughed sardonically.

'I wasn't this scared when the Mafia were after me.'

Tyler brushed a tear from her cheek.

'We'll move to another room for tonight. Barricade the door if we have to.'

'What about the bodies?' she asked.

'We can't do anything about them until morning.'

He led her across to the room where Bates had been hiding and was relieved to find the key in the lock.

'I've got to get the gun,' he said.

'We ought to check on the guy downstairs. The one who shot you.'

'Right. You stay here. Lock this door and . . .'

She cut him short.

'No way. You're not leaving me alone again. I'm going with you.'

Tyler didn't argue. They walked down the corridor to where Jo had dropped the shotgun. Tyler stooped and retrieved it, breaking it with difficulty, the pain in his shoulder intensifying. The American took it from him and thumbed in two cartridges. Both of them were careful to avoid looking at the body of the headless attacker. They made their way cautiously down the stairs, pausing momentarily as the lights flickered again and a deafening clap of thunder shook the building. Tyler had the Purdey cradled over the crook of his good arm, his finger resting gently on the fore-trigger.

As they emerged into the reception, Jo saw the bodies.

The diseased woman, nearly cut in half by the shotgun blast.

The two staff members, riddled with bullets from the sub-machine gun which lay nearby.

And Fanducci.

He was lying spread-eagled, arms outstretched in the pattern of a crucifixion. His stomach and chest had been ripped open and what remained of his intestines and other internal organs were scattered over the blood-soaked carpet around him. The .357 lay close by, the hammer still pulled back.

'Oh my God,' muttered Jo.

Tyler crossed to the eviscerated corpse and, reining back his revulsion, began fumbling inside the dead man's jacket. The stench which rose from the body was overpowering and Tyler was forced to pause for a second to suck in a reasonably unpolluted breath. Resuming with his task he finally discovered a wallet in the Italian's inside pocket. Tyler wiped the blood from it and flipped the slim leather folder open.

It contained about fifty pounds, mostly in fives, some dollar bills stuffed at the back, a receipt for something and a few other inconsequential pieces of paper.

The I.D. card fell out almost by accident.

Tyler picked it up, looking first at the slim plastic strip.

'Jo,' he said. 'Look at this.'

She appeared at his side, trying to keep her eyes off the riven corpse. Jo read aloud the details on the card.

'Carlo Fanducci, Number 23958. Born 1930.'

And below that was the all too familiar logo with the red and silver initials joined at the curve of the C.

'Vanderburg Chemicals.'

Jo looked at the body then at Tyler.

'Jesus H. Christ,' she murmured.

'Someone at Vanderburg wants us dead,' Tyler observed. 'Why I wonder?'

'Whoever it is thinks we're important enough to go to the trouble of hiring a hit man,' she murmured, looking across at the discarded .357 and the Ingram.

'And we don't know if he's the only one,' the farmer said, nodding towards Fanducci's body. 'When they find out this one's dead they might send others after us.' He slipped the I.D. card into his jacket pocket and turned to pick up the nearby Magnum. The pistol felt heavy in his fist and he passed it to Jo.

'Have you ever used one of these things?' he asked.

'I'll learn,' she told him.

The farmer put one hand to his throbbing shoulder.

'We've wasted enough time,' he said. 'We must get inside Vanderburg Chemicals.'

'Not with your shoulder in that state,' she protested.

'We've got to,' he snapped.

There was a long silence, their eyes locked, neither flinching.

'We've still got five or six hours before daybreak,' said Tyler.

Jo nodded slowly.

'Let's get you patched up first,' she said, wearily.

Outside, there was a whiplash crack of lightning and, in the momentary brilliance, they both glimpsed figures moving in the blackness beyond – writhing and moving like monstrous automatons.

And then there was only darkness again.

Thirty-three

Tyler lay on the bed, watching as Jo cut away his bloodied shirt with a pair of scissors. As she pulled at the gore-stiffened material it stuck to the ragged edges of the wound and pulled some tiny slivers of skin away with it. The farmer winced.

'Sorry,' said Jo, picking up the wet towel which lay beside her. She cleaned the rust-coloured area around the bullet hole, asking Tyler to lean forward while she attended to the exit hole which was slightly larger than her thumb. 'You were lucky,' she told him. 'The bullet couldn't have hit you direct, it must have ricocheted. The deflection took most of the power out of it otherwise it would have taken your arm off.' She wiped away the blood from the exit wound, apologizing once again as she accidentally pulled away a piece of ragged flesh. 'I don't think there's anything broken, it went clean through.'

He worked it around tentatively, making a fist of his right hand as he did so.

'How does it feel?' she asked.

'Sore,' he told her.

They looked into each other's eyes for long moments, then Jo wadded up a clean handkerchief and pressed it to the wound. She did the same at the back, securing the makeshift dressing with lengths of sheet which she had taken from the bed in their room. It lay, torn up, in the corner.

'Tie it tight,' the farmer told her.

When she'd finished he lay back again, one large hand reaching for hers. She looked tired, her mascara had run in places, her hair, normally so lustrous, was matted with blood and her jeans were spattered with dried gore.

She looked down at herself and sighed.

'I feel like shit,' she said. 'I'm going to take a shower.'

He nodded, watching as she walked wearily to the bathroom. Tyler could hear the sputter as the water began to flow from the shower spray. He picked up the .357 which lay beside him and inspected the weapon before finally laying it on the bedside table. The shotgun, together with a dozen or so cartridges, lay beside the bed.

The farmer looked at the I.D. card which bore Fanducci's name and photo and also that red and silver

VC. Their suspicions about Vanderburg Chemicals had obviously been right and also, doubtless, their fears about Geoffrey Anderson. If someone at the chemical plant was willing to kill *them* then Anderson had most probably suffered the ultimate fate. Was the secret of the feed *that* important? Important enough to kill for? Obviously it was, he reasoned. And how many of the townspeople had died or were dying? How many of the people he had known all his life had been transformed into savages by the effects of the contaminated feed? In the past few weeks Tyler had seen his entire world crumble.

He dropped the card and swung himself off the bed, padding across to the door of the bathroom.

Jo had not bothered to pull the shower curtain and the farmer ran appreciative eyes over her tanned body as she stood naked beneath the spurting shower. He watched as she soaped her hands, running them over her breasts and neck, shaking her head to allow the water to run through her hair.

'You're a very beautiful woman,' he said.

Jo turned quickly.

'You scared me,' she said, not attempting to hide herself. 'I didn't know you were standing there.'

'Sorry,' he said, smiling.

She turned off the shower spray and stepped out onto the mat, water dripping from her hair. Tyler noticed how it glistened invitingly on the tightly curled mound beneath her navel. He walked across to her and pulled her close to him, feeling the water on his skin.

Jo shuddered in his arms, her hands fumbling with his trousers which she hurriedly unfastened. Tyler stepped out of them and they stood naked, facing each other, her left hand gently squeezing his penis. It began to stiffen. They kissed and she felt his hands stroking the wet skin of her back, pausing there a second before gliding to her breasts. He kneaded the firm globes,

203

bending his head towards her nipples which had risen to red peaks. She gasped as she felt his tongue licking around thém, flicking water away in the process.

She knelt slowly, her hand still on his hard shaft and Tyler ran his hands through the silky slickness of her wet hair. She took one testicle in her mouth and sucked gently before transferring her attention to the other one, then she moved back slightly, fastening her lips around the bulging purple head of his organ.

Her own fluid was flowing now, mingling with the water from the shower and she slid one hand between her own legs as she sucked Tyler's penis, teasing the nub of her clitoris until it too stiffened and grew erect.

Jo stood up slowly, a strand of saliva dripping from the end of Tyler's organ. He felt her hard nipples brush his belly and then his chest as she straightened up and his hand replaced hers in that most delicate area between her legs. She felt only liquid pleasure there, her excitement growing stronger as he pushed two fingers inside her.

Jo pressed her pelvis hard against him, bucking hard on those fingers which probed so deeply. She slipped one leg around his, resting herself on the hard muscle of his thigh, grinding herself against it.

He realized what she was doing and bent his knee slightly, gripping her buttocks in order to add to her movements. The water from the shower dripped onto his thigh but it was her warm moistness which lathered his flesh. Her breathing became more rapid, her movements more frenetic and Tyler held her as tight as he could.

He slid one more finger into her slippery cleft, running the index finger of his other hand over the smooth skin of her back.

She pressed her head against his chest and speeded up her movements, her entire body shaking as the orgasm swept through her. Tyler gripped her tight, still moving his fingers inside her, pressing his thumb to her clitoris, prolonging the moment of pleasure for her until she cried out huskily. She muttered something under her breath and kissed him, now moving slowly against his hard thigh. Finally she pulled free, her face flushed, the upper part of her body glowing pink.

Immediately she began stroking his throbbing penis, tracing the outline of the bulging veins with her long nail. She raised herself onto her toes, allowing him to seek and then find the entrance to her burning sex with the head of his organ. He slid into her and she stepped back, taking the weight against one wall as he moved inside her and, from deep within, she felt that wonderful glow blazing in every fibre of her body.

Their mouths locked, tongues entwining, stirring the warm wetness within.

Tyler gripped her waist and began to thrust urgently. As he reached his climax, Jo felt renewed contractions between her legs and, for the second time, she was enveloped by the most powerful of physical explosions.

They clung to each other for a long moment, then Tyler gently withdrew.

Jo picked up a towel which was lying nearby and began to dry herself.

They both changed into fresh clothes, Tyler slipping on a black shirt, grunting in pain as he pulled it over the makeshift bandage. He clenched his fist, relieved that the numbness and burning sensation had diminished considerably. Then, he checked that the guns were loaded.

Jo glanced at her watch.

'Ready?' he asked.

She nodded.

They had four hours of darkness to hide them. The drive to Vanderburg Chemicals would take them about fifteen minutes.

Thirty-four

The grass was wet beneath his feet and, more than once, Tyler almost slipped over. Hs shot out a hand to steady himself, grasping a nearby tree branch. The wire cutters fell from his belt and he cursed under his breath.

'It's OK,' Jo whispered, stooping before him. 'I've got them.'

She handed the implement back to the farmer who stuck it in his jacket pocket along with the handful of large crocodile clips he'd taken from an electrical store near the centre of Wakely. Jo held a long coil of insulated wire which came from the same source.

They paused, hidden by the enveloping darkness, gazing at the tall wire fence which confronted them. Every fifty yards there were large spotlamps but between these radiant oases the desert of night was impenetrable. Tyler looked to his right and left then, satisfied that nothing was moving, he scuttled towards the fence. Forced to lie on his belly, he could feel the wetness soaking through his clothes. Jo crouched beside him and hastily wound lengths of wire around the ends of the crocodile clips, attaching the mouths to the fence. Then she watched as he slid the wire cutters from his pocket and fastened the sharp jaws on the fence between the crocodile clips.

The wire was thick and it took all of Tyler's considerable strength to cut through it. Fresh pain began to gnaw at his shoulder but he continued with his task, cutting a hole big enough for them to crawl through. If there had been an alarm attached, it had not been activated. Perhaps, Tyler thought, the knowledge that over 60,000 volts coursed through the protective barrier was deterrent enough for most intruders. Not so for Jo and himself.

He finished cutting and wriggled through, turning

on his stomach to help Jo. They both straightened up, Jo brushing the moisture from her clothes as best she could. Tyler stuck the wire cutters back in his belt, his hand brushing against the .357 as he did. The weapon was fully loaded although he doubted his ability to use it if the need arose. Shotguns were one thing, high-powered pistols another.

They both squinted through the gloom, their eyes picking out the massive bulk of the Vanderburg buildings about two hundred yards ahead of them. The ground between them and the buildings was open and Tyler was aware of the spotlights. He ducked low, pulling Jo down with him and, hunched over, they ran as fast as they were able.

They were half-way towards the nearest building when they heard the dog bark.

As if at a given signal, both of them froze.

The barking was close, perhaps fifty or sixty yards to their right. It was coming from the direction of the fence.

Beneath the light from one of the lamps, a Security guard, clad in the familiar Vanderburg dark blue, stood and lit a cigarette. With his other hand he kept a firm hold on the leash of a large black Alsatian. The animal was turned towards Jo and Tyler, its loud barks splitting the stillness.

The guard seemed to pay it no heed. He jerked on the lead and wandered on, casting just a cursory glance in their direction.

The noise the dog was making gradually receded.

'Come on,' Tyler whispered and they continued their sprint, finally coming to a halt against a cold stone wall.

Both stood panting for long seconds, surveying the scene before them.

The gigantic bulk of the main building faced them across a tarmac area about eighty feet wide. There were lights on in one or two of the rooms but most merely reflected the dull glint of the stars above. The main entrance beckoned but Tyler hesitated, sucking in a troubled breath as he saw two Security men walk across the tarmac, one of them holding a Dobermann pinscher by a thick chain. The men were chatting happily, oblivious of the two onlookers.

Jo swallowed hard, frowning when she saw them come to a halt outside the main doors.

'Shit,' she murmured. 'What now?'

Tyler didn't answer, his gaze was fixed on the men and the dog which, he noticed, had pricked up its ears and was looking back and forth. He motioned for Jo to move back further into the shadows.

The dog looked in their direction, froze for a moment, then barked loudly three times.

The farmer slid the sheath knife from its leather scabbard and gripped the handle tightly.

'Have they seen us?' Jo whispered, unable to see the Security men from where she was.

'I don't know,' Tyler answered but he had his suspicions.

The dog continued to bark, straining hard on its chain now. The guard who held it, a tall thin individual, bent and released it and, immediately, the dog bounded towards Tyler and Jo.

'Don't make a sound,' said Tyler, crouching down as the dog drew nearer. He held the knife steady and waited.

The Dobermann came hurtling around the corner of the building, its nose full of scent, but it skidded to a temporary halt in the darkness. The few seconds' respite was all Tyler needed. He threw himself at the animal, raking the knife down its side until it struck bone. He grabbed for its muzzle, trying to avoid the sharp teeth and also to shut the creature up. He succeeded in neither task.

Strong jaws clamped around his forearm for fleeting

moments and, as he struck upwards with the knife a second time, the Dobermann let out a high-pitched wail.

Tyler pushed the lifeless carcass aside, his ears detecting the sound of running feet as the Security men approached.

They, like the dog, came around the corner and paused as they were met by a solid wall of blackness.

The farmer caught the first one across the forehead with the wire cutters, the blow felling him immediately. The second man turned to run but Tyler ran after him, kicking his legs away. The man went down heavily on the tarmac, cracking his head on the wet surface. Yet still he tried to rise and the farmer was forced to drive a boot into the man's face to immobilize him completely. The guard flopped onto his back like a beached fish, blood running from his shattered nose.

'Search them,' said Jo, moving across to the prone bodies, rummaging through their pockets. She found a bunch of keys in the breast pocket of the taller man.

'C-5 report.'

The metallic voice cut through the stillness like a razor blade.

'C-5.'

There was a two-way radio lying nearby.

'Bill, if you're having a piss just say so will you?'

Tyler looked first at Jo and then at the two-way.

'C-5 come in,' the voice demanded. 'Bill, for fuck's sake, what are you playing at?'

Tyler picked up the hand-set.

'C-5' he said, praying that the static on the set would be sufficient to disguise his voice.

'What the bloody hell are you doing down there? Why didn't you answer?' the voice demanded.

'Sorry,' Tyler said, cautiously.

'Is your sector clear?' the voice asked.

'Yes.'

There was a long silence. Jo and Tyler exchanged worried glances.

'Sector is clear,' Tyler repeated, trying to hide the tension in his voice.

There was a harsh chuckle.

'You've been humping that fucking dog again haven't you?' the voice said, merrily.

Tyler gripped the set tightly.

'Sector is clear,' he repeated.

'Yeah, right, I heard you first time. Check back in an hour.' The two-way went dead.

The farmer breathed an audible sigh of relief and wiped his forehead with the back of his hand. Taking another look at the motionless guards, he and Jo crept through the shadows towards the main building.

The massive edifice towered above them, a mass of concrete and glass which looked as impregnable as a fortress. Tyler wondered how they were going to get inside. The entrances, he reasoned, would be alarmed. They couldn't break in without alerting every guard on the site. He glanced behind him. The two unconscious men weren't going to stay out forever. He and Jo didn't have much time.

The farmer reached for the small two-way which he'd slipped into his pocket. He held it before him for a second, his finger poised over the 'ON' button.

'What the hell are you doing, Vic?' Jo gaped, watching as he switched it on.

He waved a hand for her to be quiet.

'C-5,' he said.

Jo shook her head, glancing around anxiously.

The radio crackled.

'C-5' Tyler repeated. 'I have a request.'

'Come in, C-5,' said the metallic voice.

Tyler swallowed hard.

'Intruder sighted,' he said.

'Where?' the voice demanded.

'Main building. Request permission to search.'

'Do you need any help?'

'No,' said the farmer, perhaps a little too quickly.

The radio went silent again.

'Come in,' he said.

Silence.

A bead of perspiration popped onto his forehead.

'Come in,' he said again.

'The alarms are off,' the voice told him. 'Report back immediately if you find anyone.'

He flicked the set off and proceeded towards the main door, followed by Jo. They found that the doors opened easily. Both of them walked into the reception area of Vanderburg Chemicals. The shadows swallowed them up. Jo could feel her heart beating faster as they moved quickly but quietly towards one of the many corridors which grew, spoke-like, from the central hub of the main reception.

'Where do we start?' whispered Tyler, exasperatedly.

'What about the laboratories?' Jo offered.

He nodded.

'If we can find them.'

They walked the length of the corridor, each door which faced them was firmly locked. Tyler suggested searching the first floor. They found the stairs and began ascending, stepping as lightly as possible on the cold stone.

'C-5 report.'

The metallic voice sounded thunderous in the silence of the stair-well.

Tyler grabbed for the hand-set and switched it on.

'C-5, any sign of intruder?'

'No,' said the farmer.

'Check the second floor, if any one *is* inside make sure you stop them before they get to E-1.'

'E-1?' Tyler sounded vague.

Jo shot him an anxious glance, then started up the

stairs to the second floor. He tried to hold her back but she was already disappearing through a set of fire doors at the top of the steps. He followed and found himself in a corridor, at the far end there was a large oak door. Jo was in the process of turning the handle.

'Stop them reaching E-1,' the voice repeated.

'Check,' Tyler snapped.

'I'm going to send more units to help you.'

'No,' the farmer blurted.

There was an ominous silence.

'C-5 identify. Number and code name.'

Jo pushed open the door of the room.

The radio rasped in Tyler's hand again.

'Identify. Number and code name.'

He held the hand-set for long seconds, then hurled it to one side. It smashed against the wall.

'Jo, come on, we've got to get out,' he yelled but she was gazing around the room in amazement.

Computer terminals, filing cabinets and all manner of blue-prints vied for space in the large room which was completely windowless. Thick ring binders were stacked as high as a man in places where they wouldn't fit on the wooden shelves. There were half a dozen large oak desks in the room too. Jo crossed to one of the manilla files laid out on the nearest desk and flipped it open:

BIO-SYNTHETIC MUTATION

She read the top sheet to herself, reaching for another file.

'Jo, for God's sake, this place is going to be swarming with Security men in a minute,' Tyler told her.

'But Vic, it's here,' she said, grabbing up another file headed:

PROTEIN CONSTRUCTION

'Everything we need is here.'

'Come on,' he snarled, gripping her arm, pulling her forcibly from the room.

They ran back down the stairs, the far off sounds of dogs drawing nearer.

'Not the front way,' said Tyler as they reached the reception. He pushed her towards another corridor which ran off to the right. They hurtled along it, the farmer throwing his weight against a flimsy wooden door which barred their way. The impact nearly tore it from the hinges and, as he dashed through, Tyler was thankful that he had hit it with his good shoulder. The wound in his other one was throbbing anyway.

They reached a window and he flung it open. Moist air rushed in and Tyler helped Jo through, then scrambled after her.

The Security men were in the reception by now and two of them let their dogs loose. Confused by the mixture of scents, one ran up the stairs, the other scampered towards the room where the intruders had been.

Outside, Tyler and Jo jumped to the ground, Jo falling on the slick surface but the farmer hauled her upright and they were running again. He prayed that they would make it to the fence.

Lights were beginning to flash on inside the main Vanderburg building now and, from somewhere in the darkness, they heard a siren, its strident wailing filling their ears.

Jo was gasping for breath but she found new strength as she saw the fence drawing closer. Tyler urged her on, glancing around to see dark uniformed men following them. He made sure that she scrambled through the hole in the fence then crawled after her. They got to their feet and rushed into the trees, welcomed by the enveloping darkness. Not until they reached the landrover did they stop running. Tyler wrenched open the door and leapt behind the wheel, starting the engine. Jo slumped into the passenger seat, thrown back as Tyler stepped hard on the accelerator and the vehicle shot forward like some kind of projectile. He spun the wheel, guiding it onto the road back into Wakely, glancing in the rear-view mirror to see if anyone was following.

They weren't.

'Vic, it was there in those files,' Jo gasped, trying to catch her breath. 'I'm sure that was the proof we needed.'

He nodded.

'The Vanderburg scientists *must* have conducted tests. They *knew* the feed was harmful but they went ahead with the project anyway,' she said.

Tyler didn't ease his foot off the pedal, not even when the needle on the speedometer touched sixty.

'Vic, are you listening to me?' she demanded. 'What are we going to do?'

'What we should have done in the first place,' he said. 'Tomorrow morning we'll search the town, see if there's anyone else unaffected by the virus. Then, we'll get out. Leave Wakely.'

Jo nodded.

'Then we'll call every fucking newspaper and TV station we can get hold of and see what they make of Vanderburg's little game.' There was a hard edge to his voice.

Jo sat back in her seat and closed her eyes. She knew she should sleep, she needed to but her mind was too full of ideas, overflowing with thoughts. And fears?

She opened her eyes again and gazed out into the night.

In two hours it would be daylight.

Thirty-five

'Shouldn't we bury them?'

Jo ran a distasteful eye over the pile of corpses which faced her. She had helped Tyler drag them out into the car park of the hotel earlier, now she stood gazing at the untidy heap of bodies. Fanducci's gutted corpse lay face down on top of the others. There were six, counting his.

'We can't take any chances,' said Tyler, reaching for the can of petrol which he'd found amongst many in a shed to the rear of the hotel. There was a cellar beneath, approachable also by a service entrance inside the hotel itself. While he'd been down there he'd discovered a great deal of canned and dried food, hundreds of bottles of wine and a small generator which, he guessed, acted as a source of auxiliary power should anything happen to the mains supply. He began to splash the amber liquid over the corpses.

'We've got to destroy any traces of the bacteria,' he told her, the smell of petrol mingling with that of putrescent flesh. 'If Hawley said it lived on in the dead animals there's every reason to believe it'll live on in the victims.'

Jo shivered, despite the fact that she wore a thick sweatshirt. The watery sun provided little warmth and the early morning dew still lay like a glistening cowl over the ground.

It was 9.17 a.m.

Tyler emptied the last of the petrol over the bodies, then tossed the can onto the make-shift pyre with them. He stepped back, striking a match. For long seconds he hesitated, the sightless eyes of Mark Bates pinning him in a reproachful stare, then the farmer tossed the match onto the pile of corpses.

There was a loud whump as the petrol went up, the

215

flames eagerly devouring the still forms. Like a collection of obscene effigies on Guy Fawkes night they blazed, the acrid stench of scorched flesh now filling the air, rising with the thick black plume of smoke which billowed from the mound.

Tyler touched his right shoulder, rotating it slightly to remove some of the stiffness. He felt Jo's hand grasp his and he looked at her.

'Are you all right?' he asked.

She nodded, her eyes still fixed on the burning pile of cadavers.

They watched the greedy flames for a moment longer, then turned and headed back to the landrover. They both climbed in, Tyler checking the three shotguns which lay in the back of the vehicle. He had the .357 jammed into his belt.

They looked at one another and there was steel in that gaze. Tyler started the engine.

The streets of Wakely were deserted, the sound of the landrover's engine seeming louder than usual in the stillness. Tyler drove slowly, looking to both sides as well as ahead, not even sure what he was looking for.

'Vic, over there.'

Jo's shout startled him and he stepped hard on the brake. She was pointing at something to the left of them. They both got out of the landrover, Tyler picking up the Franchi as he did so. He left the engine idling and walked slowly across to the shapeless thing which was hunched in the nearby shop doorway.

It was a man. He was squatting, knees drawn up to hide his bowed head, arms dangling limply on either side of him.

Jo looked first at the man and then at Tyler who had not taken his eyes from the motionless figure. He approached within five feet, ensuring that Jo stayed behind him.

The man did not move.

The farmer worked the pump action of the shotgun, chambering a round. He took a step closer and prodded the man with the end of the barrel, one finger hooked around it. Just in case.

The body toppled sideways, face to the sky.

His throat had been cut.

There were three or four ragged tears in the skin, each about the size of a child's fist. Lying close by was a broken bottle, its razor sharp edges stained with dark fluid. And yet, around the body itself, despite the savagery of the cuts, there was little or no blood. Only the front of the man's shirt was stained crimson.

Tyler remarked on it to Jo.

'Maybe the rain washed it away,' she suggested.

Tyler didn't speak. He looked closely at the gaping wounds, noticing a darker, purplish discoloration around them. Like bruising. He stood up.

'Why is there no blood?' he pondered aloud.

Tyler and Jo walked back to the landrover and he drove off, keeping to a steady fifteen as they cruised the deserted streets.

'Maybe all the unaffected people have already left,' Jo suggested.

Tyler shook his head.

'The bloke back there with his throat cut, he wasn't infected. There must be others. Not everyone eats red meat.'

'So where are they?' Jo wanted to know.

'They're probably frightened.'

'I know the feeling,' she muttered.

There were more bodies.

Two of them lay prone in the middle of the road. A man and a small child. The man had been stabbed, his ripped shirt revealing numerous wounds in his chest and stomach.

The child, a boy about five, had been bludgeoned to

death. His head was a shattered ruin. There were pieces of skin and fragments of bone close by, indicating that he'd been killed by having his head slammed repeatedly into the tarmac of the road.

Once again, there was a noticeable lack of blood around the bodies and also, Tyler noticed, the discoloration which tinged the extremities of each wound.

Neither victim was diseased.

Flies swarmed frenziedly over both corpses, entering each orifice eagerly and the farmer watched in disgust as two of them crawled over the child's blackened tongue.

As before he remarked on the lack of blood.

'What are you thinking, Vic?' asked the American.

'I don't know what I'm thinking,' he said. 'If I told you you'd probably laugh.'

'Try me.'

'From what I saw of those infected people last night and what we've found today, I think this disease forces its victims to drink blood.'

He waited for her to say something but she didn't.

'With wounds like these,' he indicated the stabbed man, 'there'd be blood all over the place, the same as that other bloke we found. He'd bleed for ages with a cut throat. There wasn't enough rain last night to wash *that* much blood away.'

'The piglets at the cattle market,' said Jo, 'they attacked the sow. They could have been trying to drink her blood. What we thought was cannibalism was blood-lust.'

There was a long silence.

'Vampires,' Jo murmured, softly.

Tyler didn't hear her. His eyes were fixed on the wounds on the dead man's torso but, more particularly, on the dark areas around the gashes. The flesh looked as if it had been sucked; the wound milked of its crimson fluid by hungry mouths. The very thought disgusted him.

They both stood there looking at the bodies for a moment longer, then Tyler turned and headed back to the landrover.

Jo hesitated, looking first at the corpses and then at the windows of the shops which surrounded them. She wondered what was waiting inside.

The thought made her shudder and she hurried back to the waiting vehicle.

'Let's try Dan Hawley,' said Tyler.

Jo counted half a dozen more bodies on the drive to the vet's surgery. Tyler merely slowed the landrover down as they passed. Neither of them bothered to get out and inspect the corpses.

The farmer finally brought the vehicle to a halt in Hawley's driveway. He clambered down, taking care to bring the shotgun with him, looking up at the drawn curtains of the building as he approached it. Jo was close beside him, her heels clicking noisily on the concrete approach.

Tyler knocked on the door, a little surprised when it swung open at the first impact. He held the shotgun across his chest and stepped into the reception. The curtains downstairs were open, the weak sun lighting their way as they moved cautiously into the surgery itself.

'Dan,' Tyler called, his voice echoing off the white walls.

There was no answer.

Jo paused in the reception and picked up the phone. It was dead. Not even the hiss of static on the line.

Tyler nudged open the surgery door and found that the blinds were down, the room having been plunged into stifling gloom.

He muttered under his breath as he surveyed the mess before him.

The surgery had been wrecked. Instrument trolleys were turned over, specimen jars smashed, filing cabinets upended. Glass crunched beneath his boots as he walked further into the dusky room. The pungent odour of formaldehyde was strong in the air. Scalpels, probes, saws and all manner of other instruments lay on the floor, combining with ripped and discarded pieces of paper to form a chaotic jigsaw of destruction.

Jo joined him in the room, her eyes widening in shocked surprise. While Tyler moved around the surgery, the American opened the door which led through from the main room into the living quarters beyond.

She found herself in a hallway which, in turn, led through into a spacious living room.

The scene in there was the same. The sofa was upended, a large bookcase had been pulled over, spilling its load on the carpet. Even a fish tank, once a proud possession, had been torn from its base and hurled across the room. There were pieces of broken glass everywhere and, amidst the shattered crystal and tiny stones, lay the stiffened bodies of tropical fish. The room smelt damp. Jo passed through it into a kitchen and from there to the stairs.

She climbed them cautiously, ears alert for the slightest sound of movement. She reached the dim landing and headed for the door closest to her.

She paused in the doorway.

The room had been devastated. As with those downstairs, it looked as if someone had systematically gone through the house and destroyed everything they could lay their hands on. Jo moved cautiously into the room, noticing that several china figures lay smashed at her feet. She bent to inspect one.

Behind her, the door of the wardrobe opened slightly.

Jo held the tiny figure in her hand, shaking her head gently. It seemed as if nothing had escaped the fury.

The hinges on the wardrobe door creaked loudly and Jo spun round.

She saw the knife as it was lifted high above her.

When he heard the scream, Tyler burst from the surgery, not even pausing in the wrecked sitting room. He blundered up the stairs, shotgun held at the ready.

The sight which met him caused him to freeze.

Jo was sitting on the edge of the bed and, beside her, sobbing uncontrollably, was Mandy Potter. She still held the long knife in her shaking hand.

'What happened?' Tyler asked, softly, lowering the gun.

Mandy looked up to see him. She dropped the knife, using both hands to wipe away the tears which were streaming down her cheeks.

'Mandy,' he said. 'The surgery. Did Dan do that? Did he wreck the place?'

Mandy nodded.

'He tried to kill me,' she blubbered, revealing several deep indentations near the top of her arm. They looked like claw marks. Her blouse was ripped and there were flecks of blood on it. Her throat too bore scratches and there was a nasty gash on her left cheek.

'I stabbed him,' she said, her voice a harsh whisper. 'I don't know if I killed him. He ran away. She began to cry once more and Jo slipped a comforting arm around her shoulder. 'He was like an animal. Mad.'

They stood over her for long moments, Tyler watching as she removed her glasses and wiped them on the sheet.

'I'm sorry,' she said, holding up the knife. 'I could have killed you.'

'I'd have done the same thing,' said Jo, smiling.

'We've got to leave here, Mandy,' said Tyler. 'Will you be all right?'

'You're not leaving me alone,' she gasped.

He shook his head.

'I mean all of us, we've got to leave Wakely. Now.'

Mandy nodded.

While they waited downstairs, she cleaned herself up and changed into some fresh clothes. When she joined them in the hall way she looked more assured. Stronger.

'I'm OK,' she said, sniffing slightly.

The three of them walked out, back into the welcoming glow of the sunlight.

'What's happening?' asked Mandy as they climbed into the landrover. 'First the animals, now the people?'

Jo explained briefly what was going on. Mandy sat in silence, not even speaking when she'd finished. She just nodded.

'Are we the only ones left?' she asked, finally.

'That's what we've been trying to find out,' said Tyler. 'So far you're the only uncontaminated person we've found alive. The others have been killed.'

He swung the landrover around a corner, narrowly avoiding the body of a young woman which lay by the kerb.

Mandy looked briefly at it, then closed her eyes.

'Where are we going?' she asked.

'To the nearest big city,' Tyler informed her. 'We've got to let people outside Wakely know what's going on. Someone's got to stop it before it spreads.'

The streets seemed to crowd in on them as they drove, the houses glowering down like watching gargoyles, the sun reflecting off windows which glinted like hundreds of blind eyes.

'There,' shouted Jo, pointing towards a small group of shops nearby.

Tyler slammed on the brakes, the vehicle skidding slightly.

'What is it?' he asked.

'I saw something move in one of those buildings,' said Jo.

Tyler reached for one of the shotguns, his hand closing around the Franchi.

Four buildings confronted them: a small supermarket, a newsagent's, a confectioner's and a butcher's shop.

'Stay here,' Tyler said to Mandy. He and Jo climbed out of the landrover and approached the supermarket. The doors were closed but when Tyler struck at them with the butt of the shotgun they swung open. No alarms went off. Total silence prevailed.

It was relatively light inside the supermarket, the sun cast bright rays through the large windows at the front of the building.

Jo wrinkled her nose. The place smelt of bad food. The fridges were off and some of the frozen produce had begun to rot, as had the fresh vegetables. She passed a pile of apples which were now brown and putrescent. Flies swarmed hungrily over them.

There was a large storeroom at the back of the building but they found it empty. Tyler stood in the middle of the stacked boxes and cans of food and shook his head.

'I know I saw something,' said Jo before he could speak. 'Maybe whoever it was is afraid to come out.'

'Let's try the other buildings,' he said.

The newsagent's was empty. So was the confectioner's.

They moved on to the butcher's.

'There has to be someone here, I know I saw them,' Jo insisted. He nodded and pushed the door.

It was locked.

Without hesitation, the farmer put his weight against the glass and wood partition and drove his shoulder into it. The door flew open, the glass rattling in the frame as it crashed back on its hinges. The blinds were down so Tyler reached for the nearby light switch, waiting until the fluorescents overhead had sputtered into life before walking inside the shop. Both of them moved cautiously, having learnt to fear darkened rooms over the last few days. Now the only sound was the intermittent clicking of Jo's heels on the wooden floor and the steady hum of a fan. It must, Tyler assumed, be on the same circuit as the lights.

The shop itself was large, the two long glass counters forming an 'L' shape. The counters were full of display trays bearing different types of meat. Jo shuddered involuntarily as she looked at the array of beef, lamb and offal, thinking how much damage food like that had done to the residents of Wakely. Once more, there was a smell of decay, a sickly sweet odour which made her wince. Maggots writhed frenziedly on a piece of rotten steak.

Tyler walked behind the counter, touching a couple of discarded knives as he passed a large wooden chopping board. It was stained darkly with blood.

At the back of the shop was the freezer, a large room almost as big as the shop itself, where the carcasses of countless animals hung from meat hooks. There were also several large white fridges at the far end of the room and another work bench where the joints were actually prepared.

There was a man lying on the wooden surface.

His arms were dangling limply from either side of the bench and there was a meat cleaver embedded in his chest. His throat had been sliced open – probably, Tyler thought, with the large knife which lay on the floor beneath him. Apart from a small puddle of frozen blood around the man's head, there was little of the crimson fluid to be found.

'Vic, look,' Jo whispered, pointing to one of the fridges.

Several long slicks of blood had dribbled from the top of one fridge, freezing half-way down.

Tyler crossed to it and hooked two fingers under the lid, the shotgun lowered.

He flipped it open.

The fridge was empty.

Jo shrugged and opened the next one.

The man inside seemed to sit up and grab her as if he possessed some uncanny form of radar. He snatched handfuls of her hair in his clawed hands and pulled her towards him.

Jo shrieked, trying to pull away from the madman's grasp, but she felt him rising.

Tyler dare not use the shotgun for fear of hitting Jo. He could only watch for agonizing seconds as the butcher rose from the fridge and grabbed Jo around the throat. She struck out at him with one hand, her nails raking his dry flesh. Tyler ran at the man and reached for his face, clawing at his eyes. He punched hard and felt brittle bone splinter under the impact but the man merely hurled Jo to one side and turned his full attention to Tyler. It was then that the farmer noticed his adversary held a meat hook.

Jo, thrown by the butcher, had crashed into the nearby bacon slicer which promptly burst into life, its circular blade spinning at over 500 revolutions a minute. She looked up, the droning sound loud in her ears. The diseased man was out of the fridge now, between Tyler and the discarded shotgun. He swung the meat hook in a vicious arc, missing the farmer by inches. Tyler leapt to one side, trying to keep the butcher away from Jo who was still dazed after her fall.

The drone of the moving bacon slicer filled the room, covering the low raspings which the diseased man made as he came at Tyler once more.

225

The farmer avoided another swipe of the hook, this time managing to grab the meat cleaver. He tore it free of the corpse and brandished it before him. The butcher was grinning, thick streamers of saliva dripping from his mouth as he advanced on the farmer. The hook lashed forward again, this time burying itself in a nearby carcass of meat. Tyler took his chance and brought the cleaver down with bone crushing force.

His aim was good. The vicious blade thudded into the butcher's shoulder, shattering the scapula, scything through an inch or two of muscle. Blood burst from the wound and the injured man backed off.

It was his groping hands that found the shotgun.

Tyler realized that he must act fast. He hurled himself headlong at the madman, knocking him backwards. The gun clattered to the floor and the two of them toppled over. The butcher roared in pain and anger and grabbed Tyler's head between his huge hands, pressing inward. The farmer struck out wildly in an attempt to free himself but the butcher, despite the wound in his arm, was an enormously powerful man and, inch by inch, Tyler felt himself being pushed back.

The man was grinning insanely and, in a moment of panic, the farmer realized that the butcher was forcing his head towards the spinning blade of the bacon slicer.

Jo dragged herself upright moaning aloud as she saw what was about to happen to Tyler.

She looked around desperately for something to attack the butcher with and, she too, found the cleaver. Hefting it in both hands, she went at him.

Tyler gripped the big man's wrists, trying to prise them apart, attempting to relieve the pressure on his skull. It seemed merely a matter of whether his skull was crushed like an egg or his head sliced in two by the swiftly rotating blade. In a few seconds it would all be over. He could actually see the blade out of the corner of his eye.

226

Screaming in desperation, Jo struck out with the cleaver. It sank into the big man's back just below the nape of the neck. She dragged it free and struck again, this time lower. The swipe laid open his lumbar region and, through a haze of pain, Tyler saw blood begin to dribble from the butcher's mouth. His eyes rolled upward in their sockets and he released his pressure on the farmer's head.

Tyler scrambled clear, grabbing the big man by the hair, forcing his head downwards onto the spinning blade.

There was a sound like sharp nails on a blackboard as the bacon slicer shaved off a sizeable portion of the butcher's skull, exposing the sticky grey matter beneath. The large body bucked violently, blood gushing from the numerous wounds, then he rolled over, the blade of the bacon slicer taking off a chunk of his bottom jaw. He fell to the ground and lay still.

Tyler turned to see Jo standing motionless, the dripping cleaver still held firmly in her hands. She swallowed hard and looked at him, dropping the weapon as she saw the blood spilling out around the corpse at her feet.

He reached out and switched the machine off. Silence descended once more.

'Jo,' he said, softly.

'Yeah, I'm OK,' she told him.

She gazed at the body of the butcher for a moment longer then dropped the cleaver.

Tyler took her in his arms and held her tightly.

After a moment, they walked back out of the shop, leaving the two corpses.

'What happened in there?' asked Mandy.

Tyler told her, keeping details to a minimum.

It was Mandy who heard the far off roar of a car engine. The sound travelled easily in the silence and it didn't take any of them long to realise that it was coming from the centre of town. Without hesitation, Tyler leapt behind the wheel and brought the landrover full circle.

He stepped on the accelerator and drove back into the town centre.

Thirty-six

Tyler brought the landrover skidding to a halt opposite the hotel.

There was a silver-grey Capri outside, its engine idling. The driver's side door opened and a short, tubby man with brown hair and a thick moustache got out to confront Vic who held a shotgun firmly in his grip.

'Do you intend using that?' said the man, his voice as crisp as November frost.

'Who are you?' said Tyler.

'My name is Clayton. Doctor Alec Clayton,' he motioned to the woman who sat in the passenger seat. 'That's my wife, Maria. Might I ask who you are and what you're doing with a shotgun?'

'I'm Vic Tyler, I used to run a farm on the outskirts of Wakely.'

He introduced Jo and Mandy.

'You're not from Wakely,' Tyler said, looking the newcomer up and down.

'No, we've come from Sussex, we've been driving most of the night.'

'What do you want?' asked the farmer.

228

'I think that's my business, Mr Tyler,' Clayton told him.

'That's true, but we don't get too many strangers around here.'

The doctor's wife got out of the car.

'The town seems deserted,' she said. 'We didn't see a soul on our way through the streets.'

'Where is everyone?' Clayton echoed.

Tyler sighed.

'It's a long story,' he said.

'We've got time,' Clayton told him.

It took Jo and Tyler over an hour to explain what had been happening in Wakely, or at least as much as they knew. Mandy was lying down in the lounge of 'The King George', but the remaining quartet sat in the bar, with the destruction of the previous night still visible, speaking in subdued tones as if in reverence for a town which was no more.

When the whole story had been told Clayton merely sat gazing into the bottom of his wine glass, as if seeking inspiration.

'It's incredible,' he said, softly.

'That's one word for it,' said Tyler. The farmer studied the features of the newcomer. He guessed that Clayton was in his middle forties, his wife about the same age. She was a tall, willowy woman, elegantly dressed in a black two-piece.

'So,' Jo asked. 'Why are you in Wakely?'

'My brother, Edward, and his wife,' said Clayton. 'They live here. We hadn't heard anything from them for a couple of weeks. When I tried to phone two days ago there was a recorded message on the line saying that the number was unavailable.'

Jo looked at Tyler, anxiously.

'I tried two other numbers, friends of Edward, but every time it was the same. A recorded message saying those numbers were no longer in use.' He took a sip from his wine glass. 'I wondered what was wrong. I was worried about Edward anyway. He usually phones or writes regularly. Eventually, we decided to come and see for ourselves.'

'Have you been to his house?' asked Tyler.

Clayton nodded.

'There was no one there but all their belongings were in place. It was as if they'd just walked out. Or vanished.'

'Most people have left the town,' said Tyler. 'Those who haven't are either infected or . . .' He let the sentence trail off.

'Dead,' said Clayton.

There was a long silence. Clayton plucked at his moustache.

'A disease passed on by eating red meat,' he mused, 'it may be some form of food poisoning. You said the strain of bacteria which produced the virus was new, so it stands to reason the symptoms are going to manifest themselves in new ways as well.'

'Food poisoning my ass,' snapped Jo. 'What kind of virus do you know that turns people into vampires?'

Even Tyler looked at her in surprise.

'Vampires?' said Clayton, frowning.

'The contaminated people only come out at night, they have claws, they have large teeth. They drink blood.'

Clayton smiled humourlessly.

'So do haematophiliacs, Miss Ward,' he said.

Jo looked puzzled.

'Have you ever heard of Haigh? John George Haigh?' asked the doctor.

'I've heard the name,' Jo said.

'He was a murderer wasn't he?' added Tyler.

The doctor nodded.

'He was executed in 1949. His defence council tried

230

to claim he was insane because he confessed to drinking a wine glass full of his victim's blood before he dissolved them in acid. Haigh was haematophiliac. He was aroused by blood. There was a case similar to his in Germany in the 1920s. A man named Peter Kurten killed at least a dozen people and drank their blood. They nicknamed him "The Vampire of Düsseldorf".'

'Could the people in Wakely be suffering from the same disease as Haigh and Kurten?' asked Tyler.

'No. They were not physically ill. An obsession with blood whether it involves drinking it or not, is a psychological problem, not a pathological one,' Clayton explained. He looked at Jo. 'As for your theory about vampires, Miss Ward, they're creatures of folklore. What's happening in Wakely has nothing supernatural about it.'

'Well, whatever the answer is, we've all got to get out of here. Now.'

'I can't leave until I've found my brother,' Clayton protested.

'Doctor,' said Tyler, quietly, 'if your brother is still in Wakely then the chances are he's infected with this virus. I wouldn't advise you to hang around.'

'If my brother *is* infected then he needs help, all the people suffering need help. I can't just turn my back on them,' Clayton said.

'If you're staying you'll need this,' said Tyler, handing him the nickel-plated Purdey.

The doctor regarded the shotgun with horror, drawing back from it as if it were about to strike out at him.

'Take it,' urged Tyler.

'And what am I supposed to do with it?'

'Kill any of them that find you.'

'Tyler, for God's sake, they're human beings. They're ill.'

231

'They're animals,' snapped the farmer. 'Homicidal maniacs.'

'And your solution is to murder them?' said Clayton, sardonically. 'How many have you already killed?'

'You haven't seen what they're capable of,' growled the farmer.

'What in God's name gives you the right to act as judge, jury and executioner on these people?'

'If you want to find your brother, fine. But if he's infected then he's better off dead and he'll try and kill *you* if he can.'

'Is mindless violence your only answer?' asked the doctor.

Tyler turned to Jo.

'Get Mandy, we're leaving,' he said.

'Tyler,' Clayton shouted. 'We're talking about people, not cattle to be slaughtered. Is that what you'd do with every rabies victim? Shoot them?'

Jo returned a moment later with Mandy who looked on as the two men faced each other.

'You should come with us too,' said Tyler, looking at Maria Clayton.

'My wife's staying with me,' Clayton said, defiantly.

'Suit yourself,' Tyler said and tossed the shotgun onto a nearby chair. Then he turned his back on the doctor and, followed by Jo and Mandy, left the hotel.

They all climbed into the waiting landrover and the farmer started his engine.

The hotel gradually disappeared from view.

Thirty-seven

Tyler looked down at his watch and noticed that it was almost 5.00 p.m. The trees which flanked either side of the road from Wakely to Arkham crowded in like dark battalions, their leaves stirred by the strong breeze which had sprung up. Grey clouds scudded across the late afternoon sky and birds looked like black arrowheads against the dull background.

Dusk was approaching fast and, as if sensing this, Tyler put more pressure on the accelerator, coaxing extra speed from the landrover.

'What do you think will happen to the doctor and his wife?' said Mandy.

Tyler shrugged.

'If they stay inside they should be all right,' he said. 'But, they were warned.'

The road sloped upward sharply, simultaneously curving to the right.

'Jesus Christ,' gasped Tyler, slamming on the brakes.

The road block was about fifty yards from them and he could see uniformed men moving about near to a large truck which was parked on the verge. The men were wearing army uniforms.

As quickly and unobtrusively as possible, the farmer stuck the landrover into reverse and swung it off the road into an outcrop of trees. He let the engine idle and squinted towards the barrier.

'Troops?' said Jo, uncomprehendingly. 'To keep people out?'

Tyler shook his head.

'If they wanted to keep people out they'd have the road block facing the other way,' he said, cryptically.

'You mean it's to keep us *in*?' Jo whispered.

Tyler pointed to a dark-coated man who was talking

to a couple of the soldiers. The man wore the unmistakeable uniform of a Vanderburg Security guard.

'It looks like they're even more thorough than we thought,' said the farmer.

He turned his wheel and drove back the way they'd come, branching off at a junction, taking the road which led to Ducton.

'How the bloody hell did they manage to drag the army into this?' he pondered aloud.

Jo had no answer for him.

Mandy gazed out of the windows in bewilderment, watching as the trees sped past and, beyond them, rolling fields.

Clouds were gathering in greater abundance now.

It took them nearly thirty minutes to reach the Wakely–Ducton road.

The second road block consisted of two large trucks parked bumper to bumper. The troops who manned the obstruction could not have failed to see the approaching landrover but they merely stood, immobile, watching it. Tyler and the two women stared back. They sat there for what seemed like an eternity, then he swung the vehicle around once more, banging the wheel angrily as he drove away.

'We'll have to go across country,' he said and, with that, drove through a gorse hedge which fringed the road. The wheels of the landrover spun on the wet ground for a moment, then gained a grip and the heavy vehicle sped on, bumping over mounds and divots in the earth as it went.

About half a mile ahead of them was a range of low hills, the clouds already gathering ominously above them. Like dusky fingers, they crept over the hills, darkening the sky.

'They can't have covered everywhere,' Tyler said as the landrover reached the top of the hill. He peered through the windscreen and was relieved to see that there were no troops, no trucks. Nothing. A slight smile creased his face. It was clear.

'Next stop Arkham,' he said, triumphantly, and put his foot down. 'We can get back on the road in a while. There's a track about two miles further on, we'll by-pass the block.'

The vehicle moved easily through the mud and grass but after a minute or two Jo gripped his arm.

Ahead of them, clearly visible in the earth, were five or six freshly dug places each about a foot in diameter. Mandy, looking out of the back, noticed more behind them.

'Vic,' said Jo, pointing to the mounds. 'What are they?'

Tyler stepped on the brake and stiffened as if an electric current were being pumped through him. He gripped the wheel until his knuckles turned white.

'We're in a mine-field,' he said, softly.

Thirty-eight

'Sector One report.'

John Stark held the walkie-talkie in one hand and stood poised over the map of Wakely and its surrounding districts which was spread out on the desk before him.

The radio crackled loudly, then a voice came floating into the room.

'Sector One secure,' said the voice.

Stark nodded to himself and drew a large cross on

the black line which represented the Wakely-Arkham road.

'Sector Two report.'

He got a similar answer from the remaining four men he contacted and, at each affirmation, the American drew another cross at the appointed location on the map. The main roads which linked Wakely with the towns around it were blocked, the remainder of the town was ringed by troops.

They had arrived less than three hours ago. Stark didn't know what the troops had been told by their superiors. He didn't really give a shit anyway. The only thing that mattered was that they were there. Wakely was sealed off.

With each unit of troops was a Vanderburg Security man, just to keep an eye on things and, if the need arose, to quell any speculation as to why the troops were where they were. For all they knew, it was some kind of exercise. The only thing which might have puzzled them was the fact that they had been ordered to load up with live ammunition.

Stark wondered how many people *were* still alive in Wakely. He drew a large ring right around the town then dropped his pen. However many there were, they sure as hell weren't going anywhere.

He smiled and took out his hip-flask.

'How long do you propose to keep the troops there?' asked Sir Oliver Thorndike, who was also looking down at the map.

'Until this little mess is cleaned up,' Stark told him.

'And when is that likely to be?'

'What am I, a fortune teller? How the hell do I know?'

'You can't keep troops around the town indefinitely.'

Stark rounded on him.

'Don't tell me what I can or can't do, Thorndike,' rasped the American. 'I wasn't the one who put them

236

there, remember. It was *your* Government. I asked for assistance, they sent troops.'

'It seems rather like using a sledgehammer to swat a fly,' Thorndike said.

'Stop talking in riddles, dammit,' Stark snapped.

'You're after Tyler and the girl. Don't you think using a battalion of troops is being too . . .'

Stark cut him short.

'Look, there could be other people alive in that town. I don't want any of them leaving.'

There was a long silence.

'I'd like to know why the hell Fanducci isn't back yet,' Stark said, finally, unscrewing the cap on his hip-flask. He took a hefty swig.

There was a knock on the office door.

'Come in,' Stark called and looked up as Charles Muir entered.

The Scot had his pipe in his mouth but it wasn't lit. He was carrying a large clip-file.

'The reports on the new additive,' he said, passing the file to Thorndike. 'It should be ready for introduction into the feed in a day or two.'

Thorndike nodded and passed the file on to Stark.

'Any problems?' asked the American.

Muir shrugged.

'It's early days,' he said. 'There didn't seem to be any problems, at first, with the initial batch did there?'

Stark looked at him through eyes narrowed to steely slits.

'You were hired to work here, Muir, not to pass moral judgement on what you're doing.'

'Well,' said the Scot, 'let's see how much damage we can do with the second batch shall we?' His voice was heavy with sarcasm.

Stark slammed the file down.

'I've had it with your complaining,' he snapped. 'If you don't like the work then clear out.'

237

'Just walk away?' said Muir. 'You'd let me do that, knowing everything I know?' He smiled humourlessly and shook his head. 'I'm not that green *Mr* Stark.'

'Charles, the tests done this time were far more exhaustive,' said Thorndike, trying to put a wedge between the two men.

'I know,' snarled the Scot. 'I've just come from the laboratory. My God, have you seen what it's done to some of the specimens?' His own anger was now rising. 'This . . . "miracle feed" is lethal. How many more towns do you have to wipe out before you realize that, Stark?'

'Why don't you just get the fuck out of here,' Stark rasped. 'You came to work here in the beginning because you were offered a lot of money. What's wrong? Is your conscience starting to get at you? *You* helped wipe out that town, Muir.' Stark pointed an accusatory finger at him. 'You and the rest of you fucking geniuses.' He looked at Thorndike too. 'Well now *I'm* clearing up the mess you made. And I'm doing it my own way.'

A heavy silence filled the room, then the Scot turned and headed for the door.

Thorndike tried to call him back but Muir was already gone.

'He's your friend, right?' said Stark.

Thorndike nodded.

'Then keep him quiet or I swear to Christ he'll wind up like Geoffrey Anderson.'

'Does that apply to any dissenting voice?' asked Thorndike, warily.

Stark looked him in the eye.

'Yes,' he said flatly.

Charles Muir rode alone in the lift. He chewed agitatedly on the stem of his pipe and exhaled deeply.

Conflicting thoughts and emotions raged through him.

Anger. Frustration.

Guilt?

He knew Stark was right about his involvement in the Wakely catastrophe and that made it worse.

Guilt.

Hatred.

Charles Muir had taken all he was going to take from John Stark and Vanderburg Chemicals.

He chewed his pipe and wondered how best to approach the idea he had.

Thirty-nine

Mines.

The word blazed like a beacon in Tyler's mind. No wonder there had been no troops in this area. There had been no need for any. He sat behind the wheel of the landrover staring at the small mounds of earth all around them. They were spread quite well apart and the farmer shuddered as he thought how they had driven so easily and unsuspectingly into the trap. The thing was, how far into the mine-field were they?

'Get out,' he said, pushing open the passenger side door.

Jo hesitated.

'Get out, both of you,' Tyler said more forcefully. 'You'll have to guide me through it.'

Mandy sat immobile in the rear of the vehicle.

'Come on, Mandy. Now.' Tyler felt a bead of perspiration pop onto his forehead.

She shook her head.

'Move,' he bellowed, his voice a mixture of rage and desperation.

The shout seemed to galvanise her into action and, carefully, helped by Jo, she climbed out of the vehicle. The two women stood beside the landrover, looking at the ground around them, moving cautiously towards the back of the vehicle when Tyler instructed them. He pushed open his own door and peered over his shoulder.

Mandy was clinging to Jo's arm and, as they reached the back of the landrover, she slipped.

For interminable seconds, Jo thought she was going to be pulled off balance, only to topple onto one of the waiting booby traps, but she managed to steady herself and, gripping Mandy's hand, she picked her way backward. They both stepped over the mounds carefully.

'All right,' called Jo. 'Come back, slowly.'

Tyler stuck the landrover into reverse and pressed down as lightly as he could on the accelerator. The vehicle began to move.

He could see the first of the mines and tugged on the steering wheel to manoeuvre past it.

'Keep coming,' Jo called, herself backing off, careful to avoid the lethal traps. Mandy was shivering uncontrollably.

Above them, the sky was darkening. Clouds rolling across the heavens like fearful portents.

'There's one to your left,' Jo called, watching as Tyler adjusted the vehicle's path slightly.

He was breathing heavily now, his throat dry.

Mandy screamed as she slipped and fell.

Tyler slammed on his brakes and looked round.

Mandy was lying prone, her head less than a foot from the nearest mine. From where she lay she could see the two prongs which nudged up from beneath the earth. If anything should brush against those. . . .

Jo helped her up.

Tyler cursed under his breath and stuck the vehicle into reverse again, having put it in neutral when he heard the commotion from behind. Now, it edged back tortuously, guided by a combination of Jo's directions and his own careful driving.

'There's another to the left,' Jo called.

To avoid it, Tyler was forced to swing the landrover to his right, up a sharp incline.

His foot slipped from the accelerator and the engine stalled.

The landrover began sliding towards the mine.

'Vic,' screamed Jo.

The farmer grabbed his ignition key and twisted it madly.

The vehicle wouldn't start, it continued sliding inexorably towards the mine.

'Come on,' he shouted, turning it once more.

This time the engine fired and Tyler swung the land-rover back, praying that the ground was clear behind him.

Jo leapt to one side, pulling Mandy with her, both of them watching as the rear offside wheel missed a mine by a matter of inches. Tyler brought the vehicle to a halt and sat stiffly behind the wheel. He tried to swallow but couldn't.

Jo too found that her breath was coming in gasps.

Mandy could only stare, wide-eyed as the landrover continued its snail-like progress backwards.

'Another few yards and it's clear,' Jo told him.

At least she hoped it was. The ground behind her was free from any bumps or mounds. Unless, she thought, with a shudder, some other, more insidious form of booby-trap lay hidden beneath the dirt. One invisible until it was too late. It was at that point the thought struck her. The mines had been left conspicuous. As if they were waiting to be found. Silent warnings.

'Keep coming,' she called and Tyler finally reversed to safety.

He allowed his head to sag forward onto the wheel. His palms were sweaty on the plastic which he still gripped as if threatening to break it. Mandy, aided by Jo, clambered back inside the landrover and then the journalist herself got in. They all sat in silence for long moments.

'There's no way out of the town,' said Tyler, quietly. 'We're trapped.'

'What are we going to do?' Jo wanted to know.

'We'll have to go back into Wakely, to the hotel. We've got no choice.'

He spun the wheel, completing a 'U' turn, then he drove back towards the road.

'But it'll be dark soon,' Mandy protested. 'What about the infected people in the town? They'll be on the streets.' She was becoming more and more distraught. 'They'll kill us.'

'We'll make it,' said Tyler, forcefully.

He glanced up at the sky and shuddered. Rain clouds were forming in vast black banks, hastening the onset of evening. He found he was forced to flick his sidelights on as he drove back towards the centre of Wakely. The trees, bustling in the strong wind, seemed even more menacing in the dull light. They bent and snatched at the speeding vehicle as it roared past, skeletal branches tapping on the roof every now and then.

The outskirts of the town loomed nearer and Tyler allowed one hand to drop to his side where the Franchi lay.

Jo gripped his arm momentarily and he could feel her shaking.

A dark shape moved ahead of them, disappearing into the deep shadows.

'I told you they'd be around,' Mandy babbled.

No one answered her.

Tyler swung the landrover around a corner and saw more of the townspeople emerging from shop doorways. They looked at the vehicle as it hurtled past, hunger in their eyes.

'How far to go?' Jo asked.

'About three-quarters of a mile,' he told her. They had been forced to enter Wakely from a different direction. One which, Tyler knew, would add to the journey time.

The man ran out into the street as if appearing from nowhere. He raised both hands towards the speeding landrover, illuminated briefly in the dim light it cast.

The landrover struck him doing about sixty. The impact hurling the body to one side. Tyler flicked on his headlamps, able to see more of the dark shapes now.

They recoiled from the twin beams, skulking back into the shadows, only able to watch as the machine roared past.

The hotel was close now, Tyler could see its lights.

He swung the vehicle around the next corner, almost tipping it over.

Jo screamed.

There was an overturned car blocking the road.

Tyler had no time to stop, he merely twisted the steering wheel and tried to guide the vehicle around the car. The landrover bumped as it mounted the pavement, skidding on the concrete as its rear end spun round. There was a loud crash as it ploughed through the window of a shop. Glass cascaded down from the smashed sheet and Tyler cursed as the impact slammed him against the steering column.

A dozen of the dark shapes converged on the vehicle.

243

Tyler wrestled with the ignition key as the towns-people drew nearer. Jo snatched up the Franchi, stuck the barrel out of the window and fired. The noise inside the landrover was deafening and Jo shouted aloud as the recoil made her ears ring.

Mandy screamed repeatedly, grabbing the handle of the vehicle's rear doors, anxious to be out of it.

'Mandy, no,' shouted Tyler as the landrover bucked into life again. But it was too late, she had pushed open the rear doors and jumped out onto the pavement, running as fast as she could away from the attacking shapes. In the rear-view mirror, the farmer saw her disappear from view around a corner.

'We can't leave her out there,' said Jo.

Tyler stepped on the accelerator and brought the landrover full circle, speeding away from the frenzied shapes and after Mandy.

When he turned the corner there was no sign of her.

'Shit,' he snarled, scanning the darkened street ahead.

The vehicle was moving slowly now as both he and Jo squinted into the gloom in an effort to catch sight of the terrified girl.

The streets were empty.

He reversed.

'What are you doing?' Jo gasped. 'We've got to find her.'

'We're not risking our lives too,' he snapped.

'Vic, for God's sake.'

The scream came like a knife in soft flesh, ringing through the darkness. A piercing ululation which set their nerves jangling.

Tyler grabbed a shotgun and pushed open his door.

'Keep the lights trained on me,' he said and ran towards the place where the scream had come from. Jo shuffled across into the driver's seat, glancing around her anxiously. She was quivering.

244

Tyler had pinpointed the sound of the scream, realizing that it came from a house just ahead of him. He kicked open the front door and moved inside, the shotgun held at the ready.

The house smelt fusty from disuse and he wondered how long it had been uninhabited.

In the glow from the landrover's headlamps he saw something glistening on the floor ahead of him.

It was blood.

There was more of it on the stairs.

Tyler moved cautiously upward, working the pump action of the shotgun. He swallowed with difficulty, his throat dry and chalky.

He reached the landing and advanced towards one of the doors which faced him. The farmer braced himself and kicked it open.

Mandy Potter lay on the bed naked. Her clothes lay in bloodied tatters beside her like gory confetti. In her nudity, she looked even more pathetic and Tyler lowered his eyes briefly but it was the nature of her injuries which caused him to look away for a moment. She was still wearing her glasses which, Tyler noticed, had been smashed. Thick lumps of glass had punctured her eyes and blood ran down her cheeks like crimson tears. One breast had been practically ripped off, the other was covered by claw marks – deep, red furrows which made it look as if someone had pulled a rake across her torso. Her mouth was open in a soundless scream, her swollen tongue lolling from one side of it. An inch or so below her left breast there was a large hole. Clogged with black clots of congealed blood it yawned like a monstrous mouth.

On the bed beside her was her heart.

The organ looked grey in colour, parts of it having been gouged open.

Tyler crossed to the body and pulled a blanket over

it, covering both the horrific mutilation and Mandy's nakedness.

Only as he stepped back did Tyler suddenly realize that whoever had done this must still be in the house. He spun round, the shotgun lowered.

Nothing moved.

He made his way back onto the landing, then down the stairs, pausing every now and then to listen for sounds of movement.

There were none.

Above him he heard deep guttural breathing, but he kept on edging down the stairs, the light from the landrover's headlamps beckoning him.

He reached the front door, then turned and ran back to the waiting vehicle.

'Mandy?' Jo said.

He shook his head.

Jo understood.

Tyler stepped on the accelerator and drove as fast as he could in the direction of the hotel.

'I thought you were leaving.'

There was no surprise on Alec Clayton's face as he saw Jo and Tyler enter the hotel. Only Maria showed any signs of bewilderment.

'What happened?' she asked.

They told her about the road blocks. About the troops. About the mine-fields.

About Mandy.

'There's no way out of Wakely,' said Tyler, flatly.

Clayton looked a little shocked.

Tyler crossed to the bar and poured himself a large vodka.

'So what are we going to do?' asked Clayton.

The farmer shrugged.

'I wish I knew.'

Forty

Apart from the red and white collision lights which glowed on the skids and sides of the helicopter, the craft flew in darkness. The steady sweep of its powerful rotor blades cut rapidly through the air until it sounded like a loud sewing machine.

The pilot, a man in his early thirties, was bundled up in a heavy leather flying jacket, his black clothing making him almost invisible in the gloom. The lights from the complex instrument panel before him cast a weak glow across his face, highlighting the parts of his skin which were visible above his scarf. His flesh looked pale in the false light, his cheek bones standing out prominently. It seemed as though the chopper was being flown by a disembodied skull.

In the seat alongside him, John Stark pulled the engraved silver hip-flask from his coat pocket and took a hefty swig. He smacked his lips appreciatively, feeling the brandy burn its way to his stomach. Jesus, it was cold. He wore a thick, fur-lined parka but he was still shivering. He rubbed his hands together, slapping the gloved appendages against his thighs. Beneath him, a blanket of cloud had settled over Wakely, virtually blotting the town from view. There were few lights to be seen. Technicians from Vanderburg Chemicals had shut off the main power supply to the town that very afternoon.

Stark jabbed a finger earthward and nudged the pilot.

'Take her lower,' he shouted, forced to raise his voice to make himself heard above the whoosh of the rotors.

The helicopter dipped violently for a moment, caught for precious seconds in a thermo-draught, but it soon straightened out as the young pilot manipulated the controls and lowered the machine to less than 500 feet.

It skimmed through the air effortlessly, dropping ever lower as Stark demanded a better view of the town.

'I thought you said he was your best man,' said Oliver Thorndike who was sitting behind Stark.

'He was,' snapped the American.

'Then why hasn't he reported back?'

The American didn't answer, he merely took another sip from his flask and peered out into the darkness.

'Could Fanducci have caught the disease?' he asked.

Thorndike cupped a hand to his ear, finding it difficult to hear above the noise of the helicopter. He was cold too, his fingers numb.

'What did you say?' he asked.

Stark repeated his question, raising his voice as he did so.

Thorndike shook his head.

'No. He knew about the meat. Perhaps the girl and her friend were too clever for him.'

'Bullshit,' snapped Stark. 'He's never made a mistake yet.'

The helicopter danced in the air, dipping and swerving until it was just a hundred feet or so above the rooftops.

'We're on the outskirts of Wakely, Mr Stark,' said the pilot. 'Do you want me to land?'

'Are you kidding?' shouted the American. 'Just fly over the place, I want to take a look but only from up here.'

The pilot smiled.

'Just what do you expect to see?' Thorndike asked him.

Stark didn't answer. He reached beneath his seat and pulled out a pair of binoculars, squinting through them at the streets below. He adjusted the focus until everything swam into crystal clarity. In the darkness of the streets he could see moving shapes, dozens of them.

'Take a look,' he said, handing the binoculars to Thorndike. 'There are people down there.'

The scientist leant forward in his seat and looked out. 'They're the infected ones,' he said, studying the black shapes beneath them. 'There's still quite a few left.' He swept the binoculars back and forth as the chopper swung in low over the town. '*They* could have killed Fanducci.'

Once more Stark didn't answer.

He suddenly spotted something about 500 yards ahead and nudged the pilot to get closer.

'Give me the glasses back,' he said to Thorndike who willingly obliged.

As the helicopter drew nearer, Stark trained the twin lenses on the light which he had seen. He found that there were over a dozen large lights glowing in a large building a spot near the centre of Wakely. It took him just a moment or two to realize that it was the hotel.

'Son of a bitch,' he murmured under his breath.

He could actually see some of the diseased townspeople moving about beyond the glare of the hotel lights, skulking in shop doorways and standing in black-shrouded streets nearby looking at the one cursed centre of luminosity in the entire town. The hotel stood out like a beacon amidst the stifling Stygian gloom.

'If the girl and the guy are still in town, I'll lay good money they're in there,' Stark said, pointing towards the hotel. He turned to the pilot. 'Circle it a couple of times.'

The man nodded, taking the chopper up slightly before beginning the first of his sweeps.

Forty-one

The auxiliary power provided by the hotel generator had cut in as soon as the mains supply had gone off and Tyler thought again how fortunate they were to have this reserve. What would have occurred had the hotel been plunged into complete darkness he dared not think. As it was, the street lights were out. Wakely was under a blanket of impenetrable gloom – a premonitory blackness which made all four occupants of the hotel feel somewhat uneasy.

Clayton sat at the bar drinking. Maria paced nervously up and down the lounge. Jo stood close to Tyler, gazing out of the window towards the hordes of people barely visible beyond the range of the hotel's powerful lights.

'What do they want?' said Jo, quietly.

'Us,' Tyler said, flatly.

There was a long pause broken by Tyler himself.

'Fresh blood,' he muttered.

Jo frowned.

'What did you say?'

'I think they need fresh blood. Uncontaminated blood,' he explained. 'Up until now, all the victims we've found had been unaffected by the virus. I think that's why they want us.' He gripped the shotgun tighter. 'I wonder how many are out there?'

No one answered.

'I've been thinking,' Tyler continued. 'Apart from the odd victim of the virus we've found, the majority seem to disappear during the day and yet, at night, they all emerge at roughly the same time.'

'What are you getting at, Vic?' Jo asked.

'I think they're all together. In one communal . . . nest, if you like.'

'It would need to be a big building,' said Jo.

Tyler nodded.

'Are you sure this place is secure, Mr Tyler?' asked Maria, anxiously.

'As long as the lights are on they won't come near us,' Tyler reassured her. He looked down as he felt Jo squeezing his arm. He leant over and kissed her softly on the forehead.

It was Clayton who heard it first.

'Listen,' he said, raising a hand for silence.

'What is it?' asked Tyler.

The doctor cocked an ear towards the imagined sound.

'Listen,' he repeated.

The noise grew louder and they all heard it.

'It's a goddam chopper,' said Jo, peering through the window. She pointed towards the red and white lights which glowed brightly on the craft, appearing suddenly, then soaring out of sight.

'It might be someone from another town, the police perhaps,' said Maria, hopefully.

The sound of the rotor blades receded for a moment, then grew louder as the helicopter swept over the building once more.

'Isn't there some way we can signal to him?' said Clayton. 'He might be looking for somewhere to land.'

The chopper completed another circle and Tyler shook his head almost imperceptibly.

'If he wanted to land he could drop it in the street, the road's wide enough,' said the farmer.

'So why doesn't he?' Maria wondered aloud.

The helicopter passed overhead once more, swinging off to the left and hovering like some gigantic insect preparing to alight on a plant, the thrumming of the rotors sounding like a swarm of bees. In the glare of the hotel lights Jo thought she spotted something. A symbol which she had seen before – a red and silver VC. But in the gloom, could she be sure? She watched

251

the chopper as it hovered, trying to make out the markings on its sides. Was it the Vanderburg logo? She couldn't be sure. The sound of its engine gradually receded.

'Why didn't they land?' said Maria, dejectedly.

No one else spoke.

Clayton returned to the bar and began sipping at his drink once more.

'Why don't you try and get some sleep,' said Tyler to Jo.

'I'm fine,' she said, smiling.

The hands of the wall clock had crawled around to 11.26 p.m.

There was an explosion of glass as the first stone shattered the window.

Tyler jumped back, pulling Jo to one side in an attempt to shield her from the shards of crystal which sprayed inwards. He cursed as he felt a jagged splinter nick his cheek.

Another rock came flying at the glass and smashed through. And, suddenly, they were coming with increasing rapidity.

'What the hell are they doing?' said Clayton, knocking his drink over as he moved towards the window.

'Stay back,' Tyler yelled at him as another stone came hurtling at them.

There was another volley of rocks, then a lull.

Tyler peered out through the broken partition, trying to get a look at the hordes beyond the reach of the hotel lights. He could see them, moving like ghosts, almost invisible in the gloom. He could see enough to realize that a number of them were pointing at the building. Many still held lumps of stone and brick, but it was as if they were awaiting some kind of signal.

The farmer swung the shotgun up to his shoulder and aimed.

'What are you doing?' shouted Clayton, rushing towards him.

Tyler actually had his finger hooked around the trigger when the doctor pulled the barrel down.

The farmer turned on him.

'You stupid bastard, Clayton,' he rasped. 'I should use this on you.'

'I shouldn't imagine you'd find it too difficult,' said the doctor sardonically.

'I've told you before, stay out of my way,' Tyler snarled, turning back towards the window.

'Vic, look,' Jo said, pointing at the townspeople. They had unleashed their salvo of stones but they were aiming higher, many of the projectiles falling on the concrete in front of the main doors. Elsewhere, the occupants of the hotel heard more glass smashing.

'My God, they're trying to smash the lights,' said Tyler and, this time, he raised the Franchi and fired all in one movement. There was a deafening roar as the barrel flamed and he saw one of the diseased horde fall. Swiftly working the pump action of the gun, he fired again.

Maria screamed as another stone came crashing through the glass near to her whilst others were hurled at the lights which covered the front of the building.

Tyler squeezed the trigger a third time, watching as two women dragged the bleeding bodies away into the darkness. He could guess what their motives were and the thought sickened him.

He fired again, killing the first of the women.

'You mad bastard,' roared Clayton, trying to pull the gun away from Tyler. The farmer pushed him hard, knocking him over, then he hurriedly thumbed fresh cartridges into the smoking weapon.

The lights flickered once.

'What's that?' Maria gasped.

Tyler saw the shapes moving back into the shadows,

253

watching as the hotel illuminations began to perform like strobes, flickering on and off more rapidly now.

'Christ, it must be the generator,' said Tyler, anxiously. 'The fuel must be down.'

The lights glowed brightly for brief seconds then died.

The entire hotel was plunged into darkness.

Forty-two

'Get upstairs now,' Tyler said.

'Where are you going?' Jo wanted to know.

'To see about that bloody generator.' He snatched up the Purdey which was lying close by. 'Clayton, take this,' he said, thrusting the weapon towards the doctor.

Clayton merely shook his head.

Jo took it instead.

'Go quickly,' Tyler shouted, heading for the cellar door which lay to his right through the bar. He heard the sound of their footsteps as they clattered up the stairs. For his own part, he fumbled for his torch, wrenched open the door and hurried, as best he could, down the stone steps into the abyss which was the cellar. He stumbled at the bottom, sprawling on the cold stone, the shotgun falling from his grasp, the torch rolling away from him.

The impact had caused it to go out.

Like a blind man, Tyler groped around.

He heard the sounds of hammering on the outside

cellar door and realized that they were trying to break in.

At last his hand closed over the shotgun but, still in darkness, he continued groping for the torch.

The pounding on the door grew louder.

Outside, the diseased horde ran towards the darkened hotel, some climbing the rope-like ivy which clung to the walls of the building, others pounding at the doors or smashing windows to gain access.

Tyler found the torch and flicked it on, swinging the beam around until it fastened on the outside door. He could see the handle being turned, see the wood bowing inward as more pressure was exerted on it from the outside. He dashed across the cellar and up the other flight of steps, dropping the metal locking bar in place, securing the door. Then, he scurried towards the generator, running the torch beam over the various gauges on it. The needles of all three were lying limply on the red side of the dial indicating that it had indeed run out of fuel. He snatched up a can of petrol and began pouring.

There was enough natural light for Jo and the others to see where they were going once they reached the top of the stairs. Jo ushered them towards the nearest room and they locked the door behind them. The American checked that the shotgun was loaded, praying that Tyler could get the lights back on before she had need to use it.

There was a deafening crash as the window was broken and a large man came hurtling into the room.

He rolled over once, then hauled himself upright. He was followed by two others. A shorter man and a willowy woman. The taller man was carrying a hammer.

Jo aimed for him, but the massive recoil of the shotgun pulled the barrels to one side and the blast hit the shorter man. It lifted him off his feet and slammed him against the far wall where he left a large blot of crimson as he slid down.

The tallest man turned to the three terrified onlookers, the hammer gripped tight in his fist.

Alec Clayton found himself staring into the mad, bulging eyes of his brother.

'Edward,' he said, taking a step towards the man who had once been blood kin but was now little more than a raving maniac.

'Stay away from him,' shouted Jo, trying to aim the gun again.

Maria too was staring dumbfoundedly at Edward and it was towards her that he moved.

The blow from the hammer was both well-aimed and powerful. It caught Maria just below the left temple and stove in most of the side of her face, her cheek bone splintering beneath the impact. She fell sideways and Edward Clayton dropped to his knees, bringing the weapon down again. The head punched a hole in Maria's skull, exposing part of her brain. She was dead by the time he struck again, this time using the claw end of the hammer to tear open the soft flesh of her neck. Great gouts of blood rose from the rent and spattered Edward. The woman with him also moved towards the corpse but Jo squeezed the trigger of the Purdey, shouting aloud as the massive recoil slammed her backwards.

Once more her aim was off. It caused the gun to veer to one side and the blast caught the woman in the arm, almost severing it at the shoulder as it ripped away most of her chest in the pulverizing discharge.

Jo fumbled in her pocket for more cartridges, her eyes fixed on Edward Clayton who, by now, had bent his head to the jetting fountain of blood spurting from Maria's throat. He drank voraciously.

The sight finally seemed to galvanize the doctor into

action and he ran at his diseased brother, knocking him away from Maria.

Edward snarled, his mouth open to reveal dripping teeth.

Jo looked up and saw that more of the killers were attempting to clamber through the smashed window.

She unlocked the bedroom door and tugged at Clayton's arm.

'Come on,' she screamed.

He stood transfixed, gazing at his dead wife and then at his diseased brother, the awful realisation finally sweeping through him.

More of the killers were crashing into the room.

'For God's sake, move,' Jo shouted, almost pulling the doctor over and, as he looked up and found himself pinned in the stare of so many mad eyes, he finally found the strength to move. He and Jo ran from the room, charging headlong down the corridor.

Behind them, three of the townspeople followed.

'Up the stairs,' Jo said, taking them two at a time and nearly falling. She could hear the intruders drawing nearer, their feet pounding as they chased their prey.

Clayton banged into a table as he turned a corner, jarring his hip but he kept going, not daring to look behind him.

They turned into another corner, the killers less than twenty yards behind them.

It was a dead end.

Jo raced towards the door, praying that it would be unlocked.

She twisted the knob frantically but it wouldn't budge.

Clayton kicked at it while Jo held the shotgun ready, waiting for the pursuers to round the corner.

The first to appear was a woman carrying a chisel.

Jo gripped the shotgun tight and pulled the fore-trigger. The weapon bucked violently in her hand, almost knocking her off balance. The blast hit the woman in the thighs and she went down as if pole-axed.

Clayton drove his foot against the door once more and it flew open, crashing back against the wall. He dashed in, followed by Jo, then both of them struggled to pull a chest of drawers across the gap as the people outside tried to force their way in.

Jo was shaking, Clayton was finding it hard to get his breath.

'He killed her,' the doctor gasped. 'Edward killed my wife.'

Jo could hear his voice cracking but she had more important things to think about.

The door was already beginning to open a fraction and there was nothing else in the room to block it with. Another minute or so and the killers would be in and, this time, there was nowhere else to run.

Tyler threw another empty can of petrol to one side and unscrewed the cap of another. He couldn't remember how many gallons he'd poured into the hungry generator yet still the machine seemed to swallow every drop. The sound of the shotgun blasts from above had caused him to quicken his efforts and now, as he tossed yet another container aside, he reached for the switch that would activate the generator.

The needles on the dials rose a fraction, then dropped again.

The hotel remained in darkness.

Jo levelled the shotgun at the door, Clayton picked up a chair leg and prepared to defend himself as the door began to crack from the monumental blows it was receiving. The wood had already split in two places, great long vein-like seams running its full length. The hinges groaned as the furious onslaught seemed to grow in intensity and both Jo and Clayton jumped as a fist burst through the door, clawing at the splintered wood, ripping away the panels. Through the gap they could see the crazed faces, the yellowed eyes gleaming with mad desire as the intruders realized they had almost reached their prey. The chest of drawers, the final obstacle between them, began to topple.

Tyler was sweating as he poured yet another can of petrol into the generator. He hurled it aside and threw the switch. The machine spluttered for a second then hummed into life. He breathed a sigh of relief as the lights came back on, brighter than ever. He switched off the torch, stuck it in his pocket and ran towards the cellar steps.

Jo almost laughed aloud as the lights burst into life. The entire hotel seemed to glow brilliantly and from outside the splintered door both she and Clayton heard screams of pain and rage. As helpless in the brightness as their victims had been in the gloom, the infected group ran for the windows in an effort to escape the searing power of the lights. They stumbled awkwardly, falling over each other in their haste to escape back into the night.

Clayton wrenched the chest of drawers away from the door and ran out into the corridor, watching as one of the intruders writhed contortedly in front of him. Jo too watched mesmerized as the man's skin rose in large welts which burst to emit a thick mucoid fluid. His face began to turn red and the clear pus took on a crimson tinge. He opened his mouth to scream, a furred tongue lolling from his mouth, his swollen lips cracking under the lights until they were shredded by numerous small clefts, each one weeping blood. They saw his eyes bulging in pain as he continued to squirm like an eel on a hot skillet, his fingers opening and closing as he shook violently. Finally, with a last racking spasm, he coughed loudly and a foul-smelling mixture of bile and pus spilled over his lips.

Jo prodded the body with the barrel of the shotgun, looking up as Clayton hurried past in the direction of the room they had first come from.

He paused in the doorway, looking down at the body of his wife.

'Oh God,' he whimpered. 'No, no.'

He knelt beside the body, clasping her hand, tears coursing down his cheeks as he saw the extent of her mutilations.

Her clothes had been torn off, her torso punctured in a dozen different places by various weapons.

'Maria,' he whispered, sobbing uncontrollably but, as he saw another of the killers lying close by, that grief slowly became blind anger. He began kicking at the body, driving great powerful kicks into the neck and head until the bone shattered under the impact.

'No. No,' he sobbed. 'Maria.' He snarled down at the diseased body. 'You filthy bastard. Animal. Murderer.' He continued driving kicks into the body.

By this time Tyler had entered the room. He looked at Jo with relief on seeing that she was uninjured.

'Clayton?' he asked.

'In there,' Jo said, pointing towards the room. 'Maria was killed.'

'Oh Christ,' said Tyler, wearily. He looked down at the body in the corridor and then walked to where Clayton was still raining blows on the dead body of the killer. Almost exhausted now, he was on his knees, digging his thumbs and fingers into the ruined face of his adversary. Punching the still form, his body still lurched violently as the tears stained his cheeks.

Tyler shook his head as he looked down at Maria's body, then he crossed to Clayton and tried to lift him off the pulverized corpse at which he was still clawing.

'They killed her,' he rasped. 'Look what they did to her.'

Tyler nodded.

'If I'd listened to you, this wouldn't have happened,' croaked Clayton.

'It wasn't your fault,' Jo said.

He seemed to quieten down somewhat, his gaze returning to the mutilated body of his wife.

'My brother did this,' he said.

Tyler looked shocked.

'You saw your brother?' he asked.

The doctor nodded.

'He killed my wife.'

There was another heavy silence.

'I should have listened to you, Tyler,' said the older man. 'I should have listened.' He walked out of the room.

Jo put her arm around Tyler's waist and squeezed him tightly.

'Are you all right?' he asked.

She nodded, her eyes drawn to the two bodies lying before them. How easily one of them could have been herself she thought, and the realization made her shudder. Tyler crossed to the window and looked out. There was nothing to be seen out there in the oozing darkness, only the bodies of those he'd killed earlier. The breeze which blew in brought with it the smell of death. It mingled with the stench which already filled the room.

When they walked back out into the corridor, Clayton was nowhere to be seen. Tyler paused for a moment, looking down at the scorched corpse of the killer in the corridor, then he took hold of the ankles, dragged it into the room with the other one and locked the door.

'What about Maria's body?' asked Jo, apparently concerned that it was sharing a room with two other corpses.

261

'We can't do anything before morning,' Tyler said and, together, they walked downstairs.

They found Clayton in the bar pouring himself a large measure of Scotch which he downed in one, hastily refilling his glass.

He slammed the bottle down on top of the bar and ran his index finger around the rim.

'I want to bury my wife, Tyler,' he said, quietly. 'I want . . .' The sentence trailed off. He exhaled deeply and took another hefty swig from his glass. 'We'd been married for fifteen years. She was all I cared about, we had no children.' He drained what was left in his glass and poured himself another. 'I'm sorry for that little outburst earlier on,' he smiled, sardonically. 'I've had to tell about twenty patients that they were terminally ill during my time as a doctor. Twenty people in over eighteen years is quite a lot. But it was always from a distance, if you know what I mean. Death never had a tangible face until tonight.' He swallowed more of the fiery liquid. 'Death has my brother's face.' Clayton laughed humourlessly. There was a long silence finally broken by the doctor once more. 'I want to kill him. I want to kill my brother. I will destroy death.' He smiled thinly and raised his glass in salute.

The doctor pulled two more glasses from beneath the bar and filled them with the amber fluid.

'Join me?' he said.

Tyler nodded.

'Why not?' Jo echoed.

They sat on the high stools facing the doctor.

'Whatever you want to do,' said Clayton. 'I'll help you. I owe it to my wife.' He gritted his teeth, the knot of muscles at the side of his jaw pulsing.

'I don't think this is the time to talk about it,' said the farmer.

Clayton shook his head.

'I insist,' he said, his voice taking on a hard edge. 'I want someone to pay for what happened tonight.'

Tyler exhaled deeply.

'We can't get out of here, out of Wakely,' he said. 'As I see it, there's only one thing left for us to do. Something that will bring the whole country down on us.'

Jo frowned.

'What?' she asked.

'Destroy Vanderburg Chemicals,' he said.

Jo was speechless.

'And the infected people in the town?' asked Clayton.

'We've got to destroy them too.'

Jo sipped at her drink.

'You find the townspeople,' she said to Tyler. 'I'll see to Vanderburg.'

'You're not going alone,' he told her.

'She won't be alone,' Clayton interjected. 'I'll go with you, Miss Ward.'

He finished his drink and walked out from behind the bar.

'If you'll excuse me,' he said, quietly. 'I'd like to be alone for a while.'

They watched him as he walked wearily away, turning as he reached the exit.

'Tyler,' he said. 'What about that shotgun?'

The farmer tossed him the nickel-plated Purdey and a box of cartridges, watching as he hefted the weapon before him.

Outside, the dark shapes had returned but, this time, they merely stood motionless, staring at the hotel.

It would be daylight in two hours.

Forty-three

Doctor Alec Clayton placed one solitary flower on the small mound of earth in the hotel garden. Tyler and Jo stood to his right, eyes lowered. The sun had risen bright and shining, casting its warm rays over the sombre proceedings.

It had taken them less than half an hour to bury Maria Clayton. They had dug a makeshift grave using tools from the hardware shop across the street, then they had wrapped the body in a sheet and lowered it gently into the hole. No more than two feet deep, it lay beneath a small willow and, as they stood there, pieces of blossom fell like pink tears to join the flowers atop the grave.

Clayton said a short prayer, his voice cracking half-way through, then he brushed the earth from his hands and walked away.

Tyler felt an uncomfortable familiarity about the ritual, remembering the funeral of his own father not so long ago; the act which had brought him back to his birth-place, now a place of death and disease.

Before they had buried Maria, Tyler had driven alone to Dan Hawley's surgery where he had collected a couple of microscopes, some slides and other paraphernalia which Clayton had asked for. On the journey there and back he had found bodies in the streets, some savaged as Clayton's wife had been, others disfigured almost beyond recognition. And amongst those bodies he had recognized people he knew.

Reg Gentry was one of the men who had farmed around Wakely all his life. Tyler had found him with his eyes torn out and his throat cut.

He had found Ronald Faber, a man he remembered as owning a clothes shop. Faber, normally a fat individual, had wasted away to practically nothing, his skin covered everywhere by hideous growths and sores.

It had seemed to Tyler, as if he were driving through a gigantic graveyard where no one had bothered to bury the dead.

Nevertheless, he had returned with the required instruments and then set about helping Clayton bury his wife. As he had helped lift the body onto the sheet, Tyler had not failed to notice the severity of the mutilations which she had suffered. It seemed as if the ferocity of the attacks was growing worse. And, beside her, had lain the body of one of the diseased killers, the body even more broken and disfigured by the pounding which Clayton himself had given it, venting his frustration and pain on the immobile cadaver. Tyler had looked at it, at the monstrous deformity and obscene appearance and it had reminded him, somehow, of the deformed calf which he had killed. How long ago was it now? A week? Two weeks? Three? It seemed like an eternity. Memories and thoughts flooded through his mind and he was sure the others felt the same way. Each carried their own secret to be stored in the darkest recesses of their minds.

Tyler wondered how much more they would see before it was all over.

The body lay on one of the large stainless steel benches in the kitchen of the hotel. Completely naked, the skin had a yellowish tinge to it, that at least, which wasn't covered by unhealed sores and festering blisters. The stench which rose from the corpse was a pungent mixture of putrefying flesh and blood. Tyler and Clayton had carried it from the room upstairs and stripped it, wearing some rubber gloves which Jo had found in a store cupboard. Now, together with the instruments from his own black bag, Clayton had before him two large butcher's knives, a smaller freezer knife (capable of cutting through bone) and a meat saw. They were not the best implements with which to conduct an autopsy but he had little choice.

The doctor prodded the body with the end of his finger, noticing how tightly the skin was pulled across the bones. In places, it looked as if it were going to break or tear. Small pieces flaked off as he rubbed, exposing grey muscle beneath.

'Very little surface lividity,' he said, reaching for the largest of the butcher's knives. 'The skin looks jaundiced.'

Tyler and Jo watched as he inspected the body, peering closely at the face, probing at one of the gaping blisters with the point of the knife. A small trickle of clear fluid oozed from it and Clayton transferred it onto a microscope slide. 'These lesions look as if they've been caused by a reaction *within* the skin cells,' he said, peering through the microscope. He stroked his chin thoughtfully and returned to the body. Jo gritted her teeth as he pushed the knife into the abdomen of the corpse just below the sternum. With an expert movement, the doctor opened the torso as far as the pelvis.

A cloying stench erupted from the hollow and he waved a hand in front of him for a moment before reaching for a syringe. He located the bladder and ran the syringe deep into the swollen organ, withdrawing about 25ml of fluid which he also deposited on a slide. One drop of it glistened beneath the lights.

'Interesting,' he said, abstractedly. 'The bladder is undamaged yet it's full of blood and, from what I can see, there's no damage to either the liver or kidneys. Filtration of waste has been happening as it would in any normal person.' He pointed to the liver with the end of the knife. 'If the skin coloration was caused by jaundice, or hepatitis, then at least half of the liver cells would be damaged.'

266

He opened the mouth and inspected the teeth and gums.

'Gum shrinkage,' he said, moving down to the hands with their long fingernails. The doctor also looked at the hair which grew in a thick clump in the palms of both appendages. 'This is very unusual,' he said, pulling at the hairs.

'Have you ever seen anything like it before?' asked Tyler.

Clayton was silent for long moments then he nodded almost imperceptibly.

'Yes, I have,' he said. 'But, it was impossible to make the diagnosis without a full examination of a sufferer.'

'So what is it for God's sake?' asked Tyler.

Clayton looked at Jo.

'It's probably the answer to most of Eastern European myth and folklore,' he said.

'What's that supposed to mean?' Tyler said, agitatedly.

'It was Miss Ward who first mentioned vampires wasn't it?' said the doctor.

Tyler shook his head.

'Oh no, come on Clayton, you're not going to tell me that the people of Wakely have been turned into vampires? What do you think this is, some kind of joke? You'll be telling me next there are werewolves running around here.'

'Vic, let him finish,' said Jo, trying to calm the farmer down.

'This man,' he indicated the body before him, 'in fact, all the infected residents of the town, are suffering from a highly advanced form of a disease known as porphyria.'

'What's that got to do with vampires?' asked Jo.

'You've seen the symptoms yourself,' Clayton said. 'Fear of sunlight, sensitivity to light, growth of nails and teeth, swelling of the lips, yellowing of the skin.

Even the hair on the palms of the hands. The blood-lust, the psychosis. They're all symptoms of porphyria. What, in a less enlightened age, might well have been labelled vampirism.'

'My God,' said Jo, softly.

'Why the need to drink blood?' asked Tyler.

'Porphyria is basically a deficiency of iron in the blood stream,' Clayton told him. 'What is known as a disorder of haem synthesis. The blood cannot absorb iron. At first the symptoms look like anaemia and, much of the time, that's as far as it goes. We still know very little about the diseases.'

'You mean there's more than one strain of it?' Jo enquired.

Clayton nodded.

'There are at least six, each manifesting a different severity of symptoms. The people of Wakely seem to be suffering from an advanced form of *porphyria cutanea tarda*. It can be precipitated by alcohol, oestrogen as is found in some birth control pills, or by any toxic agent. In this case, it would seem to be the bacteria in the Vanderburg feed which was passed on to the humans by way of the diseased animals.'

'I still don't understand the significance of the blood,' said Tyler.

'Blood itself is rich in iron,' Clayton began, 'probably the richest source of iron in nature. As I said, anyone with porphyria would find it impossible to absorb iron but, nevertheless, they would need to replace the lost iron. The quickest way of doing that would be to drink blood. That's why the victims of those infected have been mutilated.' His voice dropped slightly and he lowered his gaze. 'The killers wanted blood.'

'Jesus,' murmured Jo. 'It's not hard to see why or how the vampire myth started.'

'There's another thing which links porphyria to myths,' Clayton told her. 'Vampires, according to folk-

268

lore, are afraid of garlic. There's an enzyme in garlic which breaks down iron in the blood. It stands to reason that anyone suffering the disease would want to keep well away from garlic. The sufferer also only comes out during the night because once the disease has reached a certain stage the iron-free porphyrins build up under the skin. Any exposure to light or sun causes a chemical reaction leading to these lesions.' He pointed to the disfiguring scars and welts on the face of the corpse.

There was a long silence, broken once more by Clayton.

'At the moment, only one person in every 25,000 suffers from porphyria but that number could increase, with or without the influence of the Vanderburg feed. That has just acted as a catalyst in this case but, as I said before, *any* toxic agent could induce it, even something as simple as alcohol or the birth control pill.'

'How is it cured?' asked Jo.

'It isn't,' Clayton said, flatly. 'So little is known about it that no one knows how to perfect a cure. I only recognize the disease because I've seen it in a much milder form many years ago, but never as virulent as this. The problem with the most common form of the disease, *Erythrohepatic porphyria*, is that people can have it and not even realize they're infected.'

A troubled silence settled over the trio, Tyler looked almost accusingly at the gutted body on the slab before him.

'Is it fatal?' Tyler asked.

Clayton stroked his chin, thoughtfully.

'Normally, no,' he said.

Tyler shook his head.

'In the early stages, the people who were infected must have realized there was something wrong with them, so why didn't they go to the doctor?'

'The disease attacks the central nervous system,' Clayton told him. 'It causes disorders of thought and

269

reason. Eventually, it leads to erosion of brain cells. That's what causes the psychosis.'

'So, theoretically, the people who are already infected may die in a few days anyway?' Jo offered.

'It's impossible to say,' said Clayton. 'Days. Weeks. Months. There's no way of knowing.'

'Which doesn't help us in the meantime,' Tyler added, cryptically.

'Thank God the infected people are inactive during the day,' said Jo.

'Inactive perhaps but, unlike the vampires of myth, they don't go into a coma during the daylight hours. Once awoken, providing they are clear of any kind of light, they're just as dangerous.'

'So, are they vampires or not?' asked Jo.

'They're as close to the concept of the mythical vampire as we'll ever see,' said Clayton. 'Or want to see,' he added as an afterthought.

'Then all those legends were created because people didn't understand about diseases like this?' said Tyler.

'Man has a habit of attaching labels to things,' Clayton said. 'It makes us all feel more secure if we can pigeon-hole people or even beliefs. Ignorance spawned legend in many cases, certainly where porphyria is concerned. If you couple the symptoms of it with the fact that there were also a great many more cases of catatonic coma and premature burial in the middle ages, it's not difficult to see how the legends of vampires, were-wolves and even the living dead came about. If we can't rationalize something, we tend to push it into the area of the sub-normal, the supernatural. We're afraid of what we don't understand. And, what we're afraid of, we tend to destroy.'

There was another long silence.

Tyler looked at his watch and saw that it was almost 12.05 p.m.

'We haven't got much time,' he said. 'Less than seven

hours of daylight and there's a lot of ground to cover. We'd better get moving.'

Forty-four

Sir Oliver Thorndike paced agitatedly back and forth in front of his desk, pausing every few seconds to look at his watch. He brushed first one sleeve then the other, as if the gesture would somehow ensure that the time passed more rapidly. He glanced over at the manilla file on his desk and swallowed hard.

There was a knock on the door.

'Come in,' said Thorndike but Stark was already half-way through the door as he said it.

The American looked at the scientist indifferently.

'OK, what's so goddam important?' he said, seating himself in one of the high-backed leather chairs which faced the older man's desk.

Thorndike walked behind the mahogany cabinet and picked up the file, brandishing it almost accusingly before him.

'This is the report on the latest batch of feed,' he said.

'I read it,' Stark told him, reaching into his pocket for the ever-present hip-flask.

'Then you'll have noticed that it too did not reach the specifications required for an adequate safety level.'

'Cut the crap, Thorndike. If there's something on your mind say it.'

'The protein additive which we are, at this very moment, adding to the new batch of feed, is no safer

271

than the first lot. And look what happened because of that. The Government won't tolerate any more incidents on the scale of the one in Wakely.'

'This Government will tolerate anything once they realize the overall financial gain. Why the hell do you think they agreed to co-operate with this project in the beginning?'

'In a covert capacity, yes, but they won't stand for much more. This incident can't be kept quiet forever.' Thorndike swallowed hard. 'Call a temporary halt to Project Erebus.'

'No,' said the American, flatly. 'The new batch of feed is treated and ready for shipment.'

'How many more people are going to die before your conscience begins to prick you?' Thorndike demanded.

'It seems to me I've heard this shit somewhere before. Have you been talking to Muir?' snarled Stark, vehemently. 'You knew the risks involved when this project was launched, you and all the other men working on it – so don't start lecturing me about conscience, you hypocritical son of a bitch.'

'Deciding to call it Erebus has become somewhat prophetic don't you think?'

'What's that supposed to mean?'

Thorndike threw down the file.

'Erebus. The God of Darkness, ruler of the region beyond Hades. Well, it seems we've created our own little hell just a mile or so away.'

Stark got to his feet.

'Don't try to hand me any of your intellectual crap. You're not indispensable, Thorndike.'

The scientist grinned but there was no humour there.

'It seems to me I've heard *that* somewhere before,' he said. 'First Anderson, then Charles Muir, then myself, is that it?'

'Forget your conscience,' the American said, his voice full of menace. 'There's no room for it anymore.'

He walked out, leaving Thorndike to stare impotently at the discarded file. He sat down, head cradled in his hands.

The file lay there like an accusation.

Forty-five

The map of Wakely which was pinned to the notice-board in the hotel was criss-crossed with red and black pen marks, entire streets had been coloured over. Tyler inked over another part of the map and stepped back in resignation.

'There's nowhere left they could be hiding,' he said.

'Have you searched everywhere?' asked Clayton.

'I think I've been to some places twice, I seem to be going around in circles.'

'What's that?' asked Jo, pointing to an untouched black square towards the north of the town.

'The old cinema,' said Tyler, quietly. He gazed at the map for long moments, thoughts tumbling through his mind.

Clayton looked at him.

'Is it big enough?' he asked.

Tyler nodded.

'How the bloody hell did I miss it?' he muttered to himself.

'You try there then, Vic,' Jo said.

'Are we decided on what to do now?' the doctor added, running over the plans which they had formulated earlier.

'I'll search the rest of the buildings, any that I haven't tried,' said Tyler. 'You and Jo drive out to Vanderburg Chemicals, see what you can find.' He reached into his pocket and pulled out the I.D. card which he'd taken from the body of Carlo Fanducci days earlier. 'Use this to get past the guards,' Tyler said, handing it to the doctor.

'And what if they know who Fanducci is?' asked Clayton.

'Then you'll have to find some other way of getting in.'

'It seems like madness doing it in broad daylight,' said the doctor. 'We'd have a much better chance at night.'

'You know as well as I do that we daren't risk being outside in the dark, not until these . . . creatures have been destroyed.'

Tyler fumbled in his coat pocket, checking that he had enough cartridges for the Franchi. His landrover was already loaded up with a dozen cans of petrol. He felt as secure as he was likely to.

'And we meet back here at eight?' said Jo.

Tyler nodded.

The trio stood in silence for long moments, then Clayton excused himself, walking out of the front door of the hotel. Jo and Tyler gazed into each other's eyes, questions hovering there. Unspoken fears.

He finally reached out and pulled her towards him. She responded fiercely.

'Vic, I'm scared,' she said.

'Join the club,' he mused.

'I don't want to lose you. Not now.'

'You won't,' he reassured her, wishing he could add more conviction to his voice.

'Please be careful,' she said.

'You too,' he told her, smiling. Then they kissed, mouths joined firmly, tongues probing urgently.

When she pulled away, there was a single tear trickling down her cheek which Tyler wiped away with his index finger.

'What happened to the tough lady reporter?' he asked, smiling.

'I think she stayed in New York,' said Jo, angry at herself. When she looked up at him, her eyes were glistening. 'I love you, Vic,' she whispered.

He looked momentarily surprised by the exclamation but then he pulled her close once more.

They remained like that for what seemed like an eternity then, without speaking, they walked outside and around to the rear of the hotel where they found Clayton. The doctor was on his knees, head bowed, beside the small mound of earth which marked the resting place of his dead wife. Tyler could see the man's mouth moving as he spoke silent prayers, muttering inaudible phrases.

Feeling like intruders at the private ritual, Jo and Tyler slipped away to wait for him.

He returned minutes later looking somewhat drawn.

'I'm sorry,' he said, smiling, thinly. 'There was something I had to do.'

Tyler nodded but didn't speak.

The three of them walked out to the car park together, Tyler watching as Clayton unlocked the boot of his Capri, ensuring that there was enough room inside for Jo to lie comfortably. It was an unfortunate necessity. The security men at Vanderburg had seen her. They may not recognise her again but it was a chance no one was willing to take.

Tyler climbed into his landrover and laid the shotgun on the passenger seat. In the rear of the vehicle were several cans of petrol which he'd taken from the hotel cellar.

He watched as Jo slid into the boot of the Capri.

Clayton shut it and walked around to the driver's side door.

He looked at his watch and then up at the sky.

Rain clouds were gathering to the west, a vast grey expanse which stretched across the sky like a shroud, drawing nearer by the minute.

The two men exchanged brief glances then, without speaking, Tyler drove off.

Clayton watched the landrover disappear around a corner, then he too started his engine, guiding the Capri out into the road.

The drive to Vanderburg Chemicals would take less than fifteen minutes.

Forty-six

Tyler glanced anxiously at the sky as he pulled the landrover to a halt. More and more of the blue canopy above him was being obscured by smoky grey cloud which moved in rolling banks towards the town. A light breeze had sprung up and he shivered a little as he stepped out of the vehicle, gripping the Franchi tightly.

The cinema stood before him, a towering red brick building built over forty years earlier. It had been allowed to fall into disrepair, its stonework chipped in places, windows broken here and there. There were still posters up outside, advertising forthcoming attractions and, as Tyler approached the building, he glanced at them. There would be no audience for them this time, he thought. Tyler rattled the glass doors, seeing that they still bore chains and padlocks. If he was going to get in he would have to find a different entrance. He wandered slowly around to one side of the large edifice and tugged on the bar of the twin wooden safety doors.

They wouldn't budge.

He decided to check the rear.

Skirting the building meant passing along a narrow alley way which ran between the cinema and the yard of a furniture store next to it. Tyler had already checked out the store, but it had not struck him to search the cinema until now. He moved slowly down the alley, glancing up at the overcast sky every so often.

Old cans and newspapers lay around his feet as he walked and the breeze whipped one up at him. Tyler pulled it away from him irritably and turned a corner.

The woman's body was lying amidst a pile of rubbish, almost hidden from view. Just her feet and the lower part of her torso were visible.

Tyler crossed to the untidy heap and prodded the corpse with the end of the shotgun, knocking some boxes away in order to get a better look at her. She was lying face down but her head was turned to one side. A woman in her thirties, her hair had come out in thick wads, even her eyebrows were mere tufts. Her eyes, dark rimmed and bloodshot, were open, as was her mouth and Tyler saw that there were several flies crawling eagerly over the corpse, their attention focused on the festering wound just below her right ear. It was already beginning to turn gangrenous, mottled blue and green in places. The knife which had been used to inflict the wound lay a foot or so away, its blade rusty with dried blood. Tyler could see that her throat had been slashed in several other places too.

He exhaled deeply and walked on, past the large incinerator where rubbish from the cinema was burned, finally reaching the other side exit.

It was slightly ajar.

Tyler approached it cautiously, noticing how clammy his hands felt against the wood and metal of the gun. He prodded the door with the end of the barrel and it shrieked alarmingly as it swung open. The farmer paused for long seconds, reaching for his torch, then he moved cautiously inside.

He found himself confronted by a set of stone steps which, he knew, led up to the balcony. As he began to climb them his boots echoed loudly within the cold passageway and Tyler cursed under his breath. It was dark on the staircase but there was enough natural light coming through the frosted glass window ahead to prevent him using the torch. He trod carefully, the shotgun lowered.

The steps finally flattened out into a landing. He needed to turn a corner to climb the other flight, which would take him into the balcony itself. Tyler could hear water dripping from the pipes in the toilets behind him. The steady 'plink, plink' jarred his nerves as he slowly ascended the second flight of steps. The darkness grew more pronounced, closing around him like a glove as he finally reached the doors which were his final obstacle.

He flicked on the torch and leant against the door.

It wouldn't move. Something, Tyler decided, was stopping its passage.

He stepped back a pace then drove a boot into the partition and, this time, it swung open to reveal the gaping black maw within. It was like walking into a coal mine. Even the beam of the torch had difficulty cutting through the all-enveloping darkness. He shone the beam down, bringing it to bear on the object which had been blocking the door.

It was another body, a man this time. His shirt and jacket lay open to reveal a pulped rib-cage and the tattered remnants of intestines. A fetid odour of decay filled the farmer's nostrils and he stepped over the corpse, moving slowly across the balcony, sweeping the torch beam back and forth. The place smelt damp and fusty but there was the ever-present odour of death and decay which he'd come to know only too well in the past week or so.

Something brushed against his ankle.

Tyler almost shouted aloud in surprise, swinging the torch around in an effort to discover what had touched him.

He held the shotgun in one hand, not daring to put the torch down but aware that, if someone did come at him, he would more than likely break his wrist firing the weapon with one hand. He felt a bead of perspiration pop onto his forehead as his eyes scanned the unyielding gloom.

He shone the torch around his feet.

'Oh Christ,' he murmured, softly.

A dismembered hand lay close by, the fingers outstretched. The hand had been torn, not cut, off. Long tendrils of flesh hung from it and Tyler swallowed hard. From the hair on the back of it, the hand looked as if it had belonged to a man.

He heard a slow, rhythmic thudding and it was drawing closer.

The farmer stood bolt upright, the torch moving wildly in his grip as the beam sought out the source of the movement.

The soft thudding grew louder.

It was close now. Very close.

His finger tightened a fraction on the trigger.

Something heavy struck his leg and he almost fired. He swung the torch down immediately, his breath stuck in his throat.

Lying at his feet was the severed head of Ben Thurston. The old man's eyes were open, gazing past Tyler as if looking for his killer. His own movements, he guessed, had dislodged the head.

Tyler gritted his teeth and shone the torch ahead of

him. The rest of Thurston's body lay a few feet away. The head had been severed by a small axe which was still embedded in the back of the corpse. The hand was missing too.

'You bastards,' Tyler shouted and his voice echoed around the cavernous interior, bouncing off the walls until it seemed to rise to a high-pitched scream of anguish.

Only silence greeted his outburst.

He was shaking slightly, as much from rage as from shock. The discovery of Thurston, the man he had loved like his own father, had shaken him more than he'd expected, and what made things worse was the fact that the old man had not been infected. He had been another helpless victim of the diseased killers. Vampires. The word drifted into Tyler's mind. Standing here in this deserted cinema with the severed head of a friend at his feet, surrounded by impenetrable darkness, the word seemed to have a terrifying reality about it.

'Vampires,' he said, quietly.

He stood for long seconds, now sure that the creatures were not hiding in the cinema. But where were they? He'd searched everywhere in town.

The thought struck him like a thunderbolt.

What a fool he'd been. It was so obvious it was ridiculous. He felt, simultaneously, elated and angry. Angry with himself for not having thought of it earlier. He turned and ran for the door.

There was only one place where they could possibly be.

Forty-seven

Clayton wound down his window as the first of the security guards approached, the familiar red and silver Vanderburg logo on his breast pocket.

'Afternoon, sir,' said the guard, running appraising eyes over both Clayton and the car.

The doctor nodded a greeting. He didn't want to speak but even if he'd needed to, he doubted if he could. It was as if someone had clamped a steel vice around his throat and were turning it one notch at a time. He tried to swallow but couldn't.

'There's no unauthorized personnel allowed in,' the guard said. 'If you want to see someone you'll . . .'

Clayton reached into his pocket and produced the I.D. card which had been taken from Fanducci. The guard took it from him, not noticing that the doctor's hands were shaking slightly. He looked at the card and then at Clayton. After a moment he handed the card back, his eyes still fixed on the doctor.

'OK,' said the security man and signalled to his partner. The barrier which blocked the drive was lifted and Clayton drove on. As he guided the vehicle up the long driveway, he peered into his rear-view mirror and saw one of the two guards pointing at the car. Clayton swallowed hard, still watching as the man disappeared inside the yellow porta-cabin. His companion followed closely.

Clayton wiped his sweating palms on his trousers and drove on, finally bringing the car to a halt next to one of the large manufacturing sheds. There was a narrow gap between the shed and the main building and he reversed towards that.

Inside the boot, Jo heard him switch off the engine.

She waited a few moments then slipped the catch, climbing out.

She felt appallingly conspicuous for a moment as she stood behind the car but she rapidly ducked down and sprinted along the narrow passage towards a window in the main building. Clayton watched her in his rear-view mirror, then he scanned the area before him.

A large container lorry had just pulled up in front of the main building. The driver got out.

He looked across, saw Clayton and headed towards the car.

The doctor was frantic as the man drew nearer, glancing at his piece of paper and then at the parked Capri.

Clayton shuffled nervously in his seat. What the hell did this man want?

Jo had disappeared from view behind him. He was alone.

And the man was getting closer.

Clayton heard a loud whistle and looked to his right where another man, dressed in a white overall, was signalling to the driver of the lorry. The man in the overall beckoned the driver to him and Clayton saw them chatting animatedly. The driver returned to his lorry and started it up, guiding the massive juggernaut into its appointed position near the loading bay of the closest manufacturing shed.

The rear end of the lorry now blocked Clayton's exit.

Jo knew the lab coat was too big and she felt conscious of it. She tried tucking the sleeves up but they kept coming down, covering her hands. She pulled it tightly across her and waited for the lift to descend.

She was standing in the main foyer of Vanderburg Chemicals, muzak filling her ears as she waited impatiently, for the metal doors to slide open.

The window by which she had gained entry into the building had led her into a deserted office. She had found the lab coat hanging on a hook on the back of the door. It bore the red and silver VC on the pocket

282

but, from the weight and size of it, Jo was convinced that it belonged to a man. She hoped he didn't come looking for it. However, as she stood watching the numbers light up above her, signalling the approach of the lift, she found that her heart had stopped pounding so hard. Few people had looked at her and, those who had, had cast only cursory glances at her. Hold onto yourself, she thought. Don't get paranoid now.

'Where are you going?'

The voice startled her and she turned to see another young woman standing beside her. The woman, in her late twenties, was carrying several thick files. She too wore the monogrammed lab coat.

'I was looking for the research labs,' said Jo, the lie ready on her tongue. 'I'm new here, I can't find my way around too well yet.'

The other girl smiled.

'I know what you mean, I was like that for the first few *weeks* after I started. This place is like a maze.'

'How long have you worked here?' asked Jo.

'Two years,' said the girl. 'My name's Ruth Wicks by the way.'

'Hi, I'm Janet Grant,' Jo lied.

The lift bumped to a halt and they stepped inside.

'Which floor?' asked Ruth, finger hovering over the buttons.

Jo swallowed hard.

The other girl continued to smile.

The American glanced at the array of buttons.

'Three,' she said, praying she'd said the right thing.

Ruth jabbed the button marked '3' and the doors slid shut.

'You're working with Glendenning then?' she said.

Jo nodded.

'He's away all day, there's no one in the labs,' Ruth said.

'I just thought I'd have a look around, familiarize myself with the place,' the journalist said.

Ruth eyed her, the smile fading slightly.

'I don't think they like people just walking in and out of the labs, not with the work they're doing.'

'Well, like I said, I wanted to get the feel of the place. What kind of work *are* they doing exactly?'

'Didn't they tell you that when you were interviewed?' asked Ruth, the smile now completely gone.

'Not everything,' said Jo, sensing that she was losing her grip here. 'Do *you* know?'

'Yes.'

There was an awkward silence. The lift came to a halt at the second floor and Ruth stepped out.

'Perhaps I'll see you later,' she said.

Jo nodded vigorously, anxious for the girl to leave.

As the doors slid shut, the American breathed an audible sigh of relief. A sound which caught in her throat as, a second later, they opened again.

'By the way,' said Ruth, the smile having returned. 'I'd get them to find you a lab coat that's the right size.'

Jo laughed exaggeratedly, watching as the girl walked away. She jabbed the '3' button again and the lift rose one more floor.

When she stepped out she found that she was in a windowless corridor, fluorescents blazing brightly above her. The passageway ran arrow-straight ahead of her for about twenty yards, then it angled sharply to the right. Jo began walking, her eyes scanning the doors on either side of her, expecting one to open at any moment. There were names on some of them, numbers on others. She sought out the door with Glendenning's name on it. She knew that name from somewhere, she knew him, had spoken to him. Of that she was sure and, as she turned the corner, the realization gradually spread through her. He had been the man she'd spoken to when she'd first visited Vanderburg Chemicals in search of Geoffrey Anderson.

One of the doors she passed was thick, sheet steel and on it was the yellow and black sign which warned of radiation. Jo paused beside the door, looking in front and behind her, listening for the slightest sound of movement. Then, she moved on.

Still the doors showed no signs of Glendenning's name. She tried the handle of one but it was locked.

Jo spun round as she heard a low whimpering sound.

In the stillness of the corridor, with just the steady hum of the fluorescents, the sound seemed louder.

She listened and it came again. It sounded like a dog in pain but a big dog and even then the whining was curiously resonant. She put it down to the acoustics in the corridor.

Jo crossed to the door from behind which the sound was coming. She twisted the knob, surprised to find it unlocked. The blinds in the room were drawn, it was difficult to see. The overcast weather outside offered her very little natural light either. But she was able to see that the room was about twenty feet square. One wall was completely covered by filing cabinets, the centre of it was divided into aisles formed by three workbenches and dozens of cages.

In each of the cages there was a different animal. They were surprisingly quiet as Jo approached them, only the dog continued to whine.

She peered into the first cage where a rhesus monkey lay motionless on the floor, its tail twitching slightly.

It had no eyes.

Where the glistening orbs should have been there were just red-rimmed holes. And yet, when Jo moved, the monkey sat up, following her with those bloodied pits as if tracking her with radar. She shuddered, almost shouting aloud as the bats in the next cage flapped their wings excitedly at her approach. There were two of them, fruit bats or flying foxes she guessed from the size.

Both were completely white, their eyes glinting with a vile pink lustre.

And then she saw the dog.

It was a labrador, at least she thought it was. Its coat had no brilliant sheen to it, rather a dull appearance which made it look dirty. Its muzzle was virtually non-existent, its mouth consisting of a huge gaping maw from which long fangs protruded. One ear was missing and, as Jo looked closely, the dog moved.

There was a long growth sprouting from one of its rear legs and the American was sure she could see claws growing at the end of it. The dog had five legs. It shuffled helplessly in the cage, that cavernous mouth dripping saliva as it watched her with eyes that glowed red.

Jo passed the last of the cages and found two or three files laid out on the nearest work-bench. One of them was open. She scanned the title page:

GENETIC RE-CONSTRUCTION

She looked at the cages behind her, then back at the file. Another lay beside it marked:

PROTEIN SYNTHESIS

Something at the back of her mind clicked. It had been Dan Hawley who had first mentioned proteins. An artificially created protein. The plague carrier. The thing which had transformed the residents of Wakely into the vulpine denizens of legend.

These files were what she sought.

There was another marked simply:

DISTRIBUTION

She picked that one up too, stuffing all three under her arm. As she turned to leave she noticed the steaming mug of coffee on the work-bench nearby. Someone had obviously been working in here and might well return.

Jo swallowed hard and made for the door.

She had taken less than two paces when it opened and Richard Neville stepped inside.

'What are you doing in here?' he snapped. 'This is a restricted area.' He noticed that her lab coat did not fit and, something which Ruth Wicks had not noticed, the absence of an identity tag on her lapel. 'Who are you?' he demanded.

Jo took a step back, her hand brushing against the mug of coffee.

As Neville advanced towards her, she hurled it at him.

The boiling liquid hit the scientist full in the face and he shrieked, clawing madly at his eyes.

Jo side-stepped him and ran for the door.

'Stop,' screamed Neville, his skin blistered by the red hot coffee, his arms flailing about uselessly.

Jo wrenched open the door and ran for the lifts.

The scientist dragged himself upright and staggered blindly across the room towards the alarm on the far wall, crashing into some of the cages as he did so.

There was an explosive cacophony of squawks, shrieks and buckling metal as the cages went flying, some of them bursting open to release their occupants.

A cat with a large tumorous growth on its back scampered free and hid beneath the work-bench. The monkey began to howl, baring long fangs, gripping the bars with the stubby nubs of fingers.

Neville reached the alarm and broke the glass with the heel of his hand. Immediately, the strident wail of a klaxon filled the air, reverberating throughout the entire building.

Alec Clayton heard the siren and he gripped the wheel of the Capri tighter, feeling the plastic slip beneath his sweating palms. The sound could have been started by anyone he reasoned. It may even be a fault in the mechanism, a drill which the employees were obliged to endure every so often. He sought desperately for explanations but his mind could accept nothing but what he knew must be the real reason for the sirens. He wondered if they had caught Jo. Should he start his engine and get away? What if he was wrong? Questions piled up in his tortured mind. Perhaps if he created a diversion of some kind . . . The thought trailed off. He looked anxiously around him. What could he do?

He twisted the key in the ignition and started his engine.

'Security alarm,' said John Stark getting to his feet. He crossed to the window of his office and looked out. Nothing moved. He returned to his desk and flicked one of the switches on the console before him.

'What the hell is going on?' he demanded. 'Who set that alarm off?'

The voice which answered him sounded metallic over the intercom. It belonged to Thorndike.

'There's been a disturbance in one of the laboratories,' he said. 'Neville said that a woman stole some files.'

'A woman?' Stark exclaimed, angrily. 'What does she look like?'

'Neville didn't get a good look at her,' Thorndike said. 'He seemed more concerned about the files. She took the files on the Erebus project.'

The American gritted his teeth and flipped another switch.

'Security, this is a general alert, there is an unauthorized person in the building. No one is to leave. Repeat, no one is to leave.' He flicked the switch off and supped deeply from his flask, grunting angrily. 'Fucking bitch,' he rasped to himself.

Jo gripped the files tightly under her arm as the lift descended. The sound of the siren was loud in her ears, even inside the enclosure. There was a loudspeaker in there too and she heard Stark's angry words. She wondered how she was going to get past the security men downstairs.

Indeed, as the lift doors slid open she stepped out into the cavernous reception area to find blue-uniformed men standing at the exit doors. One was speaking into a two-way radio. Jo hesitated for long seconds, wondering what to do. She dared not try and slip out through the window she had gained entry by, and yet she couldn't stand helplessly staring at the guards. The files suddenly seemed enormous and she felt painfully conspicuous, dressed in her ridiculously ill-fitting lab coat.

She was still trying to decide what to do when one of the security men began walking towards her.

Alec Clayton stuck the Capri into gear and guided it slowly towards the front of the main building. The siren continued to wail and he could see the blue-coated security men blocking the exits.

His shirt was sticking to his back, the perspiration beaded heavily on his face. He gripped the wheel tightly and peered through the double sets of glass doors, his roving eyes finally spotting Jo.

He could see that one of the security men was approaching her. Clayton swallowed hard, realizing what he must do. He put the car into reverse and stepped on the accelerator, pulling back about thirty yards.

Already he could see other security men approaching in his rear view mirror.

He ignored them, gripping the wheel even tighter, ducking as low as he could behind it. Then he pushed his foot down hard on the accelerator, glancing down to see the needle touch forty. There was a scream of burning rubber as the back wheels spun for long seconds, then the Capri shot forward as if fired from a gigantic cannon. It sped towards the glass doors and Clayton opened his mouth in a silent scream as he saw them rushing towards him.

The Capri hurtled into the double doors with the force of a steam train. There was an ear-piercing explosion of glass as the car obliterated the entry way. Huge shards of crystal flew through the air, pieces of wood and metal buckling under the impact. The Capri skidded inside the reception, the rear end swinging round to thud into a security guard. The impact catapulted him several feet and he rolled over in the cascade of glass splinters. The windscreen of the car was cracked but not broken, the front bumper bent badly. Clayton himself sat for long seconds gasping to regain his breath, groaning as he touched his chest. The steering column had slammed into him as he hit the doors but he was sure he hadn't broken any bones.

Jo took advantage of the shattering entrance and lashed out at the security man nearest her, driving her foot hard into his groin. He went down in a heap at her feet. She vaulted him and ran for the car, wrenching open the passenger side door and leaping in.

'Go,' she shouted and Clayton reversed, back over the jagged splinters of crystal, through the pulverized doors.

There was a loud bang and the side window exploded into a thousand pieces as a bullet struck it.

Clayton floored the accelerator, anxious to get away from the two security men who had appeared from another building and were pointing guns in the direction of the Capri. He saw one actually sight the pistol and fire. The bullet ripped off a wing mirror and ricocheted off the bonnet, gouging a deep furrow in the paintwork.

Another security guard emerged from one of the

manufacturing sheds, levelling a .38 at the speeding car.

Clayton spun the wheel, slamming the car into the man before he had a chance to fire. The impact catapulted the guard into the air. His body seemed to hang there for interminable seconds, as if suspended on invisible wires, then it crashed down on the roof of the vehicle before bouncing off.

Clayton drove for the main gate, trying to urge more speed from the Capri.

Both he and Jo saw that the barrier had been dropped. The two guards were both kneeling down, aiming their pistols. A salvo of shots hit the car, one shattering the windscreen. The glass spider-webbed, leaving Clayton momentarily unsighted. The Capri skidded violently and Jo clutched the door handle as the car lurched across the driveway. The doctor punched his fist through the shattered glass, enabling him to see out. He twisted the wheel, ducking low once more as they approached the barrier.

There was another salvo of shots and one of them caught Clayton in the shoulder.

The impact slammed him back in his seat and he yelped in pain as the bullet punched its way through his back leaving an exit hole the size of a fist. His right arm went momentarily numb and the Capri skidded but the doctor gripped the wheel as tightly as he could with his good hand and, seconds later, the car hit the barrier.

What was left of the windscreen was smashed in by the impact and Jo screamed as she was showered with glass. A sliver cut her arm as she shielded her face and she heard the groan of metal as the roof of the vehicle was almost torn free by the collision.

More bullets ploughed into the back of the vehicle as it burst miraculously through the barrier. Behind them,

291

Jo could see the two security men clambering into a rangerover.

'They're coming after us,' she yelled, watching as the large vehicle roared away in pursuit.

Clayton didn't answer. His face was the colour of rancid butter, blood running freely from the wound in his shoulder. But it was the pain which kept him conscious and, as he too saw the rangerover speeding after them, he seemed able to coax yet more speed from the Capri until the needle on the dashboard nudged eighty.

The Range Rover kept on coming.

Forty-eight

Tyler stood before the main gates of Wakely football ground, the Franchi cradled in his arms.

Above him, the grey clouds were gathering ever more rapidly and, as he pushed open one of the gates, he felt the first light spots of rain begin to fall.

The farmer realized that he would have to move fast. He was no longer safe in weather like this. The floodlights loomed menacingly over him as he walked slowly towards the broken rail which separated the stone embankment steps from the pitch itself. The ground was enclosed by a high wooden fence but, as a child, Tyler could remember sneaking through the gaps to watch the Wakely side play. Now he moved across the steps cautiously, eyes alert for any sign of movement.

There were stands on either side of the pitch and one behind each goal, only the part of the ground which he now patrolled was not under cover. As the rain began to fall more heavily, Tyler hurried to the canopy which overhung the nearest stand.

He pushed open the rusty iron gate and walked through, past the turnstile and the tiny box-like structure which had once been the ticket office. A mouldy yellow sign still proclaimed:

MAIN STAND: ADULTS £1.00 CHILDREN 25p

Tyler looked up at the stand, its roof battered and holed by the ravages of years gone by. However, at the very top, up a flight of covered stairs, was what looked like a press box. It was a room about fifteen feet long and twelve wide, its windows now crusted with dirt and broken in many places.

He had been allowed up there once when he was ten. His father had known most of the ground staff at the club and, as a special treat, young Tyler had been taken up to that special room to see how the floodlights were activated. He could still remember even after all these years.

He stood by the stairs which led up to the first row of stand seats and inhaled. The air smelt of wet grass and decay. He gripped the shotgun tighter and decided to check out the other stands first.

The farmer chose to walk across the pitch itself, coming to the smaller stand directly opposite. It had about 200 seats in it, most of them now rotten, some torn from their brackets and tossed into the aisles. Tyler scanned the delapidated structure hastily then clambered over the rail back onto the pitch.

The goal posts were still standing, the paint peeling and chipped from them like scabrous flesh.

He checked the area behind the right hand goal, it was little more than a covered embankment, then he walked the full length of the pitch and did the same at

293

the other end. Weeds had fought their way up through gaps in the concrete and, here and there, rusted tin cans lay in piles or rolled gently, coaxed by the breeze. A piece of paper, the team sheet from a programme, fluttered mournfully in the air.

Tyler turned and headed back towards the main stand, pausing at the players' tunnel.

Twelve stone steps led down into the maze-like catacombs of changing rooms and showers below. It was as black as pitch down there and the farmer reached for his torch, flicking it on when he was half-way down. An overpoweringly fetid odour rose from the subterranean tunnels but it was not the familiar fusty smell of damp and neglect. It was the pungent, nauseating odour of dead flesh.

Tyler paused as he reached the bottom of the stairs, shining the torch ahead of him. It cut through the blackness, revealing a tunnel. It ran for about twenty yards, then branched off at a sharp angle to both right and left. Tyler advanced cautiously, reigning back his revulsion as the stench grew stronger.

The walls were coated with mildew and he could feel it slimy against his hand as he felt his way along the tunnel.

As he turned to the right he almost tripped over the first of the creatures.

It was a man in his early twenties, huddled up in a foetal position, his mouth open to reveal his long teeth. But for the almost imperceptible rise of his shoulders, Tyler could have mistaken the immobile form for a corpse.

He stepped over the young man, moving as slowly as he could, desperate not to make a sound. As the torch beam cut through the darkness it picked out six, seven. A dozen more sleeping forms. Two dozen.

The tunnel was widening, opening out into another

294

corridor and, sprawled on the floor were more of them. Many more.

To his left in what had once been the showers he saw three dozen of them huddled close by. To his right, more. The entire place was full of the infected townspeople. Tyler re-traced his steps, careful not to wake any of the sleeping creatures. He tried the other way.

It was the same story. Dozens and dozens of contaminated killers all sleeping in the reeking blackness.

At his feet lay Stuart Nichols. Tyler fought to control himself, a combination of fear and loathing welling up inside him until he felt he would have to scream. The silence was broken only by the occasional rasping ululation, a liquid gurgling. Thick, mucoid snortings.

The farmer tried to control his breathing, to still his hammering heart for fear that they would hear it.

The smell was unbelievable.

All around him they lay, some dead, killed by their own. There were the remnants of corpses lying with those who still breathed and the sight made Tyler feel even sicker. It was like standing in hell itself, in the dank, reeking subterranean gloom surrounded by these monstrosities.

He moved backwards slowly, trying to avoid the numerous sleeping forms, the shotgun hovering in his grip. If he woke them now . . .

Tyler forced himself to think of something else.

He sensed that he was near to the tunnel bend, just a few more yards and he would be back in the players' entrance, able to flee upward from this pit of horror. He could feel the perspiration on his forehead. His throat felt dry and he couldn't swallow.

He would burn them, he decided. There was enough petrol in the landrover, all he had to do was seal the exits from beneath the stand and then set light to the place. Burn every one of them.

Ten yards and he would be able to run.

His torch went out.

Tyler could not restrain himself. A cry of panic escaped him as he shook the useless light, blind in the Stygian darkness.

He turned to run.

A hand caught his ankle and tripped him.

He went sprawling but managed to retain his grip on the shotgun. As he felt the deformed figure clawing at him, he tightened his finger on the trigger.

The blast not only gutted his attacker, it also gave him a second of precious light. In that second, Tyler saw that they were rising. But, there was no slow deliberation to their movements, almost as one they were awake, alert and on their feet. Dozens of them spilled from their hiding places to fill the corridor, hungry eyes fixing him with baleful stares.

Tyler turned and ran, the monstrous horde after him. He hurtled up from beneath the ground, slipping on the wet grass, rolling over in time to see the first of them emerge from the tunnel. The farmer swung the shotgun up and fired, the blast ripping away most of the man's face. The body was catapulted backwards, momentarily blocking the entrance, giving Tyler time to get to his feet.

He was moving without thinking, sheer instinct kept him going and he vaulted the rail, heading for the steps which led up to the main stand.

He could hear the fastest of them clattering up the steps behind him and he turned to see Don Mason approaching him.

Tyler didn't hesitate. He squeezed the trigger, watching as the wad of shot cut through the policeman's chest, splattering those behind with gobbets of lung and fragments of bone. But they kept coming, clambering over Mason's body in their frantic effort to reach Tyler. To reach fresh blood.

He could see the others spilling onto the pitch, looking up at the grey sky as if in gratitude.

If only the sun had been out thought Tyler as he leapt up the next flight of stone steps, the ones which would take him to the little room on top of the stand itself. He took them two at a time, slipping once, looking back to see that there were three of the creatures following him. Led by Stuart Nichols. His face was almost unrecognizable, disfigured by the ravages of the disease but, through all that, his eyes gleamed madly as he sought to catch Tyler.

Tyler reached the door of the room and twisted the handle.

The door was locked.

Nichols was about ten yards from him now and Tyler tugged hard on the recalcitrant handle.

Finally, he realized he had no choice. He spun round and fired. The close range blast eviscerated Nichols, the impact catapulting him backward, blasting him off the steps. He fell screaming.

Tyler realized he had just one cartridge left in the gun. He blew the second attacker's head off, then using the butt of the shotgun as a club, went for his final opponent. The man was in his forties, overweight and a little sluggish. Tyler easily avoided his clumsy gropings and ducked under the first punch, bringing the stock up under the man's chin. The blow staggered him and Tyler struck again, feeling bone splinter as he crushed the man's nose. Blood burst from the ruptured appendage and the farmer pressed his advantage, kicking his opponent hard in the groin.

The man overbalanced and tumbled heavily down the steps. Tyler turned and kicked at the lock of the door, driving desperate blows into it until it finally surrendered to the pressure and flew inwards.

He dashed in, finding himself confronted by a bank of switches and dials. The accumulation of dust made him cough but he scanned the array before him, glancing periodically out of the window down to the pitch below.

Every square inch of grass seemed to be occupied. He could only guess at how many of them there were.

Two hundred? Three hundred? More?

They stood glaring up at the room where he remained. Not one of them attempted to move now. They knew he had to come down eventually. They need do nothing but wait.

Tyler's breath was coming in gasps, as much from frustration as exertion. He looked desperately for some sign on the large control panel which might help him. His fingers traced patterns in the thick dust, brushing it away from the controls.

There was a switch marked:

POWER

He flicked to 'ON' and, somewhere, far below him, there was a rumbling. Like thunder only it sounded as if it were going to erupt from the earth itself. The thrumming grew louder.

Now he saw other switches:

COLUMN ONE
COLUMN TWO

And through to six.

He swallowed hard, the floodlights. The switches had to control the floodlights.

He looked out of the grime-encrusted window once again. The diseased creatures were still standing, looking up at him.

'Just stay there you bastards,' he whispered, fingers poised over the first three switches.

He prayed that the lights would work.

The rumbling from below was now shaking the room. It was time.

All Tyler heard was a maniacal scream and then

298

something heavy crashed into him, driving him into the control panel, knocking the breath from him.

He looked up to see Dan Hawley standing over him. At least what had once been Dan Hawley.

The vet's face was a patchwork of sores and blisters, some of which had burst and were weeping clear pus. Elsewhere, patches of skin had peeled off to reveal raw skin beneath. He had lost most of his hair, his scalp was now infested with suppurating boils. Nails stained darkly with dried blood curved from the ends of his fingers and he snarled at Tyler in a gesture that was more animal than human.

For what seemed like an eternity, they faced each other, then, Hawley launched himself at the farmer. Vic rolled to one side. He lashed out at his attacker as he did so, driving a powerful kick into his stomach.

The vet grunted and rolled over, his bony hand closing over the leg of a broken chair which lay nearby. He brought it down with bone crushing force, missing Tyler by inches, the nail which protruded from the end striking sparks on the control panel.

Tyler grabbed Hawley's arm and twisted it hard against the joint, trying to make him drop the weapon but the vet merely tore at Tyler's face with his long claws, drawing blood.

The farmer backed off, looking for his shotgun.

He snatched it up, hefting it before him like a club. Hawley struck again but Tyler deflected the blow, striking out himself, catching the vet on the temple. The impact sent him reeling and Tyler swung the gun once again, using it like a baseball bat. He drove the stock into Hawley's face, shattering his bottom jaw. But still the vet kept coming, ignoring the blood which oozed from the vicious rent in his flesh. He ducked beneath Tyler's next blow, striking for the farmer's thigh.

Tyler yelped in pain as the nail punctured his flesh.

Blood spurted from the hole and he felt his skin and muscle being torn as Hawley wrenched the spike free.

The farmer had cartridges in his pocket but he knew that he'd never re-load in time and, as he glanced out of the window down onto the pitch, he saw that the others were beginning to move. They could see what was happening in the room on top of the stand and they were becoming restless. Hungry.

Tyler hurled his gun at Hawley but the vet merely ducked and ran at him, bringing the chair leg down in a wide arc.

More by luck than judgement, Tyler managed to grab his assailant's wrist, gripping as hard as he could. Then, using all his strength, he swung Hawley around and hurled him towards the window.

Propelled by Tyler's throw and his own momentum, the vet could not stop himself.

He crashed through the glass with a scream of rage and horror. For what seemed like an eternity, he clutched at empty air, then, with a last caterwaul of despair, he plummeted down, smashing through the rusted roof of the stand and thudding to earth more than fifty feet below. He rolled over once, then lay still in a widening pool of blood.

Tyler threw all six switches.

The floodlights burst into life, bathing the pitch in powerful white light. Thirty bulbs, two hundred watts each, shone from every tower. In all 180 searing points of energy were trained on the vampires of Wakely, pinning them like moths in a candle flame.

Tyler saw them start to fall, hands raised to the offending brightness as their skin blistered and innumerable screams of agony began to rise like a swelling organ note from the contaminated hordes. They writhed helplessly as the light burned them, scorching their flesh as surely as if they'd been put to the torch. Some ran back and forth in an effort to escape their agony but there was no way out. They were trapped by the beams, paralysed into immobility by their pain. Like rabbits before a snake, they remained hypnotised by the blistering lights, unable to look away but dying in consequence. Their eyes were seared in the sockets, their skin stripped away as if by acid and, on all of them, the welts and sores rose like blossoming flowers. The brilliant light blazed down over the field like some purging fire – a white blanket which brought death to all beneath it. Like hundreds of artificial suns, the bulbs poured out their energy.

Tyler watched mesmerised as the last of the infected townspeople died, flopping around like beached fish until, finally, there was no movement at all.

He bowed his head, his breath coming in gasps.

The puncture in his thigh was throbbing madly and he pressed his handkerchief to it as he walked, hobbling from the little room to stand in the rain.

Tyler stood there for a full thirty minutes, eyes scanning the piles of corpses stretched out on the pitch. His whole body ached but he knew that there was one more thing he had to do.

After turning the lights off, Tyler hobbled down from the control room and wandered out to the landrover. From there he drove the vehicle inside the football ground and, working as thoroughly as possible, used up the cans of petrol, sprinkling the golden fluid over as many corpses as possible.

Now he stood watching as the bodies roasted, the acrid stench of burning flesh filling his nostrils, great black plumes of smoke rising above the scene of death.

It was another hour before he left.

Forty-nine

Charles Muir heard the sirens but he paid them no
heed, nor did he stop to ask anyone what had
happened. He continued walking purposefully towards
the oak-panelled door at the end of the windowless
corridor. A technician passed him, running, but the
Scot didn't spare the man a second glance.

He entered the room and found two other Vanderburg workers there. One, a man in his late thirties, was
looking through the maze of filing cabinets. The other,
a woman, was seated at one of the computer consoles.

Muir smiled politely at the woman.

'Could you fetch Mr Stark for me,' he asked.

The woman looked puzzled for a moment, then got
to her feet and left the room. Muir took her place at the
console.

'If you wouldn't mind leaving?' he said to the man.

The technician put down the file he had and followed
the woman outside. The Scot heard the sound of their
footsteps receding down the corridor. Stark, he
guessed, would arrive in five or six minutes.

Perfect timing. He smiled thinly.

The sirens continued to screech but Muir ignored
them, turning his attention instead to the keyboard and
V.D.U. before him. He pressed a button and the screen
went blank, then, after pausing a second, he tapped in
the first commands.

Luminous green letters appeared on the screen:
> INTERFACE 3095. READY FOR ENQUIRY

Muir hastily relayed his next instruction.
> REQUEST PROGRAM

The computer acknowledged.
> ALL TERMINALS ERASE

He sat back, looking at what was displayed before him.

DOES NOT COMPUTE

The display unit glowed.

Muir chewed on the stem of his pipe.

ALL TERMINALS SELF-DESTRUCT

NEGATIVE

Muir hit the keyboard harder.

EMERGENCY COMMAND OVERRIDE. ALL
TERMINALS SELF-DESTRUCT

FULL POWER

He sat back, watching as the letters on the V.D.U. began first to flash and then to turn red. The room began to fill with a high-pitched whine, drowning out even the siren, but Muir just sat there, the unlit pipe clenched between his teeth.

KEY

He typed:

COMMAND IRREVERSIBLE

Now there was no turning back.

Consoles all over Vanderburg Chemicals began to display the same two words and more than one employee began making for the nearest door.

Muir knew what he had done. He was even quite proud of himself. Once the power began to overload, every electrical circuit in the building would go up. Not just short out but the huge amounts of power running through the circuits would cause fires and, eventually, explosions.

The Scot sat and stared at the screen.

He had known for a while now that it must come to this. The feedstuff programme had to be stopped somehow but, more importantly, John Stark had to be stopped. What he had said to Muir had struck a note deep inside him. As he sat staring at the flashing screen he realized that this was his atonement. It was the only way he could hope to find peace after what he had helped to create. The Vanderburg feed, as he had told Stark, was indeed lethal.

303

The door opened and John Stark blundered in.

Muir turned slowly in his chair to greet the American.

'What in God's name are you doing?' snarled Stark, peering at the console.

It was beginning to flash wildly:

OVERLOAD

Muir said nothing.

'Stop it, now,' shouted Stark, trying to raise his voice above the sirens and the high-pitched screech which was reaching ever greater intensity.

'There's no way of stopping it, *Mr* Stark,' said the Scot. 'It's all over. Your plans. Everything.'

Stark leapt at Muir and fastened both hands around his throat.

'Turn it off,' he snarled as the first crackles of overloading circuitry began to fill his ears.

Muir tried to force the American's hands away but there was a furious desperation in Stark's grip, something which gave him added strength. The two of them crashed onto the console, Stark slamming the Scot's head repeatedly against the desk top.

'Turn it off,' he roared.

As if a switch had been thrown the entire room suddenly exploded in a searing welter of blistering flame. The walls, as if pushed by gigantic fists, erupted outwards. Huge lumps of stone flew through the air like shrapnel.

Elsewhere on the second floor other terminals exploded, hungry tongues of flame licking through their circuitry. A chorus of deafening blasts rocked the main building as every electrical appliance overloaded. Screams began to punctuate the growing roar of fire. Those fortunate enough to be outside the building ran for their lives as glass from the upper storeys rained down in lethal crystal showers. Long, spear-like shards sped to earth like clear javelins.

A security guard, mesmerised by the sight before

him, was transfixed by a razor sharp length of window which buried itself in his chest.

On the third floor, a blast of seismic proportions sent bodies hurtling through windows as the chemicals in the labs also caught alight. The cries of animals now joined the cacophony of sounds as specimens were burned alive in their cages.

Men and women were picked up, as if by invisible hands, and flung through the air, slamming into walls or crashing through glass. A woman, her hair and clothes ablaze ran screaming down a corridor until another explosion brought the ceiling down on her. Metal began to melt under the intense heat and even the stone steps grew hot as the fires continued to sear everything they touched.

Here and there, people were attempting to fight the fires with extinguishers but it was like trying to put out a forest blaze with a thimbleful of water. Two security men, using extinguishers, tried to make a path for several women through the hungry flames but the fire seemed to rear up at them and they were forced back towards a room near the end of a corridor. It housed several hundred bottles of chemical and, a moment later, an ear-splitting blast simply brushed aside everyone within a hundred yards. Bodies were tossed like bloodied rag dolls, hurtling through the air as if fired from cannons.

In the forecourt below, a lorry exploded, the driver catapulted through the windscreen as the vehicle disappeared beneath a shrieking ball of red and white flame. Lumps of metal went spinning in all directions.

It seemed as if the entire complex which made up Vanderburg Chemicals was ablaze, a roaring beacon which could be seen for miles around.

Powerful explosions continued to rock the place, tearing it apart. Those who could, ran. Those trapped inside were either incinerated or blasted to atoms.

And, above it all, a gigantic mushroom cloud of black smoke rose fully two hundred feet into the air. Like some massive man-made cloud it hung, shroud-like, over the remnants of the complex.

Then, finally, as if the other blasts had been mere portents, there was an explosion which threatened to split the very earth itself: the final, cataclysmic death knell which brought the remnants of Vanderburg Chemicals down like a house of cards. A concussion wave flattened everything within a 500 yard radius and then, almost as an after-thought, there was a vehement detonation which levelled anything left standing. Flames screamed defiantly in the air, shrieking geysers of fire which rose like blazing fingers to point accusingly at the sky.

Even the clouds seemed to be on fire.

Fifty

Jo ducked low in her seat as Clayton swung the car around a tight bend in the road. Behind them, the driver of the rangerover slowed slightly to take the corner but then stepped on the accelerator as the road straightened out once more. His companion was leaning out of the side window trying to aim a gun at the tyre of the speeding Capri.

Jo heard the report but, thankfully, the bullet missed its appointed mark, scraping the side of the vehicle instead.

The doctor gripped the steering wheel as tightly as

he could, blood from the wound in his shoulder seeping down his arm. As she looked at him, Jo could see a shining nub of bone protruding from the ragged wound. The bullet had smashed his scapula.

She peered out of the back window to see that the rangerover was gaining.

'Oh no,' murmured Clayton.

'What is it?' she demanded.

'We're nearly out of petrol,' Clayton told her, indicating the gauge.

He swung the car around another corner and stepped on the brake.

'What the hell are you doing?' Jo asked, in amazement.

'Get out,' he said, watching the rear view mirror.

'Why?'

'Get out,' he bellowed at her. 'Take the files. One of us has got to get away.'

'I can't . . .'

He cut her short, pushing the door open and practically shoving her out. He passed her the files.

'Run,' he told her. 'Go on. There's nothing left for me now. You save yourself. Get to Tyler if you can.'

Before she could protest, he had reached across and slammed the door, spinning the wheel of the Capri, bringing it around in a 'U' turn until it was facing the opposite way.

A second later, the rangerover came hurtling round the corner.

The driver was a little puzzled at first to see the Capri heading back towards them, and that puzzlement turned to horror as he realized what Clayton was doing.

Jo, too, saw what was to happen.

'No,' she shouted but, a second later, her voice was drowned out by a thunderous explosion.

The two vehicles hit each other head on and blew up immediately. There was a blinding ball of fire followed by a billowing orange and black cloud of smoke. Lumps of red hot metal flew into the air and Jo blenched as she saw a severed arm rise on the funnel of flame which erupted from the roaring blast. A wave of pressure rocked her and she shielded her face as the heat rolled over her. The air was filled with the roar of raging flames.

She stood gazing at the pulverized vehicles for as long as she dared, then clutching the three files, she set off across the fields towards town.

It was nearly 6.39 p.m. when Tyler walked into the hotel. He found Jo sitting at the bar, the files before her. As he limped in, she ran to him, throwing her arms around his neck. He responded with equal warmth and relief.

'Thank God you're alive,' she said. Then, stepping back, she asked: 'Is it done?'

He nodded.

'I killed them all,' he told her. 'At least I think I did. There's no way of knowing for sure.' He swallowed hard. 'Jo, I knew so many of them.' He was silent for a moment.

'Clayton's dead,' she told him.

'How?'

Jo explained everything, finally showing him the files.

'But you destroyed Vanderburg Chemicals,' he said, wearily.

She shook her head.

'Not us.'

'I saw the fires,' he said.

'Vic, I don't know *what* happened. But, they're gone.'

Tyler picked up the file marked:

DISTRIBUTION

There was a column on the left hand side of the page which bore the names of cities.

'London. Manchester. Liverpool. Glasgow,' he read.

'Paris. Bonn. Brussels. Vienna.' Tyler swallowed hard. 'New York. Houston. Quebec.' He looked at Jo. 'Jesus, do you realize what this means?'

'They're all places where the new Vanderburg feed is supposed to be distributed, to be sold by their outlets in those cities,' she said. 'Now we have the files we can stop the shipments.'

Tyler shook his head, running his finger across the page.

'The despatch dates on most of these are weeks old,' he said, anxiously.

The smile faded from Jo's face.

'These shipments have already gone,' the farmer said, softly.

'My God,' murmured Jo. 'The virus will spread.' Her voice took on a note of desperation. 'Isn't there any way of stopping it?'

Tyler dropped the file onto the table before him.

'Vic, there has to be a way,' she gasped. 'There must be something.'

He sat down heavily.

'There's nothing,' he said, flatly.

Outside, it began to get dark.

Author's Note

All characters in this novel are figments of my imagination, as are the towns of Wakely and Arkham. There is also no company called Vanderburg Chemicals.

The disease porphyria, on the other hand, *does* exist and the facts given, in *Erebus*, by Dr Alec Clayton are correct. While it is true that one person in every 25,000 suffers from this rare affliction, it is not expected that figures will increase much beyond that particular statistic.

However . . .

Shaun Hutson

STAR BOOKS BESTSELLERS

THRILLERS

SHATTERED	John Farris	£1.50*	☐
BLOODSPORT	Henry Denker	£1.75*	☐
THE AIRLINE PIRATES	John Gardner	£1.25	☐
THE INFILTRATOR	Michael Hughes	£1.60	☐
IKON	Graham Masterton	£2.50*	☐
TERROR OF THE TRIADS	Sean O'Callaghan	£1.50	☐
HUNTED	Jeremy Scott	£1.50	☐
DIRTY HARRY	Philip Rock	£1.25*	☐
MAGNUM FORCE	Mel Valley	£1.50*	☐

WAR

BLAZE OF GLORY	Michael Carreck	£1.80	☐
CONVOY OF STEEL	Wolf Kruger	£1.80	☐
BLOOD AND HONOUR	Wolf Kruger	£1.80	☐
PANZER GRENADIERS	Heinrich Conrad Muller	£1.95*	☐
THE RAID	Julian Romanes	£1.80*	☐
GUNSHIPS: NEEDLEPOINT	Jack Hamilton Teed	£1.95	☐
THE SKY IS BURNING	D. Mark Carter	£1.60	☐
TASK FORCE BATTALION	Tom Lambert	£1.60	☐

STAR Books are obtainable from many booksellers and newsagents. If you have any difficulty tick the titles you want and fill in the form below.

Name _____

Address _____

_____

Send to: Star Books Cash Sales, P.O. Box 11, Falmouth, Cornwall. TR10 9EN.

Please send a cheque or postal order to the value of the cover price plus: UK: 45p for the first book, 20p for the second book and 14p for each additional book ordered to the maximum charge of £1.63.

BFPO and EIRE: 45p for the first book, 20p for the second book, 14p per copy for the next 7 books, thereafter 8p per book.

OVERSEAS: 75p for the first book and 21p per copy for each additional book.

While every effort is made to keep prices low, it is sometimes necessary to increase prices at short notice. Star Books reserve the right to show new retail prices on covers which may differ from those advertised in the text or elsewhere.

***NOT FOR SALE IN CANADA**

STAR BOOKS BESTSELLERS

CHILLERS

CHAINSAW TERROR	*Nick Blake*	£1.80	☐
SLUGS	*Shawn Hutson*	£1.60	☐
SPAWN	*Shawn Hutson*	£1.80	☐
CARNOSAUR	*Harry Adam Knight*	£1.95	☐
SLIMER	*Harry Adam Knight*	£1.95	☐
BLOWFLY	*David Lowman*	£1.95	☐
THE PARIAH	*Graham Masterton*	£1.95*	☐
THE PLAGUE	*Graham Masterton*	£1.80*	☐
THE MANITOU	*Graham Masterton*	£1.50*	☐
SATAN'S LOVE CHILD	*Brian McNaughton*	£1.35*	☒
SATAN'S SEDUCTRESS	*Brian McNaughton*	£1.25*	☒

STAR Books are obtainable from many booksellers and newsagents. If you have any difficulty tick the titles you want and fill in the form below.

Name *Helen Garner*

Address *2 Cumberland Close, Rhodes Est,*
Dalston, London E.8. 3TF.

Send to: Star Books Cash Sales, P.O. Box 11, Falmouth, Cornwall. TR10 9EN.

Please send a cheque or postal order to the value of the cover price plus:
UK: 45p for the first book, 20p for the second book and 14p for each additional book ordered to the maximum charge of £1.63.

BFPO and EIRE: 45p for the first book, 20p for the second book, 14p per copy for the next 7 books, thereafter 8p per book.

OVERSEAS: 75p for the first book and 21p per copy for each additional book.

While every effort is made to keep prices low, it is sometimes necessary to increase prices at short notice. Star Books reserve the right to show new retail prices on covers which may differ from those advertised in the text or elsewhere.

*NOT FOR SALE IN CANADA